THE DRIFT

SUSANNAH WISE

First published in 2025 by Bloodhound Books.

www.bloodhoundbooks.com

Print ISBN: 978-1-917705-34-9

For Kit

CHAPTER ONE

By now, Annie felt nauseous.

Four hours heading north from London on the brightly lit motorway followed by the twisting inky A-road, and her stomach was about to give way. She shouldn't have had that service station crap for lunch.

Grace was fast asleep in the passenger seat, her shining curtain of hair flat against the rise of her chest. In the rear-view mirror, Caleb's face slumped against the window, silver in the glow of the Kindle on his lap. There'd be a greasy print left on the glass when he finally surfaced. His mouth was open. Annie could imagine the slick of spit glistening around his bottom lip. Still, he looked so young, barely a man, no longer a boy. There was something reassuring about driving her stepchildren whilst they slept – almost as if she knew what she was doing. Which she did, in a way: taking them somewhere new, as instructed by her late wife. In the corner of her eye, Annie saw Grace's breath condense, then disappear from the window.

Rain beat against the windscreen. The repetitive moan of the wipers marking time, the headlights' beams swinging as the car turned, left, right, left again.

She was a nervous driver; it was Issy's car, after all. Had been Issy's car. Past participle. Her wife had been superior ('superior' being Issy's word) behind the wheel. Inversely, Issy had been an awful passenger, and it should have been Issy sitting in the place Annie now occupied, guiding the BMW smoothly towards Colthwaite. Issy's driving had never made Annie feel sick.

She briefly removed one hand from the steering wheel and patted her shirt pocket; yes, The Letter was still neatly folded inside. This journey represented new beginnings. A chance to spring clean her spirit, the spirits of the kids; like opening windows in an old house.

The last few miles. Until then, the air inside the car thick as it made its way along the ever-snaking road. The rain was heavy, visibility poor, and pockets of water gathered in dips. Rain never stopped falling in the Lakes.

It wasn't possible to spring clean grief, of course – she slowed as she took a sharp bend – however many analogies about windows one made. She wanted to remember every molecule of her late wife anyway, not erase her. To preserve her in aspic, perhaps – no, that was a horrible image – preserve her as the great painting masters preserved their subjects: year on year the paint ageing, the subject growing more beautiful, the art more precious.

She wanted a change, in truth. Needed one.

She brought her attention back to the road. The flat twilight this far north had given way to the blackest night. Through the deluge, the car's lights picked out the conifers that marked the edges of the verge. The trees fell steeply towards the road on one side, and down and away on the other, their straight trunks cut-outs from a theatrical set. Further off, the dark hills rose.

Her eye caught Grace rearranging her endless legs in the passenger footwell. Her stepdaughter had had to push the seat right back into Caleb's equally long pins to stretch out. Thank God the car was an estate.

Annie's own seat felt too firm. There were lumps in all the wrong places and now her back ached. She hoped she wouldn't have to do too much driving once they'd settled. That's what the bikes were for, after all; the three frames squeaking on the rear rack. She would become fit enough to cycle to the nearest shop four hilly miles away.

Caleb made a little snort. In the mirror, his eyes were closed but she had the distinct impression he was awake. She could smell salt and vinegar crisps.

Well, he'd be able to wash the tang of Chipsticks away in the massive bathroom in their new cottage, Chapel Croft, wouldn't he. She liked the name: 'Chapel' reminded her of Grandma Halmi, which meant safety. And 'Croft' sounded cosy. A cosy, safe place. The bathroom was big enough to allow all three of them inside at once – not that *that* would ever happen, the kids were so private these days. Chapel Croft had one of those long steel baths, where even Grace would be able to luxuriate head to toe in foamy water. It also had a decent stand-alone shower, and a bidet. She couldn't imagine anyone in Hackney owning a bidet.

The turn off to the bridge wasn't far now. She wouldn't wake the kids – if they were indeed asleep. Were they worried about their new life up here? She couldn't tell. Most of the time she had no idea what they thought about anything.

She steered the car carefully across the bridge's narrow passage, empty at night-time. Annie knew the route only sketchily because on their bi-annual trips to visit Issy's parents – her wife's childhood home – it would be Issy driving, as per.

Annie turned left, and the car resumed its winding pattern. Her eyes felt dry. Meanwhile outside, more rain. More blackness. These two elements always. She wondered if she'd ever get used to it.

The other thing on her agenda was her play. The play she was writing. Well, about to. Eleven months of hiatus and now she was ready. At least, she hoped she was. Busy thinking about it, she took the approaching bend too fast.

There was something in the middle of the road. Her foot slammed the brake, the wheels locked, she let out a yell, the car skidded wildly and, in what felt like slow motion, swerved towards the verge. The reality was sudden movement, which threw her neck to the left as her hands gripped hard on the steering wheel. The car's chassis hit the grass, shunting them back onto the tarmac before the engine stalled.

In the silence that followed, Annie registered three things in this order: the kids were okay – bolt upright in their seats – that she was okay, and that the car had missed whatever was in the road by metres.

It hadn't moved: the sound of the wheels, the frantic skidding, the thing hadn't noticed any of it.

The wipers going back and forth. The rain falling more gently now, upon the road, upon the bonnet, Annie slumped in her seat, heart beating wildly. 'Everyone all right?'

The kids made assenting noises before Caleb whispered, 'What *is* it?'

It took several moments to pull it into focus. Illuminated through the water-logged light, she could see now it was a medium-sized animal with its rump thrust rudely in their direction.

A *pig*. She'd nearly killed them, for a pig.

They stared at it through the windscreen. What it was doing out here, God only knew. Its hocks glistened, slick and meaty, corkscrewed tail twitching back and forth, barrel body expanding and contracting.

As if sensing them at last, the pig lifted its head and looked over its shoulder at the car. It gave a slight start.

Grace let out an involuntary sigh of dismay on seeing its face. The poor thing was grossly disfigured, with only one eye and its features all pushed to the left. Where its nose should have been, a gaping hole.

The creaking of leather upholstery as Caleb, from the back seat, leant in for a closer look. 'What's wrong with it?'

'I don't know,' Annie said. Could it also be deaf? Was that why the car hadn't bothered it?

'What are you doing?' hissed Grace, as Annie restarted the engine. 'We can't *leave* it here.'

'We can.' She let the car slide slowly past the animal. 'And we will.' It was only after another minute, when Grace had buried her head in her phone, that Annie felt the need to say, 'Try not to worry about it.'

Grace said nothing.

Was 'try not to worry' the right thing to tell a teenager? Issy would have come up with something better. Caleb turned and watched over his shoulder through the rear windscreen as the pig disappeared. The car picked up speed.

The final two bends. A couple of slate-roofed dwellings to one side. Another hundred metres beyond these and they passed Blea Crag, Issy's parents' – Annie's parents-in-law's – home, a small sombre-stoned dwelling. The lights burned upstairs. She hoped William and Elizabeth – such *English* names – would be safely in bed and not waiting for them in Annie's new cottage with their dogs and their long vowels.

Almost opposite Blea Crag to the left, the turning to their new home; a small gate with the slate sign 'Chapel Croft' propped against the gatepost. She swung the car in, and up the bumpy track about fifty metres to the cottage.

They were to live closer to her in-laws than she'd have liked, though the track provided privacy at least, the two cottages invisible to one another unless you stood right down at the entrance to the lane by the gate.

They rumbled up the last few metres. The cottage looked picture-book perfect at night, like a child's drawing, and for a moment Annie didn't feel quite so... apprehensive. No, excited. Sometimes it was hard to tell the difference.

Smoke chugged from the chimney. Low lights burned beyond the windows. Her mother-in-law must have come into the cottage earlier to prepare. Annie weighed up the chances of Elizabeth being inside.

They'd reached the patch of grass in front of the cottage. She cut the ignition. The ticking of the engine cooling. Grace, still on her phone, hadn't registered their arrival. Or perhaps she had but was pretending not to. Caleb stared out the window. Annie flicked her eyes at the clock: five hours and five minutes precisely from Hackney on a Friday night. Not bad. Not bad at all.

The rain had stopped. Annie took that as a good omen. Nature itself was welcoming them. She punched her stepdaughter's leg affectionately, prompting a tut, and popped the door. 'Get out, lazybones. And you,' she said to Caleb. 'Out, lazybones junior.'

Nobody moved. Annie sighed and climbed out. The night air was wet earth, woodsmoke, and the recent downpour. It was chilly, but not uncomfortable. She leant on the hot bonnet, letting the rainwater soak her clothes, her nausea receding.

She'd left the removals company strict instructions to be gone by 7pm. There'd be boxes everywhere, but it didn't matter; here they were, the three of them, her family – hers alone now – safe and in one piece.

The kids dragged themselves out, all limbs. It was almost

funny, their performative weariness. Caleb groaned as his feet touched hard ground.

'You're fifteen, for God's sake,' she said. 'Not sixty-six.'

'I might as well be ninety-six after your driving.' He eye-rolled at his sister, but Grace wasn't in the giving vein.

'Desperate for a wee.' Grace crunched across the gravel to the little porch and waited for the door to open, her weight on one hip. Her skin appeared wan, almost yellow, in the flickering porch light.

Annie added 'new bulb for porch' to her list of things to do. She'd need to write it down or she'd forget. Issy wasn't here anymore to remind her.

Caleb had joined his sister, standing in the strobe of the on-off light. He was whistling softly, a new and perplexing habit he'd developed. Annie got lost for a moment, staring at her own feet: her trainer laces had come undone.

'Annie, come *on*.'

Between them the children carried two mobile phones, a small over-the-shoulder bag, and the Kindle. Annie gave them a look as she fished the front door key from her jeans.

'What?' Grace demanded.

'Don't worry about the luggage.' Annie made sure to smile because Grace took offence if you even breathed the wrong way. 'The butler'll do it.'

Grace lifted her chin at the bikes fastened to the back of the car. 'Well, whoever he is, he'll have to take those off first.'

'Whoever *she* is.' Annie chucked the key to Grace.

Grace let herself in, and Caleb followed, still whistling. Annie heard the door to the downstairs loo open and shut.

Annie lingered for a second on the porch stone, breathing with the night, listening to the children's voices drifting now from the living room. Let the children be the first to scout the rooms, let them take ownership.

The rusty cluck of a pheasant somewhere up the hill at the back of the house. Or maybe it was grouse. Quite a few stars out: Orion. His belt anyway. Issy had taught her, more than once, how to find the Pleiades. The world needed all the sisters it could get, she'd said. Another pheasant from the wood, further up the hill this time.

That pig, the gaping hole at the centre of its face. It would almost certainly be one of William's. Her in-laws owned hundreds of them – and sheep, too. She should probably tell him one had got loose. But not now. Picking up her feet, she headed inside.

The removals people had done a decent job. Most of the boxes were unpacked and the cardboard taken away. The remainder were neatly stacked in corners. Elizabeth wasn't here. Perhaps the removals company had taken her away too. Annie felt her shoulders relax. The kids were already upstairs.

'Who stacks shoes on top of books?' Caleb was complaining. 'Those removals people are totally annoying. I'll probably have footprints on *Tintin in the Congo*.'

'In the *Congo*?!' Grace's voice was distorted by its journey through the thick ceiling. 'I'm glad it's damaged. That shit is profoundly racist.'

'"Profoundly racist"?!' Caleb scoffed. 'What does that even mean? Whatever its politics, the book is a piece of *history*. First edition, four hundred quid.'

'Oh, don't even bother, big-word man,' said Grace. 'It's not a book, it's a comic, and it belongs in the bin, you penis.'

Caleb yelled, '"Penis" isn't an insult, you penis!'

'Stop arguing!' Annie yelled up the stairs. 'You've only just arrived.'

'We're not arguing!' they bellowed back.

They were always like this. Annie grinned, giving up.

The cottage was as lovely as she remembered. Traditional in

style, it was the sort of place Grandma Halmi – when she was alive – from their little flat in New Malden, used to go crazy for. Annie could do with Grandma Halmi right now. Could do with her hugs and some of her cooking, at the very least.

She took a breath in the wide low-ceilinged hall. A small flagstoned kitchen to the right, living room to the left, bathroom in the corner. A set of stairs covered in seagrass led up to the top floor. The aesthetic benefits of seagrass were inarguable, but the truth was it was uncomfortable on your feet and shit got lodged in its holes. Not literal shit. Though in this place, with all the farm animals and the fields, who knew.

Also, it was too cold in here.

Issy would have loved it: the night-time arrival, the mean slivers of warmth sliding into the hall from the wood burner in the other room, the kids' distant bickering. Her wife's body had always run hot. She'd have taken Annie's hand, led her into the kitchen, kissed her, and asked what Annie planned to cook for dinner.

Perhaps she'd rip the seagrass out? The cottage wasn't hers though; it belonged to Andrew, Issy's brother, who lived just down the lane in the Big House. Annie and the kids were merely renting, and she was sure he wouldn't appreciate her pulling things apart. He'd made sure the rent was miniscule, and she was extremely grateful for that, even if something about the whole thing struck her as whiffy – a sort of serf-and-squire feeling. Or maybe that was her own stuff. Always the only non-white person in a five-mile vicinity, their previous visits here hadn't exactly made her uncomfortable, but she'd always come away feeling more tired than when she'd arrived.

Annie caught her reflection in the wall mirror. She was frowning. She was also a little bit chubbier than she remembered, but she had plans for that.

Apart from the boxes beside the table, the kitchen was tidy

and smelled of cleaning products. The butler sink had a folded J-cloth, and a pair of pink Marigolds draped over its edge. There was a box of PG Tips with two lonely tea bags inside on the counter, and an egg cup full of white sugar. Just enough for two, Annie thought. How very Elizabeth. There was also a handwritten note:

Welcome! Hope your journey wasn't sticky? We thought we'd let you relax and settle in this evening. Some bits in the fridge for dinner.
Drinks at ours tomorrow 6pm?
Love E & W /Granny and Grandpa

Annie felt immediately guilty. Her in-laws had not only lit the fire, but they'd also remembered that she'd mentioned the car would be too full for a big food shop. That was kind, though nothing would persuade Annie to drink tea right now. She'd driven for five hours; she deserved something stronger. She found the box marked *Booze* amongst the tower of cardboard, cut it open with her penknife and pulled out the soju. She filled half a teacup and glugged it down. Her throat, then chest, grew warm. Her mind turned, as it always did, to food.

The fridge contained one of her mother-in-law's defrosted, home-made meals in a smallish Tupperware. She peeled off the lid. A cottage pie. It was Elizabeth's strongest dish. No good for Annie as a vegetarian, but the kids could have it. She returned it to the shelf, remembering with a shiver the 2014 Christmas trip: the defrosted chicken mousse and peas in aspic. Beside the Tupperware, there was an earthy cabbage and potatoes from the garden, a pint of milk, a loaf of sliced white bread, three apples, a tin of sardines and some eggs.

There was also the small collection of Annie's essentials, the things she'd ensured she *had* made space for in the car: packets of rice noodles, bottles of gochujang, kochukaru, soybean paste, rice wine, sesame oil and spices. They were crammed into a large bag in the boot.

Humming softly, she strode back out of the house and untied the bikes from the rack, not easy in darkness, especially with the on-off porch light. After five minutes she slashed the red straps with her penknife. It had been her own great idea to bring it. She'd only been here ten minutes and she'd used it twice already. She lifted the bikes to the ground and wheeled them up against the front wall.

The boot now opened. Annie stared at the luggage. A feeling she was sinking.

There would be swimming in lakes, she reminded herself, long walks, cycling in the Bluff valley, the new school for the kids. There would be space and peace, and the writing shed in the back garden. The pen was mightier than the sword. She was going to start, and *complete*, her new play.

Piece by piece Annie hefted the luggage inside. Grace's bags were by far the heaviest. *Local osteopath*, Annie added to her mental to-do list.

The car's food supplies clutched lovingly in her arms, she padded silently to the foot of the stairs, one ear turned to the ceiling. More chatting going on upstairs.

'Is it bigger?' Caleb was asking.

'Yeah.' Grace. Clomping of feet. 'It's like Narnia in here. You can literally get everything in this cupboard.'

'It's not a cupboard, moron, it's meant as a *dressing room*. But it has a slope-y ceiling,' Caleb said. 'Nowhere at home had a slope. I'll do my back in by morning.'

More clomping. 'Nowhere at home had a slope because we lived in a basement flat, you absolute cretin. And it's *not* a dressing room, Jesus. You're not in *Brideshead*.'

'What's *Brideshead*?'

'On my *God*! Look: you're five foot ten. I'm way taller, and I can stand up in here fine, see? Just stand in that corner if you wanna put your clothes on.'

There was a silence before Caleb said loudly, 'But that's where my bed's going.' Then Grace's expansive throaty laugh echoed around the cottage. It was a gorgeous sound, not at all related to her teenage sparring voice, the constant phone scrolling or the world-weary attitude. Hearing it, Annie couldn't help but smile: she must enjoy the coming years while the kids still needed her. Well, 'needed' her. She wasn't quite sure what she was providing.

She plonked the food bag on the kitchen counter. Refilling her cup with soju, she left thoughts of dinner and allowed herself to be drawn, inexplicably, to the living room. A fire crackled merrily in the wood burner. Once there, she realised what had summoned her: amongst the piles of boxes, the special box, the one containing all seven of Issy's novels in both hard and paperback. She took the fourteen books out and arranged them carefully, in order of publication, on the middle shelf above the TV.

There. She stood back, proud for her wife. This was what a body of work looked like. Seven award-winning novels. Here was the mark of success. Accomplished plots within which nothing happened, where people talked about feelings and life floated like a boat on Pacific waters.

That sounded mean; she hadn't intended it to.

Her fingers trailed each spine in turn, special editions with matt covers, detailed inlays and sprayed edges. 'Spredges' Issy had called them. 'Galleys', 'ARCs': a lexicon of authoring Annie had come to learn over the years, just as she would now come to learn, she supposed, the language of rural living.

She pulled out Issy's most recent novel, *The Passing Shadow of the Sun*, parked herself on the sofa and turned to the flyleaf.

There was Issy's photo, taken under the bridge at London Fields: skin alabaster; wool scarf around her neck to keep out the cold; smiling, but not too much, in the accepted fashion for literary authors of her standing. Annie looked up, as if she might find her wife in front of her. The light from the fire cast a soft glow, which Annie preferred by far to the harsh single hundred-watt bulb dangling on its wire overhead. Without it though, it was too dark to read. Tomorrow, first thing, she'd unpack the lamps. No one thrived in an interrogatory atmosphere.

She pulled the dust jacket from the book and held it aloft like an air stewardess demonstrating the safety card from the seat-back.

'Not bad, eh?' She introduced Issy's photo to the room, the room to Issy's photo. She propped the cover upright against the back of the sofa beside her, laced her hands behind her head and reclined. 'I'll do my best,' she told it. Her eyes closed.

The soft mouth, the faint speckle of blonde hairs above her top lip. Her ordered, lucid mind. Her smell. The *feel* of her. Sending Annie here. With two teens. Hers, yet not hers. Behind her lids, her eyes grew hot. She must practise disidentifying. She was *not* her mind. A person could be simultaneously angry and sad.

Could they, though, really?

Thundering footsteps on the stairs. 'You okay?' Grace appeared directly in front of her, her voice too loud for the low ceilings.

'I'm fine.'

'You're quite red. Why is Mum's book jacket next to you like that?'

'I'm showing her the house.'

Grace shook her head. Caleb scratched thoughtfully at his cheek. 'I'm hungry,' he announced. 'But first I'm gonna call Dad.'

'Say hi from me,' Annie told him. 'Your grandmother's left food in the fridge but I'm doing noodles.'

'Ooh yeah, definitely noodles.' Caleb wandered off.

They'd always loved – if she may say this about herself – her *remarkable* cooking. A fact that had been a source of great reward and satisfaction.

From the other room, Caleb's voice said, 'Hello? Dad...? Hey... Uh-huh. All our stuff... Yeah.'

Grace, who'd lain herself tummy-down on the floor in front of the fire to phone scroll, sprang up to join him, her mobile abandoned on the carpet. Annie tried not to peek at the comment bubbles popping up one after another.

Caleb was relating the incident with the pig now, Grace giving him running corrections in the background. Annie imagined Patrick at the other end, distracted as he always was around his children, trying to take the story seriously. For a medical doctor, he was suspiciously genial. Never present, but genial.

Seizing her opportunity, Annie jumped up and snuck out the back. There was just time to fit in a few tokes on her spliff. It was ridiculous, her trying to hide the dope smoking from the kids, but how could she lecture them when she was a major culprit?

She pulled out the joint, rolled many hours before whilst still a resident of Hackney, and lit it. She took a heavy drag, enjoying the head spin it gave her, willing the kids to take their time, to continue their chat so she could build up a heavy appetite for dinner. She'd fry the eggs, finely chop the cabbage, add noodles, sauces, lots of chilli. Her mouth watered. There was no kimchi, which was a shame, but it would do.

The end of the joint glowed red as she drew on it. She'd sealed it up that morning as she'd watched the new tenants lug their boxes, their pieces of furniture, into her London home.

She reached for The Letter – Issy's letter – in her shirt pocket and reread it for the twenty-sixth time, squinting in the grudging light from the kitchen window.

My love,

I know we were entirely pissed when we wrote our wills, but I want to be clear that I really meant it. Was anything to happen to me, I'm reiterating here what I set out in the legal document: that you will promise to pack up London and take the kids to live near Mother and Father, close to my old school, so they have a sense of continuity (might seem a strange request given we only visit the old buggers twice a year) – after the brackets Issy had drawn an emoji; a face with a sort of gurning expression.

And I have another very large ask of you, my darling. Given that currently I'm not, in fact, dead – Annie grimaced *– I'm going to ask... (wait for it) that we seriously consider moving to Colthwaite anyway, as a family, in a year or so? Sorry, I hardly dare mention it – and now I've told you and we have a whole year to be scratchy about it. Grace will have finished her A levels by then, and... arrrgh... I know it'll come as a shock – I've never held things from you, but oh, Annie, I've feared your giving me a flat 'no'. And of hurting you – I know how dearly you love Hackney, and I'm aware Colthwaite isn't exactly a beacon of diversity. I'm tired of London – its constant turbulence is giving me the blues. I'm running short of inspiration, and I need a change. Call it a midlife crisis, if you like (another gurning emoji). I keep thinking that were we to have a different horizon, albeit one from my childhood but with a fresh perspective now I'm adult, it would feed us both creatively – and emotionally. Not that we need the emotional bit: I love you more than life itself. Don't hate me. Please, dearest Annie, whaddaya think (a* drawing here of a gangster in a trilby, trench coat and smoking a fat cigar).

Let me know,
Your Issy xxx

Issy had never given her The Letter. When she'd written it exactly, Annie couldn't fathom. Sometime after they'd made their wills, certainly; but the exact day, the exact time, haunted her. What had been the catalyst for its creation? Had she, Annie, done something to prompt it? Had they argued that day? Gone for a meal? Had sex? Having written it, what had made Issy keep it from her?

Annie had discovered it amongst a slab of papers stashed in Issy's desk a month after she'd died. She hadn't been able to face sorting anything on the desk until thirty days had passed – its air of half-finished creative efficiency destroyed her. Halfway through, her head had collapsed onto the desk's surface; she'd smelled Issy's dry green perfume stuck to the lip of the wood and wailed. The perfume must have rubbed off her wife's wrist, that exquisite slender limb that curled out words like smoke onto paper.

Minutes after, Annie had sat up, opened a drawer and found The Letter; after that, everything changed. Issy's instruction utterly confused her: the request was so out of character, the tone so unusually formal and confessional, it was almost as if Issy hadn't written it at all.

Annie read it and read it, ruminating on it for weeks, until something solidified in her mind: she *would* take the kids to live in Cumbria after all. The reason for its writing, Issy's hiding it from her, was irrelevant. She knew what to do – they would have come to Colthwaite anyway, had Issy lived. And she knew that because Issy always got her way.

The will itself – Issy's wishes that they come to live here in the event of her death – might not have been enough, in truth, though Annie hated to admit it. Had it been only the will, hastily scribbled that drunken evening between them, she might have doubted Issy's conviction.

Life was unfairly complicated. In *her* will, all Annie had written was: *I leave all my worldly possessions to Issy Dillane.* Easy. So easy she'd used Grace's Mr Men pen to do it.

Annie stared out at the night, nodding softly to herself. The lease on their Hackney flat was only for a year: if anything went wrong there was a six-month break clause. It was all good.

CHAPTER TWO

When Annie was just five or six years old and living in New Malden, her favourite thing was to wake up before everyone else – before her elder sister, Lumi, before Appa, and certainly before Grandma Halmi who had, for an old lady, an unusual penchant for lie-ins. Annie would open the back door in their flat and step onto the tiny balcony to listen to the sounds of the city: the hiss of traffic; the melancholy hoot of a train; the neighbours' kettle boiling. Standing alone, a blanket wrapped around her narrow shoulders, she believed she was the first person to experience the day.

And *this* morning, her first as a resident of Colthwaite, Annie had risen just like her six-year-old self, dressed, and exited the door before so much as a mouse stirred. Well, perhaps not a mouse, she was sure there were plenty of those scurrying about, but the villagers certainly. She wanted to reclaim that childhood feeling, the part of her capable of wonder.

A dampener on proceedings – she was painfully aware of the pun – was the pelting rain. She was to run. In the rain. *Running.* A thing she'd always hated but was now driven to do.

The wind pasted her hair to her face like wet paper as soon as she made her way down the little track from Chapel Croft to the lane. She was leaving the kids behind, still in bed. It was almost rude, their capacity for slumber.

She stopped at the gate and took her bearings. She'd had the privilege of this – admittedly rainy – vista twice every year for the last decade or so, and it still had the capacity to both astound and confuse her, to the point of becoming lost.

Blea Crag, her in-laws' home, stood directly opposite. To her right, the lane ran back in the direction she'd brought the car in last night: past the slate-roofed dwellings, over the bridge, and onto the main arterial road out of Colthwaite village. To her left, Colthwaite House itself, known as the Big House to residents, sat grandly in its own grounds less than a quarter of a mile away. Beyond the Big House were other village dwellings – modest slate-roofed cottages – and the village church, a tiny thing snuggled into a dell half a mile away. The village in its entirety was a small, fragmented scatter, spreading along the single lane hugged by ancient forests and green fields: God's own country.

No, that was Yorkshire. She didn't know what they called Cumbria, but it was bloody beautiful.

Annie set off left down the lane in the direction of Colthwaite House and beyond, confident now she'd reminded herself of the route: High Tarn for a run then a swim, just as Issy used to.

You couldn't see far, the clouds hanging low as they liked to do almost all the time here, settling in the bowl of the valley, blurring the dramatic vertical rise of surrounding hills. Only the pitch and roll of the nearby fields remained visible, the dazzling snooker-table green zigzagged by drystone walls, the occasional rock thrusting from the earth like a broken tooth.

Caleb's small rucksack banged against her shoulder blades.

She'd borrowed it without asking, but he was asleep and couldn't object. It was too heavy for something that contained only her new wetsuit and a bottle of water. Never mind. She was doing it, whatever 'it' was – getting fit, attacking the day, proving she was *worth it*.

Last night she'd lain in bed worrying for hours after Caleb had woken shouting at 3am. She'd hurried into his room, stroked his head as if she was his mother. Which now she was, in a way. There was nothing either of them could do about that.

Her breath clouded in front of her. It was Issy who'd been the fit one, she of the extra-long mesh leggings and bafflingly intricate double-layer tops smelling of washing powder and deodorant. 'Like a dog,' she'd say, 'I require exercising.' Annie preferred cooking, which was lucky because she was excellent at it. Yet here she was, puffing along the splashy lane. The plan: to reduce girth and bring Issy closer by doing the things her wife had loved.

Behind every crumbling wall, water poured from the hill, flowing from lakes and springs at the top of the fell. A carpet of ferns hid the ground. Moss grew along every branch. The smell was damp and loamy. This ancient world was hers now, thanks to Issy's *mandate*.

The word popped into her head uninvited, making her dizzy; she flicked it away. No one had forced her hand. She was here of her own accord; well, mostly. She had the money from the rental of the flat in London. She also had – she could hardly bear to think about it – Issy's life insurance as well as royalties from Issy's literary estate. Despite their great tragedy, Annie and the kids had been blessed.

The stench of the pig field arrived long before she had eyes on it. She jogged by handsome Colthwaite House – 'the Big House' she would start calling it, like the locals – its Georgian windows like watchful eyes, its grey walls cracked, its gutters clogged with leaves.

She wondered if Andrew was home: Issy's brother had been the latest in a long line of Dillanes to become guardian of the place. He could be watching her puff past right now. Possibly laughing.

The walled farmyard spread out at the far end of Colthwaite House, open to view from the lane. Her in-laws still insisted on managing the attached farm, despite no longer living in the Big House themselves, which was impressive and possibly mad given their combined ages. The yard was a mucky concrete square, empty save for a tangle of rusted metal piled against one side, and a rectangular pallet with gate attached for dipping the animals' feet, which, now it was no longer attached to anything, looked like a guillotine.

She glanced at her sneakered feet making tracks, taking her the half mile towards High Tarn. She was certainly dipping her own trotters today – in puddles. Why had she chosen a white pair? And hot already: she'd only been going – she checked her watch – twelve minutes.

Directly following the farmyard, she came upon the stinking pig field at last, with its low arched-metal shelters, its turned clods of earth, and the pigs themselves, snuffling the ground or lying on their sides like exhausted Roman emperors. She gave them a wave. She ran on, passing Colthwaite church, where they'd held Issy's funeral. But she wasn't going to think about that now.

She stopped to catch her breath. At last, the turn off to the left and High Tarn. The Tarn itself was a body of water perched high on the crest of the hill; a portion of Issy's ashes had been scattered in the water as per her request in the will. Annie's head felt weird again when she thought of it: she might swim right through Issy, might swallow a part of her, Issy's atoms sticking to her wetsuit. She might carry her back to the house on her skin. The idea was at once both lovely and repulsive.

The Tarn's small car park was empty. No one here this time in the morning. Except her, Annie Jane Park, about to take on the climb. She looked up the hill track. *High* Tarn: they hadn't lied when they named it. The gradient was about to get real, and she needed to master herself. Her spirits faltering momentarily, she reminded herself of the fearsome beauty, the whole damned rawness, and then set off upwards at a lick.

A hundred metres later, she was in amongst the towering conifers, her breath staggered and uneven, her chest wet with sweat. The dark canopy kept everything beneath it in a state of murk, even the air felt bottle green. At least the leaf cover protected her from the rain's more enthusiastic drops. The needles were letting off their medicinal-scented oil. Pine cones rolled underfoot. She could give up, go back for eggs on toast. Or not.

Her steps were the only sound – that, and her laboured breathing. How had Issy done it? Annie rounded the fourth hairpin. Up ahead, stones graduated into mossed boulders, fern fronds like melted wax hanging over their edges. She threw a glance down the hill.

The steepest part of the ascent, the last sixty metres, rose in front of her. She was almost at walking pace, but at least she'd built up a good heat before submerging herself into that icy water. Her steps slowed until her body came to a halt, as if giving up entirely. Hands on hips, back arched, she recovered as the rain pattered on her forehead.

Bit spooky out here on your own. The ghosts of her past might be with her now. The thought wasn't entirely reassuring. Mum; Grandma Halmi; Appa; Issy.

Some distance to her right, a sound, then movement. Annie's breath stilled. At the base of a tree snarled with ivy: *something*. She edged higher up the path away from it.

Snap. A creature, one large enough to break sticks in the undergrowth. As a reflex, her hand went into her pocket for her penknife. It wasn't there; it was back home, in her jeans.

Hadn't there been rewilding going on in the north recently? Could there be bears? Wolves?

She shot off again, running faster, harder this time, upwards towards the lake. It wasn't logical, it was the direction her feet took her. She was closer to the top than the bottom and she'd decided what her life would look like here, and regardless of dangerous animals, Issy was in the Tarn, waiting.

Not a soul at the top, which was both a relief and, given the mystery animal, a bit of a worry. The long, uneven body of water stretched black along the flattened plane of the hilltop; its silken surface broken by arrows of rain.

The Tarn was popular with cold-water swimmers, providing a shallow entry point around its entirety. She dropped her stuff beneath a tree, squeezed herself hastily into her new wetsuit drawn from Caleb's backpack. The suit had been bought online by Annie with the secret intention that it wouldn't fit. Now she stared at the soft dome of her neoprene-coated stomach. It was surprisingly comfortable.

A goose squawked across the water, forcing her head to lift. It was grey, like the day, its feathers fluffed against the cold.

Proximity to the animal back down the slope lent her entry into the water a sudden urgency, and within minutes she found herself in the arctic water up to her waist, her toes buried in the slimy lakebed. With a breath, her head submerged.

'Oh!' She came up gasping for air. 'What were you *thinking?*'

Panting with cold, she looked back at the bank. Whatever that thing had been, it wouldn't follow her in for a swim.

Would it? There were fish in these parts big enough to take your toes off, people said. *Pike.* She could only ever picture them in a diving position.

She breast-stroked her way towards the island at the centre. Easy. Easier than she'd imagined anyway. She felt oddly protected inside the wetsuit.

'Where are you, sweetheart?' She pushed the water away with the flat of her palms. 'Issy?'

Ridiculous. If Issy had been here, she'd have laughed.

She kicked a little harder as the raindrops hit the water then bounced at her chin. Soon the island was close, and the water shallow again. She let her legs drop until her feet reached the gelatinous lakebed, hauling herself out to the bank, scaring some large birds with a wave of her arm. She flopped onto her back. The rain smacked her face. Two hundred days of it a year, according to Google.

The canopy swayed above. People would have lain where she was now throughout history, staring at these trees. Issy, certainly, and Andrew as children. Annie stroked her wet-suited stomach tenderly. Maybe they'd have come here with a boat, like *Swallows and Amazons*, their stick-thin arms rowing furiously. Maybe they'd have fished. Caught a pike or six.

Her thoughts turned to Lumi, forever in New Malden. Why was she thinking of her sister now? It was annoying. She had other things to think about.

But she could have brought Lumi here to experience these new textures, this light, if they'd been on good terms, couldn't she? Lumi might have loved it, if she'd dared. Her sister hadn't been there for her, though, in the last year; not in the way Annie had needed. She wasn't interested in new experiences; she lived in their childhood town, in a characterless new build with her solicitor husband. Her sister didn't care about trees.

Annie sat up. The island was smaller than it had appeared from the lake edge and home only to a few low shrubs, several broad-leafed trees and a knot of birds. Those little black duck-like ones with white beaks – were they moorhens?

She wondered how much of Issy she had met so far on her swim. A small portion of her ashes were safe in a drawer beneath Annie's bedside table at the cottage. The lake didn't need all of her wife.

Annie squinted at her dry clothes, abandoned on the mainland. *Come back!* they seemed to be saying. And: *breakfast!* Another enormous bird swooped low. Its wings beat heavily as it banked steeply to the left and headed over the treeline. The air was becoming colder, her hands began to shake.

She slid into the water and paddled back, rubbing furiously at her calves with a 'quick-dry' camping towel. Close by, more sounds of sticks cracking.

'Hello?' Her voice held a dead-flat quality in the earthy forest. 'Anybody there?' She walked a little to her right, putting space between herself and whatever it was. She *could* run. Even half-dressed. 'Hello?'

Hot breath escaped from nostrils somewhere nearby. The hairs rose again along her arms.

'Come out and show yourself!'

As if in understanding, something flesh-coloured inched from behind a boulder.

The pig. That *same* pig – she could tell from its face – from the road last night. Emerging from its hiding place, she could see air puffing not from nostrils, but from the hole at its mouth.

'Okay, okay, it's okay. We're okay.'

What if it was a male, a… what did they call it – a boar? They were often violent. She dipped her head. Two lines of teats ran along its underbelly. A female, thank God: a *sow*. She knew the name for that one.

The sow staggered a little closer, ears forward as if listening, though after last night, Annie felt sure it couldn't hear. Perhaps it could feel the vibration of her voice through the ground?

The pig was filthy and had a limp. It parked its bottom on the path leading down the hill, its one eye challenging her. Slowly, without breaking its gaze, Annie pulled on her jogging bottoms, socks and trainers. 'Ssh, ssh. It's okay now. I'll just...'

She picked her bag up and hitched it on her shoulder. The sow made a little noise, not so much a snort as a whine and staggered to its feet.

'What now?' Annie demanded. 'Because I haven't got all day.'

The pig dropped its head. It seemed to have a change of heart because it began to limp away into the trees to the right. Annie felt instantly guilty. Years of conditioning, where she was taught to worry about other people's feelings – even an animal's – before her own meant she wasn't okay with this.

'You don't *have* to go,' she called at its departing back. 'I need to get home, is all.'

It seemed to have no appreciation of Annie's childhood experiences, however, and once the pig was out of sight, she started downhill at twice the pace she'd ascended. The remaining adrenaline made her legs light. The rain drummed at her head and squelched in her trainers. When she hit the road, the concrete battering the soles of her feet was satisfying somehow, as if she deserved it. That poor pig, alone on the fell, wet and cold. She was lucky it hadn't had piglets to protect.

She was stupid, getting spooked about a pig. She'd need to get used to chance encounters with animals up here.

She reached home, the cottage silent, the children still fast asleep. She dragged off her wet socks and bunged them in the wash. Imagine Lumi's expression at all this mud. She went into the living room to discover she'd left the door to the wood burner open all night. That was a dangerously silly mistake. She fell onto the sofa and stared at the wall on the other side of the room.

Those new tenants would be waking warm and cosy in *her* bedroom in Hackney. They'd be making coffee in *her* kitchen. They had a child of their own, a newborn. There'd been a cot, a bottle sterilising machine, a play mat. They'd been overly solicitous, as if they knew what had happened to Issy.

She hoped they didn't use those soaps in the bathroom cupboard. They'd smelled of vetiver: Issy's favourite. She'd left them behind by accident. Another mistake. Not a dangerous one, but a mistake all the same.

Annie hurried about the house decanting boxes, unwinding bubble-wrap from pictures, placing them on the floor. She and the kids orbited one another, Annie with a smile on her face, a little forced, not saying much. They ate tinned sardines with chilli on toast for lunch, Annie still craving the added bite of good kimchi.

About half two, Annie received a text from Patrick:

> Hope the move went smoothly and the kids happy? They sounded well on the phone last night. Patrick x

> Thanks! Yes, all fine. Drowning in unpacking. A x

He hadn't responded. When Issy had first introduced Annie to Patrick, he'd been a Senior House Officer at The Royal Free and a heavy smoker, always in scrubs and continually tired.

Nowadays he was a big deal, always busy: gynaecology, mainly private practice. That wasn't the reason he was absent though; that was just privileged male single-mindedness – an intrinsic feature, and possibly not his fault.

Trying not to think about Patrick more than was necessary, she headed to the writing shed at the end of the upward-sloping garden.

She hadn't written for fourteen months – a lifetime – and she felt almost sick with trepidation. What if she couldn't do it anymore?

The shed's rear wall abutted the hillside, a slab of rock topped by gorse and matted shrubs. She placed the hard-copy theatrical manuscripts onto the shelves. It was cold and damp in here from the unceasing rain but quiet and calm too, promising the chance for new works, unbroken thought. Back home, writing had been underscored by the sonic chaos of London.

Some things Issy had written in The Letter were true: the turbulence of London, its enervating quality – something was happening inside Annie's nervous system already, she could tell. She wouldn't go so far as to say *relaxation*, not with the running and the pig and it being only twenty-four hours, after all, but something. Her out breath felt longer.

She arranged her desk against the low windows trying, but failing, not to think of Issy in the study in Hackney, the light from the Anglepoise glossing her hair. Now she felt sad again, and she'd hoped for the absence of it for these next few hours. But it was childish, wasn't it, to hope for *only* anything. She was allowed to hope, she decided, but not expect it.

From here, she could see both the back of the house, and the old stone hut dug into the rock on the garden's far side. An empty rectangle stood where its door used to. Most likely it had been a shelter for animals. She'd stepped inside a moment ago, the hut quiet and smelling of moss, but hadn't come up with a use for it.

Annie pushed her chair against the desk and plugged the bar heater into the socket. She opened her laptop and paired it to the internet: answered emails, paid bills from utility companies. No writing happened, but there was time.

She wasn't sure how long had passed before Caleb's and Grace's faces appeared in the misted window, making her jump. They smiled and waved.

'Can we ask you something?' Caleb mouthed, though she could hear him perfectly well through the thin sheet of glass.

'Of course.' She loved it when they needed her.

Grace stuck her head around the door. 'Wondering if you'd let us watch *Halloween?*'

Annie blinked. 'It's three in the afternoon.'

'Yes, but we've never seen it before.' Her stepdaughter loved a horror film.

'I'm not sure it's suitable.' Annie winced internally. 'What if it gives your brother more nightmares?'

'It won't,' Caleb protested. She could tell even he didn't believe himself.

The children waited, eyes round. It was two against one, which wasn't fair.

'I think,' Annie rose from her seat, attempting to give herself an advantage. 'You'd better give *Halloween* a rain check today. What about *Sicario?* Or *Carlito's Way?*'

Grace sighed. 'Seen them. Come on, Cal. Let's find something *suitable.*'

Annie watched them trudge back into the house, long legs like pencils.

Annie's timekeeping had never been impeccable but had become worse since Issy died. She seemed to be always too late or too early: parties, job interviews, birthdays, it didn't matter the occasion, she never failed to disappoint. Someone was either running to answer the door to her in only their socks and half their make-up or looking at their watch in ill-disguised disapproval as she arrived at dessert.

On this day, she chose 5pm, an hour before the invited drinks at her in-laws' as a sensible moment to set off food shopping at Gillyhead. The village was a decent drive from Colthwaite and its sole shop was a substandard Co-op manned by a grumpy teenager called Alex with no discernible customer-service skills, but it was the nearest by some miles, and they needed provisions. Her in-laws' drinks could wait a few minutes. Maybe fifteen at a push. The kids had asked only for a Cadbury's Fruit and Nut, and some Doritos as she'd left – their long bodies half-slumped in front of the TV. She'd made sure she loudly approved their choice of *suitable* film, but not their legs on the coffee table.

She took the road's sharp bends with caution; the car was too responsive for the slapdash nature of her driving. Annie didn't even learn to drive until she'd met Issy: Grandma Halmi hadn't approved of cars, she'd said they were just another way to eat up your money, and what was wrong with the bus? Secretly, Annie agreed. She'd never needed a car. Playwrights – especially ones that made little to no money – did not require cars, and all her hairdressing clients, the job through which she made an actual living, had only ever been a Tube ride away.

Five twenty pm. The falling autumn sky, the edges of the hills becoming outlines, the siren call of distant vehicles lighting her way. Up and down the rolling roads the car went, past the Fossemere estate, taking in glimpses of both Colthwaite and

Ethdale lakes. Annie let her eyes wander. Little fishing boats were anchored in Ethdale, the water matt brown.

They'd paid to go fishing once, she and Issy, in that very lake. Sitting in a boat, frozen but spellbound by the light on the wavelets, she'd wondered what the point was. Soon after, fish guts on her fingers, she'd got her answer. *But I'm a vegetarian,* she'd cried as the accompanying fisherman looked the other way. The moment had birthed one of their only arguments. She could still see Issy's disappointed eyes, the downward turn of her mouth.

Annie's eyes flicked to the road.

'Jesus!'

The car was over the midline and heading fast towards a hedge on the wrong side. She braked, overcorrected, and swerved back into the left-hand lane before levelling up. Unable to control her shaking hands, she pulled in at a lay-by, cut the ignition and rested her head on the steering wheel. The wind blew in the trees.

That was the second time in as many days she'd nearly had an accident, and not even a pig to avoid. Perhaps she should give up driving altogether.

She restarted the engine and drove slowly into Gillyhead, reversing into a parking space beside an outdoor walking shop. Wordsworth had lived in this village. His old school now sat right next to the car park. The poet's initials were carved into a wooden bench. Issy and Annie had taken the tour. The guide explained that lessons had lasted eleven hours of the day. Annie had whispered in her wife's ear that it was no wonder the poor boy wandered lonely as a cloud after so much study, and Issy had snorted, annoying the other people.

The village also had a Tibetan charity outlet amongst other things, pleasingly out of place in this most traditional of areas, selling knitted goods from a hall. Photos of sweet-faced children, silk flags, and a sign that read 10% OFF EVERYTHING decorated the window. Men and women in pastel-coloured hiking gear came and went through its entrance: they smiled at Annie, she smiled back. She knew that was she to go in, some tourist would ask if she worked there. It had happened more than once.

She turned a corner onto the lane with Boots, the Beatrix Potter Museum, and the Co-op. An old man stood outside the entrance to the supermarket. He held the door open for her with his walking stick. She thanked him, picked up a basket and made her way around the aisles.

Alex the teenager was behind the counter, head down, as if he hadn't moved since her last visit.

'Hey, Alex.'

He looked up.

'Annie.' She put her hand out. 'Issy's partner? Remember?'

Alex seemed confused. He held her fingers in his, limply.

'*Issy*, Elizabeth and William's daughter?' she urged. 'From Colthwaite?'

'Oh. Yeah.' His face reddened.

Annie cleared her throat. 'Sorry to disturb you but do you by any chance know of a shop that might sell kimchi?' she asked.

'Kim who?'

'Kim*chi*. It's a Korean side dish of salted and fermented vegetables.'

He looked down. 'Maybe the health food shop in Ambleside? They've got weird stuff.'

'Thanks. Maybe you could ask your manager to get some in, for next time?'

She filled her bag, paid Alex and left him in peace. 'You have a good day now.'

Why had she even asked? She'd known he wouldn't have it. *Weird stuff.* Kimchi wasn't weird. Patrick was weird: he had

OCD. He checked and rechecked everything, arranging objects into neat lines: plates, socks, tennis balls. He had vocal ticks, repeated actions in even numbers. That was weird. Kimchi was... *normal*. And she, Annie, was stubborn.

Leaning against the glass outside, the old man with the stick, still there, struggling to slide a bag of milk and oranges inside another, larger carrier.

'Allow me.' Annie set down her shopping. She fixed the bags for him and turned away.

'Thanks, Annie.'

She spun to face him. 'Do we know each other?'

'But of course!' The old man smiled. 'We met at the shoot, remember? The Boxing Day shoot?' He gestured at the darkening sky. 'Last year at the Big House?'

A shoot. Boxing Day. Colthwaite House.

'Ah. Yes,' she lied. 'I remember! Good to re-make your acquaintance...?'

'Vincent,' prompted the man. 'Vincent Prime. I live at the far end of the village, the other end to Chapel Croft, past the turning to High Tarn and closer to Collermere Lake.'

A lot of detail. Perhaps he was lonely. Perhaps he wanted a visit.

'Nice to re-meet you, Vincent Prime.' She glanced at his legs. They didn't look strong enough to carry him to the end of the street, let alone all the way to Colthwaite. 'Can I offer you a lift?'

'You're kind, but David's driving me.'

'Right. And David is your... son?'

'My son!' Vincent's eyes bunched in amusement. 'David is the vicar, dear. He's in Boots, picking up a prescription. The rectory sits directly behind my house.'

''Course it does.'

There was a pause in which Vincent's smile remained firmly fixed and Annie didn't feel it polite to leave.

'I hear you're a resident now,' he said at last. 'So good of you to honour Issy's last wish.'

A hot feeling travelled through her.

'Welcome to the neighbourhood.' He moved off slowly.

It was only once she'd driven halfway home that she remembered she hadn't been to that pheasant shoot, on principle. That Issy had gone alone. Vincent Prime had got that wrong. They must have met elsewhere.

CHAPTER THREE

Darkness had fallen by the time she arrived at Chapel Croft. It was five past six; not even fifteen minutes late. She must have raced the last mile. Badly done, Annie.

She'd barely stepped out with her bags and made for the porch, when a door at Blea Crag slammed open then closed, a gate creaked, a dog barked, and footsteps approached, crossing the lane. She'd not seen her mother- and father-in-law since she'd recced the place back in August and she hastily shoved the shopping into the hallway as if caught doing something she shouldn't, before walking back outside, ready and smiling beside the car.

'Hallo!' Elizabeth's voice was equal parts aristocratic and chilly. She approached up the track, a slender giant in pearls. She had an uncanny resemblance to Issy, their likeness starker now Issy was... gone.

On her mother-in-law's feet, rubber gardening shoes. She had make-up on, and Annie remembered it was Sunday, and therefore, church. Her hair was neatly styled to the shoulder and brush-dried at the bottom. Annie became aware of how she must appear in turn; gelled spikes with undercut. Slouch jeans, hoodie. Her shortness. Her general air of the city.

'Welcome, welcome.' Bodily contact was two light pecks on the cheek before her mother-in-law's fingers encircled half of Annie's bicep.

'I'm sorry we're late – I got stuck at the shop,' Annie began. 'Thanks so much for warming the place yesterday. For the food and everything. It was so kind.'

'My pleasure.'

Elizabeth's dog appeared, sniffing around Annie's Doc Marten's. Issy had referred to it as The *bloody* Jack Russell and that meant Annie had too; now she couldn't remember its real name. It seemed to be always magnetically drawn to her; it stood on its hind legs now, fussing at Annie's calf. She tried her best not to kick it away.

'Grandma!'

The kids were out the house, thank goodness, diluting things. Though a seven-day visit twice a year wasn't enough for them to have formed solid bonds, and at the last moment Caleb hung back, forcing his sister to take the lead.

Elizabeth pulled Grace into a warm embrace. Warmer than the one given Annie, she noted a little sourly. Grace could stand head-to-head with her grandmother now. They looked so similar: Elizabeth, Issy, Grace: the newest shiniest cut-out from the family cloth.

'Let's have a look at you.' Elizabeth pushed Grace away, holding her by the shoulders. 'How thin you are!'

Grace looked to Annie, eyebrows raised, but at the same moment there was the sound of feet slapping the lane, and William's deep voice said, 'That my grandchildren?' He appeared at the gate, then loped up the track, arms wide. 'Annie! Sticky journey last night?' Before she could answer, his attention had fallen on the children. 'God, but you've grown!'

He ruffled Caleb's hair, who was still a good head shorter than both his grandparents. Annie was shorter than all of them. It was like being a sapling amongst a forest of redwoods.

William took his grandson's arm and propelled him back down the track towards Blea Crag. Like Issy, William loved a reason to celebrate.

He looked back over his shoulder. His right eye had been damaged in a farming accident, resulting in the upper lid losing its muscle function, and now it drooped permanently, giving the impression he was struggling to stay awake. 'What are you waiting for, you ghastly lot? Glass of wine?'

'I'd prefer whisky,' Annie heard Caleb reply.

'Don't be stupid, idiot.' Grace flicked her hair as she and Elizabeth headed after him. 'I'd *love* a glass, though.'

'Lizzo, will you listen to that?' William laughed, to his wife. 'I've aired the Bordeaux, now the blasted grandchildren want a whisky.'

How often did he think of his daughter? As often as Annie? It couldn't be more.

Footsteps going away, a door squeaking open, then closed. Annie stood alone in the dark landscape, almost but not quite a part of it. She wanted to dissolve into the night or, failing that, unwind and drink soju in her own cottage, on the green sofa delivered from the London flat.

This was only the first day, for God's sake. Good things took time – something every experienced cook knows well.

The sound of rustling amongst the shrubs at the side of the garage. The *bloody* Jack Russell emerged from the undergrowth, something grey and nasty in its mouth. The dog gave her a look and trotted off home, pleased with itself. Its legs were even shorter than hers. She went after it down the track and through the gate, steeling herself as she made the short journey across the lane.

There were photos of Issy everywhere in Blea Crag: balanced on bookshelves in the snug, on side tables, on the walls. They had been up when Issy was alive, of course, but to Annie they seemed larger, brighter now, as if someone had turned up the volume. Issy as a toddler in a blue snowsuit; a twelve-year-old Issy hanging around the necks of two drooling Labradors; Issy at her graduation from UEA looking exactly as Grace did now, sandwiched between proud parents, neither of whom appeared to have aged in the intervening time. There were images of Issy's brother, Andrew, too, one of Annie and Issy together, and one – irritatingly – of Patrick.

A bit of ash floated from the fire and lodged in Annie's throat. She started to cough. William eyeballed her. 'All right over there?'

Eyes watering, she nodded. The kids were in the kitchen stroking the dogs – as well as of the terrier, there were two working sheepdogs, one old and one affectionate. Annie liked them far more than the yappy Russell. She cupped her goblet of wine. 'Sorry. Delicious.' She felt a bit like a museum exhibit standing in the centre of the room on her own.

The wine *was* good, though. William had passions for animal husbandry, food, drink, and attractive women. At least that's what he'd once told her with a wink after too much sherry. She looked at him now, perched on that strange piece of furniture; a red leather seat above a metal rectangle surrounding the fireplace. A 'Club Fender' the family called it. Annie tried to think of the club it historically might have fended, and from what. A gentlemen's, no doubt. From women, perhaps.

Elizabeth wasn't saying much. She seemed watchful, straight-backed in the narrow armchair, elegant in repose, her gazelle legs neat and at perfect right-angles to the floor.

Annie searched her mind for a conversation starter. It was as if, in this context, without the children or Issy beside her, she forgot who she was. She had plenty to say, just not to these particular people. She glanced at the fire. The logs smoked and hissed in the grate, sucking oxygen from the room. She'd left the door to the wood burner at the cottage open last night. Maybe she should enquire after a Club Fender of her own. She stifled a yawn.

William's eyes shone like marbles; the one that worked, anyway. Annie cleared her throat. 'So–'

'So,' William bellowed in return, as if he'd been switched on. 'How long 'til the children's school term begins?'

'Two-and-a-bit weeks,' she said. 'Time for us to settle in.' The words felt empty. Everything without Issy had become slack, unmoored. Weekly boarding had not been Annie's idea, but part of the deal: Issy's plan, as set out in the will. The kids would go to Issy's old school. Tradition. Green fields. Blah. Annie had given up trying to work out why. 'Thank you again for your generous support. It means a lot.' It had meant a lot to Issy; she supposed that was what mattered now.

'You're welcome.' Elizabeth gave her a smile, which made her mouth turn down instead of up. 'I'm hoping they'll enjoy it as much as ours did.'

Annie doubted that. Had Issy even enjoyed it, anyway? Not wildly, to Annie's memory, and yet she'd asked for Grace and Caleb to go there.

'Would anyone like crisps?' Her mother-in-law stood quickly and went to the kitchen, leaving William and Annie alone.

'I met Vincent Prime earlier,' she began, to break the silence. 'Outside the Co-op in Gillyhead.'

'Did he tell you,' William grinned, 'that you and he had met before?'

'Oh,' said Annie. 'Yes. But I didn't think we had.'

William chuckled. 'He's a swine. Worse than my actual swine out there.' He gestured behind him with a chunky thumb. 'It's his little game, see? Nothing coming out of the man's mouth is true.'

'What? Why?'

From the kitchen, Grace let out a little cry and said something about the dogs' saliva.

'Just one of his many ways.' William shrugged. 'People make their own traditions here in the countryside.' His chin dropped to his chest, and he fiddled with a shirt button entangled in its own cotton.

'Willy!' Elizabeth called from the kitchen. 'Which cylinder of crisps has been open longer than a week, please?'

William rose with a groan as his knees unbent. 'Duty calls.' He exited the room.

Vincent always told lies. Bizarre. Annie wondered if there were any more peculiar traditions she would be subjected to. Perhaps the 'game' was some sort of induction into local society: wind up the new person or whatever. Well, she wasn't going to be bullied or made fun of.

She began a quick shuffling tour of the room, navigating sofas, and side tables, rolling her eyes at the biographies of David Cameron and Nigel Havers. She passed the veterinary certificate hanging on the wall, a string of letters after Elizabeth's name. She sighed. Her in-laws were the sort of people who stood to attention when the national anthem played.

Her gaze snagged on three identical-looking animal skulls lined up along a top shelf. She'd never noticed them. Three long narrow snouts and cut-outs for eyes.

'They sheep?' Annie looked at William, freshly returned

from his crisp mission. He stood in the low doorway, his phone at arm's length.

'Who's that messaging me? I can't see a blasted thing.' His glasses were on his head, but she resisted telling him. 'Sheep?!' he said without looking up. 'They're piglets, girl.'

'Oh.'

He laughed and loped over to the Club Fender, his eyes going directly from phone to shelf, missing Annie out altogether.

She did wish he'd stop calling her a *girl*. 'What was special about those three piglets in particular that you kept them?'

William blew air through his lips. 'Triplets. Identical. Very rare. Elizabeth birthed 'em.'

Annie's hand went to her throat. 'What happened?'

'Didn't make it.'

'Well, but how? And how could you tell they were identical? I mean, don't piglets pretty much all look the same?'

'Nonsense.' He waved the wine bottle at her. 'Not if you know what you're looking for. Top up?'

She held out her glass and watched as the liquid rose until it touched the rim. William had remarkably steady hands for someone so old. She wanted to ask again exactly *why* the poor piglets hadn't made it but worried it would come across as the wrong sort of interest.

Elizabeth returned with the crisps. Pringles presented in a china bowl with painted cats prancing its circumference. Annie took a disc between thumb and forefinger, inserted it gingerly into her mouth and let it dissolve on her tongue. 'Lovely. Thank you.' She took a slug of wine.

Elizabeth resettled herself in the armchair.

'Just hearing about your late triplets,' Annie said.

Elizabeth's brows shot up. 'What?'

Annie pointed to the skulls. 'Sorry, the piglets. Just hearing about them. So sorry they died.'

'Ah.' Her mother-in-law gave her a funny look. 'Yes. Terribly sad.'

Annie glanced again at the skulls. It was then that she decided against mentioning the escaped sow. She didn't think she could cope if they laughed at her and told her it was meant to be wandering out there, or worse, that it should be captured and killed.

Caleb and Grace clomped into the room, Grace's head bending deeply as she navigated the two steps down, the sloped ceiling. The three dogs were right behind her, the *bloody* Jack Russell curling itself into a ball in front of the fire. It was chewing something. Possibly that dead animal it'd unearthed from beneath the shed.

William winked at Caleb. 'And if you think the pigs are bad, you should see the sheep.'

Caleb giggled. 'What are you talking about, Grandpa?' He sprawled next to Grace on the floor, rubbing the tummies of the two sheepdogs, pulling at lumps of mud caught in the animals' fur. It set Annie's teeth on edge to think of it gathering under his nails.

'Your father called,' Elizabeth announced suddenly, making Annie start, wondering how and why Appa had rung her in-laws, before remembering that Appa was dead and it was Patrick that Elizabeth was referring to, and the children to whom she was speaking.

'Oh?' Grace looked up. 'Why?'

Yes, Annie thought, annoyed, *why*. Why would Patrick ring his in-laws rather than her? Or the actual kids themselves?

Elizabeth waved a hand. 'He rang to talk about arrangements for the start of school.'

Now Annie was properly cross. How dare Patrick, living

hundreds of miles away in London and never around even when his kids had been nearby, feel he had agency over any aspect of their lives? How dare he go over her head. He'd given up that privilege years ago. *She* was their guardian. He sucked up to his in-laws, always had done. Probably hoping they'd leave something to him in their will. God knows, he had enough money of his own.

What was she doing here in this cottage eating horrible crisps and being made to feel shit? There was soju back at the cottage, and the rest of her joint. 'Oh Lord.' She stood, with affected surprise. 'I left the door to my wood burner open.'

'Well, that was silly.' Elizabeth seemed to buy it. 'Your glass is full.'

'Just pop back and shut it, old girl,' said William.

But the children were already on their feet too, arranging themselves, tugging on jumpers, making Annie sure they were as keen to get away as her. 'Well, I think the younger members might need their beds.'

'Yeah, sorry, Granny, Grandpa,' Caleb said winningly, picking up the baton. 'We're actually really tired.'

Annie pulled on her jacket, hiding her smile behind her zip. 'Thank you so much for having us.'

William and Elizabeth showed them to the door. 'Brief, but perfectly formed,' said William.

'It's been lovely,' Annie said.

'It has.' Elizabeth's smile was all teeth.

Annie walked back to Chapel Croft thinking about the pig skulls on the shelf. Who were her in-laws, exactly? She honestly had no idea. She'd seen William hold sheep down by their heads whilst Elizabeth pierced their ears with plastic identifiers. She'd seen syringes in rumps, needles, lots of shouting. They might as well have been aliens.

Issy had known all this – that Annie was different to them:

vegetarian, loved animals, was poorly schooled in farmyard things – and had wanted them to live here regardless. Perhaps Issy had had plans to educate Annie herself in the ways of the countryside, had she survived? Yes, that must have been it.

CHAPTER FOUR

The next few days were spent feverishly unpacking.

Annie tackled the kitchen first, her second sanctuary after the shed. She was doing well until, unable to decide where the ramekins should live, she found herself at the table, head in hands.

Caleb discovered her there. She felt his hand go on her shoulder.

'You okay?'

'Uh-huh.' It wasn't good for him to see her like this. The sadness must be saved, with all the other stored-up feelings, for another time. She stood quickly. 'Just taking a breather.'

She unpacked the living room, the bathroom, and finished the writing shed. She hadn't even started on the bedroom: she had clothing of Issy's, still smelling of her, folded in a suitcase in the wardrobe. She'd leave those. For an indeterminate time, perhaps when the children had started school.

During all the unloading, the kids seemed okay. They were undemanding, barring calls for food and the keys to the bike shed, after which they took off along the lane without helmets, legs lifted against puddles. She'd even persuaded them on a shopping trip into Ulswater and Amblethwaite on the pretext of not knowing what exactly they'd like to eat, but mainly because she preferred their company to her own thoughts.

She'd also managed a second run-swim at High Tarn, where the water felt marginally less cold and her body more able. There'd been no sign of the pig.

Now it was 10am and Friday, and Annie was wearing her tracksuit, the one that doubled as pyjamas. She was back in the shed, which was both too hot thanks to the bar heater, and unpleasantly damp thanks to the rain. Her plans to rise at dawn and bash out five pages of the new play's structural plan before breakfast had been ruined by an overriding need to sleep. After this, the habitual creative voice of doom started up in her head:

What if it was a dead horse?

No, it was good.

But what if it wasn't, really?

She already had a title: *Kimchi Trout Sandwich*. Aware it didn't exactly trip off the tongue, it would do for now. A 'kimchi trout sandwich' was something Grandma Halmi inexplicably requested as a treat on her birthday, thirty years into her life in England. Appa told his mother she could eat anything anywhere, but no, that was what she chose.

Annie raised her head. The sky – what she could see of it – was dour. Across the garden the leaves dripped from an earlier downpour.

Her writing spot in Hackney had been at the kitchen table, carving out space amongst the condiments, bills, and kids' detritus. The image was fading already.

She must concentrate. She dragged her eyes back to the page.

The plot was closely based on Grandma Halmi's late romantic preoccupation with the local vicar at Christ Church, New Malden, whom Annie felt sure had been gay. What wouldn't go into the play was that Mum had already left – well, had been taken away – by the time the action was set. Sectioned hours from home, a place Grandma Halmi described as 'somewhere to get a nice rest', Annie hardly saw Mum after that. She used to find her used needles hidden around the flat: on a top shelf, in the toilet cistern, a locked box. She'd turn it into a game, make a point of searching for them. To a six-year-old, the needles were treasures, proof of her mother's existence. *Kimchi Trout Sandwich* was going to be a very real play. But not that real.

A movement inside the cottage drew her off the page again: Grace, upstairs in the bathroom. Annie watched as Grace's naked body bent over the sink. She was staring at her reflection in the wall mirror as she mopped at her face and armpits with a flannel. An electric toothbrush whizzed across her teeth. Her stepdaughter replaced the brush on its shelf and took several paces back, turning this way and that, then all the way around for a rear view. Annie smiled, dropped her eyes to the page, but a moment later felt a presence and looked up again.

'Issy?'

Condensation on the windows. The patter of rain.

Pushing air through her lips, she googled Issy's *Wikipedia* page. Someone who wasn't Annie had updated the entry.

Issy (Isabelle) Dillane was the author of seven award-winning novels. Her first, Calling Home won the Desmond Elliot prize for emerging writers, 2003. Her second, A Banner for the Heart, was nominated for the Man Booker 2005. She was also winner of the Women's Fiction Prize 2008 for her third novel, Eleven in the Afternoon.

It went on listing books and prizes. At the end it said:

> Issy Dillane lived in East London with her two children, Caleb and Grace (from her first marriage to Patrick Cook, a doctor) and her long-term partner, Annie Park, a playwright. She died of complications following a rare catastrophic aortic aneurism, a genetic condition, in Homerton Hospital, London, on 15th June 202–

Annie clicked off the page. She felt sick. Who wrote this shit. Didn't they have better things to do?

For comfort she sought Grace's outline in the bathroom window again. There she was: lissom as a ribbon. She'd taken out her phone, snapping a selfie and drawing the screen toward her. Annie watched as her fingers typed a message.

That floppy-haired boy back in the East End – what had his name been – Dougal? Douglas? Something Scottish sounding. Issy hadn't liked him.

The cottage's back door opened. Caleb stepped out in his boxers, cotton and elastic hanging from his hips. He lit a cigarette and shivered; sinewed arms at his chest as he puffed out smoke rings. She'd thought kids these days were too smart for tobacco. She'd report the smoking and selfies to Patrick when they next spoke: she couldn't be sure what view he'd take. Hopefully a dim one. Telling tales was what parents – and step-parents – did for one another. Apparently.

Caleb finished his cigarette and went back inside the house. Annie glanced at her laptop. The cursor flashed on a blank page. The paper on the desk with the words, STRUCTURAL PLAN underlined in black Sharpie had – she counted – thirty words on it. The voice of doom told her: not good enough. At all.

At least the kids were up, cleaning themselves. Well, more *preening*, really: smoking, posing for the camera.

At this point, the voice of doom became very strict and told her if she didn't focus, she'd be banned from soju and weed for a week.

For two hours she wrote freehand, a rough outline of the plot. Well, 'plot'. It wasn't a high-concept thriller. Halfway into bullet-pointing the fourth act, there was a squeal on the lane, followed by William's piercing whistle, then, 'Belle, fall back! Don't bite her bloody ankles!'

Annie tried to shut the noise out, but the whistling and dog barking continued until she heard William bellow, '*Annie?*'

With a feeling of dread, she closed her laptop and hurried to the gate at the end of the track.

Staff in hand, William was waiting for her in a knitted hat, mud-splattered khaki boilersuit, and wellies. 'Ah, there you are. Lie *down*. Not you, Annie, the dog. Wretched things.' He appeared to have been herding a single hairy sow with pendulous teats who'd come to a standstill in the middle of the lane. 'I've a message for you.'

Annie nodded at the sow. 'Taking it to pasture?'

'Say something?' He cupped a hand to his ear.

'Taking it to pasture?' she repeated loudly, remembering William's hearing wasn't the best, and that she was still in her pyjama–trackpants combo and braless. She crossed her arms over her chest.

'Pasture? Dear me, girl, it's not a sheep.' William approached the gate, rested his staff against the wall and removed his hat. 'Off to the knackers.'

'What's wrong with it?' It looked normal enough. Whatever 'normal' meant. The dogs were barking at its rump. Annie told them to bog off in her head.

'Nothing's wrong with it. It's what it's *farrowing*.' William pressed his palm to his cheek, squashing his face to one side.

'Farrowing?'

'Producing. Birthing.'

'Oh. You mean...?' She didn't know how to phrase it delicately and instead found herself pressing her own face to the side. 'The pigs with...?'

'Exactly.'

Could the sow currently on strike in front of her in the lane be mother to the disabled gilt she'd seen twice? This one here had a brown heart-shaped birthmark on its left flank. The other sow hadn't had that, but then perhaps it wasn't like humans where you inherited features from your parents. The sow was looking at her, as if hoping she'd argue on its behalf. Annie smiled at it. The sow looked away.

William pulled a handkerchief from his pocket and blew. 'Shame really. Expensive loss. And not the old girl's fault, but better in the long run.'

'Right.' She studied the floor. 'But couldn't it be the father of the disfigured pigs that has the faulty gene, or whatever? How d'you know it's the mum?'

'The boar? Not a chance.' William tapped his nose. 'He's out of Old Major. Water-tight lineage. Nope, this came down the mother line.'

The mother line. Like a shipping company.

The dogs were getting restless and William gathered himself. 'Now, I've a missive. The Saturday after next, there's drinks. You're invited.' He stuffed the 'kerchief back into his pocket, replaced his hat and picked up his staff.

She waited for more. 'At Blea Crag or...?'

'Ah yes, no, my son Andrew's drinks. Colthwaite House. 7pm. One of his boys was supposed to have put an invite through your door.'

Annie shook her head. 'I don't think–'

'Thought not, the lying bugger. Useless boy. Nothing like his brother. Whole village is coming. The Paines too, remember them? You and Issy liked the wife.'

'We did?'

William tossed his head around like a horse. 'Yes. Directs plays at Kendal. Blue hair.'

Annie had a vague recollection. The wife chatty, the husband tall and fair and sporting stray whiskers that curled from his eyebrows into his eyes.

More drinks. The parties here were relentless. The village must be permanently pissed. Probably the only way they could deal with the rain.

'That's the day before the kids leave for school,' she said, suddenly realising.

'All the more reason. Come and celebrate.'

'Right. Ha. Yes, I won't be celebrating.'

'Commiserate then.'

William moved off with the animals. Before the sow disappeared round the bend, it stopped and looked back at her with small accusing eyes.

That afternoon, Annie took a walk. It was important to expose the skin to as much light as possible; she'd already achieved her writing goal for the day. Now she must stretch.

She elected for a route up the fell, one she'd done with Issy several times. Her intended destination was random – just the top, really. She set off along the lane, catching her reflection in a cottage window; her hair was growing out. She'd need to take the clippers to it. The sky was grey of course – she probably wouldn't be getting any vitamin D after all.

Someone was coming along the lane towards her. A man in a long scarf, white trainers and black trousers. Something about him didn't look local. Apart from anything, he was walking too slowly, the way tourists do on their first visit to a place. The man and Annie passed one another. She smiled and the man smiled back distractedly. He was about sixty, with a grey crew-cut and kind eyes. She hoped he wasn't planning any excursions up the Fell in *those* shoes. Soon he was behind her and a minute after that she turned off at a signpost pointing into the woods, forgetting him entirely.

Drinks at the Big House in two Saturdays' time. Ugh. She liked Andrew but he always seemed nervous, as if something bad was about to happen.

The woods were silent and very, very damp, the trees the deciduous kind. Was that the right word? She was hopeless at nature. She and Issy had been through here at night once. They'd stood on the slope staring through the gaps in the canopy, a hip flask going back and forth between them. Issy had detailed the constellations. Annie always struggled with stargazing. What was the point of all that 'oohing' and 'ahhing' over pinpricks of light that weren't even in existence anymore?

Now she stood on the very same spot alone, in the grey light of day, and Issy was gone forever. Liking someone was as intense as loving them, and they'd both liked and loved one another. She bent in half to lay sticks in a star shape on the ground, a memento mori, before walking on.

Five minutes later she was lost, and the green overgrowth was high as her shoulder. It was her own fault: she'd failed to take her bearings before setting off. Her head had been too full of thoughts. Issy would laugh if she could see her now.

She took out her iPhone: Google Maps to the rescue. The blue dot flashed her location in an ocean of green. Fat lot of good that was. She followed the dot, which was useless; she was essentially following herself. She stepped over rotten bracken, careful of any hidden burrows, hoping for a landmark to jog her memory. She thought of the lost pig, trekking this terrain with its limp and its one working eye.

In front of her, a large broken-down section of drystone wall ran up the side of the hill. Someone, or something, a long time ago judging from the moss growing on the rubble, had driven a large hole through it. Beyond was a wide path overlaid with pine cones and needles fading into ordered lines of evergreens. It was a darker, eerier route, but the lines of trees meant she could at least walk a clear path with her head up instead of staring at her feet. The path traversed the hill diagonally upward. She looked at her phone again, the blue dot moving slowly northwards.

Out of nowhere, a flurry of excited clucks started, her foot struck something, and a pulse of electricity shot through her. The force propelled her onto her back with a yelp, and she dropped her phone. She watched as a gaggle of pheasants took off.

She sat up, blinking with shock. She'd struck an electric fence. How had she missed seeing *that*? Beyond it lay a huge pheasant pen, its pale grey metal almost invisible in the dim light. On the other side were the pheasants, now running ungainly away, as if she'd had nasty things planned. A solitary feather was left on the electric tape.

The pen stretched in all directions as far as the eye could see. Large blue barrels were dotted about inside. Annie knew they contained seed for the birds. There were neon yellow pellets, she noticed now, scattered around the base of the fence. She got to her feet, put her ear to the wire. Yes: crackling. She'd been distracted, that's why she hadn't seen it. One day soon she'd properly come a cropper if she didn't focus.

She flung her neck back at the canopy. Which way now? She felt small and useless. The wind blew above. On the ground, the air was still.

The tinny buzz of a vehicle. It sounded as if it was coming towards her from inside the enclosure. A khaki buggy came into view. She recognised it at once as belonging to Stephen, the estate ranger. Annie waved. 'Hey!'

The buggy pulled up on the other side of the fence. Stephen idled the engine and climbed out. A flat cap pulled down over his forehead obscured his eyes.

'Ranger' wasn't the right word for him, she remembered now. William had once put her straight on that. *'The Keep, girl: we say the Keep here.'*

Now the Keep and Annie faced one another on opposite sides of the fence.

He nodded. 'How do.'

'I'm good, thanks. How... how are you?'

'You're a long way from home.' His voice was deep, his accent pleasing to Annie's ear.

'I'm a crap orienteer.'

'You want to be careful. Not safe up here.'

'You're telling me. Nearly electrocuted myself.' Her smile faded. 'Or do you mean bears and stuff?'

'Bears?' Now it was his turn to smile. 'Nowt but birds up here, lass. Electricity and poison more like.' So that's what the yellow pellets were. 'Very good at keeping badgers, foxes, poachers and rustlers out.' He let out a staccato laugh. 'Likes of you.'

'I'm vegetarian.'

Stephen sucked air between his teeth. 'Ooh, locals won't be happy about that.'

She chuckled. 'Which ones?'

'You'll be wanting to go back the way you've come. Owt up this way but pens. Be wandering around 'til dark, you will. Wouldn't want to get caught up here during...' He turned away, busying himself.

'During...?' she prompted, but he didn't say any more. She

looked behind her down the path. 'I've never taken this route. How big is this pheasant pen?'

'Two miles square, give or take.'

'Two *miles*?! I didn't know pheasants needed so much space.'

'Aye.'

She squinted into the distance, at the trees fading into blackness at the pen's top end, pinpricks of light piercing its edges. It looked like there might be a clearing up there. Yes, she could just make out its circular shape. 'I'll retrace my steps,' she said. 'I mean, I was going to head for the top but–'

'Not this way, you're not.'

'Guess I'll just go home then.' When Stephen didn't respond, she said, 'Wish me luck.'

'Good luck.'

Annie wheeled about, praying she'd remember the way. Back through the pine forest she went.

She held a decent opinion of Stephen, despite his offhand manner, mainly thanks to Issy who thought him wonderful. Annie didn't know why but had decided to trust her wife on this: she'd spotted him across a crowded room numerous times over the years surrounded by a sea of local lads, and sometimes when Annie had walked the lane with Issy, Stephen's buggy would fly by and he'd salute.

She picked her way down the hill, the return easier than anticipated. On the last section of the route, the star-shaped sticks she'd laid not thirty minutes previously had been moved and piled up at one side of the path. She stared, wondering if she might have kicked them there herself without realising before moving on. She looked over her shoulder into the trees. Perhaps another walker. Or an animal. Maybe it was the pig.

CHAPTER FIVE

The days seemed to be rolling into one another with increasing speed. Annie couldn't remember if it was Wednesday or Thursday, but was making vegetable bulgogi, the kids' favourite. Annie's number one hobby had always been cooking. The process of chopping and prepping soothed any bumps in life, a skill she'd learned from Grandma Halmi, despite the addition of atrocities such as kimchi trout sandwiches.

She was also doing four banchan dishes to go with the bulgogi because they looked pretty, tasted delicious, and had a bunch of ingredients in common. But mainly because she was sad. She started with oi muchim and sigeumchi namul, slicing the cucumbers finely, covering them in salt to bring out their water, then turning to blanch the spinach and chop scallions into tiny cubes.

No wonder she was sad, she told herself huffily: she'd left London, she was lonely, she had no clue about the ways of the people here, *and* the children's departure for weekly boarding was almost upon her. And her wife had died, for God's sake. *Died.*

She put down the knife she was holding to wipe her eyes.

Everything just felt so... empty. And it would be even emptier soon. And apart from fear of the kids' absence, there was the issue of Annie needing to care solely about herself for the first time in years. It left too much air everywhere. How was she supposed to fill it?

She took a small bowl and threw in a handful of sesame seeds, minced garlic, sesame oil, vinegar, sugar, gochutgaru, and soy sauce.

In the hallway, she could hear the kids readying themselves for another bike ride. 'See you later!' Grace yelled.

Annie called for Grace to use less volume; she was right there, only ten feet away. And for them to be careful on wet lanes and back 2pm sharp for lunch. When they'd gone, she said, 'I love you. I love you so, so much,' very quietly to herself and started to cry again.

Three minutes later, her eyes had just stopped swimming when there was a knock on the door. 'For goodness' sake.' She wiped her hands on her apron and went to answer. 'What have you forgotten now... oh.'

It was Andrew standing on the porch stone, shuffling from one foot to the other, reminding her oddly of Caleb.

'Hi.' His hands were in his pockets, awkward as she was. 'Didn't want to disturb you, but *did* want to say welcome. Sorry I haven't been before, it's been ridiculously busy, what with one thing and another.'

'Hi.' From the kitchen, the sound of water beginning to bubble on the stove. She forced herself not to turn around. 'Please don't worry. It's fine.'

'Dad said my boys forgot to drop in the invite for our party?' he said. 'We'd love you to come. It's this Saturday, 7pm at the Big House.' He smiled. 'D'you think you might make it?'

'Definitely. Thank you.' That was that then, no getting out of it now.

He made to leave but turned back at the last moment. 'Do holler if you need help.'

'Oh, thanks.'

'With anything.'

'I will.' She went back into the kitchen. That was touching, what he'd said, but there'd been something else, she felt, on his mind. From the set of his shoulders, perhaps. She turned the heat down on the pan of water.

Now for the aubergines. There were no Asian aubergines available, of course, but bog-standard ones would do. She chopped them into two-inch pieces, flung them in the steamer and stared at the pot.

If she felt more comfortable around him, she'd call Andrew up there and then, demand to know what that other thing was.

She watched as the lid of the steamer went cloudy. She'd completed the first scene of *Kimchi Trout Sandwich* this morning. She'd felt pleased with it when she'd finished, but more than likely she'd return tomorrow, reread, and judge it terrible.

She finished dressing the banchan. She laid chopsticks and bowls on the table and put placemats out for the hot dishes. Eyes on her handiwork, she deliberated for a moment about soju at lunchtime, and decided it was a 'no'.

Talking of which: the kids were out the house. She brought Patrick's name up on her phone.

'This is Doctor Patrick Cook. Please leave a message after the tone.'

'Er... oh hi. It's Annie. I hope you're well. Just calling because there's a little matter to do with Caleb and smoking that I'd like to talk to you about. Nothing major but... Give me a call when you have a minute. Cheers.'

Patrick giving her a call. Like *that* was going to happen. She put her phone away and wondered how the runaway mutant pig might be doing. She hoped it was okay.

She stepped out for her now-habitual afternoon constitutional, turning left on the muddy lane towards Colthwaite House. Sheep spread like a dot-to-dot up the ridge. She'd head left along the lane beyond the Big House, turn right down the track to the church, and walk into the woods at the rear of the churchyard – somewhere she hadn't been for some time. Not since Issy was alive.

She'd barely seen Elizabeth and William – *Lizzo and Willy* – since the drinks round at Blea Crag that second night, but tomorrow was Saturday and the drinks party for the entire village and she'd definitely see them there. Maybe Vincent Prime would be invited? He'd be someone else she knew. Sort of.

She got twenty metres or so along the lane from Chapel Croft, when she had a panic attack. She placed her hand on her racing heart, gulping deep breaths. Where was Issy? She couldn't just be gone. Why wasn't she here to help? She wasn't going to cry. She was going to breathe through it. After twenty seconds, which she counted on her watch, her breathing steadied and she could stand upright again. A lone sheep stared at her through a barbed-wire fence.

What kind of stupid name was *Willy*, anyway?

Dogs began to bark nearby, around the next bend. Not wanting anyone to catch her like this, she turned on her heel and hurried in the opposite direction back along the lane past Chapel Croft and Blea Crag towards the bridge.

From behind, she heard, 'Annie!' Too late: it was William. She dropped to her haunches and pretended to tie a shoelace in case that made him change his mind. He caught up with her anyway. She lifted her head. William stood over her, tapping his shepherd's staff on the ground like an impatient god. 'Free?' he demanded.

'I–'

'Good. Need help with some serving.' He turned and headed away in the direction of Colthwaite House.

She ran after him. 'Um...?'

'Yes?'

'Serving as in for the drinks party?'

William roared with laughter. 'Good God, no! Farm work, girl. Farrowing, handling, serving. Gilt that needs mating. Her first time.' He marched on.

'Gilt?' When one of the Dillanes said it, it always sounded like 'guilt'. 'That's a female that hasn't bred yet, right?' She was half-running to keep up, his stride was that much longer than hers.

'Right.'

'Which bit...' she panted, 'of the *serving*, exactly, do you need help with?'

'You'll encourage the gilt into the pen. She's jumpy. From a litter out of Old Major. Help her relax, keep her calm. We've lost one of that litter already: an escapologist. Not a looker, mind.'

'Not a...? I think I saw her up at High Tarn.' It just came out.

William stopped. 'When?'

She shouldn't have told him. 'Can't remember exactly.' If she kept it vague, maybe it wouldn't ruin it entirely for the poor thing.

'Up at High Tarn, eh?' William nodded to himself. 'Well, her wandering days are over. No, the gilt we're serving today is the same batch, but not a mutant.'

Annie felt herself shrink. 'What do you mean, "her wandering days are over"?'

'We're going to try this gilt today for breeding,' William ignored her question, 'or it'll be off to the knackers with her like her mum, in case she also carries the bad gene. Huge waste of money, but there you are.'

The dogs had stopped to sniff the verge. He tapped their legs with his staff.

They walked on in silence for a while, Annie praying that whatever was going to happen, it wouldn't involve a syringe and a needle.

From behind, the rumble of a large vehicle racing along the twisted roads in their direction.

'Heads!' William yelled. The dogs circled into him, obediently. He hooked the crook of his staff around Annie's arm and pulled her to one side. 'Look out!'

'I'm not a sheep!' she said, only half-joking.

A plain white Transit van whizzed past, bass thumping from its speakers. The young driver's head bobbed to the music. She could smell diesel – and skunk.

'Always happening,' William grumbled. They moved on.

A little way ahead, the engine and the beat cut out. William and Annie rounded the corner to the driveway of the Big House and there the van was, parked to the rear of the farmyard by the shed where Elizabeth kept her veterinary supplies.

The driver leapt from the vehicle, flinging the rear doors wide. Elizabeth emerged from the barn in a blue plastic apron, a pair of goggles on her head like a mad professor. The shed had a coded numerical locking system rather than a key, which struck Annie as surprising for such a run-down farm. Perhaps, like the pheasant pens, they'd had problems with burglars in the past. The driver handed over two brown boxes, which Elizabeth signed for then went back inside. The van's engine fired. It whizzed out the far end of the yard in the direction of Gillyhead.

'Well, *he* certainly seemed to have urgent produce,' Annie commented, as William headed sideways to the larger barn.

'Fresh swine supplementation. Comes in every now and then.' He poked at the ground with his stick. 'Can't raise a drift on this blighted pasture and a few scraps.'

'A drift?'

'Goodness me, girl, didn't Issy teach you anything? A drift is the name for a group of pigs.'

'Oh.' It was funny, really: their solid, hairy bodies seemed anything but drifty.

The sows were out in the pig field, slick with mud. They snuffled busily in the grass outside their corrugated homes. 'Good day, ladies!' she called.

The animals looked up. As far as their heads allowed, anyway. William got to freeing a ball of wire snagged in the wall. Annie leant against the gate while she waited, careful not to touch the electric strip. She was hoping to catch sight of some piglets. They were always so sweet.

'How old are this lot, then?' she enquired.

William wound the wire round his arms like an extension lead. 'Yearlings mainly. Hardly out of nappies. That one,' he pointed at an especially rotund pig with mud around her mouth, as if she'd been at the chocolate, 'she's older. She's auntie to the one you're about to help.'

Annie did some family-tree arithmetic. 'That means she's also auntie to the one I saw up at High Tarn?'

'That's right,' he said. 'The ex-wandering mutant, currently penned in the barn.'

'In the barn?' That poor deaf pig, with its limp and hole for a nose was right here in the farmyard, a prisoner.

'Captured her a couple of days ago, the little tinker. She was hiding behind the vicarage. David lured her out with fried bacon.' He chuckled. 'She's off to the knackers too, after...'

Annie felt sick. 'After...?'

'Elizabeth's checked her over.'

'Checked her over in case of...?'

'In case she's pregnant.' He shook his head. 'Obviously. That *would* rather complicate matters.'

'But how would she have become pregnant?'

'*How?*' William raised an eyebrow in amusement. 'Annie, I'd have thought by now you'd have learned how.'

That wasn't what she'd meant, and she felt sure he knew it. The dogs had gone ahead. In the area behind the sows, the boars – housed in separate pens so they didn't fight – were kicking up a racket.

'Also, why would it complicate matters?' she asked. Couldn't they just let the poor thing give birth and *then* take her to the abattoir? This wasn't Annie's world at *all*. It hadn't even been Issy's. Not really.

'Eh?' William drew an arc in the air with his staff. 'Time to stop talking, start toiling.'

She trundled after him into the barn, a sense of dread mounting in her chest.

The barn was dark and warm inside with small pools of orange lamplight illuminating straw-covered pens. It smelled of petrol, and greasy sheep fleeces.

'This way.' William strode toward the rear where the light didn't reach.

Annie followed, stepping around the jumble of farmyard equipment. Poorly sheep bleated from their makeshift pens. The farm cat pranced by her empty food bowl.

Daylight shone between a chink in two slats in the wall.

Annie couldn't resist putting her eye to it as she passed: she could make out the pig field, beyond that the hills.

She'd travelled half the building's length now and no sign of the sickly pig so far. Then her hands brushed cold metal and something snorted. Behind a gate, a lump. She squinted: it was the disfigured pig. She felt disproportionally pleased to see it.

'Hey!' Annie whispered.

Its open mouth gaped a dark hole in its shadowy face. She reached a hand through the rungs and the pig shuffled closer, its breath gusting at her fingers.

Above them, the neon strip lights suddenly flickered on. Annie snatched her hand back and the pig retreated to a corner. 'Annie, dithering!' William shouted.

She left the pig and joined William at the back. It was a large area divided in two by movable metal gates. A contraption sat in its centre, like the one in the yard for the sheep dip with an unnerving resemblance to a guillotine. A long metal chain attached to a smaller metal slat acted as a barrier and when it was lifted, the animals could pass through, and vice versa. The chain was operated by hand from outside the pen. On one side of this large rear pen a young female – the gilt – stood, eyes rolling in fear. The other side was empty. A closed door in one wall led ominously outdoors.

'Right.' William rubbed his hands. 'I'm going now.'

'Going?' Annie was startled. 'Where?'

'To prepare the boar, girl. I'll only be five minutes. Get in the pen. Give her this.' He lobbed something over, which Annie caught.

A tube of white cream in a syringe with – mercifully – no needle but a flat teat at one end. 'What is it?'

'Pig soju.' He grinned and took off, opening the door in the wall, the dogs at his heels.

She stared at the space he'd left behind. She couldn't remember ever telling him about her love of soju.

Throwing a leg over the pen, she climbed in. The gilt slunk away, backing itself against the wall.

'Come on, it's okay.' She proffered the syringe. The gilt wasn't convinced. Annie pretended to suck on the teat. 'Mmm, delicious.'

Its little eyes closed. Annie looked around, helpless.

A series of meat hooks dangled from an automated metal runner high above. She followed the runner with her eyes to where it met the wall and fed into a metal box. There was a red lever at the box's centre. Outside, William was cursing.

'Ignore him,' she whispered, coming to kneel in front of the gilt on the dirty floor. 'I won't hurt you.'

The gilt sidled toward her, underslung jaw agape. Annie stayed quite still until it reached the syringe. The pig's mouth wrapped around the teat, and it began to suckle. Annie was just beginning to enjoy the moment when there was a furious squeal from outside and the gilt jumped back in fear. Annie scrambled to her feet, the door flung open and in raced the boar, all tusks, hair, and testosterone. It ran straight up to the divider, pawing the ground. The gilt gave an ear-piercing cry of its own and galloped away to safety at the far reaches of her own side, head through the outer railings in an attempt at escape.

The boar panted. Drool hung from its mouth. 'Righto!' William bellowed, as the boar began to headbutt the barrier. 'Annie, climb out! We're to leave them alone until the virgin's less hysterical.'

'Leave them?' She watched the interlocking barriers tremble under the boar's considerable pressure.

''S'good for her.' The dogs were circling outside the pen like hungry wolves. 'Make a woman of her. Hurdles'll protect her.'

'Hurdles?'

William raised his arms in exasperation. 'The barriers, you ninny.'

With a last look at the gilt, she followed William out the rear door, leaving the boar to do its thing.

A light spit had started. They stood side by side under shelter of the gutter, the dogs at their feet. The dreadful noises continued inside. William drove circles in the mud with his staff.

'Not used to this, eh?'

'Pig rearing? Not really.'

'The "ways of nature".'

Her fingers curled around the slats at her back, the wood splintering into her skin.

'Men and *women*,' William went on. 'Through the centuries.'

Annie looked at him.

Inside, things had gone quiet.

'Right.' William leant a shoulder against the door. 'Follow me.'

There appeared to have been some sort of truce between the gilt and the boar. They now stood not far from one another on either side of the hurdles. 'See?' William said. 'You city gals need to stop worrying.'

William told her to stand by the guillotine-slat chain contraption and pull at his instruction. He climbed into the gilt's half of the enclosure, put on some gloves and readied himself at the gilt's rear, like a backstop in a game of rounders.

'*Now, Annie!*'

Annie yanked on the chain. The guillotine-slat lifted. The boar bounced through. Foam leaked from its lips. It hurried round to the female's rear. The panting female backed sideways until its rump met William's hands, then panicking, it pinballed forwards between the dividing hurdle pursued by the boar. Half of the gilt's body was now on one side of the pen, half on the other, with the barrier slat hanging ominously above her back. The boar nudged her forwards a little and mounted. William moved to one side, but the gilt wriggled free and let rip a horrendous squeal, so loud that, shocked, Annie let the chain go. The slat dropped like a knife, making William yell. The animals dodged the slat, jumping apart just in time, and stood separated once more on each side of the pen. Mercifully, neither had been hurt, but William was now marooned on the side with the furious boar. Her father-in-law vaulted the barrier and landed on his feet beside her. She'd never seen anyone move so fast. The boar thundered round the pen.

'Bloody idiot!' William pulled the gloves off and stuffed them in his pocket.

'It was an accident.' Annie stepped out of his way. 'I'm sorry.'

'Not you! The damned gilt!' His face was puce. He led the disgraced female to a smaller pen beside the lame sheep. '*Women*,' Annie heard him mutter.

She didn't think it was the gilt's fault. She looked at the boar. He'd come to a stop now, tail down, crestfallen.

'Come on, old fella. Next time, eh?' William encouraged him outside while Annie waited anxiously at the back of the barn.

When William reappeared, he'd calmed down. 'I feel I've rather put you through the wringer,' he said. 'My fault. Shouldn't have expected so much when you're not used to it.' He hit the lights, plunging the barn back into almost darkness, and walked off.

'Is that it, then?' she called after him.

'That's it.' His voice sounded far away.

Annie followed his steps towards the rectangle of daylight filling the door at the front. She reached the disfigured pig's pen.

'Hey,' she whispered. 'Look.'

William was already out the door and didn't see her lift the pen's latch, leaving its gate ajar.

'Go,' she encouraged. 'Be free.'

CHAPTER SIX

It was the day of the drinks party at the Big House. It was also the day before the children's departure for weekly boarding school. Annie felt her mood blacken as she stared, from her position on the sofa, at the logs crackling in the wood burner. Grace and Caleb were too preoccupied to notice. For the last few hours, they'd been shut in their rooms, the odd thump passing through the ceiling to the living room. For something to do, Annie picked up Issy's final novel.

She scowled at the words on the page. Issy was stealing the kids away, and she was doing it from the grave. Private school had not been part of their shared ethics or parenting style, and she bet her in-laws had had something to do with the decision. Them, or bloody Patrick.

She'd read the same paragraph five times. The book was brilliant, which was even more annoying right now. Brilliant writing, brilliant pacing. She flung it down and flumped up the stairs. She stood outside Grace's room and knocked at her door.

'Huh?' called Grace.

'It's me.'

'Come in, then.' Grace was in the centre of the room,

perched on top of a suitcase. Annie surveyed the mess of clothes squashed between zips that didn't meet. The case was too small. That was Annie's fault, she should have bought Grace a new one.

'Oh, sweetheart, are you going to wear all that?' Annie said. 'They do have a uniform, you know.'

'I know.' Her stepdaughter bounced up and down on the case. 'I feel like an extra from *Malory Towers*.'

'Shall I make you a tuck box?' Annie laughed, then turned away. She wanted the kids here. Needed them. They were her heart, even if they didn't love her as much as they'd loved their actual mother. Or as much as Annie loved them. Whatever, when she turned back Grace was on her phone again. Annie felt a stab of irritation. 'Who you texting?'

'No one.' Her stepdaughter put the mobile face down on the bed.

The naked selfies in the bathroom. Annie took another pace into the room as the atmosphere went taut. 'What?' Grace demanded.

'Are you okay?'

'About?'

'Well, about everything.' Annie took a breath. 'How you feeling?'

'*Feeling?*'

'Grace, please.' Annie's shoulders lifted. 'School, for example? How're you feeling about starting?'

Why was this always happening?

'Fine.'

'And...' At a loss, Annie glanced at the ceiling.

'What?' Grace snapped. 'Whatever it is, say it.'

'About *Mum*.' Annie dared to sit on Grace's bed. 'Sorry to be... annoying, but I just want to reiterate that it's all right to feel sad.' She put an arm round her stepdaughter, her eyes accidentally passing over Grace's phone as she did so.

Grace stiffened. 'What you doing?' She snatched the phone up.

'Gracie,' Annie said. 'For God's sake, I wasn't looking. But if I was, c'mon, it's my business too.'

'Is it? Why?'

'Because I have sole responsibility for you, and the internet can be a dangerous place for a young woman. Who was it?'

Grace looked mutinous. 'A boy.'

'I guessed that much.' Annie smiled in spite of herself. 'Which one?'

'From the new school. And before you say anything, no we haven't met in real life. On Snapchat. His name's Adam. He's in my year. He's a friend of my cousins, of Andrew's boys. They put us in touch because we're going to be in the same class. He seems nice. Not a nutter. Satisfied?'

'Okay. Great.' Annie fought to keep her patience. 'How d'you know he's not a nutter?'

'Oh my *God*,' Grace said. 'Have you listened to anything I've just said? He's friends with Uncle Andrew's boys. I'm not a child.'

But Grace was a child. *Her* child now, and it was Annie's rules whether Grace liked it or not. Even though Annie had no idea what her actual rules were. 'As long as you're being careful,' she said eventually.

'What does *that* mean?' Grace's voice went up an octave. 'I just *said*, I haven't met him yet.'

'It *means*, not sending him compromising photos of yourself.'

Grace's expression closed off.

'There's plenty of time,' Annie stood, out of her depth, 'to get to know one another, starting in two days. In real life.' She dared a sympathetic pat on Grace's thigh. It was like dealing with a skittish horse. 'Love you.'

Grace said, 'Yeah okay. I need to finish packing.'

Annie left and waited on the landing, arms at her sides. She'd probably over-reacted. Nothing would be going on with this boy: Adam.

And fucking Patrick *still* hadn't returned her call about Caleb smoking.

She found Caleb at the window in his bedroom, staring down the track to the gate, suitcase half-packed.

'All right?' she said. 'What you doing?'

'Are you going to be okay here all by yourself?' he asked.

''Course I'll be okay.' The question both touched and rattled her. 'Why wouldn't I be?'

'Dunno.'

He was only fifteen. Perhaps both children saw more of her than she gave them credit for. She watched his back, long and narrow like his mother's, bent over his packing, throwing jumpers in without folding. 'I'd be happy to go to the comp,' he said.

Annie went to put an arm around him, as she'd done with Grace. Caleb softened against her. She could have wept.

'Your granny and grandpa are very kind giving you this opportunity,' she said. A lot of parenting seemed to be fibbing to protect those you loved. 'I mean, you guys wanted to come here, you and Grace? And to Mum's old school? That's what you told me. You agreed.'

'I did. I do.' Caleb gazed at his socked feet. 'Just don't let anything bad happen. Promise?'

'Promise.'

'I don't fancy being an orphan.'

Annie smiled. 'Don't be silly. What about your dad?'

He gave an amused, '*Him*.'

'It'll be difficult, the first few days, but after that you'll have such a wonderful time you won't want to come home at weekends.'

'Been to boarding school, have you?'

'Come here.' She hugged him hard. She could feel his ribs through his sweater.

Needing air, she stomped alone along the lane to the churchyard. She hoped to feel close to Issy there. She'd make sure to get there without interruption from William and his stupid pig work.

She passed the Big House and spotted Andrew's wife, Carolina, through the window arranging wine glasses on the piano lid ready for later. A piano didn't seem a sensible place for liquids.

It was good to be outside. Nature was non-judgemental and she liked the church, the view pretty from the grassed grave-stoned area out front. A couple of weeks after Issy died, they'd held the small family funeral and the cremation up here. The village vicar had conducted the funeral; she couldn't remember his name – David, was it? Elizabeth had organised it. A couple of Bible readings; a hymn or two. A eulogy from Elizabeth, quoting widely from Issy's novels, a small speech from Annie. She had saved most of her words for the London memorial several months later. She got through the whole of it without crying. When she thought about that now, it seemed impossible.

A lone blue Renault two-door was parked in the gravelled area at the front of the church. Ramblers, probably. She sank onto a bench, her back to the west wall, facing a cluster of houses in the village proper. A shadowy yew spread its branches to her left. She and Issy used to stop here to rest and share a joint. Now Annie's breath alone clouded the air.

Issy in the hospital, unconscious. No, she didn't want to think about that, thank you.

She pulled out a joint and lit up. She'd brought an ounce of strong weed with her from London. Her head was spinning after one toke.

'Something for the weekend, madam?' she slurred, then snorted. Crows massed in a copse further off.

It had been a summer's day when Issy had died; bright and hot outside.

Annie gazed at the gravestones, gunmetal grey and slick with water, so old they'd sunk into the ground entirely, as if the bodies beneath were sucking them down. A few looked relatively new: straight angled, with smart legible engravings and glossy faces. Stonemasonry was a dying art, according to her late wife.

Up on the lane, another white van thundered past. More deliveries no doubt, for Elizabeth and her ghastly goggles. Annie was so stoned now that the words 'ghastly' and 'goggles' together like that made her fall about. The rain started. She let the water trammel her face, licking it from the creases either side of her mouth. Standing into a fog of her own smoke, she picked her way around the churchyard while she finished the joint.

She'd never walked amongst the graves before. Issy hadn't recommended it; said some belonged to children and to see their names would make anyone maudlin.

John Carey, who passed from this world 14th April 1768. Also, Millicent Carey, his wife, who passed from this world...

Where the stone met the grass, there was a wet green line.

She moved on: *Joseph Paine.* She wondered if he had been an actual pain, and started laughing, then stopped suddenly when she remembered that Paine was the name of the female director and her husband who were attending drinks later. And anyway, that wasn't how you spelled 'pain'. She collapsed into giggles again until her eye caught on two gravestones, smaller than the others and further off against the south wall. She swished through the grass towards them.

RIP Penelope Dillane December 5th, 1966 – October 23rd, 1968

Eh? Annie read the inscription again. Dillane? A relative of Issy's, dead at eighteen months old. A simple grave without embellishment, no farewell, no platitudes. Annie moved to the second little gravestone.

RIP Flora Dillane December 5th, 1970 – January 15th, 1971

Another Dillane family child, and so young. Whose children had they been? Were they cousins of Issy? And how was it that they were both born on the same day of the same month? That was weird.

Wait, Annie told herself, her brain moving more slowly than usual: Issy was *also* born on the 5th of December. In 1969.

Annie stared at the grey sky. Her wife never mentioned these girls.

She moved on, the joint falling from her fingers, drawn towards a small mausoleum sitting in the corner. The outside was plain, just a few flowers carved in stone at its edges and a woman's head, garlanded with flowers. She went around the side.

RIP Thomasina Bell December 7th, 1971 – March 28th 1982
RIP Carol Yearly December 9th 1971 – September 3rd 1982

RIP Molly Swifton November 29th 1971 – July 18th 1982

RIP Sarah Prime December 11th 1971 – October 20th 1982

RIP Rebecca Paine December 3rd, 1971 – October 16th 1982

Now hang on a minute. Annie reread the inscriptions.

Five girls from separate families born within days of one another. That wasn't possible, surely? She studied the names through narrowed eyes.

Sarah Prime – that would have to be a member of Vincent's family, wouldn't it? His daughter, maybe? And what about Rebecca Paine? Was she related to both Joseph Paine on the grave over there, *and* the theatre couple she was to meet again at the drinks party? So much grief in so tiny a place.

She walked around the rear of the mausoleum, legs wobbly, where she found a collection of stubby little gravestones belonging to pets. She made her way back to the bench. The sky felt heavy, bearing down on her head. Who could she ask about all of this? She shouldn't have had that joint.

A heavy noise from inside the church, as if a book had hit the flagstones. She stood quickly. 'Hallo?' A pulse started in her ears.

Her mobile trilled loudly in her pocket, making her start. It was Patrick. She swiped right.

'Annie?'

'Hi.' It was so quiet in the graveyard, she dropped her voice.

Patrick produced one of his many tic sounds, then, 'Sorry for the delay getting back to you. Been flat out at work.'

'That's okay.'

'How're you all getting on. Everything okay up there?' The

bleep of hospital medical equipment in the background. Another tic.

'We're fine.'

'You somewhere public? You're speaking very quietly.'

She rubbed the tip of her shoe against a grave. 'Not really.'

'You wanted to talk to me about Caleb? About smoking?'

'Oh, that.' It hardly seemed important now. 'I mean, I caught him at it. He doesn't know I did, but...' She flicked a glance at the mausoleum. 'Patrick?'

'Mmm?'

'Very briefly: I'm in the churchyard and–'

'What are you doing *there*?'

'There are all these... Did Issy ever talk of cousins? Who died young? Or, like...' Her voice dropped to a whisper. 'A brother or sister? Other than Andrew?'

'Of course not.' At Patrick's end, an alarm began to wail, and a tannoy appealed for 'Resus in Bay 4'. There was rustling in the earpiece and Patrick said, 'I've got to go. I'm sorry. I'll talk to Caleb on the phone later.'

'Okay,' she said. He wouldn't call later, she knew. She didn't want to talk about it, anyway. She wished she'd never come to this church.

Threatening granite clouds massed on the horizon. Unsettled, she left for home, the sky slanting darkly across the land.

CHAPTER SEVEN

Annie stood in Colthwaite House's huge flag-stoned kitchen clutching a champagne flute. It was 7pm, black outside, and she was no longer stoned. Water beat against the high windows. The long room was filled with gassy light from a medieval circular iron chandelier. Its little holders were dotted with candles, their small flames dancing.

Most of the guests were over seventy. Their ageing frames moved across the flag-stoned floor, the women in court shoes, the men in Hush Puppies, like pawns in an enormous game of chess.

An open range dominated one end of the room. To its side, a sink made from a rectangle of crackled ceramic. The draining board, currently hidden beneath trays of glasses and wine bottles, was an endless piece of sloping black oak, troughed and pocked by never-ending piles of washing-up. The overriding smell was of dog.

There was the Paine wife several feet away, she of the blue hair. Vincent Prime stood talking to her. He was so small and frail, as if at any moment he'd snap. He caught Annie's eye and gave her a nod. She smiled back, trying not to think about his relative – possibly his daughter – bones brittle beneath the earth. The Paines' relative too and perhaps more relatives connected to present company.

Annie was drinking too fast, half listening to the things happening around her. She longed to ask someone questions about the churchyard, but children's gravestones weren't exactly party talk.

The Paine husband was amongst a group nearby, as tall as any Dillane, and with the same light hair and eyes. 'Tough, isn't it, wintering here?' he was saying. It took a moment before she realised he was talking to her.

'Oh. I suppose,' she said, 'what with the rain and everything. Though I'm enjoying myself so far.'

'We heard you encountered the spastic pig?' he continued.

'The–?'

'Pig with the funny face?'

'Oh. Right.' Annie chewed the inside of her cheek. 'Yes. We nearly ran it over.'

'Gave you all an awful fright, I shouldn't imagine?' said a woman whose name Annie didn't know.

'Well.' Annie laughed. 'Only in that it was in the middle of the road, which was a bit of a surprise, but otherwise we just felt sorry for it.'

'Quite right,' said Mr Paine. 'Not its fault, is it? Can't change what we're given.' He nodded at the floor. 'Take that poor bitch.'

Annie looked around in confusion, an unpleasant sensation spreading through her. Everyone roared with laughter.

'The dog, Annie!' the woman said. 'He's talking about the dog!'

Hidden by a forest of legs, a fat black Labrador. Annie bent to give the dog a stroke. Its nose was cold.

'Lost her leg on a shoot in 2011,' Mr Paine was saying.

'I see.'

'Colin.'

Annie stood. 'The Lab's called Colin?'

Another peal of laughter.

'Dear me, no. *My* name.' The Paine husband offered his hand. She shook it. 'The dog's called Virginia. I'm Colin Paine. We're not easily muddled.' His grin broadened. Virginia was a seriously shit name for a dog. 'You and I have met before.'

'Yes, so sorry.' The act of trying not to go red only made it worse. 'I do remember. At a Christmas party. Just... lots of new people.'

'I'm sure.' He rubbed his hands together. 'Ready for the eclipse?'

'I'm sorry? The...?'

'Eclipse,' Colin said, as if the words 'ready' and 'eclipse' together were perfectly normal. 'Haven't they mentioned it, Lizzo and Wills? They haven't told you?'

'Er... nope.'

Colin looked at the others, eyebrows raised.

'Oh, leave her be, Colin.' The woman laughed. 'They're probably busy settling her in, I shouldn't imagine.' She turned to Annie. 'A total solar eclipse on the 29th of November. It's been in the news, dear. A total only happens every seventy years, give or take.'

'Wow,' Annie said. It *was* kind of interesting. 'You guys are into star gazing up here, then?' This must be where Issy had got it from.

'Oh yes,' Colin said. 'We're praying for good weather.' He studied her for a moment. 'It happens to fall in line with our traditional winter festival.'

'Traditional...?' Issy had never mentioned a winter festival. Or any festival come to think of it.

'You shall have the pleasure,' Colin said with a smile, 'of

experiencing our celebrations and the eclipse for the first time in person at the *same time*. Lucky you.'

'What's the... er... the tradition in honour of?'

'Ah.' He wafted a hand. 'You know the sort of thing: ancient village stuff. All Christian, of course. None of that Pagan nonsense.'

Annie almost laughed. 'Of course.'

'And,' the woman said, eyes slitted with pleasure, 'we *all* love an eclipse because it's a "supernatural" event, Annie. The whole place will be thrown into darkness for two whole minutes; can you countenance such a thing? God's magic! What d'you think about that?'

Annie didn't know what she thought about it. It was going to be dark in the daytime: big deal. Up here it was practically dark all day anyway. And she certainly didn't need six weeks to prepare for a festival, whatever its history.

'If you'll excuse me.' She moved towards the back door. She wanted another joint. The kids would be gone tomorrow, and the people here were all loud and rude and strange. Perhaps they *were* the sort of people you could talk to about dead children after all.

Maddeningly, the back door was locked. She did a one-eighty, forced to face the room again. She sipped her drink, preternaturally self-conscious, listening to two women beside her.

'Wast Water?' one was asking in strong Cumbrian tones. 'D'you mean the piece about the disgruntled husband? Dropped his wife from a helicopter?'

'*That's* the one, yes,' the other replied. 'Wrapped in a bin liner filled with stones, the silly marra. But caught on a rock beneath the water, discovered by frogmen. The fool hadn't removed the wedding ring from his missus's finger. It had their names inscribed on the inside.'

The first's head was shaking. 'Barmpot.'

'Deepest lake in the district and he goes and forgets something like that.'

'Best part, remember,' the first woman was saying, 'is that divers had only been diving the lake because a student had disappeared, and they suspected *she* was dumped in there. Helicopter woman was a total surprise.'

'Serves him right for owning one. Not a wife. The helicopter, I mean.' They fell into companionable silence.

Laughter erupted from another corner of the room: Andrew and Carolina stood smoking beside Elizabeth, Elizabeth's hand resting on Carolina's shoulder. Annie couldn't imagine a day when her mother-in-law would feel familiar enough to rest a hand on Annie, or when Annie would feel comfortable enough to allow it. Patrick had always been on far better terms with them all. They had more in common, she thought, what with him being a doctor and Elizabeth being a vet. Also, he was posh, white, and voted Conservative. Issy confessed that he still visited Colthwaite even now, which Annie found outrageous when you considered he barely found time to see his children in London.

She studied everyone's feet again: why did the women feel the need to wear heels at all when they were about six feet tall already? Andrew was in his regulation brown brogues. Issy called it 'his uniform': brogues, cords, a nice pink shirt.

'Feeling lonely?' It was Colin Paine's wife with the blue hair.

'That obvious?' Annie smiled, relieved to be rescued.

'Only to me.' She kissed Annie's cheek, which felt nice after all the chilly hand shaking. The hair, though. Strong choice. 'Margaret. Remember?'

'Absolutely I remember. Issy and I met you and your husband at Christmas one year, right?'

'Right.' Margaret's accent was local, similar to the two women discussing the bodies in the lake, the sound both plain and melodious. 'I saw a play of yours, years ago in London, Annie. The Old Red Lion, was it? *Peculiar Hairs.*'

'Oh.' Annie giggled. She must stop blushing. *'That.'*

'No, no. It was good. I was down for a night costuming for *The Dream* at Angels. I only didn't come say hallo cos you were surrounded. By people.' She chuckled and rolled her eyes. 'Listen to me. What else would you be surrounded by, eh? Elephants?'

'You should have said hi!'

'Issy was there and...' Margaret put a hand on her arm. 'I'm very sorry. For your loss.'

'Thanks. I mean... thanks.' Annie took a breath, let it out.

There was a scream from the far end of the room. Three of Andrew's four children, along with Grace, Caleb, and a couple of others, were hanging on to one another in either horror or delight. You could never tell with teenagers when they screamed if someone had broken their arm or won the lottery. Andrew's three here in front of her were the boys, large-boned and confident, each one as tall as Grace. Their fourth, the only girl, wasn't there. Annie had a quick scan for her elsewhere in the kitchen, but she wasn't there either. Something was wrong with her: an illness, genetic. MS. Or was it ME? Perhaps she was upstairs in bed.

Grace looked around briefly, caught Annie's eye. The pleasure on her stepdaughter's face dropped away. Oh dear. Annie turned to Margaret. 'Would you like a drink?'

'I'm fine, pet.' Margaret drew closer. Their heads were almost touching. 'Don't let them muck you about.'

'My kids, you mean?' Annie laughed. 'They're okay.'

'No. These lot.' She gestured at the room.

'What d'you mean? Who?'

'We're a tight bunch.' Margaret smiled and stepped away. 'Ignore me. I'm what we call "mithering".'

'Issy taught me that word. She always says–' Annie caught herself. '*Said.*' There was an awkward silence. 'Habit,' she said eventually.

'Of course.' Margaret was looking over at her husband draining his glass as he stepped through the door to the hall. 'Fifty years.' She sighed, not altogether fondly. 'Colin and I met at a dance. Nineteen, we were. Only went cos my grandmother made me.'

Annie chuckled. 'Grandmothers can be like that.'

'Had my fair share of him, haven't I?' Margaret rolled her eyes comically. 'And this community.'

'That's a long time to live in a place this small.'

But Margaret hadn't finished. 'Don't let 'em make you do things you don't want to.'

'Have no fear, Margaret, I won't,' Annie said, as Margaret headed out to find her husband. She had no intention of being pushed around.

She went to the sink, grabbed a bottle of wine and poured to the rim. Might as well get pissed if she couldn't get stoned. A man in a lemon cashmere jumper and checked trousers was making a beeline for her. He looked like Rupert the Bear.

'Annie!' His cheeks were speckled with vermillion veins. Perhaps he had a heart condition.

She had no clue who he was. She'd just have to style it out. 'Welcome!' He clinked his glass against hers.

'David.' He held out his hand. 'Vicar of Colthwaite. And Gillyhead and Ethdale, of course.'

So *that's* who he was. The vicar who'd done Issy's funeral. 'Of course. Nice to meet you.' She corrected herself. 'Meet you *again.*' She'd seen his work at other times too: once at Midnight

Mass, a long service in candlelight involving talk about cycles of life and, unusually for a Christian church, reincarnation.

'Did I catch you,' he pulled a pair of reading glasses from his pocket and put them on, 'in the churchyard earlier?'

'That was your car?' The blue Renault. The noise from inside the church.

'Didn't want to disturb you,' David said. His eyes dropped. 'I'm deeply sorry for your loss.'

'Thank you. Yes, it's awful... I... excuse me.' She made a dash for the bathroom.

The stone hallway was cool and dark and surrounded by wooden doors. She searched for the bathroom, opening first a small cupboard, then almost falling into an enormous bottle-green dining room.

There were three people at the far end of a long table, bent over a dresser, their backs facing her. One she recognised as Elizabeth, the second was Colin Paine, the last Stephen, the Keep.

'Again?' she could hear her mother-in-law saying. 'When?'

'Three or four days ago,' Stephen said. 'Give or take.'

'On the lane, you say?'

'That's right.'

'You're sure it was him?' Colin was asking.

Annie tried to sneak away, but the door hinge let out a squawk as she pulled it to. The others turned sharply. 'Sorry. Looking for the bathroom.'

'Lav's across the way.' Elizabeth sounded irritated.

Annie let the door close behind her and crossed the hall, passing an empty saltlick repurposed to collect drips from a leaking ceiling.

The bathroom contained a lavatory and a sink and was plastered in floral yellow wallpaper. Annie locked the door and sat heavily on the wooden seat, chin in hands. Rain spattered at the window.

Why was she not able to talk about Issy? Each time it was as if something crawled up her throat and took hold. And those poor babies and girls buried in the church. If anyone understood death, it would be the villagers. She still couldn't get her head around why no one had ever mentioned them. She should ask the vicar; he'd know.

On the wall at her shoulder hung a metre-long framed and faded school photograph. Hundreds of students in uniform in a line stared straight-faced into camera. *Collermere School* the brass plate read at the bottom. She recognised it as the seventies from their lapels and hairstyles.

She searched for Issy in the line-up, but her eyes kept swimming. Giving up, she stood, tugging roughly at her trousers. The kids were going to be at that school tomorrow.

They'd be tired and grouchy in the morning; it would be Annie bearing the brunt of their mood, their nerves, as she drove them to the gates. At least they'd have their cousins there for support. Two of Andrew's kids were still at school and weekly boarders too. That would be reassuring for Caleb and Grace – a sense of continuity, of understanding.

She pulled the ceramic handle at the end of the chain. The cistern gurgled, and a cupful of water swished through the toilet bowl. She scrubbed her hands with soap, glaring at herself in the silvered mirror.

Their favourite bar, Drinks of Hackney, had had lovely mirrors with lights all around the edges. Issy always ordered the Dutch beer that tasted of old socks. Annie wished she was there, right now.

She tugged at the door. When it opened, Vincent Prime was outside, grinning. 'Heard you got lost on the way to the khazi.' He clicked the tip of his cane against the stone floor.

'News travels fast.' She gestured at the hall. 'In my defence, there *are* a lot of rooms.'

'There are.'

Elizabeth, Colin Paine, and Stephen stepped out from the dining room. Stephen departed immediately for the kitchen.

'You found it,' Elizabeth stated to Annie.

'I did.'

Standing side by side, her mother-in-law and Colin Paine were the same height, to the centimetre. Annie wondered what it would be like to be that tall, to always be able to see over people's heads. Good for gigs, at least.

'Vincent?' said Elizabeth. 'Why don't you take Annie on a tour?'

'A tour?' Annie and Vincent echoed in unison.

'Of the house.'

'But why?' Annie blundered.

'*Oh, reason not the need,*' her mother-in-law declared. 'I don't believe you've seen upstairs?'

'No.' Annie shook her head. 'But I wouldn't want to put Vincent to any trouble.'

'Deary me.' Elizabeth sighed. 'You're spoiling it. There *is* a need. There's a painting I think you might be interested in.' She tapped the side of her nose.

'Oh, yes,' Vincent agreed, catching on. '*I* see. *I* know what you're talking about, Lizzo. And it's no trouble.' He turned and headed for the stairwell. 'Come along, Annie; you'll like this.'

'Prudent to learn your way around.' And with that, her mother-in-law strode into the kitchen, Colin behind her.

Vincent had already begun his laboured ascent of the stairs. Annie trotted after him.

'Why would I need to learn my way around?' she asked, worried in case he fell.

'Well,' Vincent's eyes were on the treads, 'you never know.'

'Never know what?'

'Ha. You don't know yet.' He stopped, looked over his shoulder and winked, like William. 'That's the point.'

Annie walked up beside him, one arm at the ready. 'What's the painting of?'

'You'll see.'

'William told me not to believe a word you say.'

Vincent chuckled.

'That you tell newcomers you've met them before, regardless, as a joke?'

He gave her hand a squeeze. 'But how ironic,' he said, wheezily. 'It's William who tells the porkies.'

It was like the riddle of the lying twins. Perhaps Margaret was right; she mustn't let them push her around.

Vincent was now pulling his way up the banister like a mountaineer. 'Legs aren't what they used to be.'

As she waited for him to conquer the stairwell, Annie had plenty of time to take in the paintings on the walls, their small brass nameplates at the bottom: stern-faced Dillanes in Edwardian clothing, their chests puffed out; thin-lipped Victorian Dillanes. She'd been to the house in the past of course with Issy, but never upstairs. In truth, she'd never been bothered – she didn't really care about inherited wealth – and Issy had never offered, perhaps because she knew this about her wife. With Issy gone, it was probably time.

The Dillane name came from Elizabeth's family line. Annie found it unusual that William's family name had taken a back seat to his wife's, he was such a traditionalist; but no doubt Elizabeth had grander heritage. Titles and grandeur stuck fast in England, like glue.

Annie passed a portrait of a light-skinned blonde woman and stopped. It was Issy, in flared jeans and T-shirt, legs flung over the arm of a chair, one hand dangling. The position, the expression, it was her for sure. She looked for the nameplate, just to make sure, but there wasn't one. The exquisite torture of stumbling across her like this. It must be the one Elizabeth had wanted her to see.

'Beautiful, wasn't she?' Vincent said at Annie's shoulder.

'I never knew she'd...' She clenched her jaw to stop herself from weeping. 'When was it done?'

'Couldn't say.'

Issy had never mentioned having her portrait painted and hung in the family house. It must have taken ages. Unless the artist had worked from a photograph? That happened sometimes, didn't it?

Annie touched the varnished paint; it was hard, lumpy. She ran the pads of her fingers over the slick of yellow hair. 'Who painted it?'

'Local man. Dead now, sadly.'

'Strange that Issy never said.'

'"Never said..."? Annie dear, you do know that's Elizabeth you're looking at?'

Annie snatched her fingers from the canvas. 'No. It's–'

'I assure you; that's your mother-in-law.'

It *was* Issy. That pose, the mole on her left bicep, that half-smile that told the story – were you to know it, as Annie did – of loving weariness, contentment. She leaned in.

But it was as if the painting was a Magic Eye, and now that Annie knew it was Elizabeth, she couldn't see it any other way. The clothes were a little dated, she noted now: the flares; the T-shirt with scalloped collar. 'She looks *exactly* like her.'

'A dominant family likeness.' Vincent continued up the stairs ahead of her. 'Strong genes.'

But they were not strong genes. Not strong enough.

The painting directly above Elizabeth's was of a young man,

also in jeans, on the same armchair. Again, no nameplate. But certainly a Dillane.

'That's Andrew, right?'

Vincent turned. 'Andrew? Yes, that's right.'

A few inches above the portrait of Andrew there was a dark rectangle where another painting of the same dimensions would have hung. Annie pointed. 'And this one? Whose portrait stood here, and where've they gone?'

Vincent lowered his voice. 'Ah, now *that* is the one Elizabeth wants you to see. Someone's taken it down and put it elsewhere, ready for you.'

'Oh.'

That must be the one of Issy. She wasn't sure she'd be able to hold it together when she saw it; not tonight. Hadn't anyone thought that she might like to be presented with it by Elizabeth herself in a quiet moment and not at a fucking party?

Vincent puffed air from his cheeks. 'It'll be in the house, fear not. It's our mission to discover it.'

And why she was expected to go on a treasure hunt for the damn thing, she had no idea. The whole operation was meant to be kindly; she reminded herself. She mustn't be ungrateful.

'Vincent?' she said. 'Do you mind me asking what the deal is with the village festival next month?'

'"The deal?"' They faced one another in the shadow of the stairwell. 'Oh, it's just a trifle. An excuse for a dance. There's a shindig in the field behind the church every few years. Little bit of ceremony. Certain Novembers mark a celebration.'

'Of what? And according to whom?'

'Of agriculture and fertility.'

'But which religion? Or is it not religious?'

He beamed at her. 'Ha. Who can remember that sort of important fact?' He crossed his eyes, and she laughed. 'This year the celebration falls in line with a full solar eclipse. David will give out special glasses so we can view it without burning our retinas.'

'Right.'

'Love or hate tradition,' he continued, 'villages are just like that.' And with this, he moved on.

She followed Vincent on to the first-floor landing, waiting beside him in the darkness until he caught his breath. It wasn't enough information. She wanted more. 'I just don't get–'

'Off we go!' He moved along the long passage that appeared to stretch from one end of the house to the other, the floorboards groaning beneath them. It was chilly away from the heat of the kitchen fire. Through the windows, rhomboids of moonlight streaked the floor.

'Hold on.' Vincent's voice, weak in the blackness. 'Just locating the light switch.'

A clicking sound and above them, lamps flickered on one after the other. A dim glow seeped through the corridor. 'That's better.' He turned left into a room. Annie stepped after him as he hit another light switch.

A bedroom: large and decorated in more floral wallpaper, this time patterned with little pink flowers with green stalks, peeling at three of its four corners. One flap of ceiling hung where a leak had broken through. A wooden four-poster draped in a grubby quilt sat at the room's centre.

'Massive room,' Annie commented.

'There's ten of them this size.' Vincent pinged the light and trudged from the room head down. 'And as your gift doesn't seem to be in this one, we've got nine more to investigate.'

Downstairs a squeal of laughter travelled up the stairwell.

'Vincent, where's Andrew's middle one?' Annie asked. 'The daughter? I haven't seen her tonight.'

'Polly?' Vincent looked to the ceiling. 'Away at a medical centre, I think they said. New treatment.'

'She won't be at school with Caleb and Grace, then?' Vincent shook his head. That was a shame: she wasn't much older than Grace. 'What is it exactly that's wrong with her?'

'Don't entirely know.' He shot her a rueful smile. 'I'm not a doctor and I'm very old and forget everything.'

He *was* old. Perhaps it might turn out he'd got it wrong, and that *had* been Issy staring back at her from the wall after all, and then they'd have been needlessly wandering about up here in the dark for no reason. She stroked the wall with her palm. It felt soggy. 'Maybe Elizabeth will know?'

'Polly has an inherited disease,' Vincent announced suddenly. 'Caused by a single-allele gene mutation affecting the nervous system.'

Annie whistled through her teeth. 'Vincent! For someone who isn't a doctor, you certainly *sound* like one!'

'I do, don't I?' His shoulders lifted. 'Clever old me.'

Sounds came from a television downstairs, and a young voice shouted, 'Get him! Use the roundhouse kick!'

Vincent moved off again. 'I like a bit of study now and then, now that I'm retired. Keeps the brain sharp.'

They peered into one room after another. Along the first floor lay the dilapidated sleeping quarters of generations of Dillanes. The water-damaged wallpaper hung like tongues, especially in the adjoining bathrooms, its sloping floors giving the impression the house had had one drink too many. The children's rooms were here too: a strange mix of laptops, stereos, smelly bedding, and old cups of tea, alongside shelves of meaningless – to Annie at least – trinkets. On the walls, pop bands kept company with paintings of pigs or sheep foregrounded against gloomy landscapes. No wonder Issy had extricated herself from this place. Polly's room – Andrew's absent daughter's – had an open wardrobe stuffed with girly clothing. It was noticeably tidier than the boys' rooms. On one wall, someone had mounted a squat ceramic statuette of an unnaturally wide-hipped woman. It looked old, and a bit creepy.

'Who's *that*?' she demanded.

Vincent squinted in the half-light. 'Who's what?'

'That woman thing.' She pointed at the wall. 'Who is she?'

'Good Lord, Annie.' Vincent flicked the light off and walked out. 'You ask an awful lot of questions.'

Annie went after him into the corridor. 'But who *is* she?'

'My dear, I have no clue. Far be it for me to understand the machinations of the teenage mind.'

'Wait. But okay, where's the medical centre Polly's at, then? I'd like to write to her.'

'Oh dear.' Vincent gave a non-committal shake of his head. 'I don't know that either.' He looked apologetic. 'Not doing terribly well, am I?'

In Andrew and Carolina's bedroom – judging by the amount of face creams on the dresser and a second pair of brown brogues lines up at the end of the bed – there, mounted on the wall, another identical wide-hipped statuette.

Annie turned. 'Vincent?'

He smiled, sighed. 'Fine. She's an old goddess. She's meant to bring luck and hope. Everyone needs hope, eh? The land of the living can be a lonely place.'

No one needed to tell *her* that, but she wouldn't say it to Vincent; he might think she was being rude. It was clear now, though, that he knew far more than he let on and this would surely be the perfect time to ask about the grave of the dead Prime girl. She opened her mouth to speak, but caught him looking at her, his face all worn and vulnerable, and couldn't bring herself to do it. She didn't want to upset him.

'Right.' She clapped her hands. It was ridiculous really, the two of them hiding their misery from one another. 'Where's this mystery portrait, then?'

'Do you know, Annie, I'm stumped. I fear you're fast discovering that I've no clue about anything.'

'It's okay.' She couldn't help but like him. Annie followed him to the end of the corridor where they found a room with a closed door. It was positioned next to a winding staircase that led to the attic. 'What's in there?'

Vincent rattled the handle of the door demonstratively. 'Library.'

'Why's it locked?'

'Questions, questions!'

'I'm interested!'

'You playwrights,' he said. 'These old houses *are* fascinating, aren't they? The library contains rare first editions of *The Encyclopaedia Britannica*, as well as veterinary science bibles dating from the eighteenth century.' He turned to her solemnly, eyes wide.

'Who's going to steal those?'

'This house has been burgled more than once. Lizzo comes from a long line of medics. Generations of Dillanes made this their ancestral home.'

'But Liz... Elizabeth doesn't live in this house anymore. Why didn't she take the valuable books with her when she moved to Blea Crag?'

'And store them where exactly? Some damp garage lock-up in Barrow? Blea Crag's too small.' He had a point. 'I imagine the library is where Andrew has placed your painting, for safekeeping. We'll ask Wilko to open it.'

There was a pause. 'You call William "Wilko"?' she said. 'But Elizabeth calls him—'

'*Willy.*' His face dissolved into giggles. 'They're awful raggers, this lot.'

Annie grinned. 'Were you at school together?'

Vincent shook his head.

'So how do you know one another?'

'For another day,' he said.

'Whatever you say.' She peered into the dark of the attic stairwell. 'What's up there?'

'Too steep for me, dear.' He headed back along the corridor. 'Third floor's for another day.'

'Like everything else?'

'Exactly.' He was already huffing and puffing down the main stairwell.

Before they reached the kitchen, he stopped and pulled a card from his trouser pocket. 'My number,' he said. 'Coming to a new place can be a stinking business. Do call if you need anything or have questions. Anything at all.'

'Thank you so much.' Touched, she stowed the card in her wallet.

He squeezed her arm. 'Ready to re-enter the fray, comrade?' They smiled at one another.

The kitchen was even hotter than when she'd left. Annie wiped her top lip and prayed someone would open a window. Vincent asked Elizabeth about the location of the mystery portrait, and Elizabeth in turn asked Andrew, who went off and came back saying it was in the library, of course, and why had no one told Vincent and Annie *before* they'd had to traipse all around the house looking for it? Someone would fetch it after the food.

'There, see?' Vincent patted Annie's arm. 'As I suspected.'

More wine. The food was miniature Yorkshire puddings filled with beef, and smoked salmon over triangles of bread served on silver platters. For the vegetarians – no one said it, but this seemed to be only Annie – there were cucumber, apple, and cheddar cheese kebabs. They were surprisingly good. She stuffed several in her mouth, hiding the toothpicks in her jeans in case she'd taken more than she should. Caleb appeared at the door with bloodshot eyes saying he felt tired, and could they go, and Annie said yes, would he please rouse Grace from the other room, and Caleb said, what d'you mean 'rouse' her? I thought she was in here.

Annie felt a little jolt, like a doorbell ringing in the middle of the night. 'Wasn't she with you?'

'Yeah.' Caleb shook of his head. 'She *was*. Then Granny came in an hour ago and Grace went with her.'

It was 11pm. Annie glanced around the kitchen. There was Elizabeth, talking to Stephen. 'But where did they go?'

Caleb shrugged. 'Granny said she wanted to give Grace a book from the library. A piece of writing Mum had done as a child, Granny said. To take to school with her or something. Oh, and to get a painting.'

Annie put down her glass. 'No problemo. Find your coat and shoes, I'll ask Granny where Grace is, then we'll leave.'

Elizabeth was chatting to someone. 'Have you seen Grace?' Annie interrupted, as tactfully as she could. 'It's super late and we're going to have to leave, I'm afraid.'

Elizabeth regarded her blankly.

'We're going to have to leave,' Annie repeated. 'Sorry. School's tomorrow. Caleb said you'd taken Grace to the library?'

Elizabeth looked into her drink.

'Don't think you'll find her in there,' Annie quipped, but Elizabeth didn't laugh.

'Oh yes, but I took Grace to the library over forty-five minutes ago,' she said. 'I thought she'd rejoined the others in the television room. I can look for her if you like?'

Annie shook her head. 'Thanks. I'll go.' She checked the TV room, the dining room, the two enormous reception rooms. She checked the downstairs bathroom. No Grace.

She climbed the stairs for a second time. How was it eleven already? The kids would be unbearable tomorrow and it would be Annie's fault. She passed the painting of Elizabeth and looked the other way. She stood at the top of the stairs on the first-floor landing, swaying slightly in the darkness. 'Grace?'

She felt around the wall with her hands for the light switch because someone had turned it off again. The hall flickered into life. Annie chose to go right.

'Grace? Where are you?' She returned to the stairwell and took the corridor along the left wing. 'Honestly,' she said, sticking her head into a bathroom. 'This has gone beyond a joke, young lady.'

The last room at the end was the locked library. It was now unlocked, the door ajar.

'Grace?' she whispered. It was pitch black inside. 'You in here?'

The empty darkness made the back of her neck prickle. She found the light switch. The library was wood-panelled, deep red, and surrounded on three sides by shelves. The fourth wall was occupied by Georgian windows that looked out to the front drive. Two leather armchairs with long backs hid potential occupants from approaching visitors. There was a moth-eaten sofa and a round reading table. An antique clock on the mantel above the fireplace ticked the seconds. The floor was covered in a holed Persian rug. There was no Grace.

'It's okay, Annie!' Elizabeth's voice travelled up the stairs like wind. 'We've found her!'

'Down in a minute!' Hastily she pushed the door closed, shutting herself in, and crept towards the shelves.

A quick scan of the spines revealed none of Issy's old writings, but there were dusty collections on animals, as per Vincent's assertion. She pulled one out. A brown leather hardcover with gold embossed writing. *The Yadil Veterinary Book.* The pages smelled of fungus.

Published by Clement and Johnson in 1923. Yadil is the antiseptic sought for by Lister. The careful study of this book, and the use of 'Yadil' in all infectious diseases of Live Stock will save thousands of pounds now lost annually

Poor Mr Yadil: no doubt he'd gone out of business shortly after. She moved on. Old directories on veterinary science, veterinary encyclopaedias, medical journals, the venerated *Encyclopaedia Britannica.* Eighteen volumes of thick pale-bound leather so old she feared they would crumble in her hand. Downstairs there was laughter.

On a bottom shelf, something caught her eye. A series of crimson volumes, their spines smooth and shiny and far newer than the others. The labels at the sides of each one penned in spidery hand read respectively:

1963–63 The First
1965–65 The Second
1967–67 The Third
1968–73 The Fourth

She dropped to her heels and slid *The First* out. The cover was synthetic and felt weird after the soft leather of the valuable encyclopaedias, but there was the satisfying sound of unsticking plastic as it opened. It was a photograph album.

Preserved beneath more bubbled plastic, a faded and blurry Polaroid of a newborn piglet, perfectly raw and vulnerable looking, on hay beneath a heat lamp. It had freshly slithered from its mother's rear, the sow's blooded backside just in view, along with someone's leg in a wellington boot. The same spidery handwriting beneath read: *One day old, April 10th, 1963.*

On the next page, the pig had grown, and its backside faced the camera. *Six months old, October 10th 1963.* A female, its head bent over a feeding trough.

The Dillanes kept records of their animals as if they were children? Was that usual for farmers?

On the third page, Annie's smile died. *One year old, April 10th, 1964.* The photograph was close on the pig's face, its lower lids drooping, pus weeping from the corners, nose full of mucus. Its tongue lolled from an open mouth. She thought of the pig on the road, its one eye, its missing nose, its current situation as prisoner in the barn. Unless it had escaped.

From downstairs, a man called her name. It sounded like William. She slid the album back into place and leapt up, as feet thumped up the treads of the main stairwell.

Annie raced for the exit, hit the lights and squeezed onto the landing, leaving the door ajar just as she'd found it. It was Elizabeth on the top step, her head looking left, right. 'Annie?'

Annie almost skated along the wood to meet her. 'Yes. Hi. Bathroom. Sorry.'

'*There* you are. We thought you'd fallen in!'

'Ate something funny.' Annie heard her own words too late. 'Not here at the party, obviously. Your food's lovely. I meant, earlier in the day.'

'The children are waiting in the kitchen. Along with your painting.' Elizabeth turned and headed downstairs. Annie followed, her face burning.

The kitchen had emptied slightly. Grace was on a kitchen chair, relaxed and sleepy. In front of her on the table, a black binder. Elizabeth came to stand behind her, like a bouncer.

'Gracie!' Annie strained to keep her voice at its usual register. 'Where were you hiding?'

'Hiding? Don't be ridiculous. Where have *you* been, more like?' Grace yawned. 'I've been down here ten minutes.'

Aware of others' ears, Annie spoke more quietly. 'But where were you before you were here?'

'Nowhere. I fell asleep upstairs.'

'But I searched every bedroom,' Annie persisted.

'She was in the attic,' said Elizabeth.

'The attic?' Annie looked searchingly at Grace.

'Third floor?' Grace said. 'D'you look up there?'

'No. I–'

'Well, that's where I was.' Grace rubbed her eyes. She nodded at the folder in front of her. 'Granny gave me this. It's a keepsake. Mum wrote it when she was young.'

'That's nice.'

'I popped up to the nursery. It felt like the right place to read it. Must have fallen asleep on the bed.'

'The nursery is in the...?' Annie turned to Elizabeth. 'Issy's childhood bedroom was in the attic? I didn't know that.'

'Possibly Issy didn't imagine the location of her childhood sleeping quarters of particular importance?' Elizabeth chivvied Grace from her seat. 'It's a lovely room. Vincent didn't show it to you?'

Annie shook her head.

Her mother-in-law sighed. 'His legs aren't the best.' She turned to Grace. 'Off you go, poppet. Big day tomorrow.'

'The... painting?' Annie dared. 'Can I–'

'Golly gosh.' Elizabeth palmed her forehead. 'What a silly! I took it from the library then left it in the breakfast room. Hang on.' She hurried from the kitchen.

Annie caught Stephen's eye. He stood alone, beer in hand.

He gave her a curt, almost imperceptible nod. She felt sure he'd been eavesdropping.

Grace stood up with the folder and Annie saw she was swaying. She looked dazed, was moving oddly, as if somewhere she was hurting. Annie went to her. 'Caleb, get yours and your sister's coats,' she instructed. Caleb did as he was told.

'Everything's fine,' Grace snapped. 'Why are you being weird?'

'I'm not being weird.' *You are though*, she thought.

William was tapping Grace on the shoulder. 'Might you have had one too many shandies, my girl? Alka Seltzer for you tonight, or it'll be a nasty headache tomorrow.'

'I'm not drunk, Grandpa,' Grace said. 'I'm *tired*.'

Elizabeth returned with the mystery portrait. It was large and looked heavy and its face was turned the other way. Andrew took it from his mother, and she blew him a kiss he didn't appear to want. 'The library is still unlocked, by the way,' she told him. 'No free hands to close it.'

At mention of the library, Annie blushed again and looked away.

'We wondered if you'd like this in Chapel Croft?' Andrew asked her. 'I took it off the wall in case.' He offered her the painting, the front still hidden. 'I hope you like it.'

'That's incredibly kind.' Annie turned it the right way round and almost did a double take.

It was Issy, as she'd guessed, but in the same chair as Elizabeth had been in her portrait, and in the same position, one leg over the armrest, one hand dangling. The mole, the expression identical. The only differences were the jeans and T-shirt she wore, and her hair was slightly longer than her mother's. The whole experience, the similarities, the fact of Annie seeing it without Issy present, made her want to faint.

'It's beautiful. Thank you,' she stammered. 'They look so... similar. You all do.'

Andrew flashed an uncertain smile. 'Strong genes.' She wished they'd stop talking about strong bloody genes. He put his hand out. 'We can keep it here for now if you like? Wouldn't want it getting wet on the way home.'

She didn't want to have to return to Colthwaite House again to get it, but he was right: the weather was bad. 'That would be great.'

'Annie,' Grace said. 'I thought we were leaving?'

'Yes, sorry.' She tried to commandeer Issy's story folder from Grace's arms, but Grace held on firmly. Something about this wound Annie up: *she* wanted to take possession of it. Needed to. Issy's writing was her domain. Everyone here seemed to have something of her wife, except her.

She stepped away from her stepdaughter with a sigh. She was being selfish, wrong. Issy belonged to all of them. 'Thank you so much for everything,' was all she could manage. She waved to the room in general. People called goodbye from across the kitchen.

She stepped into the night, the kids close behind. It was blustery outside, the wind skinning the heat from Annie's skin, carrying it up and off to the swaying branches.

'Are we walking?' Grace was sagging.

'Well, we're not driving three hundred yards.' It was meant as a joke.

There was no moon and they fell silent as they concentrated on the dark lane, Grace leaning heavily on Annie's arm. This sudden proximity felt good, as if Grace had forgiven her for whatever Annie had done.

'Mum's story.' Annie nudged her gently as they passed Blea Crag, The *bloody* Jack Russell yapping from the other side of the window. 'What's it about exactly? That Granny had to give it to you now?'

'Hard to explain.'

'Shall I take it?' Annie tried again to wrestle the folder from Grace's arms. 'It'd be easier for you to walk.'

'No. It's fine.'

'How old was your mum when she wrote it? I mean, what skill level's the writing, would you say?'

'Good level.'

'Okay.' Annie kept a lid on her mounting frustration. 'But good how? Like scary good? Happy? Funny?'

'I'm really tired.' Grace pushed the gate open on the track leading up to Chapel Croft. 'Can we talk about it tomorrow?'

'You'll be away at school tomorrow.' Annie felt a lump forming in her throat. Halfway up the track, Grace stopped suddenly.

'You okay, sweet pea?'

'It's mine, this story.' Grace's mouth was tight. 'Something of Mum's that's mine.'

'Of course it's yours, I just want to–'

'It was given to *me*,' Grace's tone was sharp. 'By *my* granny. Written by *my* mum.' She waved the folder in Annie's face, then marched ahead. 'Perhaps you could respect that.'

'Respect you?' Annie did nothing *but* respect Grace. She spent most of her life tiptoeing around so she wouldn't piss her off.

Annie looked at Caleb. He shrugged. She ran to catch Grace at the door. 'Sweetheart, what's wrong?'

Grace forced her key into the lock. 'Nothing. We'll talk in the morning.'

Something gave in Annie, like a branch snapping. 'No,' she said, her arm barring the way. 'We'll talk now. You're off to school in the morning; you'll be *gone.*'

Grace fell against the door frame. 'I'm tired.'

There was a moment of suspension. One in which Annie knew she had a choice: she could either shout, escalating this clash of wills, or back down. She chose the latter. 'I'm sorry,' she said, letting her arm drop. She was the adult. It was the right thing to do.

Grace pushed past. Annie watched her shuffle upstairs, the precious folder tucked into her armpit.

'I'll wake you at seven, 'K?' Annie called.

But Grace didn't respond. Caleb was still on the porch step. He waited until his sister had gone before saying, 'Don't worry. She'll have forgotten by the morning.'

'Sure.'

Annie headed to the kitchen to fetch herself a glass of water. It wasn't just Grace; it was everything tonight. Once Caleb was in bed, she stomped through the back garden to the writing shed. She plonked herself down and huffily reread what existed of her play. It was shit. Shit shit shit.

She scribbled *rewrite this SHIT tomorrow* in her notebook, then slammed it shut. She glared at the photo of Issy, her image ghostly in the blue night.

'Why didn't you tell me about the Christian-Pagan effing festival and the eclipse?' Annie asked. 'And your portrait? And the story you wrote as a kid that's still at Colthwaite House in a locked library?' Issy stared back. 'Why didn't you tell me your bedroom was in the attic? And that your parents kept albums of deformed pigs?' Annie splayed her hands in the half-light and examined them. They looked puffy. 'Your family are a bunch of weirdos.'

It was freezing in here. She banged the laptop lid down and made her way back into the warm cottage to find she'd left the fucking door to the wood burner open again.

CHAPTER EIGHT

Rain. The squeak of windscreen wipers. They rode in silence, the car racing towards school. They were running late, and there'd been no time for coffee, and she was driving too fast. Grace stared out the window, prim-looking in her uniform, perched next to Caleb in the back seat so that Annie felt like a chauffeur. On the empty passenger seat there were two envelopes stuffed with cotton name tags: *Caleb Christopher Dillane, Grace Rose Dillane.* Annie had forgotten to sew them into the children's clothes. Of course she had.

And Caleb had been wrong: Grace *hadn't* forgotten things by morning, and before leaving had made a great show of taking Issy's story with her to school.

'Nearly there now, eh?' Annie said now. The kids grunted.

They swung round a corner. Ahead, black gates marked the entrance to an imposing Victorian gothic building with narrow windows. So much for Malory Towers.

She pulled up next to a fleet of cars as Grace sat forward, suddenly alert. Woozy all morning and complaining of a bad night's sleep and aching tummy, she now leapt from the car like she'd been plugged into the mains, dragging her suitcase from the boot and skipping up the wide steps to the entrance. It irritated Annie all over again. Why did she save all the best bits for other people?

'So long, then!' Annie called. 'See you at the weekend!'

Grace returned for a peck on the cheek. 'Bye.' She took off again, scanning the students. Perhaps she was searching out her cousins, perhaps that Snapchat guy.

Annie put a hand behind her and found Caleb's knee. 'It's going to be fine. Promise.'

He smiled at her, uncertain, in the rear-view mirror. 'See you Friday.' He climbed out to fetch his suitcase, hugged her and went after his sister who was already in conversation with a boy even taller than Grace herself. He looked friendly. Maybe this was the guy? What was he called? Adam?

She watched them chatting, Grace's arms animated, her mouth wide open as she laughed, until her face bunched suddenly, and she doubled over.

Annie hurried from the car, but the young man – whoever he might be – was already at Grace's back and it seemed as soon as whatever was causing her pain had started, it was over. Andrew's youngest son appeared out of nowhere and within seconds, Grace was surrounded by solicitous faces. Annie hung back. Caleb looked over at her and smiled apologetically. She didn't want him feeling he had to take a paternal role. She was the parent, that was her job. She smiled back, waved and retreated, glancing around for Andrew as she went.

A bell rang and the students poured into the building. She watched from the car as parents and guardians melted away. No Andrew. Their cousin must have hitched a lift with friends: Annie could have taken him. She flicked the ignition, and the car roared into life. Grace had looked so like Issy, standing there.

Now Annie was to live entirely alone. It wasn't an unfamiliar feeling. Losing Mum to the psych ward at six, the overdose at seven: yeah, Annie knew about alone. It was true she'd had Grandma Halmi, Lumi and Appa, but still, it had felt like a lot of empty space.

She drove past the school grounds and through the gates, joining a long line of cars at traffic lights. Would Patrick remember to call the kids and ask how they were getting on? He'd been so keen to *talk through arrangements* with Elizabeth and William. Fuck him.

The countryside flew by in a blur. She tried to imagine what Appa would say if he could see her now, living in relative luxury in a white, rural village, driving a Beemer, surrounded by pigs and sheep. He'd always hated being any distance from the city.

She'd almost reached home, the window wound down, when she heard noises – strange sounds, like that of a distressed animal – coming from the barn next to Colthwaite House.

William had better not be euthanising the disfigured pig. In her current mood, she wasn't sure what she'd do if she found out he was.

She pulled in along the lane and sat listening to the squealing, uncomfortable though it was to hear, the wind blowing hard at her cheek.

In the barn, everything went silent.

Then another noise: electric, maybe a drill? She thought of that poor pig, its terrified face, a large metal prod heading for its forehead. At this, she was out of the car and head down into the bluster, the car's door-open alert pinging loudly behind her.

She hurried through the farmyard and slid around one side of the building. She walked its length until she located the gap in the slats she'd come across during the abortive *serving*. She put her eye to the hole.

The overhead lights burned inside. At the far end, William, along with Vicar David, stood behind a freshly slaughtered sow. It hung from a hook on the automated line, upside down, blood squirting from its neck. She'd been right. Nausea shot up the back of her throat.

But *no*! There was a distinctive heart-shaped brown patch decorating the animal's back: it wasn't the one Annie now thought of as her pig. It was the sow she'd met on the lane with William: the mother, the one producing disfigured litters. That was odd; hadn't that sow been taken to the abattoir on that very day?

William was dressed in a rubber apron and goggles like the ones worn by Elizabeth in her work shed. He raised some sort of machine to hip height – it looked a lot like an electric saw – and began shearing its legs off one by one. Fresh blood spattered his apron. Once he'd finished, he killed the power again. 'Awfully messy job.'

'Extraction now?' David asked, holding out a silver kidney-shaped hospital bowl. 'It's rather warm in here.'

'Not yet.' William bent to retrieve something. He stood up holding a flat-bladed steel implement. 'Flense first. Don't waste the skin.'

'"Flense".' David chuckled. 'Pork scratchings for Christmas?'

'Couple of lampshades, more like.'

The skin came away in shavings like an apple, the sow's belly an exposed patch of livid red tissue threaded with bone and sinew.

'Right, David-o,' said William. '*Now* we go in.' He cut into the pig with a large knife. The blade looked almost Japanese. 'Easy does it.' He withdrew one of the organs and plopped it onto David's dish. The size and weight caused the vicar's arms to drop. Annie's stomach heaved.

'Good God,' David said. 'But that's enlarged. What've you been feeding her?'

'The usual,' William grunted. Perhaps the heart was to be sold separately, as a delicacy? He pulled out a pair of steel weighing scales from a cupboard and plonked the organ onto the plate. 'Weight?'

David squinted at the scales. 'A kilo, is it? I can't quite...' He bent closer. 'Yep, a kilo.'

'That should do it,' William replied. 'Get it down in the book or the missus will have my balls off.' They moved out of sight to the side and Annie lost the conversation.

The place looked like a murder had been committed, which it had, even if it wasn't called that. This wasn't her world. She should leave.

But then the men came into view again, and she couldn't tear herself away. What were they *doing* exactly? William removed his apron and goggles. The vicar switched on a hose attached to a wall-mounted tap and washed the floor down, sweeping the blood into a drain with a stiff broom.

'Andrew's boys used that to scrub the wheels of the ruddy tractor,' William said. 'Don't think it's up to much.'

David upended the broom and pulled the bristles to his face for inspection. 'It'll do.'

William collected his jacket. 'Ready?' They headed for the door and Annie sprinted to the car, keen to avoid them at all costs. Something told her that what they'd been doing wasn't quite... legal.

The door alarm was still pinging and the rain pelting now. She was sure you weren't supposed to butcher your own meat. She'd read it somewhere, or Issy had told her. She wished she hadn't seen it, because what was she supposed to do with the information? She didn't have the first clue who to report it to, even if it *did* turn out to be off-limits. Farm life was brutal:

perhaps she was being naïve. Farmers dealt with death and guts every day. It was just the distinct sense they'd been enjoying themselves that really bothered her.

Annie was at her desk in two pairs of trousers, two sweaters, and several pairs of socks. The little bar heater in the freezing writing shed was blasting out hot air as fast as its element could manage and the windows had steamed over. It was like working in a greenhouse. She was on scene 3 of *Kimchi Trout Sandwich*. She'd channelled the extra time alone into her work. She was making headway. Of sorts.

As she tried to remember her childhood Korean and place it into avatar Grandma Halmi's mouth, her mobile rang, making her jump. A London number.

'Hallo?'

'Am I speaking to Annie Park?'

'Yes?'

'It's Aku Ngwenya, from the Finborough Theatre here.'

Her mouth went instantly dry. 'Yes?' Why were they calling? They'd had *Bambisexual*, for a year and nothing.

There was some preamble chat from Aku asking how she was, none of which she really listened to because – the Finborough! The Finborough was one of her favourites. How could they keep her in suspense like this?

'We've read your work,' he was saying now.

She almost missed it. 'Sorry what?'

'We're so sorry for the delay. We had the most ridiculous backlog.'

'No problem, um...' They must want it, or they'd never have called her. No, they *mustn't* want it, because if they did, they'd be–

'We *loved* it, Annie.'

'Eh?'

Aku laughed. 'We loved it.'

'You did?'

'Yep. We'd love to add *Bambisexual* to our programme for the end of next year if possible.'

Was this even *real*?

Aku added, 'Unless in the interim another theatre has bagged it?'

'Oh sorry, no! Not bagged. To my knowledge.' She should stop talking now.

Aku talked about edits, his thoughts on the play, Annie furiously jotting down notes while a magpie squawked importantly in a tree.

'So would it be okay?' Aku was saying. 'To slot it into our winter schedule?'

Would it be okay? Was he *insane*? 'Definitely okay by me.' Her heart was going like the clappers.

'Great! And could you come in for a meeting next month? Sam and I would love to meet you.'

'Yes, *I'd* love that. Who's Sam? Oh yes! Thank you!' She sounded like an overexcited child. 'When were you thinking?'

'Sam's the assistant A.D.'

'Oh yeah, I knew that, sorry.'

'We'll ping you some dates,' he sounded amused. 'We can talk in more detail.'

The call ended. Annie stared at the reflection grinning back from the black screen of her laptop. She looked ridiculous, as if she was on drugs. An off-West End theatre! The play she'd completed before Issy died. It was a symbol, an omen. She allowed herself the briefest fantasy of five-star reviews, crowded houses, a possible extension before killing it out of superstition. She modified it to the trip to London for the meeting: lunch in a restaurant, the smell of the Tube, dodging pedestrians on pavements.

She couldn't possibly do any more writing today. She saved today's work, emailed it to herself, executed a little skip and caught her head on the corner of the desk lamp. Ouch, but her play was going on!

She wanted to tell the kids, but they were at school, and she'd not heard from them. If Caleb was homesick, her calling might make it worse.

Who *could* she tell? Not Elizabeth and William; they knew nothing about theatre and had never shown any interest in her work. Not her sister, either. Lumi just wouldn't get it and things were frosty between them, anyway. Annie still wasn't quite sure why. She'd the impression she'd done something, said something – or *not* said something – but hadn't had the battery power these last few months to care enough to find out.

She could tell one of her and Issy's actual friends back in London? But if she spoke to them, they'd ask how she was getting on and then she'd have to lie.

She replaced the jotter pad on the shelf, dropped her pens into the pot. Her face split into another grin. Her play! She turned to Issy's photo. 'Good news!' She remembered suddenly that her wife had been uncharacteristically equivocal about that play. The word she'd used on first reading was 'extraordinary'.

Annie neatened the stack of papers beside her and placed them next to her computer. She switched off the bar heater. A pheasant began its two-note call up in the woods. Issy stared back at her from the wall.

The hot bright hospital, the long airless corridors, kind doctors. Scans, blood tests. Issy in a coma.

Oh God, not now, Annie begged. Please not this memory now. She saved her work, sent it to herself and shut the laptop.

It was no good, the image kept swimming right back up to the surface.

The kids crying. And Patrick, not crying but wild-eyed like a child, touching and re-touching everything, his OCD in overdrive. Hours waiting. Issy wetting herself, Annie not thinking to bring spare underwear.

'Christ's *sake!*' She pressed a piece of A4 in front of Issy's photo, then felt terrible and pulled it away. 'Sorry,' she grovelled.

The coroner's report said a tangle of arterial mass balled in the left ventricle, a genetic abnormality from birth. '"Strong genes",' Annie mimicked at Issy's bland, impassive face.

A sound in the garden, a swishing. A gentle bump against the back of the shed.

'Hello?'

Nothing to see beyond the misted windows. She rubbed the glass with the back of her sleeve, but the area re-fogged instantly. Another bump, to the side this time. Snuffling. It was an animal of some sort. She got to her feet, opened the door.

The deformed pig appeared around one corner of the shed. It had escaped its pen in the barn, after all! Just as she'd intended. Everything about this made her mood lift and she greeted it warmly, like an old friend. It stood still, weight unevenly distributed, head supplicant as she patted its back gingerly. 'Have you been hiding in the woods?' she asked it. Saliva dribbled from its mouth as it made a pitiful sound.

'You've got a *lot* to thank me for,' she told it, thinking of the other pig – its mother! – legless, hanging from a hook.

The pig turned its head, staring off into the woods like a tortured poet, before throwing Annie a look with its one eye. Its belly was terribly distended. 'But I can't keep you here,' Annie told it. 'Where would I put you?' She tried to shoo it away. It wouldn't budge.

She looked around the garden, at the crumbling hut cut into the rock. 'Okay, you win, fatso. Luckily for you, I'm generous. We have this suite available for rent. And one of my plays is about to be staged at the Finborough. So...' At least now she'd told someone: some*thing*. 'Don't move.'

The sow grunted.

Annie swooshed through the wet grass to the cottage and returned with a saucer of bread sopped in milk. She'd no idea if bread was the right thing to give a pig, but it had worked back in the day with stray cats in New Malden. The sow guzzled the lot, then looked up, eyeballing her. Annie went back inside and brought out another saucerful. 'Greedy guts.'

While it finished that, she returned to the cottage a third time to fetch a table she'd brought from London; one she'd not yet found a use for, turning it upside down, using it to corral the pig towards the open door of the hut. Once the pig was inside, Annie lay the table on its end, blocking the exit, threw a blanket into a corner as a substitute for straw, and placed a bowl of drinking water just inside the entrance – though God knows, in Cumbria water was one thing the pig wouldn't be short of. It rootled in the dirt, then hobbled towards the blanket, where it settled definitively, eye closed.

Annie left for the warmth of the cottage, keeping watch through the kitchen window as she brewed a pot of coffee. She stood, the mug warming her hands, imagining the press night for *Bambi*. How many did the Finborough seat? Was it two hundred? The pub downstairs was large; the cast, everyone, could have drinks afterwards. Maybe she'd hit up Issy's friend at *The Guardian*? A broadsheet review would be incredible. The pleasing thought spread through her like molasses.

Right. She knew what she could do today, could face: sorting Issy's clothes. It was time. The pig was fine for now.

She thumped upstairs. The suitcase was waiting for her in

the cupboard. She unzipped the lid a couple of inches. Familiar perfume wafted through the gap. Annie looked away, mooring herself to the present, to the chair strewn with her own clothes. The clothes of the living. 'I fucking *miss* you,' she told the case.

She opened it fully. Everything had been neatly folded. Possibly by Annie, she couldn't remember the order of events: which friends had come to help, and when.

Her wife's running outfits, sweaters, a blue scarf, some smart black trousers.

Pulling off her own jumper, Annie put on Issy's tracksuit top. It was chocolate brown terry cotton with yellow piping. They'd bought it in New York, at a thrift store in Williamsburg. It was too tight on Annie, and the sleeves too long.

Yeah, well. It was hers now. Slowly, methodically, she hung each item up, sliding the hangers in next to her own clothes. 'I'm going to have a bloody play on,' she told the trousers as she clipped them tidily onto the rail. Then she started to weep.

Her mobile rang. It was Caleb.

'Mum?'

Annie's heart missed a beat. He'd never called her Mum before. 'Hey, darling boy!' She hoped he wouldn't pick up the jagged tone in her voice. 'How are you?'

'Yeah.'

'Everything okay?'

'I'm a bit... what they call "homesick".' There was a pause and then he laughed. 'I'm a moron, right?'

'Oh, love.' Her first instinct, which she sat on, was to say she missed him like mad and wished he was with her right now. Her second was to mention the play to cheer him up, but that would be making the moment about her. 'Give it time,' she soothed. 'You'll be back before you know it.'

'Yeah.' He sighed. 'But then I'll have to leave again.'

'It's lovely to hear your voice. How you getting on?' A ball of

Issy's socks were still in the case, she noticed. They could go in with hers. 'Is it nice?'

'Not sure "nice" is the right word. It's busy. Grace is being a bit weird.'

'Tummy ache weird, like ill? Or another kind of weird?'

'Moody and emotional.'

'I think that's girl's stuff,' Annie reassured.

Caleb cleared his throat. 'You mean her period?'

She tried not to smile. 'That's exactly what I mean.'

'I heard her tell Adam, that boy you saw her with when you dropped us off, that she's late.'

So, that *had* been Adam. 'Well, periods are often late. Don't worry about Grace, love. You take care of yourself.'

Another pause. 'What are you doing right now?' he asked.

If he could see her in the cupboard, her face streaked with tears. 'Working,' she lied. 'Then going for a walk.' She wouldn't tell him about the sow, either. He might mention it to Elizabeth and William before she could warn him not to. 'What are *you* doing?'

'It's a study period.' She wanted to reach her arms through the phone and hug him. 'See you Friday then.'

'Yes, Friday. Can't wait.' She took a little breath, the news of the play hovering. 'Love you.'

She *did* love him. So, so much. Grace too. His call disarranged her, though, and she found she couldn't finish Issy's clothes. Instead, as if to honour her lie to Caleb, she went to the hall and pulled on her walking boots, then hurled herself out the front door and down the track through the puddles with the remnants of Issy's perfume in her nose. She was still wearing Issy's tracksuit top as well, and had forgotten a coat. Never mind.

The lane was empty. Her only company, the steady patter of water on sodden leaves, the roar of the beck. The lonesome bleats of sheep came off the fell. She was to have a play in production. Caleb had called her 'Mum'.

There was a long meadow to her left. Usually home to William's flock of Herdwicks, today it was empty, the grass tufted by the animals' bottomless appetite. William must have moved them at first light. She had a hazy recollection of hearing, as she'd turned in bed, buzzing quad bikes, sheepdogs barking.

A vehicle blaring rap music was approaching fast along the lane. She'd guessed what it was before it appeared around the bend: a white van, the same as the other day. It whizzed past, nearly clipping her heels as it passed. She shouted but what was the point? He couldn't hear over the racket. Annoyed, she decided to follow him. She knew exactly where he was headed.

When she arrived in the farmyard, the guy was already in the storage area at the van's rear.

'Excuse me?' she called. The man – a boy really, not much older than Caleb – looked round. 'You nearly ran me over just now,' she said. 'You do know you're going too fast?'

The boy stared at her with bloodshot eyes. Perhaps he was stoned? Without a word, he returned to his work pulling polystyrene boxes from a large in-built refrigerator. The boxes had stickers on the sides labelled *Dillane*.

That photo album with the dead piglet, the unusual slaughtering; there was something going on. She wanted to know what.

'If you don't mind my asking...?' she said, louder this time. 'What's in those?'

'Huh?'

'What are you delivering to Elizab...' Something occurred to her. Elizabeth was almost certainly nearby. She dropped her voice. 'What are you bringing to Dr Dillane?'

He stepped out of the van, almost invisible behind a wall of polystyrene. The rain pattered hollow sounds onto the topmost one. 'I'm just the driver,' he said.

'I can see that. How about this, then: where do the deliveries come from?'

'Backbarrow.'

'And before that?'

His eyes narrowed, 'Who are you anyway?'

Who *did* she think she was? 'Dr Dillane's daughter-in-law,' she said, which was true, at least. 'I'm supposed to be helping out on the farm, but I'm from London so...' She shrugged, smiled.

The boy sighed, rocked back on his heels, and Annie knew she'd won. 'The top one says from Munich, Germany. Look, see?' He pointed at another, smaller label. 'Here. The three below are from...' he pushed the top box aside. 'America.'

'And how often do you make these deliveries?'

'Wouldn't you already know that if you're helping out?'

'I *should* but...' Annie tapped her temple with her finger. 'She's a bit funny, my mother-in-law. Bit old-fashioned.'

His face split into a grin. 'My dad calls her The Witch.'

The *bloody* Jack Russell began to yap; they both turned towards the sound. It was coming from Elizabeth's work shed. If Elizabeth saw Annie, she'd want to know why she was being nosy. She mustn't be seen here like this. Making a snap decision, she hid behind the tractor.

The boy turned to say something else, found Annie gone, and hesitated. The shed door opened, and Elizabeth's head popped out.

'Ah, wonderful,' she heard her mother-in-law say. 'Just leave them on the ground, please.'

'You don't want me to bring 'em in?' he asked.

'I'm not as ancient as I look.' The dog barked from between Elizabeth's ankles. 'Inside, Noah! Thank you.'

Noah! That was the dog's name. Finally.

From her hiding place, Annie could see the boy amble back to his van, rolling his eyes. He climbed into his cab and fired the engine, bringing another wave of techno crashing into the yard, then roared down the drive.

Annie peeked around the front of the tractor. Elizabeth was carting the boxes into the shed, one at a time. In a minute, she'd be done, and Annie could make her escape.

Noah appeared at her feet, back legs aquiver. Annie mimed for him to leave, but this seemed to excite him further and he barked twice, then ran forwards to nip her neatly on the shin.

'Ow!'

'Annie?' Footsteps, then Elizabeth was right in front of her. 'Are you quite all right?'

'Sorry, yes.' Annie shook herself. 'I was walking, and then came over all faint.'

'But what on earth were you doing back there?' She took Annie's elbow.

'I... I wasn't *hiding*.' Annie cursed herself, silently. 'That kid nearly killed me with his van, and I thought I was going to pass out.'

Elizabeth steered her towards a bench in front of the main barn, the dog running circles around them. Annie tried not to boot it across the yard. The bench was wet, of course, and the seat of her trackpants instantly soaked. 'I was running,' she explained, though Elizabeth hadn't demanded more information. 'When the boy almost took me out. I chased him. By the time I got here he was leaving and I...' She wasn't even convincing herself.

'Dear oh dear.' Elizabeth stared down the lane. 'I must speak to the dispatch company. The deliveries have a limited shelf life and come a long way, which is, I suppose, an explanation if not an excuse.'

'Europe,' Annie commented, then caught herself. 'He told me.'

No, she'd got her timeline muddled. The boy wouldn't have been able to tell her about Europe if he'd been leaving just as she'd arrived.

'That's right.' Elizabeth smiled. 'Specialist breeding programmes require specialist treatments. It's horribly expensive.'

'Worse since Brexit, I should imagine.'

Elizabeth tipped her head to the side, like Margaret Thatcher. 'Mmm. We're famous for our swine breeding at Colthwaite, did you know? The sole farm in the UK to have American Landrace-Arapawa Island crosses – amongst others.'

'Oh. Impressive.'

'Tricky to raise in our climate, *but* with special care and attention...'

Annie looked around the dilapidated yard at its ancient equipment, the paint flaking from the barn's corrugated roof. 'Issy never mentioned you were so... successful.' That sounded rude. 'I mean–'

'My daughter did tend to take it all rather for granted.'

'Well...' She was getting cold. She got to her feet, pulled at the wet clothes stuck to her skin.

'Would you care to see inside?' her mother-in-law said, suddenly.

'Your... work shed?' Annie scratched her head. 'I mean, sure. Thank you.' She didn't care to really, but it would be bad manners to say no.

The door to the shed had locked behind Elizabeth, and she was forced to punch in the code in front of Annie. She glanced quickly at Annie before starting, and Annie pretended to look away. 'Can't be too careful.' Her mother-in-law laughed.

'Of course.'

1943. The year of Elizabeth's birth. The door clicked open.

The interior of the shed was narrow and smelt peculiarly cheesy. Windowless and low-ceilinged, it was around thirty feet in length. The walls were corrugated metal. Strip lighting ran along the central section of the roof, creating large pockets of darkness either end.

'As you can see...' The dog spatchcocked itself at Elizabeth's feet. 'We do our best, but we're constantly battling cashflow, and the weather.'

At waist height along both sides there were countertops littered with bottles, petri dishes, and several ancient-looking microscopes. Shelving units ran above these, the unpainted MDF bowed in the middle. Annie didn't know what she'd expected of a breeding farm – stainless-steel high-tech equipment; a secret assistant in a hazmat suit – certainly not this fusty hotch-potch of outdated paraphernalia. She picked up a glass beaker covered in fingerprints. A small label read: *C-4 Test 1*. She felt Elizabeth's gaze on her and put it down.

'Different language,' Annie offered.

'It *is*,' her mother-in-law said. 'And hard work. We've always had the best intentions. Unfortunately, our efforts haven't always been a success.' She crossed her arms at her chest. 'All animals are *not* born equal.'

Annie leant, not with complete confidence, on the countertop. There were so many bits and pieces, her hand struggled to find a resting place. The dog opened one eye and looked at her.

'Our drifts need vitamins and minerals they can't get from the feed in the UK.' Elizabeth returned a stray wisp of white hair to the bun at the nape of her neck. 'Importing feed from abroad is expensive. Instead, we compromise, import supplements only and add those to the British feed. The animals receive every nutrient they need, and extra richness, to encourage breeding. It's not strictly speaking a *traditional* approach.' She lifted her shoulders.

'They're terribly shy little things, pigs. Not many people know that. Unlike this ferocious beast.' She pushed the tip of her shoe against the dog's back, making its tail thump against the floor. 'Any person in this line of work will tell you we're *seekers*, continually moving forwards, discovering the new. That's the purpose of a life scientific, isn't it?'

'To make things better than they are?'

'Yes, or what's the point?' Elizabeth began to walk up and down the corridor between units.

Annie hoped her mother-in-law wasn't making claims for a broken-down farm and its workers being at the cutting-edge of science. She watched Elizabeth pacing and felt a speech coming her way. She wasn't in the mood for a farming lecture, but it came anyway.

'A farm is a bottomless pit,' Elizabeth began. 'Early mornings, late finishes, the constant demands from livestock and the land. A farm swallows everything: time, money, your health, until you hardly know who you are anymore. You need a passion for it, or you'll sink.'

'I bet.' Annie was freezing. Her thoughts leant in the direction of escape, home to food. Maybe a nice kimchi pancake for lunch.

'I gave up my career as a vet when I had a family,' Elizabeth went on. 'Believing a farm would be less demanding. How wrong I was. The children suffered as a result.'

Or a kimchi *omelette*. Wait, what was that Elizabeth had just said? Her children suffering? Annie grew suddenly focused.

Annie weighed her next words carefully. 'Is it okay,' she asked. 'To know in what way the children suffered?'

Elizabeth smiled. Annie wondered if her mother-in-law had

been wanting, *waiting* to reveal this information – it was far and away the most intimate thing she'd ever shared with her. 'Issy may have told you we had a series of poor outcomes with our first drifts when she and Andrew were small?'

'No, I don't believe she did.'

'Terribly upsetting. William and I were taken up with the animals, and the poor children neglected.'

'But Issy always said she loved her childhood here.'

'Did she?'

There was a long silence. Annie waited for her mother-in-law to say more, but nothing came.

Annie pointed to a large white item at one end of the counter. 'What's that?'

'Centrifuge,' Elizabeth said. 'But look at you! Here I am talking, while you're catching your death. Would you like a cup of tea in the Big House? I can give you Issy's portrait to take with? Wrap it in a bin liner? Andrew and Carolina are out for the day so we wouldn't be imposing.'

Annie nodded. The possibility of hearing more about Issy's childhood was too much to resist. Teeth chattering, she trudged towards the house, thinking about Issy's beautiful painted face wrapped in a bin liner.

They went through the back door to the kitchen, Elizabeth tiptoeing to the pewter stovetop kettle, opening the lid of the enormous range and sliding the kettle onto the hotplate where it began to hiss. 'Ah, already warm,' she stated.

Annie waited, uncertain, in the doorway. 'I'm so sorry...' she began. 'About Issy. We haven't really spoken, you and me. It must be so hard as her mother, and I–'

'Thank you.' Elizabeth allowed the steaming kettle to screech for a good while before pushing it off the hotplate. 'Is that her top you're wearing?'

'Oh.' Annie looked down. 'Yes. Sorry.' Why was she apologising?

She would have liked to put her frozen body against the Raeburn but that would have meant standing right next to Elizabeth. Instead, she sat in one of the rickety chairs behind the long table, resting her elbows on the oak. Jagged crumbs of leftover toast poked at her skin.

'Yorkshire tea all right?' Elizabeth asked.

Annie laughed. 'Given we're in the Lakes?'

Elizabeth looked up. 'What?'

'Nothing. Yorkshire's perfect.'

Noah sniffed busily around the skirting. For one moment, Annie considered telling Elizabeth about the play. But she'd probably never even *heard* of the Finborough Theatre.

Elizabeth went to the fridge. 'There's no milk, I'm afraid. Lemon? Though not sure there's any of that, either.'

'Just as it comes is great.'

It smelled of wet Labrador in here. She stared at the empty dog baskets. Elizabeth presented her with the tea and placed herself in the chair opposite, Annie listening to the sound as the liquid travelled down her mother-in-law's throat.

'Have you been to Gillyhead?' Elizabeth asked. 'There's a new bakery that sells pork pies. Proper large Melton Mowburys.' She checked herself. 'Oh, silly me, you don't eat that sort of thing.'

Annie shook her head. 'Thank you so much for the loan of the portrait.'

'It's Andrew you need to thank, not me. I'll fetch it in one moment.' Elizabeth set her cup down. 'How are the children getting on at school?'

'Great, I think. It's lovely they're with their cousins. Well, *cousin.*'

'It is.' Elizabeth agitated her cup, swirling the leaves at the bottom.

'Talking of which,' she said, 'how's Polly these days? She's away?'

'Ah, Polly, Polly, Polly.' Elizabeth extended her arms, frowning at her hands. 'She's at a health retreat. Or so I'm told.'

'Health retreat? Vincent said it was a medical rehabilitation centre.'

'There now! You know more than I do. Fuddy-duddy that I am, Andrew tells me very little.' Annie highly doubted that. 'Polly is, shall we say, partial to drama.'

'Vincent said she had an illness caused by mutations in her genes.'

Her mother-in-law threw her head back and laughed; Annie could see her fillings. 'Did he? Poor man.' Elizabeth wiped her eyes. 'He always fancies himself a medical expert. No, dear.' She placed a hand over Annie's, who worked hard not to snatch it away. 'It's nothing as funky as *genes*. That's what Andrew will have told everyone, for Polly's sake.'

'What is it then? If you don't mind my asking?'

Her mother-in-law sucked in her cheeks. 'It's depression,' she said. 'That sort of nonsense. I think they call it "bipolarism" these days.'

'Oh.' Annie's own mum's illness. One of her many.

'You know there are only seven diseases that are *solely* attributable to genetic mutation? Every other "*dis*-ease" is caused by the environment in which the genes reside. Some of them are light switches, dormant for years and just waiting to be flicked on. In simple terms,' Elizabeth looked to the ceiling, 'the more stress a body is subjected to, the more likely the cells will mutate in injurious ways. With Polly it's a *mental* issue that has a physiological expression. Does that make sense?'

'Sort of.' Polly, far from home, in a centre receiving treatment, her cells all muddled.

'Do you have the address? I'd love to send a card, wish her well.' She'd been so young when Mum had been taken away, she hadn't understood it, hadn't written once. Appa had said it was for the best.

Elizabeth sat back. 'No, no, she's under strict instructions: no contact. When a body's lame, it needs rest.'

No contact. That's what Mum had received in her psych ward: nothing. For shame. And Appa having upped sticks in the first place, to come to London for a British woman he'd fallen in love with, far from home. A woman who turned out crazy. *Far from home*: it was how Annie felt, now.

Elizabeth was on her feet, taking her cup to the sink. 'There's more than one way to skin an animal,' she said.

'Sorry?'

'There *are* other methods with which to treat the sort of predicament Polly finds herself in. Not blowing my own trumpet of course, but doctors could learn a thing or two from veterinarians. Remove emotion from the equation and there'll be superior outcomes. The brain is a powerful weapon. It mustn't be allowed to develop poor belief systems.' Annie watched as she wiped her hands on a tea towel.

'I think you might have lost me,' Annie said, then gulped her tea. She did understand, of course; what intrigued her was why Elizabeth felt the need to tell her all this. It was a lot of detail for someone claiming to be a fuddy-duddy.

A text message pinged from inside Elizabeth's clothing. She pulled her mobile from her pocket and put on her reading glasses. 'Excuse me.' There was a pause, then, 'Oh blast.' She typed a reply with one finger. 'Willy's at the end of the drive with four fugitive sheep.'

Annie stood. 'I can help.'

'No, you stay in the warm.' Her mother-in-law snatched a random coat from a hook. 'I'll be five minutes. I haven't forgotten about the painting.' She ran out the door, the dog at her heels. Through the window, Annie watched her march down the drive, as a silver Jeep Cherokee passed very slowly along the lane.

She fell back onto her chair, a strange lightness in her shoulders. Poor Polly. She drew her own phone out. It was still damp, and she checked the microphone for rain damage. Her screensaver was Issy, Annie, and the kids bunched together, grinning on the back terrace at Hackney, Annie's arm extended in the foreground to capture them. Caleb's hair was very short. He must have been about thirteen. She should probably swap the image out. It wasn't good to feel heartsore every time you wanted to check the time, or someone rang.

Outside, William and Elizabeth were bellowing at one another. Annie looked up at the stained and patchy ceiling, the weight of Dillane family history resting on it. An ancestral burden. All those expectations, those *genes* to live up to.

She typed a message to Caleb:

> Looking forward to seeing you soon! I have good news, but I'll save it for Friday! You know I love you very much x

A minute later, the phone buzzed:

> Can't wait to hear it! Love you too. Are you still working in the shed? X

Annie texted back:

> No, at the Big House. Alone!

She watched the ellipsis on the screen.

Time to go exploring: you never know what they're hiding! Heh. See you at the weekend x

Annie put the phone down. She stared at the wall for a moment. She *could* go exploring; she still hadn't seen Issy's old bedroom in the attic. The idea felt rude, and possibly a little dangerous. What if Elizabeth came back and caught her? She hopped up and went back to the window. Elizabeth was still busy outside. This was not her house. She should return to her seat. Instead, she made her way into the hall.

'Hello? Anybody there?' No answer.

Heart thumping, she raced up the staircase. The first-floor landing was gloomy even in daylight, and so quiet she could almost feel the walls vibrating. Blood pumped into the tips of her fingers. She wasn't cut out to play detective. She glanced in both directions and made her way along the left-hand corridor until she reached the library: for good measure, she tried the handle – it was locked. Here was the narrow stairwell to the attic, leading up into darkness.

Her mouth dry, she took the creaky wooden treads one at a time.

The attic landing was small and far darker even than the first floor. Sloping windows interrupted a steeply angled roof. Every now and then, slices of light interrupted the shadows. Cobwebs swagged from every corner. It smelled of damp.

On the lane, Noah was barking. She'd better be quick.

She approached the door ahead, turning the handle sharply. A tiny windowless room: LPs, books, and blankets were piled up, as well as a jumble of ornaments. Everything was coated in a thick layer of dust. A hanging rail was wedged against one wall, from which pointed hoods in brown linen material dangled. Annie gawped. Jesus, what had they been for? A fancy-dress party back in the seventies?

She closed the door and moved on. The second and third rooms were empty. The fourth was the nursery: Issy's room! Large – at least three times the length of any other so far – it was bright, with two corners occupied by narrow iron beds draped in identical crocheted quilts. On the side table next to each bed stood a mini crucifix, the Jesuses looking a little disappointed in their crowns of thorns, perhaps sad they'd been depicted so pale.

A wooden rocking horse, a large, dark wooden chest decorated with flowers and sealed with a small hinge and padlock, dozens of books, a toy fort on a low stool, dolls with genuine-looking hair staring at her. Hanging on the wall was another of those squat, ancient-looking large-hipped women. The remaining, living Dillanes clearly hadn't touched a thing.

Issy's childlike dreams had formed here, as she'd looked out at... what exactly? The windows in the ceiling were impossible even for an adult to reach. She tried to imagine Issy playing with the doll's house or sitting quietly with a book, its spine bent from repeated reading. Had she enjoyed being stuck up here with the gowns and dusty ornaments?

It seemed incomprehensible that Grace had drifted off to sleep in this room just the other night, while the party went on noisily downstairs. Annie found it almost too spooky to breathe in here.

On the floor behind her, leant against the wall, a large painting, its back to the room. She went over, turned it to face her. It was a second portrait of Andrew, almost identical to the first hanging above the stairs. Different jeans – flared. Slight change in hairstyle. Why had the family commissioned two? It seemed a bit weird. Perhaps they'd preferred the artist's work in the first piece. If so, it would have been an expensive mistake. She put it back and wandered around, running her hands over shelves, lifting books, shaking them in case anything interesting fell out. She even tried the lock on the wooden chest.

At the far end of the shelf was a small and tatty book missing its spine. Carefully, she edged it out. Issy's childish writing was scrawled across the cover: *My Diary*. Annie stared at the words with a sense of deliciousness but also dread. She desperately wanted to open it, but what if Issy's childhood musings made her cry? She was exhausted by crying, and anyway, there wasn't time: Elizabeth would be back any minute. She stuffed the book into the front pocket of her tracksuit top. She'd save it for later, in front of the fire at Chapel Croft.

She went over to one of the beds. The quilts were silky and soft as butter. The pillow looked a little mildewed. She put her nose close to it and sniffed. Yes, damp.

There, stretched across the pillowcase, a strand of flaxen hair. Grace's? She picked it up and held it to the light. It could be Issy's.

Unable to stop herself, she pulled back the cover on the bed and inhaled the scent of the sheet. Nothing but more damp. Disappointed, she threw herself onto the pillow face down, pushing her hands beneath it. The sheet felt cool against her palms, but also, there was something there, something small and cold, like metal. She pulled it out. A tiny iron key. Too small for the door. Perhaps it unlocked another diary? Or a jewellery box?

How could it have been left here like this? Had Issy or Andrew hidden it as children, and no one thought to look? Annie had to know. Absolutely *had* to.

She leapt up frantically and surveyed the room. The wooden chest. She went to it, knelt, and pushed the key into the keyhole. It fit! Outside, she heard William's two-note whistle for the dogs. She must hurry.

Annie twisted the key until the mechanism gave and the lid popped open. She peered into it.

The chest was full of photo albums. With red covers, exactly like those with the pigs in the library, but these were unlabelled.

'Oh God, please no,' she whispered.

More pigs? More 'poor outcomes' from the Dillane's off-label breeding programmes? She didn't think she could bear it.

Downstairs the sound of the back door opening then closing, then Noah yapping inside the kitchen.

Annie hastily locked the chest, replaced the key beneath the pillow and threw herself out the door, her toe catching the bedpost in her hurry. Trying not to yowl in pain, she scurried down the winding staircase to the first floor, at which point she ran into the nearest bathroom. She perched on the edge of the bath, breathing fast.

'Hello?' Downstairs, Elizabeth was already in the hall on the hunt for her. 'Annie?'

Annie sat very still.

'Your phone's on the table so I assume you're still here?'

'Just coming, sorry!' Her voice was tremulous. She pulled the chain on the lavatory, washed her hands and splashed water on her face. She dried herself on the hand towel, noticing a pair of used blue surgical gloves and a small syringe in the wastepaper basket below. Perhaps someone had diabetes. Or Carolina used Botox and asked Elizabeth to inject it. The thought was repulsive.

'Are you okay?'

Why was Elizabeth still waiting? Couldn't she use the loo in peace?

Annie cleared her throat and said with a little laugh, 'I used the upstairs bathroom for good manners.' That ought to shut the old bag up.

Sure enough, a moment later, she heard Elizabeth's

footsteps retreating to the kitchen. Annie calmed her breathing and made her way downstairs.

Elizabeth was sitting in a kitchen chair nursing a second cup of tea, Noah panting at her feet. Next to her, leaning up against the table, a black bin bag wrapped around Issy's portrait. Annie stood in the doorway and rubbed her tummy performatively.

'Guts still playing up?'

'Uh-huh.'

Elizabeth nodded at the table. 'Here's the painting.'

'Thank you so much. Did you catch the rogue sheep?'

'We did, though they *are* the biggest pests.' Elizabeth took a sip of tea. 'Willy's cut his leg. Beastly luck. It needs a stitch but of course he's decided to go with gaffer tape.' She shook her head. 'That man will be the death of me.'

'I hope not.' Annie's hand fluttered to her neck. 'I think I'd better head off. It'll probably be dark soon. Thanks so much for the tea. And the chat.' She scuttled to pick up the enormous painting and crab-walked with it to the back door.

Just as she reached it, Elizabeth said offhandedly, 'You know, if you want to borrow something, you only need ask.'

Annie's grip tightened around the portrait. 'What?'

'The book. It's from the nursery, yes?' Elizabeth's shoes clicked on the tiled floor as she approached. 'The corner's poking from your – my *daughter's* – tracksuit pocket.'

Annie looked down and reddened. 'Ah. I'm so sorry.' She rotated the painting in her arms for something to do. 'I wanted to see Issy's old bedroom.' Her voice grew small. 'The nursery. Complete the tour Vincent promised.'

Elizabeth laid a proprietary hand on the portrait to stop Annie agitating it. 'Of course. I understand. Just ask in future.'

'Absolutely.' Annie bowed slightly. 'I'll... Sorry. I'd better get back.'

She pushed at the door and a gust of wet wind hit her face.

'Which book?' Elizabeth enquired.

'Which...?'

'The book? Which one is it that you've taken?'

'Oh,' Annie said. 'Um, Enid Blyton. *Malory Towers.*'

'Good choice. Makes better reading than our collection of photo albums, at least.' Elizabeth's gaze was firmly on Noah. 'Of the lost pigs in the library. I believe you had a look at those, too. At the drinks party.'

Annie swallowed. 'I–'

'Of the breeding programmes,' Elizabeth pressed, 'that didn't go quite as planned.'

Unable to think of a thing to say, Annie glanced out the window instead.

'You put the album back upside down,' Elizabeth said, neutrally. 'That's how we knew.'

If Annie could just stay focused on the swaying trees outside. 'Again, I'm so sorry. I *really* wasn't snooping that night. The library was open. I was looking for Grace and thought she might have been in there, and...'

'There were so many books, you couldn't help yourself?'

Annie nodded, miserably.

'I understand.' Elizabeth smiled. 'You wouldn't be the first.'

'Oh. Well.'

'It's really quite all right.' Elizabeth held the door open; Annie stepped through it.

The relief of being outside. Everyone was so polite here, but sort of rude at the same time. She could have sworn she'd put the album from the library back on its shelf the right way up.

The wind and rain whipped her face. What did Elizabeth really think about Annie's adventures around the Big House? She'd seemed a combination of amused and angry. More importantly, what did *she*, Annie, think about what she'd found:

the albums of overbred piglets, the hidden key, that syringe in the bathroom bin? A little afraid, perhaps.

No, that was silly. What was there to be afraid of? Retired pensioners with an over-focus on livestock were hardly scary. But they weren't only that, were they. They were sadistic retired pensioners: there'd been nothing sweet about how William and David had dispatched that pig.

Coming up from behind on the lane, a vehicle: the Jeep Cherokee she'd seen earlier, returning. It slowed as it went past – she had the feeling the driver was looking at her – but the windows were dark, and she couldn't see who was at the wheel.

She headed home, fiercely protective of Issy's portrait in the rain.

CHAPTER NINE

As soon as she'd reached the cottage, she set the painting down
and went out the back to check on the pig. Her earlier
excitement about the play had spoiled now, replaced by a deep
sense of unease.

The pig lay on its belly in the corner. Annie snuck her nose
over the table. 'Hey, tubsy,' she said.

The pig blinked at her.

'What can you tell me about your owners, then?' she
demanded. The pig turned its head away from her towards the
wall. 'Fine,' Annie said. 'Be like that.'

She stomped into the living room, freed Issy's portrait from
its wrapping, laid it against the wall, then lit the wood burner.
Once logs hissed and crackled behind the glass, she made sure
to close the burner door and fell onto the sofa with Issy's
nursery diary. Annie looked round at the painting. 'See?' she
said, dangling the diary between two fingers at her. 'It's your
fault your mum thinks I'm a busybody. I love you, but it is.'

Issy stared back, louche, dismissive.

'Okay then, allow me to jog your memory.' Annie opened to
the first page. '"Issy's Diary: 1975–76",' she read. 'Repetition,

babe. You've already said that on the front.' Issy had penned it in curly script, with doodles of farm animals beside it.

Annie turned to the next page. 'Okay. "Chrissmass 1975. I got a bike for Chrissmass! It is red and has no staberlisers." God, your spelling was appalling!'

Annie smiled at the mistakes. She could just see seven-year-old Issy, with her left-handedness, her arm the wrong way up on the paper.

'"It is very nice. Mother says I can ride it on the lane. Andrew got a bike to and it is bigger than mine wich isn't fair becos even tho hes taller hes yonger. We went to church and david made us sing boring songs." Preach. "Also this is my new diry. It was in my stokking. I am going to right in it every day." Aww.'

Annie felt a thrill as she turned the page.

'"Boxing Day 1975: I cut myself on the fir trees up the bannisters." Oh no! "Father said it was good luck. Then he and me went to check the animmals. We had a day off yesterday becos it was Chrissmass. Claribel had dyed in the nite and I cryed." What again, why?! "She wasn't even as old as me. She looked awfull lying on her side with her eyes open. Her body was all stiff like a dolly. In a way it was good she dyed becos she was a funny shape and..."'

Annie's reading began to slow as she pushed further into the entry. '"...her face was wird and I think everyon at my new skool would hav laffed at her if they saw her. Althouhg she would never go to skool being a pig. Father said death is the way things are and I must grow a thikker skin for bording school next year, but I tryed scrubbing my arm in the bathroom this evening before bed and it wnet red and bled becos my skin is too thin".' Annie glanced at the painting of Issy in horror. '"Now I have too cuts. One becos of the fir trees and one becos of the scrubbing".'

She reread the entry silently, before turning the page.

'"Janury 1976: it is a new year and also the end of winter and I am very happy becuas I will be eight in december. I am going to bording skool in september wich will be my first ever skool and Andrew will com the year after becuas he is not old enouhg yet. Mother says becuas I am going to be eight I must lern to spell and lern how to honour God. She is a quite good teecher but I am looking forwad to meeting new teechers at shcool and making new frends".'

Annie frowned. Issy; homeschooled until she was eight – *really*? Her late wife had always had a fertile imagination, as well as being a terrible speller, so perhaps she'd made the homeschooling bit up. But why would she make it up in her own diary? What would be the point of that?

'"Februry 1976: I got in trouble today becuas I forgot to take my tablate after brekkfast. Mother was cross and worried, then she got upset wich she said is becuas she loves and cares. We are all broken in the eyes of God she says. But I am more broken BUT CAN BE MENDED".' A strange feeling was wrapping itself around Annie's chest. '"She made me clean out the pig stys as a punishment but I was secretly happy becuas I love the pigs anyway, espeshially the piglets, espeshially all the newest Claribels".'

Annie's eyes were racing ahead now. '"And reely I didn't forget my tablate. I don't like them. They are brown and taste horrid and usully I give them to the dog or put them in my nikkers when no one is looking. Andrew dosent have to take them only me. Mother says this is becuas im speshel. But im not im just me. Also, I rote a story today about a wheelbarrow that can speek and Mother said it was very good".'

She'd stopped reading out loud and simply turned the page.

March 1976: im not righting in here anymore. Its

> *boring and stupid. Im going to hide this book in my bookshelf. ANDREW IF YOU LOOK I WILL NO!!!!*

Feeling almost winded, Annie set the book on her lap. She took out her phone and googled 'Colthwaite village' and 'Colthwaite House'.

There was an entry on Wikipedia about Colthwaite church, its origins, and a site listing: Colthwaite Farm.co.uk. Annie clicked. It loaded a sunny snapshot of sheep and pigs happily grazing amongst lush green meadows overlaid with the farm's address and landline number. The picture must have been taken over three decades ago because there was a link on the homepage that led to another photo: Elizabeth and William in dated clothing, below their smiling faces a toggle marked 'shop'. It took her to a blank screen with the words, *Error 404 page not found*.

Issy would have been in her early twenties when that was taken, and already married to Patrick.

She clicked off. What 'tablate' had Issy been forced to take? Had she had a childhood illness, one she'd hidden from Annie? She tried not to think of her wife at seven, scrubbing away at her skin. And Issy *homeschooled*?

She went into the kitchen, ate half a Mars bar, then needing something else to do that didn't involve ruminating, prepared an early supper. Popcorn tofu. One hour and five minutes. It required her total focus. She'd managed to persuade the woman at the health food store in Ambleside to order packs of Korean rice cakes and they now sat waiting to be used in Annie's fridge. Issy had found 'popcorn' anything too sweet, but the kids loved it. Shame they weren't here to share it.

She flicked on the radio as she cut firm tofu into chunks and put them in a bowl with the spices, covered them in the starch and left them to marinade while she made the sauce.

Why had Issy hidden the key? Or had someone else hidden it there? Annie suddenly remembered Elizabeth, Steven, and Colin chatting secretively in the dining room the night of the party. What had they been talking about?

There was only half a bottle of gochujang left; that was another thing she needed to put on order at the shop, along with some pre-marinated tofu chunks.

Forty-five minutes later, she'd heated a large pan of oil and deep fried the rice cake and the firm tofu in batches and was feeling calmer. The oil stank out the kitchen and transported her instantly to childhood, standing next to Grandma Halmi, Appa tinkering with electrical parts in the lounge, the radio on in the background.

Ah, Grandma Halmi would say. *The Archers. Son-nyeo dear, turn it up.*

New Malden. She never thought it would happen – thinking of the area with affection, but here it was.

She mixed the tofu and rice cake in the sauce, took out a bowl, sprinkled on some spring onions and took it to the table. It smelled amazing.

She should speak to Vincent Prime. He'd help her understand. He had said to call if she needed anything, hadn't he?

She looked down at her bowl, the tofu swimming in delicious gloopy mess. Technically speaking, it should be popcorn chicken. Her grandma had practically fallen off her chair when Annie announced she'd become vegetarian. *There'll be nothing left of you, girly.* Fat chance of that.

She devoured the food in five minutes. All that prep for such a short window of heaven. She dumped the bowl in the sink and left the oil to cool in the pan while she banged nails into the wall in the hall in anticipation of Issy's portrait.

'Now we can say hallo and goodbye every time I go out,' she told it, making sure it hung straight. The artist had done a great job with the eyes. She could see the tiniest reflection of another person – possibly the painter themselves? – in the shine on Issy's pupils. She searched for a signature, but there was just a squiggle.

An old conversation swam towards her: Annie and Issy in their usual booth at Drinks of Hackney. 'Didn't it frighten you,' Annie had asked, 'you and Andrew rattling around that house as kids?' Issy had said, 'No! We slept in the same room. It's now Polly's.'

Perhaps they'd moved into Polly's room later, when they were teens? Perhaps her wife hadn't considered the nursery worth a mention.

But all her childhood stuff was in there. Her diary.

And that key.

And Polly, her room now empty, alone in some awful rehab centre. Well, maybe it wasn't awful, maybe it was smart and expensive, but still.

'Right.' Annie walked away down the hall. 'I'm writing your niece a letter, whatever your mother says about contact.'

She took out a postcard from a box, one of a young girl in Victorian clothes leading a donkey along a canal towpath, and wrote.

> *Dear Polly,*
> *I hope you don't mind me reaching out. Your*
> *grandmother told me about your struggles and*
> *recommended I don't contact you, but I have indirect*
> *experience of what you're going through (my mother spent*
> *time in a centre not unlike yours) and I wanted to let you*

know I'm thinking of you. We haven't seen one another for some time but if you ever want to chat, I'm here and an ear; no judgement. Wishing you all the best and that we see you back at Colthwaite soon.

Love,

Annie x

She popped the card in an envelope and sealed it. She'd ask Andrew for the address; she hoped he'd be more agreeable about it than his mother.

Next, she searched out Vincent's card in her jacket pocket. Blue indented print on butter-coloured paper. It was just his name and number. The lack of detail was touching.

Vincent would be the one to answer her questions. She'd call him first thing in the morning.

Annie woke with a gasp. She'd been dreaming, or maybe not dreaming – *remembering*. It had started off lovely, the two of them, she and Issy, lying on the grass in Hyde Park eating ice cream, the cream dripping off the cone onto their faces in the heat. Annie had licked some from the end of Issy's nose. But as dreams often do, it switched suddenly: Issy was complaining of a headache and Annie was cancelling an outing to a friend's book launch. Then Issy was feeling better the next morning and telling Annie they should go to the launch after all, and Annie was admiring Issy's long body in the dressing mirror as Issy applied mascara. Her arm was jerking suddenly, grasping at the air. There was Issy listing to the side, just as she had in life a year ago, then falling like a tree to the floor. There was foam at her mouth. The blood where she'd bitten her tongue, the left side of her face slack and melted-looking. Annie crying for help, her phone far away in the kitchen.

She sat up with a start. She was drenched in sweat.

She climbed out of bed, pulled her wet T-shirt from her body, and padded downstairs to dump it in the wash basket. After that she returned upstairs to retrieve her phone. She punched Vincent's number into the keypad.

It rang and rang. Eventually, a shaky voice answered: 'Colthwaite 542.'

'Vincent?'

'Who's speaking?'

'It's Annie, from Chapel Croft. Sorry to call you at...' She checked the clock. 'Seven forty-five.'

'Apology unnecessary. I'm up every day at five.'

'I was wondering if you could help me. I'm trying to... understand a few things.'

'Of course.' As if he'd been expecting her.

'Okay, great. Er... I'd prefer to meet in person, if it's not too much trouble. I could come by your house later this morning?' When Vincent didn't answer, Annie added, 'I've biscuits?'

'Ah, *biscuits*. See you at eleven.' A rustling sound signalled he was about to put the phone down. 'Annie?'

'Yes?'

'Is everything all right?'

She went to the window and parted the curtains an inch with her fingers. It was raining. The track up to the cottage was empty. 'Yes,' she found herself saying. 'Everything's fine.'

Rain drummed on the hood of her jacket. It was 10.55am, and she was killing time outside Vincent's, a packet of chocolate

Hobnobs growing slippery in her hands. Her card to Polly was tucked into her jacket. Her plan was to call at the Big House afterwards and get the rehab centre address from Andrew.

Vincent's house was larger than anticipated. She'd imagined a small place with white walls and an unkempt garden, but it turned out it was dark stone and double-fronted, heavily Victorian, elevated from the road and perched on the edge of the Fell. Its two front bays had views across the sheep fields, as if the place awaited the return of someone important.

She watched as the long hand on her watch crept towards eleven.

Vincent's house had no bell so bang on eleven she clunked the knocker on the door. The metal plate screwed to the wood was an antique head of a woman, and the act of knocking meant hitting the woman in the face. By the time Vincent came to the door, Annie's own face felt drawn and very cold.

'Oh dear,' Vincent said, taking in the state of her clothes. He moved sideways to let her in, and she stepped forward into the hall, laying the wet coat over her arm because Vincent appeared not to want to hang it up.

'Cats and dogs today.' He ushered her on, pointing his stick towards a room at the left.

It was the living room, surprisingly light despite the day, with neutral décor and sofas. A fire burned merrily in the grate and a huge old television sat in an alcove. After Colthwaite House, Annie had assumed everyone in the village must live in a state of falling-to-pieces-ness, yet here was Vincent's home, neat and beige.

'This is nice,' she said, conscious of him behind her. She put her coat carefully on the arm of a chair. 'Lived here long?'

'Forty years.' He gestured for Annie to sit. She chose the sofa. The seat didn't give at all under her weight. She rubbed her wet palms against her rain-soaked trouser leg, wondering how to begin, but Vincent started for her. 'With my wife, when she was alive, and our daughter.'

'I'm so sorry,' Annie said. There was a pause. 'Do you mind my asking when she died?'

Vincent's eyes opened wide. 'My wife?'

That wasn't who she'd meant. 'Er...' Was she brave enough to say it? She must, this was why she'd come, after all. 'No, your daughter. I'm so sorry. I saw her gravestone in the churchyard a few days ago. I just... I wanted to say something at the party, but–'

'Ah yes.' Vincent nodded. 'When you rang this morning, I thought it might be something like that. Davido said he'd caught you sitting on your own outside the church.'

Annie looked up. '*Caught* me?'

'A turn of phrase, dear.' The old man's eyebrows began to pull down at the edges, as if his face couldn't sustain their weight.

'Vincent?' she prompted, gently. 'Are you okay? Have I upset you? I'm sorry, I didn't mean to.'

His head turned to the window, to the fields beyond. 'I don't think I...' There was an uneasy silence. 'Would you care for a cup of tea?'

'Oh.' More tea. 'Sure. Can I help?'

'Absolutely not. Sit, enjoy the view.'

He shuffled out of the room. A carriage clock ticked on a shelf; its regular stroke interrupted by the sound of horse hooves on tarmac along the lane. From the sofa, she craned her neck to see out of the window. The tips of hills. Grey skies. Rain. The clip-clopping drew near, a horse-riding helmet bounced by, the sound faded.

On the wall opposite above the mantel, three plaster

pheasants ascending in a line. Grandma Halmi had nailed plastic ducks up the wall in Annie's childhood flat. Annie spent a lot of time at the Formica table drinking Ovaltine through a straw, wondering where they were flying to.

On Vincent's mantel, a row of standard ornaments, china cats and dogs, a miniature metal handbell, a small statue of a wide-hipped woman.

Her, again.

The rattling of cups from the corridor.

'Here we go.' Vincent appeared around the frame of the door with a tray, tea towel over one arm, back stooped. She leapt up, but he told her to sit down, laying the tray on the coffee table, pouring tea from the pot through a strainer with trembling hands. The liquid came out too fast, splashing hotly into her saucer and across the tray.

'Oh dear,' Vincent said for the second time that morning.

'Let me.' She mopped up the excess liquid with the tea towel, then laid it on top of her coat because she couldn't think of another place to put it without having to get up and go to the kitchen, which Vincent had expressly told her not to do. She sat back, unable to help herself throwing another look at the statuette.

'Admiring my Astarte?' He smiled, settling himself into the armchair opposite, taking a gulp of tea.

'Is that her name?' She mimed wide hips with her hands, making Vincent smile. 'She's the one we saw at Colthwaite several times.'

'She is. There wasn't time to explain that night because we had a mission to accomplish. Have you taken possession of the painting? Safely stowed in your home?'

'Yes, thank you. Can you tell me who she is? Astarte, I mean. What she represents?'

'She's an Assyrian goddess, a proto-Christian icon. She represented fertility and abundance, amongst other things.' He looked incredibly sad for a moment. 'What was it exactly that you came to ask? About my daughter?'

She longed to ask more about Astarte now, to know why everyone felt the need to display her on their walls. But this was her chance: she mustn't blow it. 'I'm afraid this is going to sound insensitive,' she began.

'I'm very old, so I doubt it.'

'When I saw your daughter's headstone in the church, I also saw the headstones of other girls that died in Colthwaite around the same time. Such a tragedy. Not one of the Dillanes have ever mentioned anything.' She hesitated. 'Would you mind very much explaining what happened?'

Vincent crossed one leg over the other with difficulty and sat back in his chair, balancing his cup on the armrest. 'Have you heard of Dolly Blue?'

Annie shook her head.

'I didn't suppose so.' He sighed. 'There was a blueing factory up here in the fifties. Lots of the villagers used to work there. My wife was an employee, myself, the Paines too, back in the day.'

'Blueing?' Annie had a brief recollection of Grandma Halmi running clothes through the mangle, her hands dry and flaking as they swirled in sky-coloured liquid. 'You mean for bleaching clothes?'

'That's the one. There are other uses for it, of course. For whitening animal's hair, horses' manes, for example.'

'Oh.'

'It can also be used off-label, for whitening sheep's coats, if one were to say, want to achieve a higher price for wool.' Vincent's chest filled with air. 'It's hard to make money from farming, Annie. We've always been a tight community. What arrives on the table at your neighbour's house is meat for your own. Do you see? Good wool means a better return for everyone. At the end of each day, we'd return from the factory covered in the stuff – the blueing. It was on our skin, clothes, in our pores. And, tragically, without our knowledge, in our water supply and food chain. It turns out that living things, human and animal, absorb the stuff: it's highly toxic, especially to the young, to those whose immune systems haven't fully developed.'

He pulled himself from the chair and went to a side cabinet, dragging a leather photo album from its drawer. He came to sit beside her on the sofa.

Fear pressed at her temples. More photos. She hoped they wouldn't be piglets. When he turned to the first page, she was afforded a brief glimpse of a younger, sepia-coloured Vincent, standing to attention in uniform.

'You were in the army?'

'Air force.'

The pages flipped past. A babe in its mother's arms, a toddler by a tree. He came to pause at an assembly of adults in three neat rows against a stone wall, children kneeling or sitting cross-legged in front of them. At the bottom it read: *Colthwaite 1976 Silver Jubilee*. She could tell the wall belonged to the church because the old Yew was just in frame, smaller than today. She recognised several faces: Vincent, a youthful Elizabeth and William, and Vicar David standing to the right, his expression closed.

Her eyes travelled across each face. 'Oh!' She sighed. There she was: a young Issy in the front row. Around eight years old. Standing to attention next to an even younger Andrew. They were holding one another's hands. Here was more of her wife, preserved in celluloid at Vincent's house; parts of her that Annie had never seen, never known. 'Sorry, wasn't expecting that.'

Vincent took her hand. 'Never apologise for loving someone.' He tapped a wrinkled finger on one of four girls, around five years old, all with blonde hair at different lengths. 'Here's Sarah, my daughter.'

'She's gorgeous.'

Annie stared. Sarah looked very much like all the other girls in the picture. Blonde, long-limbed, Aryan-looking. 'They're so similar!'

Vincent looked up. 'Do you think so? I don't see it.'

How could he not? Annie looked again. Perhaps it was her projection; on some subconscious level she couldn't accept Issy was gone and now she was seeing her everywhere.

'We weren't blessed with another after Sarah.' Vincent was already turning the page.

Annie wanted to tell him to wait, slow down, but it was his album, his tragedy. She wasn't sure she could bear any more, but here came another, of his late wife and daughter. eighties clothing, the woman's hair swinging from her face, the girl about ten years old, in a padded coat, hood pulled forward, the mouth not smiling but solemn, as if she'd understood already that life wasn't fair.

'By this time, we knew Sarah was gravely ill.'

Another page flipped. Annie's breath caught in her throat.

It was Issy in school uniform. What was she doing there? Semi-professional studio shots, Issy's slender head and neck against a stippled background, ageing year-on-schoolyear, her hair in a ponytail, a neat fringe ending just above the eyes. These belonged to Elizabeth and William, surely?

'Vincent–'

'Sarah loved school.'

'Sarah? No, but that's...' Vincent was looking at her; she found she couldn't say the words.

'Are you all right, dear?'

'I'm...' She examined the pictures a second time. The eyes of *this* child, clear in these brightly lit shots, were different to Issy's– green blue instead of ocean. And Issy had never had a fringe.

'The blueing was catastrophic for Sarah's body,' Vincent said. 'And not just for her. For all the young girls aged five or six in this Jubilee picture. The Dolly Blue was a ticking bomb, dripping its way into their systems, poisoning them, setting up cascades of organ failure.'

'Organ failure?'

'An immune system overload,' he said. 'The body becomes confused, attacks itself.'

'Autoimmune problems?'

He looked up sharply. 'You know about autoimmunity?'

'My grandmother on my father's side had autoimmune rheumatoid arthritis. But Issy didn't. She was healthy, until...' She trailed off, miserably.

He patted her hand. 'Now you understand why we keep our Astartes close. Foolish superstitions if you like, but we cling to what we can.'

A sensation in her feet, as if a coin had dropped from a slot high up and was rolling slowly to her toes. 'I understand.'

The body attacking itself. Issy's aneurism. Mum's bipolarism. Not the same, but similar. Perhaps the villagers had it right: Annie could benefit from a spiritual guide, a belief system of her own right now. 'Why was it only the girls who became sick? Why not the boys?'

Vincent shook his head. 'No one quite understands. Several of the girls died within months of one another.'

Annie stood up, sat down, stood again. She went to the window. At the top of the ridge, a line of sheep chewed grass. 'Issy never mentioned anything about this stuff. *Ever.*'

'Can you blame her?'

'I'm trying my best not to.'

Vincent went to her, took her hands in his. 'You have to forgive her. It was an unconscionable thing that happened here, Annie. A matter of great shame to the village. Something we've tried hard to forget.'

'Why shame? It wasn't your fault; you couldn't possibly have known.'

Vincent was silent.

'Didn't you consider suing the makers of Dolly Blue?' she pressed.

'Would *you* have felt like going to court if you'd just lost a child?'

Annie knew she wouldn't.

'Dolly Blue ceased trading and the factory closed in 1982,' he said. 'Just weeks after our last tragic losses. It's a car museum now. But you won't find any mention of the deaths there.'

'I don't know what to say. It's all just *awful*.'

'Yes, I'm rather afraid it is.' He shuffled back to the coffee table. 'Oh, look. You haven't drunk your tea.' He held the cup out, rattling on its saucer. 'Terrible waste of a bag.'

'Sorry. It wasn't a tea-drinking sort of conversation.'

He glanced at his own empty cup. 'Have you more questions?'

She looked at him, helplessly. It was all such a jumble. She needed time to think. 'Not today.'

'I understand.'

'I might need to get some air now. Sorry.' She picked up her wet coat, her brain burning with unanswered questions: the piglet albums, Issy's childhood 'tablates', the strange slaughter of the pig, the second portrait of Andrew. He saw her to the door. In the narrow hallway, she stopped. 'Vincent?'

'Mmm?' But he looked so worn, so vulnerable, she didn't have the heart to ask more.

'Nothing. Thank you. For being open.' She made her way carefully down the slippery steps of his front garden.

'At least we've the festival!' he called after her. 'A party is the best tonic for faltering spirits.'

Annie stood on the lane. The sheep hadn't moved from their position on the ridge. She didn't want to think of her wife keeping things from her out of shame. It caused actual pain in her heart area.

A short distance to her right, in the driveway of the Big House, Andrew was tinkering with bags of earth.

How could those girls all look so similar? It didn't make sense.

She watched as he ripped the bags open and emptied earth into the flowerbed, blond hair flopping over his face.

What if the girls were... inbred?

Andrew stood now, brushing soil from his hands. Polly's letter burned a hole in her jacket pocket.

A sheep bleated, another answered. Andrew went inside through the front door of the Big House. Good, she couldn't face him now anyway. She was overwhelmed by a stab of homesickness for London so intense she let out an actual sound, an animal groan.

Her body needed exercise. She set off at a march towards The Pipe, a shortcut to the fell, one that followed a tributary, the water shooting down a steep gorge. She cut a path beside its edge, criss-crossing the flow at intervals, building heat, her shoes squelching in mud.

Could Issy's 'tablates' have been related to the Dolly Blue? Vincent said the girls died within months of one another, but Issy hadn't. Perhaps Elizabeth who, unlike the rest of the village, had had medical training, gave Issy something to protect her from the ravages of the blueing chemical. Annie saw the graves in her mind's eye, their sad little inscriptions, the closeness of their deaths. A terrible thing to happen. No one deserved such grief. Something else was brought into focus though, too: the girls' birthdates – they'd been *born* within days of one another. These would have had nothing to do with Dolly Blue. The very fact of this, let alone the reason, Vincent hadn't mentioned.

What if he'd made the Dolly Blue story up? But why would he do such a thing? William's assertion that Vincent lied about everything might be true. Oh God, she was sick of the lot of them.

A wood pigeon swooped between the trees. Her phone rang in her pocket: a withheld number. She swiped right. 'Hello?'

'Annie?'

'Vincent?'

'Sorry to bother you. I wanted to say, probably best if you don't mention our discussion to Elizabeth or William. Understandably, they find the whole business upsetting. We wouldn't want to jinx anything.'

'Jinx? What d'you mean?'

But he was gone. She pushed forwards, the thunderous beck at her flank. People were keeping things from her, and she didn't like it.

She came to an open section of land complete with fenced-off rusted water tanks. Sheep grazed nearby. She crossed the wet grass and continued up the precipitous track to the apex of the fell. Pillows of cloud sat heavy on the hillside, visibility was poor and worsening each second. Annie, hot despite the rain, flapped the sides of her coat like wings. The sensible thing to do would be return home but she wasn't ready. She was all jangled. Her mind was like soup; she needed the view to clear it.

Several instants later, the peak of the fell disappeared in mist; it was almost a magic trick how quickly it happened. Long clouds rolled towards her. She looked back; a second blanket settled in the plateau below. Stupid, stupid. She *should* have gone home. She turned and went back down by traversing the hillside. But on her fifth step, her foot dropped into nothingness, and her ankle twisted. Pain shot up her calf. She pitched forward into some gorse, where she lay, belly down, cursing.

She lay very still, assessing the damage, as fine drops of water pattered at her back. Her ankle throbbed ominously. She rolled over to face the sky. It was a white-grey lid locking her in. She sat up. It had been a rat hole her foot had fallen into. She examined her bad ankle, still laced in its boot; it seemed to be in the right position, thank God.

A faint whistling wind blew into her ears as the mist continued to close around her. She could see barely two metres ahead. She staggered up to a stand and leant, testily, on her bad ankle. Another bolt of pain shot through her. 'Shit!'

She rolled up her jeans; blood trickled from a wide gash in her calf. The cut was deep, several centimetres in length. Woozily, she clung to a tuft of heather. She was out here alone with no phone reception and a buggered foot.

Two fat Herdwicks appeared from a bush, then scurried up the hill. She limped towards a small tree, blown sideways by years of exposure to an unrelenting northerly breeze and took hold of a green branch, pushing it back and forth until it cleaved itself from its trunk with a reluctant crunch. Annie cut the branch to length with her penknife, carving a rough V in its top. The stick now tucked comfortably beneath her armpit. There.

The slope went on and on, her ankle getting worse. Every so often she'd stop to check the blood situation. A dark wet glob had formed around the wound. She pushed on blindly through the cloud, the fell silent save for the wind.

Soon, she spotted a wide fence beyond the mist, encircled by a line of yellow tape, and could hear the hum of electricity. A pheasant pen! If she could get into it and head downwards, she'd eventually reach the bottom end, and from there it would be a short distance to the road. She drew close, thanking fate as she spotted an entry point into the pen, a gate with a shiny metal padlock hanging from its latch. Please God, she prayed; let it be open. It was. The U-shaped bolt hung shy of its housing. Perhaps Stephen would be in here.

She staggered beneath the electric wire, careful not to catch the back of her jacket, until she reached the gate itself, pushed it open and she was in. The pine trees closed in around her. Her pulse beat painfully in her leg. Her calf felt tight. Still no signal on her phone.

'Stephen!' she shouted. From their perch in the coop, the currant eyes of six pheasants peered at her through a hatch.

She headed downwards through the pen. 'Stephen? *Stephen*! Anybody?'

Light began to bleed through the tightly packed trees as the mist lifted. She found herself in a clearing, possibly the one she'd spotted in the distance from the opposite direction some time ago. There was a hut at its centre. Or not a hut, but a small one-storey stone cottage surrounded by boggy grass and reeds. An old shepherd's retreat perhaps, though it was a little too well-preserved. Maybe Stephen used it to shelter on his break. He could be in there now, eating a KitKat, listening to the radio. She made her way towards it, but before she could reach it there was the buzzing of an engine from the woods below, Stephen made a beeline for her on his buggy. She waved wildly. 'Help!'

He pulled up beside her and leapt from the driver's seat. 'What you doing here? You'll catch your death.'

'Got lost.' Relief made her want to cry. 'Oh God, thank you!'

'I was at the bottom of the fell. I heard you yelling.'

'From all that way away? I've injured my leg.'

He propped his shoulder under her armpit. 'How d'you get in here?'

'The top gate – or maybe the side one? The padlock was

open, and...' She looked at him. He was frowning. 'Was I not supposed to? I'm sorry.'

'Don't know which marra left that open. Bloody stupid, though lucky for you.' He glanced at her stick. 'How d'you hurt it?'

'Fell in a rat hole.'

'Rat?' He smiled. 'Badger or fox, more like.'

'I'm not sure if I've broken something.' She fought to keep the pain from showing.

Stephen dropped to his haunches and took Annie's damaged foot in his hands. 'Just a sprain. That cut needs looking at, mind.'

'At the hospital?'

'Hospital?' He snorted. 'Elizabeth can do it.'

'Elizabeth?' She did *not* want her mother-in-law's hands on her injury.

'Vet's knowledge is better than any doctor, Annie.'

'She told me that herself,' Annie said, grimly.

'Because it's true. They train for longer, work on all manner of biology. Let's get you home.' He led her around to the passenger seat then nipped to the driver's side.

The little cart coughed into life, and they set off slowly, passing the stone cottage at the centre of the clearing. One square squat opaque window cut into its wall.

'That your hideout?' Annie joked.

Stephen nodded. 'Place to shelter when the weather comes in.'

Annie twisted to look at it: the cottage had a low door at its front end. There was a knocker, which struck her as odd.

'Look ahead or you'll get another injury,' Stephen warned. 'It was a shepherd's hut back in the day.'

'Right.'

'S'full of sheeps' droppings and mildew.' He grinned. 'And a radio and a couple of chairs for me old legs.'

The cart bumped over the grass and rejoined a rough track at the bottom of the clearing. Her pain was even worse now the adrenaline was dying. At the bottom end of the pen, Stephen stopped the cart and took a bunch of keys from his jacket. He opened the padlock, disarmed the electric tape, drove through, and rearmed it. She realised with horror that had she reached here on foot alone, there would have been no way of letting herself out. And – she checked her phone – still no signal.

'Nearly there,' Stephen yelled.

The buggy trundled onto the lane, picking up speed as it passed the pig pens, the Big House, until it reached Chapel Croft. It bumped up the track. Annie tried not to wince.

Elizabeth was waiting for them at the door, a black leather holdall at her feet, the picture of concern. 'How beastly! Let's get you inside.'

'I texted her,' Stephen explained at Annie's look of surprise. 'The minute I caught sight of you.' But he couldn't have known at that point that her wound needed Elizabeth's veterinary skills because he hadn't yet looked at it.

He helped Annie out, tossing her stick into the bushes. She'd liked that stick.

'I can take it from here Stephen, thank you.' Elizabeth steered her into the living room. 'I see you've Issy's portrait on the wall already.'

'Yeah.' She stripped off her wet jacket and flopped onto the sofa before attempting her bootlaces.

'Don't be a silly. I'll do that.' Elizabeth knelt before her.

Annie sat up suddenly. The pig in the back garden! Under no circumstances must Elizabeth be allowed to see it.

'Relax and lie back,' her mother-in-law complained. 'You're jumpier than a gilt.' She opened the holdall and removed a pair of curved scissors. Annie felt herself blanch. 'Don't worry, they're not for skin, but I'm going to have to ruin your trousers, I'm afraid.' She cut through the jeans and inched the material up to the knee. 'Deary me, what have we here?'

The sight of the gash, the congealed blood, and glistening tissue made Annie's head go back onto the cushions.

Elizabeth turned the leg gently. 'We'll clean it up; five or so stitches–'

'Stitches?' Needles. Oh God.

'Only a few. Some pain relief, rest for the swelling; you'll be fine. Lucky you're young.' Annie made a noise. 'I'm not joshing,' Elizabeth said. 'At my age, this could have been serious.' She pulled on some latex gloves, cleaned the wound with iodine, which was agony, and injected the leg with anaesthetic.

They waited for the drug to take effect. Annie didn't have the energy to talk. Soon enough that blissful opiate respite came, and her shoulders dropped. She took a long deep breath. 'Thank you.'

Elizabeth got to work again, stitching the wound closed. Annie tried not to look, but her eyes were drawn to Elizabeth's handiwork, the quick, neat movements across her skin.

'Bet you've done this a thousand times,' Annie said.

'Just a few.' Elizabeth remained focused on the job. 'Usually, my subjects are larger and make different noises.' She finished the last stitch, removed the needle, tied it off with her fingers, and cut away the excess thread. 'All done.'

Annie looked at her calf. Five short black horizontal lines tracked the length of the wound, the skin taut. She was numb thanks to the anaesthetic, but still, the sight of it made her want to puke. 'Thank you.'

'You're welcome.' Elizabeth rootled in the holdall. She pulled out a blister pack. 'Painkillers. One, twice a day for four days. They're strong, so no more than that, please. And no driving.'

Annie saluted. 'Yes, ma'am.'

Elizabeth clicked the bag shut and stood. Instinctively, Annie reached for her arm. 'Sorry for putting you to this trouble.'

'No trouble. Really.' Elizabeth's mind seemed half a mile away. 'I suppose you'll struggle to come on the shoot now, on Saturday?'

'The... shoot?'

'The November shoot?' Elizabeth sighed. 'Oh, not again. One of Andrew's boys was supposed to bring you the invitation.'

'I'm not sure Andrew's boys are too reliable.'

'Well, I'll bring you a brace for the pot.' Her mother-in-law shook her head. 'Silly me, I forgot; you don't eat that sort of thing. Now, is there anything else I can do?'

Annie said there wasn't.

'You'll be right as rain in no time.' Elizabeth peeled off her gloves, the latex shrivelling instantly. 'I'll just wash my hands.'

'Kitchen sink's out of service!' Annie blurted. A trip to the kitchen involved the window with a clear view of the back garden. 'Use the downstairs loo.'

Elizabeth left the room. A few moments later, there was the sound of water running in the bathroom sink and Annie relaxed.

Her mother-in-law returned, one hand behind her back. 'Take one now,' she ordered, nodding at the painkillers. 'I'll get you a glass of water.'

The kitchen again.

'No!' Annie adjusted her face. 'I mean... I prefer to take them without water.' She stared at the pill.

And reely I didn't forget my tablate. I don't like them. They are brown and taste horrid.

'I'm not poisoning you,' Elizabeth snapped. 'Just take it.'

Annie did as she was told. The tablet tasted sour and dry, and caught in her throat.

'This was beside the loo.' Elizabeth pulled Issy's childhood diary from behind her back. So, that explained her sudden mood. 'Not Enid Blyton as far as I can make out.'

'I...' Why had Annie left it in the *loo* of all places?

'Are you still reading it?' Elizabeth turned the book over. 'Or can I return it to the Big House?'

'No. Yes. Sorry. My mistake.'

'Another mistake?'

The two women glared at one another. Annie was the first to look away. 'I found it on the nursery bookshelf,' she said. She'd done enough apologising. 'I didn't want to tell you in case... well, I'm not sure really, but anyway, I'm still going through it.'

'Going through it?' Elizabeth's tone was sharp.

'*Reading* it. I promise I'll return it soon.'

Elizabeth placed the book in Annie's lap. 'As you please. Do put your leg up. And call if you need anything.' She bowed at the waist and left the room. The front door clicked.

Annie breathed out. She couldn't deny it, she sort of hated Elizabeth. She was good with a stitch though.

She looked at her leg, propped up and useless. There would be no driving, no picking the kids up from school on Fridays, no walking, no more... investigating. She turned the diary in her hand then setting it down, twisted on to her side, flicking on the TV with the remote. She longed for the kids, for their warm bodies to snuggle into. But there was no way they'd let her do that. Well, Caleb might.

On telly there was a daytime chat show, a woman with

fluffy blonde hair, her teeth Dulux white. Another woman came on to explain how her third pregnancy remained unknown to her until she went to the lavatory and the baby fell out.

Annie's eyes drooped. Pig noises came from the shed: it was feeding time. And the dead girls. Those poor things. She wanted to light the lunch, prepare the fire. No, that wasn't right. *Elizabeth's drugs are very strong*, she thought, as she drifted into oblivion.

CHAPTER TEN

With Annie out of commission, Andrew kindly picked up all the kids, his and hers, from school, drove them home, and tipped hers out at the door. Annie hobbled to the porch to ask after Polly, explain she'd written a card, ask for the address. Andrew said he'd pass the card on; he was due to visit her this week anyway. He headed off with it in his pocket, leaving Annie wondering if it would reach its destination.

Annie was goofily pleased to see the kids, though days of isolation meant she found their youthful vitality a little overwhelming.

'... and by the end of the class Professor Bomball'd said "neat" *exactly* twenty-five times, and he's not even *American*, and he's, like, *old*.' Caleb stood in front of her, hopping from one foot to the other, his hair damp with rain.

Annie smiled. He seemed much happier than when they'd last spoken.

'I mean, he's from *Birmingham*. How bad is that? He teaches *English*. Does he think it's cool? We couldn't stop laughing.'

'I bet.' She moved her leg from the sofa cushion and pulled

herself up to sit. She'd taken another of Elizabeth's painkillers this morning and her head was thick, her leg throbbing as if three times its normal size. 'Where's your sister gone?'

Caleb rolled his eyes. 'Upstairs, dumping her stuff.'

'Excellent. Grace,' Annie called. '*Grace.*'

'*What?*'

'Let me look at your gorgeous face.'

The sound of Grace's steps on the treads. She slid around the edges of the room like mercury. 'Sorry, needed a pee. Hey.'

'Hey!' Annie gave her a broad smile. 'How's it going? How was your first week?' As if to compensate for Grace's minor key, Annie's tone was too jolly, like a *Blue Peter* presenter.

'Okay.' Grace yawned, which made Annie yawn too.

'Just okay?'

'It was good.' Grace nodded at Annie's leg. 'Are you okay? Grandpa told us about what happened. You should have said on the phone.'

'But I haven't spoken to you, Gracie. Every time I've called, you're busy.'

'*In lessons.*' Grace sighed.

'I'm fine, thank you for asking. Nothing major.'

'You've put up the painting of Mum,' said Grace.

'Like it?'

Caleb said yes, and Grace said, 'It'll be weird her staring at me when I go out, but yeah.' Grace nodded at the hospital crutch Elizabeth had dropped in that morning. 'How is it, the wound?'

'It's okay.'

Grace's mouth curled up at one side. 'Just "okay"?'

'Oh, touché young lady. Have you seen our new pet?'

The children's expressions lifted. 'What? Where?' They looked around.

'The escaped pig. It's in the stone hut in the back garden.'

'The pig?' Grace's nose wrinkled, reminding Annie of Elizabeth. 'The spooky pig? It's here?'

'It's not spooky. *It* found *me*. William caught it and put it in the barn, but it must have escaped again.' She avoided mentioning how. 'It needs our help.'

'With what?' Caleb asked.

'Its *existence*, stupid,' Grace explained. 'If it was in the barn, Granny and Grandpa must have wanted to euthanise it, obvs.' She left the room with renewed vigour, legs and arms swinging. 'Poor little thing. Now I think about it, this is lovely.'

Caleb shook his head. '"Lovely"?'

The back door clicked as it opened and a gust of wind blew through the hall into the living room. 'Well, at least one of you is pleased about our new guest,' Annie said.

Caleb was looking at his shoes. He brought his eyes up to meet hers.

'What?' she demanded. 'What's wrong?'

'It's Grace,' he whispered. 'I think... I think she might be pregnant.'

Annie nearly choked. '*What*? What would make you say a thing like that?'

'Forget it.' He went out, shoulders hunched as if into a blizzard.

'Caleb!' she called. 'Don't drop that bomb and leave. Come here, please!' But the back door thumped as he went to join his sister. Annie stared at the wall, thoughts racing.

Dougal, Douglas, whatever his name was in Hackney. And those naked selfies, her stepdaughter's head bent toward that other boy, Adam, on the first day of school. Could they have met somehow, secretly, before term started? How would they have managed that?

Grabbing the crutch, she hobbled to the kitchen window. Grace was going to answer some questions, whether she liked it or not. But when Annie got there, she found the children were on their knees at the far end of the garden, heads in the hut, the table pulled out to one side.

She couldn't ask now. Grace had only just arrived home. Things were strained enough after the showdown with Issy's folder. If she timed it badly, her stepdaughter would shut her out completely. She'd ask later, or tomorrow. Caleb was almost certainly wrong, anyway.

The pig had come out and lay between the children, its wonky eye shut in contentment. It clearly preferred the kids' company to hers. Several times in the last few days she'd pulled that table out, offered the pig a chance to be free, but it hadn't been keen.

She could sneak into Grace's room and search for a pregnancy test, maybe? But even if she had used one, why would Grace have kept the thing?

What she needed, she decided, was to speak to Caleb on his own. With a little pressing, he'd let her in.

The three of them sat at the kitchen table eating what the kids called 'Annie's kimchi jjigae'. Actually, it was Grandma Halmi's recipe; Annie had taken credit for so long that she didn't want to explain that.

'So.' She squinted at Grace as if she'd just remembered something. 'How's your tummy ache?'

Caleb glanced up from his bowl. His head shook a warning at Annie.

Grace shrugged.

'Any better?' Annie smiled. The room was clouded with the scent of garlic so strong it made Annie's head fizz. 'More pains during the week, or...?'

'My tummy's fine,' Grace snapped. 'Thanks for asking.'

'Oh my God,' Caleb said, laughing with uncharacteristic bravado. 'I've just remembered about woodwork this week. So–'

'We need a name for the pig,' Grace announced. 'What about Clementine?'

Annie carved a chunk of butter from the pat and busied herself spreading it across a slice of bread. 'I like it. But can we just talk about your–'

'In woodwork,' Caleb cut her off again, 'we–'

Grace whacked Caleb's leg. 'We're *talking*.' She turned to Annie. 'Or Pomander?'

'*Pomander?*'

'Because she smells so strong.'

Annie couldn't help laughing. 'I like it.'

'Me too,' Caleb agreed.

'Also,' Grace stated, 'the pig's pregnant.'

Annie laid her chopsticks down. 'The *pig's* pregnant?!' she exclaimed. Caleb frowned at the dangerous emphasis. 'How can you tell?'

'Guys,' Caleb pressed. Annie could feel his leg jiggling under the table 'I *really* want to tell you about what happened in wood–'

'Either that, or she's getting *really* fat.' Grace returned to her food. 'I wonder if she'll have mutant piglets.'

Annie tutted. 'Why would you say that?'

'Why not? Are you ableist or something?'

'No, I'm not ableist.'

'In woodwo–'

'*Cal!*' Grace yelled, throwing her chopsticks onto the table. 'Shut *up* about boring fucking woodwork! No one cares.'

'God. Sorry.' He looked to Annie for support.

'Gracie,' Annie said, 'please don't speak to your brother like that.'

'Fine.' Grace retrieved her chopsticks.

'So what did you get up to this week, Gracie?' Annie couldn't stop herself. 'At school? Make any new friends? What are the boys like?'

Grace tore a hunk of bread from the loaf and stuffed it in her mouth. 'Good.'

Annie downed a glass of water, fed up now. 'Anyone want more?' The children shook their heads.

She stood and cleared the plates, limping back and forth between table and dishwasher, annoyed that the kids considered it okay to look on as she cleaned up. She should be harder on them, but she didn't have the energy. Or maybe not the energy, the *courage*.

She leant over the counter and peered out the window. Rain. Grey sky. A lumpy silhouette at the end of the garden. The pig – *Pomander* – could have the leftover soup, some bread and a block of tofu past its date. Her ankle pulsed inside its bandage.

'Just so we're all on the same page,' she said lightly, 'no telling Granny and Grandpa about the pig – about Pomander – okay?'

Grace went to the snack cupboard. 'Got it.'

Annie filled the sink with soapy water. Behind her, Grace was unwrapping something.

'Don't worry, Mrs Park,' Grace said, in a comical voice. 'We'll keep mum.'

'What are you eating now?' Annie said. 'You've just had dinner, for God's sake!'

Grace had stuffed a whole Snickers sideways into her mouth. She looked ridiculous. Caleb went to say something, but Grace put a finger to her over-stretched lips, and they dissolved into giggles, even Annie.

Later, Annie went to find Caleb for a talk. It wasn't to be as the children were together in the living room; their supple bodies curved over the coffee table. A fire crackled in the wood burner. The burner door was open. 'Guys,' she said, closing it. 'Shut this door. *Always.*' They didn't look up. 'What's that you're at?'

'Spilikins,' said Grace. A collection of tiny white sticks in a pile. Next to them sat a small antique wooden box with a sliding lid.

'Spilikins? Like pick-up-sticks?'

'Uh-huh.'

It was Caleb's go. The tip of his tongue popped out as he pulled another stick loose.

'How come I've never seen that box before?' Annie asked.

'Grandpa gave it to us the other day.'

Annie bent close. Each stick was intricately carved. And they weren't white, but cream coloured. 'Are they ivory?'

Grace huffed through her nose. 'Bones is what they're made from.' She checked for Annie's reaction. 'I know, grim, right? Grandpa said Granny's dad made them. Then Granny and Grandpa had the carvings put into them later.'

'*Bones?*' Annie picked up a stick from Caleb's collection. The carvings *were* beautiful: vines and animals, tiny details, but still. 'What kind of bones?'

'Pigs' bones.' Grace grinned. Annie quickly laid the stick down. 'Sorry. I mean, I don't see what's *so* wrong with it. It's an antique from the past. And we eat the things, even their trotters.'

'I don't.'

Grace tossed her head. 'You know what I mean. *People.* At least now we know great- grandpa was an upcycling sort of person.'

'Yay,' Annie said. Generations of Dillanes boiling the bones of animals to create parlour games. How disgusting.

'Annie?' Grace said. 'Does your leg mean you won't be able to come on the shoot? Granny said you were still hoping to.'

Annie certainly hadn't agreed she would come. In fact, Elizabeth had told her that she mustn't. Hadn't she? She'd been so full of anaesthetic, perhaps she'd got this wrong.

'The pheasants need culling this time of year: it's *tradition*, apparently.' Grace wanted her to come, Annie could tell. It was a nice feeling.

'There must be a more humane way than blasting them out the sky,' Annie said.

The children looked at her. It would be their first shoot as adults: they'd not been here this time of year since they were tiny. 'We kind of... have to go,' Caleb said.

William had commandeered an extra buggy especially for Annie's use, Grace explained, complete with rear seat removed allowing more room for her leg. 'The shoot's a whole village kind of thing, Grandpa says. Like that festival that's coming up.'

Annie looked at their expectant faces. She was being a city snob. How else was the pheasant population to be controlled? It wasn't like Stephen had time to go around euthanising them individually.

'It'd look bad manners if you're the only no-show,' Caleb added. 'Please?'

'I'll do my best,' she said. 'To *think* about it.'

Grace laughed. 'Right.'

'*You're* very keen, madam,' Annie teased, sensing an opening. 'It wouldn't be that a certain person whose name begins with "A" and ends with "dam" might be there, would it?'

Grace's face soured. 'You're *unbelievable*.'

Now Caleb was glaring in disapproval. Annie felt a familiar shrivelling feeling.

'Last time I looked, Adam didn't live in the village, *did* he?' Grace was saying.

Annie raised her hands. 'Okay, sorry. I just–'

But Grace was clutching her stomach, her face drawing together.

'Grace?' Annie tried to get to her. 'Is it the pain? Are you all right, sweetheart?'

'Uh-huh.' Grace stayed in contortion for several moments before looking up suddenly and saying she felt much better.

'Tell you what,' Annie was so relieved, it just came out, 'I'll come on the shoot, okay? Definitely. Now, I'll go get some Gaviscon for your tum.'

Annie's eyes fluttered open. It was dark and her brain was heavy with painkillers. A sound was coming from outside the cottage beneath her window. She hit the clock display: 4.15am.

Annoyed, she dragged herself up, hobbled to the window, opened it and peered over the sill. It was raining, of course. There it was, that noise again, in the narrow flower bed directly below. She lifted the sash up higher and leant further out.

Bloody Noah! The dog was flicking up soil with his hind legs, his squat muscly body busying himself in Annie's shrubs.

'Hey!' she hissed. He stopped digging and looked up. 'What you doing?' His ears went up. 'Bog off!'

A faint whistle came off the fell and the dog glanced over its shoulder. The whistle was followed by the swing of a torch beam far away in the trees. Who the hell was out in the woods at four o'clock in the sodding morning? Maybe it was William searching for Pomander? Or Stephen?

Noah was trotting off along the track now towards the lane in the pre-dawn blackness. Annie ducked her head inside and hopped back to bed. She stared at the ceiling, but felt wide awake and after a second, she switched on the light and yanked the bedside drawer open. There was Issy's letter:

I know we were pissed when we wrote our wills, but I want to be clear that I truly meant it, my darling.

Issy had kept things from her. Had lied. Had tricked her into coming here. Annie felt sick at the thought.

No, why would she do such a thing? Issy wasn't like that. There had to be a reason. She, Annie, was going to find out what.

The day dawned unusually bright and crisp, the sky sterile blue. She had fallen asleep again and must have rolled onto Issy's letter because the paper was now creased. Irritated with herself, she put it back in the bedside drawer.

And she'd agreed to go on the shoot today. Oh God. Why had she done that? To please Grace and avoid an argument. She was weak and easily manipulated.

At least the sun was shining. She'd just finished the last of Elizabeth's painkillers, though her leg felt a little less sore this morning. She dressed and made her way downstairs. Coffee, then eggs. Then some writing on *KTS*. Could she manage that, with everything going on in her head? And before the dreaded shoot? Probably not.

In the kitchen the kids were already up and dressed in wet weather gear, crunching cereal at the table.

'Morning!' No one said anything, so she said, 'I don't think you'll need raincoats. Look at the sun.'

'You never know,' Grace muttered.

Annie limped to the stove. 'How's your tummy?'

'Good.' Grace nodded.

Annie drank her coffee and hobbled to check on the pig. The hospital crutch was useful but also annoying, sinking into the wet ground at each step then popping back out with a squelch.

The kids had obviously been out to the pig already: a teaspoon of chocolate milk remained at the bottom of a bowl beside a crust of burnt toast and some orange peelings.

Pomander seemed pleased to see her for once, lumbering to her feet as fast as her fat legs would allow and waddling out from a dark corner, whiskers bristling. The sow pushed her snout over the tabletop. Annie patted the barrel-shaped body, thrilled to be wanted, shooting a glance at the pig's belly: it was round, and getting rounder by the day.

What if Grace was right and Pomander *was* pregnant. How had Annie not worked this out for herself? William had all but told her in the farmyard that day, hadn't he?

At the end of the track leading to Chapel Croft, green four-by-fours were already coasting along the lane, ready for the shoot.

'I've got to watch men firing guns today, baby girl,' she told Pomander. 'What d'you think about that?' The sow swung her neck down, round, and up again, her one eye focused on the woods. Her skin absolutely stank. How could pigs, with their amazing sense of smell, stand themselves? 'If you hear gunshots,' Annie told her, 'it's your feathered friends. Just pray it's not me as well.'

Pomander grunted and swayed off to her nesting corner. Annie collected the empty bowl, then, remembering the dog's night-time visit, went around to the front.

Soil everywhere. An uprooted plant lay beside the front wheel of the car. She carried it back to the flowerbed. The dog's handiwork was a hole littered with white shards, like bone fragments. A shrew or mouse, perhaps? She nudged at the soil with the ferrule of the hospital crutch. There was a tiny skull, too. She picked it up. It smelled strongly of vinegar. It didn't look as if it had belonged to a rodent.

'Annie!'

William and the sheepdogs were striding up the track towards her. The dogs stopped a couple of feet in front of her, sniffing the air. 'Feeling queer?' William asked.

'I'm fine.'

'Coming on the shoot?' He was wearing a tweed coat, bronzed cords, wellies, and a checked flat cap. 'Apologies you didn't receive the *official* invitation. That boy of Andrew's needs a bloody good hiding. Lizzo told you, yes?'

Annie could hear the kids behind her now, the rustle of their wet weather gear. She gestured at her leg. 'I'm not sure...'

'She's definitely coming,' Caleb called from the porch. 'You promised, right?'

No way out now. 'Uh-huh. But as long as if you shoot one, I won't have to cook it.'

'Deal,' Caleb said with a grin and went back inside.

'You won't have to *do* anything,' William reassured. 'Just sit in the buggy, drink hooch, and eat flapjacks at the end of the third drive.'

She smiled. 'Sounds not too bad, actually.'

William was looking at her hand. 'What's that you've got there?'

'Oh.' She didn't really want to show him. 'I think it's a skull. I found it – *Noah* found it – in my flower bed.'

'Plenty of remains lying around.' He pulled his glasses from his pocket and put them on. His mouth went into a line.

'Do you know what it is? It's not a shape I recognise,' she said.

William laughed and loped away from her along the track. 'Says the girl who can't tell a piglet skull when it's right in front of her.'

Annie made a face at his departing back. She wrapped the stinky skull in a tissue and put it in her pocket.

Ha-hoo, ha-hoo! The mournful horn, followed by a double-tone whistle being blown far away. Hundreds of pheasants beating their wings across the canopy out into the open sky, the guns whipping left to right, shots volleying out. A cracking sound echoing around the bowl of the village. The birds raining down. Annie felt slightly sick.

Half an hour previously, the village had gathered in a disused barn in one of Andrew's fields. There'd been brandy in leather hip flasks and chat about braces and bead sights. Now they were in the valley, and everyone except her seemed perfectly at home.

William asked if she'd like to travel up the fell with Stephen, and she said yes please. Anything not to have to watch the poor things dropping from the sky. Her father-in-law stuffed a bright orange tabard into her arms, with instructions to wear it *at all times*. The kids waved her goodbye.

She and Stephen journeyed up the hill, quiet but amiable. 'Déjà vu being here with you,' she joked, and he smiled. She struggled into the tabard and tried not to wince at the bumps in the terrain.

They arrived at a plateau deep in the woods. Stephen quickly reversed the buggy into position, checked her leg was comfortable and disappeared back down the hill on foot with a promise to return at the end of the third drive. It was a bit spooky being abandoned on the fell alone, but better here than down with all the noise. That whistle again, in the valley. Yes, better here.

Her watch ticked the minutes. She glanced behind her. How many animals had the Dillane family members killed in total? Thousands, probably. Before making parlour games from the remains.

She pulled out her phone to google 'Dolly blue factory near Colthwaite' but there was no reception. She put her hands in her lap and thought instead about the ideal casting for *Bambisexual*. How long to the interval, or whatever the break in the middle of a shoot was called? She could do with a hot drink, preferably alcoholic, and a snack.

Shouting. Shots ringing, the sound ricocheting. She pictured Caleb and Grace, guns aloft, ear defenders on, their shoulders struggling against the recoil.

Ha-hoo! Ha-hoo!

Time passed slowly. At one point she could have sworn she saw a glint of sun bounce off something reflective on the other side of the valley. Sunglasses, perhaps? A mirror? A window? No, no windows up here. Binoculars?

No. Silly. Unless it was one of those guys on the hunt whose job it was to look out for pheasants.

Still, she was a little relieved when Stephen arrived and delivered her safely back to the gloom of the barn. She could just make out the tops of the kids' heads on the far side. Andrew hurried by, smiled, enquired about her leg. She wanted to ask about her postcard to Polly and whether he'd delivered it, but it didn't seem the time. She spotted Margaret Paine – hair even bluer than usual, she must have had a go at it in the last few days.

'Flapjack?' William looked out of place carrying a tray.

Annie took one, put it in her mouth, took another. 'Sorry,'

she said. 'Hungry work, sitting still.' He was about to walk off. 'Can I ask you something?'

'Another question?' he said. 'Second time today. Making a habit of it.'

'Ha. Yes. Do you know if anyone was out last night, on the fell?'

'Ah.' William grinned. 'Guilty as charged. Don't worry, old thing. I was looking for the sow. The "off" one, with the funny...' He jabbed a finger at her face. 'Haven't seen her hanging about, have you?'

'No.' Annie suddenly became very interested in her second flapjack. 'Nope. Can't say I have.'

'We're sure she's pregnant. Very much need to get hold of her. If you spot her, holler.'

Elizabeth bustled in their direction, Vincent on her arm. Annie tried not to pull a face.

'How's the leg?'

'Much better, thanks to you,' she said, which was true at least.

Her mother-in-law moved off, taking William with her. That just left Vincent, who was struggling to brush mud from his walking stick. He linked a bony arm through hers. 'Fish out of water?'

'A bit.' She smiled.

'It'll be over soon.'

That made her laugh. 'Slightly hoping it was over already.'

'Oh no.' Vincent shook his head so hard she half worried it might fall off. 'There's a whole other drive yet.'

'But... what will I be *doing*?'

He leant in. 'You know you've an important job up there on the fell?'

'I do?'

'Absolutely.'

'What is it?'

But he seemed not to hear, and she didn't want to ask again in case she seemed neurotic. He was probably just saying it to make her feel better, anyway. Someone shouted that the second drive was about to start, and everyone began to move out. Vincent and Annie walked together towards the buggy, Vincent slow with his stick, Annie equally slow with her crutch. He chuckled. 'Pair we make.'

Stephen was already in the driver's seat, reeling instructions to a crowd of gun-toting boys in plus-fours and flat caps. They looked like shrunken adult men.

What she wanted to do was go home. She climbed in anyway, bid farewell to Vincent, and let herself be carried up the hillside, her leg stiffening in the cold. 'Don't worry, it's only a short drive this one,' Stephen reassured.

'Can't wait.'

The buggy reached the plateau, which had been her previous spot and passed it, continuing up through the trees. 'Where are we going?' she asked. 'Everest?'

Stephen shook his head. 'Shoot's coming through Furlong Field into Beeches.' God knows what *that* meant. A few more minutes and he killed the engine.

Annie looked around. Another plateau, more trees. They were right next to the large pheasant pen, the huge one with the clearing and the shepherds hut within it. 'Vincent says I've an important job here. Or was that bullshit?'

'Not bullshit at all,' he said. 'If the pheasants run through this area, you're to call me.'

'On what?' She pulled out her phone. 'No reception.'

He handed her an ancient mobile. 'My spare brick,' he said. '*With* reception. Don't lose it.'

Annie stared. A Nokia. She doubted it would even stretch to a text. But full bars.

'What's wrong with the pheasants running through here?' she asked.

'The guns don't like to come up this way. Too steep.'

'Right.'

Stephen was laughing.

'What?'

'Your face,' he said. 'So, to repeat, when you hear the whistle, if pheasants run through or fly overhead, *use the phone*. And put your tabard on.'

'Okay.' She struggled into the tabard. 'It all sounds very serious.'

'It is. If the birds are here, I'll need to come up toot sweet or you might find you've a nasty hole in that jacket.'

Annie felt herself pale.

'Joking,' he said. 'But we *would* need to move you double quick: the guns heading this way 'n' that.'

She looked at him. 'Stephen,' she said, 'I'm not in danger sitting here, am I? With my leg and everything?'

'Definitely not.'

'Good. And I'd really like to ask you a second question if I may. It might sound weird.'

'Oh?' He shifted.

'Do you know anything about the history of the Dolly Blue factory? The deaths of the girls in the graveyard as a result of it?'

He looked away. 'That kind of stuff's above my pay grade, I'm afraid.' He was already out the buggy and walking down the steep stone track. 'I leave all the village history to the boss. Stay sharp, Annie!' Then he was gone.

Two whistles and a horn. Annie was growing colder by the

minute and her ankle was grumbling. It had been irresponsible to put her here on lookout.

Stephen said this 'drive' was going to be shorter, but it didn't feel like it. And they hadn't even had lunch yet. The menu would be something traditionally English, probably roasted, possibly pheasant.

She looked about. Trees. More trees.

She brought her weed pouch out from her pocket. Now it was *her* being irresponsible: getting stoned when she had an 'important' job to do. Never mind. She rolled a joint, smoking it as a thin beam of sun tracked its way across her body. Comfortably baked, she checked her phone. No service: duh. And Stephen's Nokia would be useless for the internet. At least the weed deadened the pain in her leg.

Another whistle.

A sudden disturbance on the slope below. A sound like wind, the ground moving, leaves flying, and out of nowhere, hundreds of pheasants appeared from the undergrowth racing past her up the hill. She waved her arms in the air, realising too late that this was the moment she was supposed to make that all-important phone call.

The crack of multiple gunshots. Something whizzed above her in the treeline. Were those... *bullets?* She fumbled for Stephen's phone, but the joint had made her clumsy. More shots rang out. 'Stop! Please!' Another whizzed past, far too close.

'Oh my *God!*' She rolled off the buggy, banging her bad leg on the running board on her way down. 'Fuck!'

The buggy was now her defence. On her back, she searched the Nokia's address book. Oh God, why had she smoked that joint? More shots to her left. 'Stop!' Stephen must be off somewhere preparing the next thingy – the drive – or he'd never have allowed them to come this way.

Annie punched letters into the phone's search bar.

Stephen's name and number appeared. 'C'mon, pick up, pick up.'

The phone rang out.

'*Hi, this is Stephen. You know what to do.*' He was supposed to answer. That's what he'd said. Annie pressed redial. '*Hi, this is Stephen...*' She waited for the beep.

'It's Annie! Where are you? Bullets! The guns are near me! I'm behind the buggy. Please. I need help!' The guns went silent. The only sound was the squawks of a dying pheasant. Perhaps someone had got the message?

There was a large boulder ten feet away, right next to the pheasant pen's fence. That would do. She could hide behind it. She flipped onto her front, and keeping her nose to the ground, crawled uphill towards it. She tucked herself in tight. The ground smelled rich and damp, and the electric fence hummed above her. The yellow poison pellets to keep out the animals were right by her; she mustn't touch those. She didn't feel remotely stoned anymore.

Further downhill, men were whooping and beaters' sticks hacked at bushes. A last clutch of pheasants made a dash uphill to her right.

If she could just hang on a few moments more, someone was sure to appear.

Bang! A lone bullet whizzed past, hit the ground and ricocheted off a rock, pranging loudly against the buggy.

'Oh my *God!*' If she'd stayed in the vehicle... It didn't bear thinking about.

She pulled her legs in and screwed her eyes tight shut. Stephen's Nokia began to vibrate. She snatched it up.

'Annie! I'm on my way. My phone switched itself on to silent. I've been at the other end of the valley. The guns have stood down.'

'One of their shots hit the buggy!'

'It was the sound of it hitting metal that told them you were there. I'm very sorry. Hang tight.' He rang off.

It was almost as if... No. They would never. Annie stared at the buggy: the bullet had grazed the paintwork. No wonder they'd put her in a tabard. She leant back, breathing out slowly, pushed her hands beneath her thighs for comfort.

Her fingers met a stone that didn't feel quite right: warm and smooth, like plastic. She pulled it out from under her.

It *was* plastic! She turned it in her hand: a perfectly symmetrical mini 'boulder' coated in camo-effect print, weighing almost nothing. At one end, a camera eye stared back at her. On the base, a slot for a battery, sealed with two tiny screws. What was *this* doing here? Why film out in the woods? It was true that Stephen said something about poachers, but how bad was it really? And how could a camera placed this low to the ground hope to catch people up to no good? Spooked, she looked around her. Yes, there, fastened high to a pine trunk, another one.

Someone could be watching her. Recording, perhaps. There was only one way to find out.

Taking out her penknife, she unscrewed the baseplate to reveal a memory card inside. Good: she'd load it onto her computer back at the cottage. Then she'd have her answer.

Footsteps were coming up the hillside. Hastily, she screwed the plate back in place and replaced the cam on the ground.

'Annie?' It was Stephen.

She stuffed the memory card into her pocket. 'I'm here!'

She got to her feet, dismissing the thought that she was paranoid, that Mum's mental illness might be inheritable and that her genes, Annie's genes, had been waiting for the right time to switch on, just as Elizabeth had said.

'What a balls-up.' Stephen's chest was heaving. 'You must have been scared out your wits.'

'It's okay.' It wasn't, but she didn't want to cause a scene, especially with the memory card burning a hole in her coat. She climbed into the buggy as he pushed the key in the ignition. 'You'd better have this back.' She handed him the phone. The engine juddered to life.

He paused, looked at her. 'All right?'

'Yeah.'

'Ears ringing?'

'Yep.'

'That'll go. Hold tight.' The buggy's engine sprang to life. They set off down the hill. 'I should have checked my phone was on,' he said over the sound of the engine. 'It's my fault. None of this should have happened.'

'I forgot to call straight away when I saw the birds. I was...' she could hardly tell him she was stoned, '... checking emails.'

He tutted. 'No reception here.'

She didn't dare look at him. 'It came on for just a second.'

The kids ran to her as the buggy drew up next to the shooting party. Several people she didn't know by name apologised. She nodded, answered their questions, told them she was fine. Vincent patted her leg.

'Out you come, then,' William said. 'Lunch is waiting.' Annie went with him; her hand curled around the memory card. She saw Andrew watching from a distance, his brow furrowed.

Later, back at Chapel Croft, Annie took a bath to warm her bones, then hobbled into the sitting room to find the kids watching *The Babadook*.

'Guys! What did I say about horror?'

Caleb looked up. 'It's fine, really. I'm fine.'

Grace raised her palms. 'We just wanted to take our minds off the shoot. Those poor birds.'

'With *that*?' Annie came to sit beside them.

'And you nearly died,' Caleb stated.

'I wouldn't go that far,' Annie said, though secretly she agreed.

Grace turned to Annie with a forensic look. 'I don't think anyone was trying to shoot you, if that's what you're worried about?'

''Course not!'

'It was crazy with the dogs barking and running about,' Grace went on. 'And people shouting, and I think everyone just forgot you in the chaos.'

Forgot her. Annie bit her lip.

'What Grace means,' Caleb qualified, 'is don't take this the wrong way, but *we* didn't remember you were up there in that exact spot. And we're your kids.'

'Right.' Annie savoured the 'we're your kids'. They said nothing more about it, and eventually, the children went to bed.

She waited long enough for them to be asleep, then limped in darkness to the writing shed, the memory card in her pocket.

Pomander snorted in greeting as she passed, the pig's outline blacker than the other black things surrounding it. For once, Annie didn't stop for a stroke.

It was icy cold in the shed. She flicked on the heater but not the lights in case the children woke and saw her. She opened her laptop, dimming the brightness on the screen and positioning herself with her back to the cottage. Sometimes a sturdy frame was a blessing.

She slid the memory card into the laptop's USB port and waited for the file to appear on her screen: *Boulder-cam 4: enclosure, south gate.*

The number four suggested there might be others. She'd

spotted one other, but four was excessive, even for poachers, surely. She clicked her VLC player. The application launched a small window of live footage. It was of the enclosure in daylight; the point of view reaching twenty feet along the ground. The timecode read: *06.15am*. The date: two days ago. She enlarged to full-screen and let the video run.

A couple of leaves blew past the lens. A bird pecked at moss. She hovered the cursor over the file: forty-eight hours long! She'd couldn't possibly watch all of it. She pushed through at thirty-two frames a second, as day turned to night and back to day again, pausing whenever a movement caught her eye. But it was only ever a pheasant, a pair of Herdwicks ambling past, or twice – once yesterday morning and once yesterday evening – Stephen powering through the gate in his buggy. He disappeared inside the enclosure and drove out half an hour later.

The file reached thirty-nine hours. Annie needed a break. Her eyes were sore. She had no idea what she was even looking for, anyway. Forty hours, forty-two hours. Boring, nothing, nothing.

At 42.34 hours, which happened to be 5.15am this very morning, there was movement in the trees at the far reaches of the cam's capabilities. She hit pause and replayed the tape.

A person's legs. Wellingtons. The fuzzy shape darting behind a tree. She played the section again in slow motion. It wasn't Stephen, that much was clear: too small, too skinny. Too... female.

A woman poacher? A lost rambler? Elizabeth? She let the recording run. At 7.23am, two hours after the figure last appeared, Stephen arrived again, journeying through the gate. As before, thirty minutes later, he drove out. But the woman – whoever she was – hadn't left. Or at least, not through this gate. The recording ended.

Annie sat back in her chair. Sweat had bloomed at her nape. Forty-eight hours of recording. Tomorrow morning would be reset day for the memory card. If they found out she'd taken it... she'd better get it back. She flexed her bad foot, testily. She felt strangely vindicated. Not paranoia, after all.

<hr>

She set the volume on the alarm so low she almost missed it when it went off at 5.30am. Starting in the dark wasn't ideal, but she wouldn't make it before Stephen's daily morning visits otherwise. She threw on her clothes and waterproofs, grabbed a torch, the crutch, and left the house through the back door, closing it gently behind her.

It was pitch black outside and blurry with rain, only a thin triangle of world visible in the narrow capabilities of her torch beam. The pig was snoring as she crept past its shelter. She made her way to the woods beyond, traversing the lower section of the fell. What if she became lost, ended up in another fox hole? Everything smelled of wet leaves and fungus.

She reached what she estimated to be the halfway point. Dawn wouldn't show its face for half an hour. Behind the hill, things dropped away into darkness. Even with the aid of crutches, her leg wasn't good, and by the time she arrived at the enclosure, it was 6.45am and streaks of purple-orange sky were flooding the trees to the east. She swung the torch across the ground near the gate. There it was: that little plastic rock-cam. With a glance at the camera in the tree, she flipped the one in her hand over and slid the panel back to replace the memory card. She switched the torch off and simply sat there listening to the rain, settling the tingling sensation in her leg.

A sound in the trees, a hiss. Annie turned round. It had

originated from within the pheasant enclosure. Was it…
breathing? Or the wind?

'Anybody there?' She flicked the torch beam into the
enclosure as she pulled herself to her feet. At least she was
protected by the fence. 'Hello?'

She could hear Stephen's buggy setting out from the bottom
of the fell for his morning rounds. She needed to leave now. She
shone the torch into the enclosure one last time: its beam caught
a flicker of straw-coloured hair.

'Grace!' she called. 'Is that you?' But Grace was home, in
bed. Wasn't she? Whoever it was, they were running now. The
pock-pock sound of legs moving in wellies. '*Hey!*'

The figure disappeared deep into the enclosure.

'Wait!'

But they'd gone. Someone with hair like Grace. But not
Grace.

Stephen would be on her in minutes. After checking she'd
left nothing behind, she hurried down the hill.

CHAPTER ELEVEN

She'd bet her life it was the same woman on the memory card's footage.

Perhaps she should tell William, or Stephen? If the woman turned out to be some sort of poacher, they'd be grateful. Though they'd want to know why she'd been up on the fell at six in the morning. And something told her it wasn't a poacher, anyway. But then, who? And *why?*

She ate her breakfast too fast, thoughts thick with the cemetery's occupants, re-running Vincent's conversation about their deaths. She threw her bowl in the dishwasher, marvelling once again that Issy hadn't ever mentioned Dolly Blue. It was inconceivable. Her wife hadn't been a liar, which meant only one thing: Vincent was the one doing the lying. And there was a way to find this out, right now.

The kids were fast asleep. Grabbing the car keys, she headed out the door.

The old blueing factory-turned-car museum wasn't far. She shouldn't be driving with her leg but fuck it.

The early dawn light had morphed into a grim morning, the

rain falling in sheets. She passed through Colthwaite and crossed the bridge without, she hoped, being spotted. Her leg complained as she pressed the accelerator. A snarl of early morning traffic on the A-road – day-trippers mainly, heading to or from Lake Collermere. Annie sat in a queue, knuckles tight around the steering wheel and tried to think about something – anything – else.

There'd been an email from the Finborough just before she'd set off, confirming the date for her meeting in London: Thursday of the following week. She wished she could focus entirely on it, prepare properly instead of worrying, amongst other things, about forest women.

Fifteen minutes later, she pulled into an almost empty car park. The museum itself was a low stone building, with a temporary-looking modern extension perched on its top, like a bird alighting. Annie stepped through the double doors. The reception was neat, municipal, the floor moving with the shadows of raindrops as they hit the glass ceiling. She paid the young woman at the desk and walked through the turnstile.

She'd expected it to be busy on a Sunday morning, but she pretty much had the place to herself. The only other visitors were an American couple in chinos and fleeces. A soporific hush pervaded the rooms. Annie was instantly overcome by what she and Issy used to call 'museum foot', where five minutes after entering a gallery, only a sit down in the building's café could revive drooping limbs. The exhibits had been assembled with care: bygone-era cars polished 'til you could see your reflection in the paintwork; vintage vans; motorcycles with sidecars; life-size papier-mâché chauffeurs and figures in military wear, each one accompanied by a paragraph of historical text on mounted hardboard.

She climbed the stairwell to the first floor. 'THE OLD

BLUEING FACTORY' read a large sign. So that part was true, at least.

A little booth, a female mannequin with a rictus smile, in a house coat and white hat, the figure seated at a table with several bowls: the raw materials used to formulate Dolly Blue – china clay, caustic soda, sulphur. Black-and-white images of workers from the mid-twentieth century ran along the wall: smiling men and women on benches; others assembled around barrels of steaming chemicals, their skin, white aprons, and caps splatted with ultramarine dye. The hardboard signs made no mention of toxicity or death. Perhaps Vincent hadn't been lying after all – which was worse, as it meant Issy had been hiding things from her for the entirety of their relationship. Annie looked hard for his face, for any inhabitant of Colthwaite, in the photos, but found none.

She navigated the remainder of the museum accompanied by the Americans' background chatter until she found her way to the turnstile in the atrium. The woman at the desk had been replaced by another, older woman. 'Enjoyed it?' she enquired.

'I don't suppose you hold records, do you, of the people who worked in the factory?'

The woman smiled. 'Pet, we have a whole room of 'em.'

'Oh!' A stroke of luck. 'Would I be able to take a look?'

''Course. They used to be held at Ullerforth archives.' The woman pulled her chin in. 'Then when everything went digital, they ran out of space and returned the hard copies to us. Ironic, really.'

The woman pushed the flap behind the counter and stepped from her booth. Her shoes squeaked on the linoleum. 'Academia, is it?'

'Uh... yeah.'

'We get a lot of you, historians and so on.' She went out the double doors at the front. 'Follow me.'

A smaller building sat behind the main one. Inside, it was cold and overly lit, the shelves stacked with boxes. In one corner sat a desk with a lamp and chair.

'Make yourself at home.'

'I can go through anything I like?'

The woman looked at her, quizzically. ''Course you can.'

'I mean,' Annie fumbled. 'People could steal things. Not me, just–'

The woman laughed. 'It's not like that in these parts.' She went to the door. 'Each box is labelled in date order. If you want lists of workers, it's the blue folders, which means, as you can see, the irony never stops around here. Holler if you need help.' The door closed behind her.

Annie went along the first aisle, each box meticulously labelled, as the woman had said, according to year. They went back as far as 1890. They hardly weighed anything, and Annie stacked them quickly, a tower growing beside the desk. Folders in red, green, and blue were inside, the blue set divided by alphabetised markers.

Annie retrieved the 'P' section from 1971. A log of names with date of birth, address, and National Insurance number:

Parker Tom

Patterson Michael

Patt George

Pathlone Brian

Prerling Amy

She ran her finger down the page. No Vincent Prime. No female Prime. No Colin, no Margaret Paine. A pulse drumming at her temples, she searched earlier in the alphabet for Dillane, as well as the other surnames belonging to the dead girls: Bell, Yearly, something else beginning with S? She should have written them down.

She combed each year until she reached 1982. There wasn't

a single person's name she recognised. She repacked the boxes onto the shelves and made her way to reception.

The Americans had gone, and the museum was silent. The old woman behind the desk was eating a sandwich. The place smelled strongly of tuna.

'Find what you're after?'

'Not really. I was looking for the people of Colthwaite who worked at the factory in the seventies.'

The woman snorted. 'There aren't any. They've always been farmers out that way. Or comers-in, too smart for factory work.'

'Comers-in? Outsiders, you mean?'

'Yep. People not born here.' The woman looked at her sharply. 'You researching the village, then?'

Annie nodded.

'Right. Them up at the Big Hou– at Colthwaite House, too?'

'Yes.' She hoped she wasn't blowing it.

'Them's comers-in as well.'

Annie frowned. 'No, the family at Colthwaite House *were* born in the village. Elizabeth Dillane grew up in that house; generations of Dillanes did.'

The woman shrugged. '*She* did, all right, but not the others. And soon as she could, off Elizabeth went up to London, to university. Met Vincent Prime there, them lot.'

Annie went very still. 'Wasn't Vincent Prime born in the north? He worked here at the factory, I thought?'

'Give your head a wobble! Have you heard his accent? He's a southerner.'

Annie cleared her throat. 'But–'

'They're medical, all of 'em.'

'Medical? Elizabeth's a vet. The others are–'

'–medical doctors,' the woman insisted. 'Apart from

William. Him she met up here on the other side of the valley. The others all took degrees in London. King's, I think it was. Followed Elizabeth back to Colthwaite after.'

'Which others exactly? Vincent, who else?'

'Vincent and...' The woman looked at the ceiling. 'Mind's gone blank. A few of 'em, anyway.'

'Why would they do that?' Annie pressed. 'Follow her here?'

'They're awful tight, the lot of 'em.' Finished with her sandwich, the woman dropped the crusts in the bin.

'Please, sorry to be a pain, but would you mind trying to remember who we are talking about here? Vincent and...?'

The woman's eyes lit up. 'That's it! I've remembered! The vicar, David. He's one. He's not from Colthwaite, neither. Another university friend.' She nodded. 'Retrained: from medicine to God. Don't understand it myself. Quite a cut in pay, I'd imagine. Though God has his own rewards, I dare say. Then again...' The woman narrowed her eyes.

'Yes?' Annie prompted.

The woman searched in a handbag sitting on a shelf behind her. 'Don't know why I'm showing you this, but anyways...' She had a wad of photographs in her hand and fanned them out on the counter like a pack of cards. 'This is me trusting you, yes?'

'Of course,' Annie said, praying no visitors came through the door to break the spell. 'Thank you.'

A young man, and a much younger version of the woman herself, standing in a sunny garden, arms around one another. The second photo was a small girl against a backdrop of blue sea. 'My late husband. That was my daughter, there.'

'Both of them are...?' Annie felt her throat tighten.

'Yep.'

'I'm so sorry.'

The woman held the photos in front of her. She looked lost.

'And...' Annie felt terrible probing further, 'what about the other photos you have there?'

'Oh yes.' She pulled a third photo out. Her knuckles were lumpy and arthritic and reminded Annie of Grandma Halmi. 'Here we are.'

Annie recognised the person instantly: a youthful Vincent in a sixties suit, cream shirt, tie, glasses, sitting at a desk in a small room, a stethoscope hanging at his neck. Seated beside him was the woman in front of Annie now, around thirty years old. Both were smiling, their bodies turned to the camera, thumbs up.

'He was the local GP for a while, see?'

'GP? Vincent was a *GP*?'

'That's right. We'd just discovered I was pregnant. That's why I looked so happy.' The woman's eyes widened. 'Brian, my late husband, he took the picture.'

'Thank you for showing me.' Annie swallowed. 'What date was this?'

'November 1968.' Furrows appeared in the woman's forehead. She pulled the photo towards herself. 'A good doctor, Vincent was. We'd been having trouble conceiving. He helped lots of women in the area.' She leaned on the counter. 'We couldn't have had Mandy without him.'

'What d'you mean?'

'He gave us drugs.' The woman picked the photos up and returned them to her bag. 'Special ones. Foreign. This government makes them illegal, prevents peoples' happiness, he said. Criminal. It's all about money. Such a shame he was struck off.'

Annie nearly choked. 'Struck off? What for?'

'Nobody knows, but like I say, I believe it was for the drugs. They hadn't been approved by the hoojamaflip in the UK; more Vincent's *home* recipe.' She shook her head. 'Awful business.

Happened just as Mandy was born. All for helping people. Who cares what's in the drugs if it means people are going to get bonny babies?' She paused, as if listening back at her own words. 'Know him, do you?'

'He's a... friend,' Annie said. 'A new one.'

'Probably didn't want to scare you. Can you blame him? The shame of it.' Something dark passed across her face. 'We lost Mandy when she was twenty-one. Never got over it, either of us.'

'I'm so sorry. Was it... the Dolly Blue?'

'Dolly Blue?' The woman scoffed. 'Don't be soft. Cystic fibrosis. It's a tragedy, that disease. I said "bonny babies" but after Mandy went, Brian and I had to be tested at the hospital, you know, to check if we carried the gene. As if we were going to have any more children after that.'

'That's–'

'Life's not fair. You've to endure the lot you're given.'

A group of people pushed noisily through the doors and with a nod to signal the conversation was over, the woman turned away, drawn into the business of ticket sales. Annie mouthed, 'Thank you,' and left.

She made it to the car in the drizzle, fastening her seat belt, slotting the key in the ignition but failing to turn it, the front lights pushing their watery beams onto the concrete. Vincent had lied through his rotten teeth. The wipers began their agonised traverse across the windscreen. Vincent, whom she'd considered a friend, told tales of Dolly Blue and the ultramarine factory to steer her from the truth. She pushed her forehead against the window.

There would be a connection between this woman's daughter, the girls in the churchyard, and the woman on the fell. She was sure of it.

She googled *King's London* on her phone and pushed call.

When someone answered, she told them she was looking for records of past students, dating right back to the forties and fifties. The person put her on hold.

Behind a window on the museum's first floor, she saw a group of visitors pass up the stairwell.

And Grace. She'd all but dismissed Caleb's assertion; but now, well – what if it turned out she *was* pregnant? Could Vincent have had anything to do with it? No, that was insane. Grace hadn't begged Vincent for a baby. And Vincent was no longer practicing. *Jesus.*

'I hear you're looking for our alumni database?' said someone new at the end of the line.

'That's right.'

'Records are stored at the college libraries, but you'll need to make an appointment and come in person, I'm afraid.'

Annie found herself saying this was fine, she was coming to London on the train the following Thursday anyway. They took her name and telephone number, and Annie booked herself an appointment with them several hours after her meeting at the Finborough. She'd no idea if this was a good plan, but it was done now.

She fired up the engine and drove out of the car park, taking the lanes slowly, overhanging branches swaying like uncut hair. It wasn't safe in Colthwaite. What if Vincent was still... dabbling, and Grace – or Caleb, even – were to be exposed to his strange medical practices? There was no way she was going to let *that* happen. She connected her phone to the car speakers and dialled the letting agent in London.

'I just want to establish,' she fired at them, 'what the situation is with my tenants' six-month break clause? I can break it, right? It is a thing?' The agent said it was a thing. Annie put the phone down, her mind made up.

But the six months was still over twelve weeks away. She

and the kids could stay somewhere else until the time was up, but where? There wasn't enough money to rent an equivalent space.

She'd find something. The children, she thought with an intensity that surprised even her, were all that mattered.

Annie gnawed at the tip of her pen. She'd been huddled in the shed trying to research, but so far when she'd typed in *King's College London Alumni 1958–1968*, Google had given her nothing. She'd have to wait until the appointment in London.

The kids had gone back to school this morning. She'd not told them anything so far. She would, of course, but not yet. Not until she knew more. The woman at the museum might have been stirring up all kinds of things for her own edification. It hadn't appeared that way, it was true, but Annie was quickly learning you couldn't trust anyone.

And the meeting at the Finborough was approaching, and she was woefully underprepared. But how was she expected to concentrate with all this going on? It hardly seemed important.

What if Vincent had continued administering home-spun drugs, using them on female inhabitants in Colthwaite – possibly his own wife – for years following his dismissal, to encourage fertility? The graveyard girls' premature deaths, his own daughter's – Sarah's – death, might have been a direct result of his medication.

Pomander was making self-important noises from her hut.

Probably hungry. Annie rubbed at the steamed shed window and saw the pig pushing her face over the table. She rapped on the glass and Pomander fluttered the lashes of her eye in response.

Annie opened her notebook. *Rewrite this shit* was scrawled beneath a section of *Kimchi Trout Sandwich*. She'd already written a play that the theatre wanted; she should drop this new one entirely for now. There were other things that needed dealing with first. All she had to do in the meeting was listen, then talk with clarity for a few minutes. She pulled the *Bambisexual* manuscript from a drawer and reread it with laser focus. It was better than she remembered.

Wednesday. She was in the cottage laying out her things: smart shoes, laptop bag, good trousers, ready for an early departure the next morning. The journey would go like this: drive to the station at Oxdale, three-hour train to Euston, Tube to the theatre. After the meeting, she'd head to the King's College archives. As soon as the kids were back at the weekend, she'd tell them what she'd learned.

A knock at the door.

The outlines of two tall people beyond the stippled panes of glass. She recognised one: William. It was too late to turn back; he would have spotted her.

'Oh,' he said when she opened the door, as if he expected to be greeted by another person entirely. Andrew stood beside him, hands in his pockets. The sheepdogs panted at their feet.

'What a lovely surprise,' Annie managed, and Andrew smiled.

William scratched his neck. 'How are you? The leg?'

'Much better, thanks.'

'Jolly good.'

William cleared his throat. 'Came to say, Andrew here won't be able to pick the children up this weekend. There's a Tup sale at the market in Ullerforth; he's coming with. We'll be there all Friday.'

'Oh, no problem.' Why Andrew couldn't speak for himself was anyone's guess.

'Especially since you're back to driving now.'

'I'm...?'

William nodded. 'Saw you out in the car Sunday.'

'Shopping,' she said. 'Ambleside.'

William put his head on one side. 'Funny route you took to Ambleside.'

'*Anyway.*' She wasn't going to let him push her around. 'I'm heading to Oxdale station tomorrow. Going to London for a meeting about a play I wrote that'll be going on at the Finborough.' Now why had she told them that?

'The Finborough?' Andrew seemed confused.

'Fringe venue,' Annie explained. 'In Earl's Court.'

William's eyebrows shot up. 'Fringe? As in hair?'

'No, it's a term for any theatre that isn't in the centre of a city.' She ran her hands up and down her thighs. Really, why couldn't they just leave her alone?

William was peering around and behind her. 'You like to be prepared, I see.'

Her clothes and shoes, lined up in the hallway. 'That's right. I do.'

'Very good.' William slapped his palms together. 'Work to be getting on with myself this morning.'

'I bet.'

The two men looked like they were about to leave. 'How's Polly?' Annie asked. Andrew looked non-plussed. 'On your visit?' she said. 'To see her?'

'Oh!' Andrew laughed briefly. 'Sorry. Doing much better, thank you.'

'Did she like my card?'

'She did. She said thank you very much and sent her love.'

'That's nice.'

'Righto!' William turned and strode away down the track with his dogs, one long arm waving. 'Good luck with your meeting!'

Andrew hovered for a moment. 'Yes, good luck!' he said, before hurrying after his father.

Annie closed the door. She stared at her travel kit. They knew about her trip. She couldn't help feeling that was a mistake.

The moon was rising behind fat clouds. She fed the pig dinner, lifting the table out as was ritual now, allowing Pomander time in the garden to snuffle. She was very fond of nibbling Annie's belt loops and rubbing herself against Annie's quads. And she was growing ever fatter. Each evening Annie placed a gentle hand on the pig's belly, feeling for signs of life. Usually Pomander didn't like that, and would grunt and swing her backside round, forcing Annie off balance. Tonight though, when Annie ducked and put her hand there, she felt something inside the pig kick.

'Pomander!' she exclaimed. 'Your piglets!' Yes, there it was again. Annie grinned. Sweet little piglets. Ha. If Elizabeth and William had had their way, the piglets would have remained unborn, and Pomander would be just another carcass on a hook.

Her alarm shocked her awake at 6.30am: interview day. Behind the curtain, darkness. She showered, dressed carefully in her interview outfit, and went out to feed Pomander, collecting her manuscript papers, laptop, and notes from the writing shed. The train wasn't until 8.30am. She idly turned pages as she ate four slices of buttered toast with chilli flakes. She hoped getting around London with her bad leg wouldn't be a problem.

Somewhere in the distance, a quad bike and the protestations of sheep being herded.

Her phone beeped. A text from Caleb. It was only 7am.

Good luck for today! Thinking of you.

Her heart expanded. She typed back.

Thank you, my love! Hope you're okay. Surviving?

No reply.

At 7.45 she laced her brogues, checked herself one last time in the mirror, and left the house carefully to avoid getting her shoes in the mud as she loaded her bag into the boot. She turned the car out of the gate and swung right towards the bridge. The lights were off inside Blea Crag. Annie felt a kick of satisfaction. She'd slip away and return before anyone noticed.

Daylight pushed its way between the trees now. She was buzzing as she headed for the bridge, and freedom: London's coffee shops, whisky bars, tall buildings. The archives.

She rounded the bend in the lane to find a traffic jam directly ahead, and was forced to slam the brakes, her head thumping the headrest. Really, she was making a habit of this.

Ten cars in front, William's giant yellow tractor was at a standstill in the middle of the road. Exhaust fumes clouded the air. 'You have *got* to be kidding me.'

She could see Stephen, along with Andrew's eldest son, peering beneath the wheel rim at the back of the tractor. She left the car and hurried along the queue, pulling her coat around her against the chill morning air. 'What's going on?'

Stephen straightened. In his hands, a wrench and a jack. 'Quick couplers gone. Not going anywhere urgent, I hope?'

Panic swelled in her chest. 'I am actually.'

'Oh 'eck.'

'I'll double back to the other end of the village.' She spun on her heel. Of all days! They had to be taking the piss. Another car had pulled up behind hers making it impossible to move. The silver Jeep Cherokee, the one she'd seen on the lane before.

'Hey!' she yelled, walking to the driver's window and ducking her head. It was a man. He looked familiar. 'D'you think you could go back a bit? I'm in a rush.'

The man nodded and the Jeep reversed down the lane. After she'd swung the BMW into a ten-point turn, she drove back swiftly through the village to its far end. She'd take the Gillyhead road. If she stepped on the gas, she could still make it to the station with five minutes to spare. And to think she'd wasted all that time this morning making toast and eating it.

On the last bend out of Colthwaite, she came upon a flock of sheep in the road, their grubby backsides bobbing in unison. Hundreds streamed out of a field through a wide gate overseen by Andrew's second eldest boy, staff in hand, while William's dogs ran in circles. Ahead was William himself, like a standing-stone, shouting instructions. She leapt from the car, the engine running, gesturing at Andrew's son, who waved indifferently. Her leg wasn't enjoying itself any more than she was.

'William!' she yelled. He seemed not to hear. Unable to reach him without pushing through the flock, an act which would incense him beyond words, she clambered up to the highest rung on a wooden fence – another rural no-no – and waved her arms. '*William!*' He looked up.

'Annie! What are you doing up there? Can you give us a hand?'

She pointed to her watch and shook her head. 'I've a train to catch! *Train!* My meeting!'

She mimed the motion of a moving train by rotating her arms at her sides. William nodded, then returned his attention to the sheep. She felt sure he was doing it on purpose.

'William!' She crabbed along the top of the fence towards him, but the last sheep had left the field by now, Andrew's boy was closing the gate behind him, and as she jumped onto the road, she found she was caught behind the flock again. 'Oh, for fuck's *sake!*'

Her shout scared the animals, and they scattered in all directions. The dogs took off after them. William looked at her in horror. Nothing for it now: she kept going, pushing through the panicked sheep to her father-in-law. Andrew's son was calling for her to stop, but she didn't care.

William's face had grown thunderous. 'The sheep, girl!' He was a good foot taller than her.

'Yes, but I've a train to catch!' she shouted back. 'Your tractor's stuck by the bridge. It's my meeting! The one I told you about.'

William's expression softened. 'Ah. Wondered why you looked so smart.' He came towards her. 'There's nothing we can do about it. It's taken nearly two hours to bring 'em off the fell. They're to go up to Briscombe Bank off the Gillyhead road. We'll do our best.'

'How long will that take?'

'Twenty minutes?'

'Twenty minutes?' she yelled, but he'd already taken off in

long strides, shooing the sheep on, banging his stick against the road, making mud and shit fly up around his ankles.

Andrew's son and the dogs fell in at his side. 'Hup, hup! Yah, get on!'

She was to definitively and spectacularly miss her train. She looked to her car, its engine still running: it hadn't yet learned the bad news.

Movement on the drive at the Big House and Andrew appeared, wheelbarrow in hand, his calm slow movements in direct contrast to the scene on the lane. He caught her looking, waved, then turned and pushed the barrow round the back of the house. It made her want to scream.

She hurried back to the car, reversed into a lay-by and motored in the opposite direction – towards the bridge again – in case by some miracle the tractor situation had changed, but it was still there, barring the way, a queue on both sides now. Trembling with rage, she dialled the theatre and explained what had happened. If she took a later train, the one departing in an hour, was there a possibility they could still see her?

They couldn't. They apologised for their inflexibility. The next available window wasn't for five weeks. Five *weeks*. It was aeons away. Yes, she said; she'd make that date.

She returned along the lane. As she passed Blea Crag, Elizabeth waved and smiled from the kitchen window. Annie felt sure the old bitch knew exactly what had happened.

At Chapel Croft, still roiling, she rang King's College. A young woman named Melissa answered. Annie explained there'd been a death in the family – not a total lie – that she couldn't make her appointment with the archivist, but could they make an exception and send any relevant information via email? Melissa took pity on her and agreed. She didn't know exactly when she'd get it to Annie, she said, but it wouldn't be long.

Annie put the phone down and stared at the wall. She felt like breaking something. Possibly William's neck.

She made herself a delicious vegetable pancake for lunch, as if the act of filling her body could make up for the morning. Now she struck out, angular with frustration, across the fields beyond the end of the village. Her leg was less painful, at least.

Why did she have the impression they'd stopped her going on purpose? It didn't make sense. How could it possibly benefit anybody here? Unless they simply wanted to annoy her, which seemed unlikely.

A low sun arrowed its beams between clouds, polishing the grass to lustrous green. She turned and looked at the run of dense trees up the fell, the houses dotted along the single long lane, everything bathed in golden light. There was Vincent's, its double bay windows. She had the sensation he was watching her.

Unsettled, she ducked sideways, changing her route to a rough track towards the side of the field. It would lead her to a natural trough in the land, hiding her from the village. The trough fed into a sunlit grassy approach, a gateway to a hard line of pine forest on the opposite side of the valley.

She was heartsore for London, and – she could admit this to herself now – if the trip *had* happened, she'd have made a pilgrimage to Hackney too, to her flat. What would she have done then? Knocked at the door, asked the tenants if they'd consider moving out in the next few weeks.

Because she'd remembered something else: the driver of the Jeep Cherokee, the man who'd looked familiar. He was who she'd passed on the lane on her first walk up the Fell – in the scarf and black trousers. That same Jeep had driven past

Colthwaite House not long ago. It seemed strange that today it had been his car that pulled up behind hers in the queue. Perhaps he was a friend of her in-laws. Perhaps he was spying on her.

No, that didn't make sense. Or did it?

Ahead, a figure emerged from the forest on to the field's grassy path. A man with a stick and a small white and brown dog. It wasn't William; too short. It might be Vincent? She *really* didn't want to see him. The stride was confident. Not Vincent, then. What if it was the Jeep Cherokee man? It was too late to turn around, she'd already been spotted. The stick waved in greeting. It was the vicar, David, with Noah. Great. Just fantastic.

Cheeks even ruddier than usual, his blue eyes watering in the breeze, he came to a halt in front of her. 'Well, well,' he said, not entirely pleasantly. He reached into his pocket, pulled out a hanky, wiped it across his mouth.

'Well.' She glanced down at Noah, who was taking a shit at her feet, back legs quivering.

'I borrow the hound every Thursday for my afternoon constitutional,' David said. 'He's an excellent ratter.'

Annie didn't have the will to answer. A group of crows flew overhead.

'And I see you have the same idea.' He looked her up and down. 'Not the ratting. The walking. Thought you preferred the fell, in general.'

She grew instantly alert. 'What makes you say that?'

'Dreaming up new plots for your plays? I hear there was a bit of a mess-up this morning with an interview in London. Terrible shame.'

'News travels fast.'

He chuckled softly at the open field. 'My dear, you live in a small community now. Like it or loathe it, we know one another's business. You'll get used to it.' He stepped neatly around her. 'At least we've got you on camera.'

'Excuse me?'

David stopped. 'Eh?'

'You said something.' She swallowed. 'You–'

'I *said* "at least it's colder in Canada".' He bent to pat the dog. 'It's chilly, no?'

Her eyes narrowed deliberately. 'Yeah, it is.'

'Colder, no doubt, in Nova Scotia. Things to be grateful for! Toodle-oo.' He moved off, taking the dog with him.

Whatever David's game, she'd received the message loud and clear: we know what you're up to, where you go. Although what *was* she up to, exactly? She'd been to the museum, she supposed. Perhaps they knew about that. But *they* were the ones who were up to something.

The sun had dropped now, a telltale streak of mauve signalling twilight, an incoming tide of navy shadows sliding across the field. The time for a walk along the forest trail had gone. Which was fine by her, she'd lost her appetite for it anyway and her leg ached.

She turned and instantly spotted the vicar moving on to the lane. Silhouetted by the sun, she watched his outline travel towards the rectory. Annie picked the most direct path home, avoiding the lane entirely to prevent any chance of bumping into him a second time. Her route took her through marshland and around the rear of the churchyard, the gravestones like old teeth in the maw of the church itself, the bell tower black against a blackening sky.

Her phone beeped in her pocket. It was an email from Melissa at King's, with attachments and the words *Here you go* in the subject box.

Annie couldn't wait. She leant against the church fence, the freezing iron biting into her. The young girls' graves were not ten feet away. She clicked on the email.

Melissa hadn't let her down. It was the list of medical alumni from 1958 to 1970 she'd asked for. Scrolling on the phone was far easier than it had been sifting through old logs by hand at the museum, and within seconds she'd hit the class of '59.

Elizabeth Dillane, RCVS Hons Veterinary Science
Vincent Prime, MRCGP Medicine and Dphil Science and Genetics
David Carey, BSc Hons Medical Genetics
Colin Paine, BSc Chemical Engineering

Colin, Margaret's husband, was there too? Of course, Margaret had told her they'd all met at university. Annie had forgotten. The email attachment was too wide for the screen and a portion of data was hidden beyond the narrow parameters. Annie scrolled sideways: a list of dates of attendance, and beside several names – including Elizabeth's, Vincent's and the rest – an asterisk. She scrolled to the bottom of the file searching for a key, a clue to what the asterisk represented, but there was nothing.

Annie rang the college archive number and asked to speak to Melissa.

'This is she.'

'It's Annie, the woman you sent the list of King's alumni to.' She tried to walk away, to put distance between herself and the church, but the reception immediately went patchy.

'You still there?' asked Melissa. 'Get what you needed?'

'I did,' Annie said, keeping her eyes on the fields around her and not on the gravestones. 'I have a question. The asterisk beside some of the names, d'you happen to know what that means?' The darkness was spreading like ink.

'Hang on.' Melissa crunched something in her mouth. Cosy warm Melissa in her library, no cemeteries to contend with, no dead girls.

The sound of computer keys tapping. 'Here it is. The asterisk is a marker for a society...' Melissa's voice trailed off. 'Oh, yes, I see! There's a tradition of societies at the college, right? It's still going on today. The students set the societies up themselves. They change year on year.'

'What kind of societies?'

'Various. With the science and medical students for example, they'll set up research teams, name them themselves. Then if they make a breakthrough, the society name becomes famous. Everyone wants to be the new Lister.' Annie heard Melissa smile through her mouthful of biscuits.

'So, how can I find out what this particular group's society name was, the ones with the asterisks on the list; what research *they* did?'

'I'd need to cross reference the individuals with our logs. It's not really... It might take a little time. When d'you need an answer?'

'Soon as possible,' Annie said. The wind had got up, whistling around the church spire, the evergreen branches shivering like limbs. 'It's urgent. For research.'

'No problem. I'll be in touch.'

Annie pushed her phone into her pocket. It was utterly black now, no moon, just a few stars.

'Annie!' A man's voice, from inside the church.

'Who's there?' Her voice was high with fear.

'Goodness, it's only me.' A bobbing torch beam made its way towards her. It was David. 'Sorry.'

Not fifteen minutes ago she'd watched him heading in the opposite direction towards the rectory. Had he doubled back, followed her?

'Didn't mean to make you jump.' He'd better not have overheard her chat with the archivist. 'Getting a head start on my sermon for Ullerforth. It always helps, I find, to gather inspiration from the place of worship itself.' He was beside her now. She could smell sweet almonds.

The little bell struck five. Pomander would be expecting her evening meal.

'"Full fathom five, thy father lies",' David intoned. He looked out over the fence at the graves. '*The Tempest*. Know it?'

'"Of his bones are coral made",' Annie quoted. '"Those are pearls that were his eyes." Ariel, Act I, Scene II.'

'Ah, but of course.' He knocked his fist against his head. 'You're a playwright.'

'I am.'

'Do you have a favourite? Play, I mean?' he enquired.

Why on earth was he making small talk in the freezing night? 'Not in particular. I'd better get home.'

'You know this will be one of the best locations from which to view the eclipse next week.'

'Next week?' She'd been so busy googling things that she'd forgotten about the eclipse. 'Wow. I'd better get prepped.'

'I know what you're thinking,' he said. 'Why does a village make a song and dance about an eclipse? Why do they have an annual festival not marked in the Christian calendar?'

'Not really.'

'It's a beautiful event; a testament to the power of nature. Villages live or die by their rituals.' David shone his torch beam at a point in the field behind her. 'Look at that.'

Annie swivelled. A small structure growing out of the ground about three feet high. She'd missed it on her way past: planks of wood nailed together.

'That's the viewing platform. Under construction, obviously. We use our own trees, it's entirely sustainable.' He was looking at her with peculiar intensity. 'We elevate ourselves, get as close as we can to God's magic. This eclipse is very rare.'

'Amazing.'

'They called it the Eye of God, you know,' he said, 'a total eclipse.'

'The past inhabitants of Colthwaite?'

He smiled. 'The Ancients, Annie.'

'Right.'

'Right indeed. "And the sun was eclipsed, and the moon turned back, while the nation was avenged on its enemies". Joshua: chapter ten.'

Annie pulled her jacket tighter around her.

'The divine marriage between Christianity and Ancient tradition.' David patted her arm. 'The Eye of God: He is always watching, and so on.'

Annie thought to herself that as well as God, there seemed to be a lot of people watching, right here in this village. Well, she was watching too.

'I've really got to go,' she said, as friendly as she could.

'Of course. I do hope you'll come. To the celebrations. There'll be fireworks afterwards, and music.'

'Sounds great.' She was already several paces from him.

'...and a pig on a spit,' he called. 'We traditionally cull one of our own to roast and eat.' He laughed under his breath. 'Don't worry, we only terminate the old and infirm. She's currently in the freezer at the barn. You may have seen her hanging up.'

Annie went still. 'Can't say that I–'

'But you'll come?'

She frowned at him through the darkness. 'Wouldn't miss it for the world.'

She double locked the doors and windows and closed the curtains. She stood in the hall, wondering what to do with herself. Rarely had she felt so alone, so far from everyone and everything important to her.

The possibility of speaking to Lumi appeared like a ship on the horizon. They hadn't spoken in such a long time. But things had grown strange and unusual here and she needed an adult she could trust.

'Well, this is a surprise,' Lumi said, not entirely sarcastically when she answered. 'D'you need something?'

'Oh,' said Annie. 'No. I just wanted to... hear your voice.'

'It's been a while.'

'Yeah.'

'How's it going up there?'

And then, like gates opening, Annie spilled her thoughts, her theories, her unanswered questions about the village, the odd people, the misshapen pigs, the albums, everything. Saying it out loud, sharing it, was a huge relief.

'What d'you think?' Annie asked at last when Lumi hadn't reacted. 'D'you think I'm paranoid? Am I mad. Am I like Mum?'

There was a long silence.

'Jamae,' Lumi said eventually. It had been years since she'd used Annie's childhood name. 'Of course you're not mad. Course you're not like Mum.'

The generous response took Annie so by surprise that she laughed.

'I *told* you.' Her sister followed with.

Annie knew it had been too good to last. She closed her eyes. 'Oh, please no,' she muttered. 'Not the "I told you".'

'I said not to go, didn't I?' Lumi ignored her. 'I said when you first mentioned it, no good will come. D'you remember?'

'Nope.'

Annie could feel Lumi's indignation through the phone. 'But that was the main reason we fell out!'

'Lumes, I was a bit distracted back then, what with my wife being *dead* and all.' The line went quiet again. 'Lumes?' Perhaps her sister had hung up.

'You don't belong with those people,' Lumi said at last.

'Yes, but I'm here now. What do I do?'

'Get out of there!' It was delivered with uncharacteristic vehemence. 'Run! Go back to London! Now.'

'Believe me, there's nothing I'd love more, but the flat's rented.'

'Speak to the estate agent. There's always a way.'

'I left them a message,' Annie said in a small voice.

'You could always come to stay with us for a bit.'

'Thank you.' Back to depressing New Malden, back to memories of Halmi and Appa, of people she loved, gone forever? 'Truly. Can I let you know?'

'Let me know?' Lumi exclaimed. 'How long will it take you to know? Don't wait to know. Get out while you still can!'

Annie snorted. 'Now you're being melodramatic. I can't just cut and run. The kids and... they've no clue about any of this. I've got to sort things here first, with the school and stuff.'

Lumi exhaled. 'Hmm. What you going to do in the meantime?'

Annie glanced at Issy's portrait. 'I don't actually know.'

'Be careful.'

'Lumes?'

'Yes?'

'I've missed you.'

'Me too, little Jamae. Me too.'

Annie put the phone in her pocket. Issy stared back at her.

It was a balance: dragging the kids to a new build in Kent with George, Lumi's accountant husband, might finish them all off. But Lumi's place was a good option if... well, if it became necessary.

Annie padded around the cottage. She felt oddly calm. Caleb and Grace would be back tomorrow, dropped off by Adam's mum, according to Grace. Annie couldn't wait to hug them.

No need for you to schlep here, Grace had texted. *His mum says they pass our way anyway. Their car is leng.*

Annie had no idea what 'leng' meant – perhaps a posh way of saying 'long'.

The kids were her talisman. She wanted them within arm's reach.

A seven-seater Tesla thundered up the drive the following evening. It tipped the kids out and sped away before Annie even made it to the door. The previous hour she'd spent searching furiously for Issy's childhood diary. She simply could not work out what had happened to it; she was sure it had been stowed in her bedside drawer. It didn't bear thinking what Elizabeth would say if Annie lost it.

She greeted the children in the hall with an offering of different coloured dasik biscuits, baked earlier that afternoon.

Grace dragged her bag over the tiles, gave Annie a peremptory embrace, fell on the dasik with a cry – she was *starving*, apparently – then disappeared to the kitchen, touching Issy's portrait on the way. 'Adam's mum said sorry she didn't stop to say hallo,' Grace called, through a mouthful of biscuit. 'She's got a meeting to go to.' Grace being hungry was a good omen.

Caleb was skulking in the hall, moving from foot to foot in that way he did when there was something on his mind.

'Okay? How was your week?' She offered the biscuits, but he shook his head.

'You know.'

'Not so much,' she coaxed. 'That's why I'm asking.'

'Bit shit.'

'Oh?' Her hand went to his arm. Perhaps she gripped a little tightly, because he pulled away.

'Can we not talk about it now?' He walked away to the kitchen, towards the sound of Grace unloading clothes into the washing machine. Hurt, Annie locked the front door and padded after him.

Rain was spotting the kitchen window. Grace was on her knees, head in the washing drum, Caleb leaning against the counter.

'Anyone want tea?' Annie asked. 'Another snack?'

Caleb's eyes flicked up, then back to his sister.

'Okay,' Annie set down the tray of dasik. 'What's going on?'

Grace pulled her head out of the drum. 'What d'you mean?'

'Is it school?'

'No,' Grace said, with a scowl at her brother. 'I just... I don't feel so good.' She was pale, it was true. There were circles beneath her eyes. Her usually shining hair looked lank and dry. How had Annie not noticed?

'Sweetheart, I think you might need a trip to the doctor,' Annie said.

'Granny says I'm just lacking vitamins. She's given me pills to help.'

Annie felt herself tighten. 'What? When did you speak to Granny?'

'On the phone last week.'

'You rang her? From school?'

'She rang *me*. To check I was okay. Or so she said.' At least Grace was still being snarky. She couldn't be that ill.

'What kind of pills?' Annie asked. How dare Elizabeth. She'd go over there in a minute and tell her. 'Can you show me?'

Grace went to her shoulder bag. She pulled out a small white plastic tub. 'Here you go. For energy, she said.'

Annie unscrewed the lid. Large brown capsules, a particularly yeasty smell. She held one between thumb and forefinger. 'Did she say what's in them?'

'Nope.'

Furious, Annie dropped the capsule back in the tub. 'She shouldn't prescribe pills without checking with me first.'

'That's what I said,' Caleb uttered under his breath. Grace frowned at him again.

'I'd like you to stop taking them,' Annie said. 'Okay?'

Grace nodded. 'No problem.'

'We'll take you to the doctor, the *actual* GP next week.' She touched Grace's hair. Grace seemed not to mind.

'I hope the doctor won't need to stick things in me.' Grace began loading the machine again.

'What if it's cancer?' Caleb asked.

Grace looked at him. 'Oh great. Thanks.'

Annie tried her best to smile. ''Course it's not cancer, Cal. Jesus. It'll turn out to be something very simple to fix, I'm sure. Try not to worry.'

Finished with the washing, Grace got to her feet. 'I'm not worried,' she said, and left the room.

Caleb took a glass to the sink and filled it with water. He downed it, washed it with the cloth and placed it upside down on the drainer.

Annie dropped her voice, 'Cal, I need to ask you something.' She heard him let out a sigh. 'What made you say Grace might be pregnant?'

'Oh fucking hell.'

'Please. Will you just tell me?'

'I don't know!' He leant against the fridge.

'Fine. I give up.' She stomped to the cupboard and began to make hot chocolate in a pan. When Caleb didn't move, she looked up to find his eyes fixed on the pan. 'Cal, I'm sorry,' she said. 'You don't have to know. You're only fifteen.' The milk began to bubble. 'I take it *you're* not on any of Granny's medications?'

This made him laugh. 'Definitely not.'

'So...' She must be careful now, not to push him away. 'What is it that's... shit? What's going on?'

His cheeks went crimson. 'I feel like a twat even saying it.'

'You could never be a twat to me.'

He stared out the window. 'A few kids at school have been saying stuff.'

She suddenly felt so fiercely protective, she didn't trust herself to speak.

'So... yeah.'

'Who exactly, and what about?'

Caleb shook his head. 'I can handle it.'

'No,' Annie insisted. 'I'm not having anyone hurting you, or your sister. Who's saying what to you?'

'Bunch of neeks from Ambleside. Because I'm from Colthwaite.' Caleb rolled his eyes. 'And a Dillane.'

'What's to laugh about that?'

'They say Colthwaite's the "Village of the Damned". They say everyone's...' He shifted. 'The people aren't quite right. That they're inbred.'

'Well.' She gazed at the cooker. 'That's not true. Obviously. And you're not from this village, Cal. You're from London.' She poured the chocolate into mugs.

'Hmm. But Mum was.' He took his mug and left the kitchen.

'Wait! I'll talk to the school!' she called after him.

'Please don't.' The sound of the back door opening.

Annie watched through the window as Caleb crossed the garden to the hut and let the pig out. The rain fell hard, and Caleb's hair went sleek against his head. Pomander sniffed at his feet; he patted her back. She could see he was talking to her. He put his mug down and placed a hand on Pomander's belly, as Annie had, feeling for the piglets' kick, while she slurped his hot chocolate. When he picked up his mug and found it empty, he laughed.

Annie went into the hall and stood in front of Issy's portrait. 'Can you believe your mother?' she said. 'And those Ambleside kids.' She threw on her coat and called upstairs, 'Grace! There's hot chocolate waiting in the kitchen, I'm just popping out.' No response.

Annie stalked through the darkness along the track, turned out of the gate and crossed the lane to Blea Crag. She had too much to cope with. It was going to break her. A horrible thought brought her to a standstill: what if Grace's tablets had been a prescription from Vincent? Quickening her pace, she reached her in-law's front door and rapped sharply.

No answer. She followed the wall along the side of the cottage, peering into the empty snug. A single lamp burned.

Colthwaite House was where they'd be. She looked at it in the distance, its windows glowing orange like a Halloween pumpkin. On the ground floor she made out two long silhouettes passing in front of a window. Fine, she'd go there then.

She stomped back to Chapel Croft and ordered the kids grab coats and torches. Grace, mug in hand, said she'd no wish to pay her uncle and cousins a visit, but caught Annie's face and did as she was told.

They pushed through the downpour. 'Why do we have to come?' Grace moaned.

'You just do.' She wanted the children with her as her excuse. And for reinforcement.

They reached the back door of Colthwaite House. Annie was about to ring the bell, when Grace put her hand out. 'This is about the pills, isn't it?'

Annie couldn't meet her eye. 'Well. It's a chance for you to see your cousins,' she said. The children looked at her. 'Okay, I might mention the pills.'

Grace stuck her chin out. 'Just make sure I'm not in the room when you do.'

'Me too,' Caleb echoed.

The bell tinkled prettily, the sound ringing away from them along the hall before returning a demi tone lower. Dogs barked and two wet noses pushed themselves through the letterbox from the inside. Footsteps, and the door flung open. It was Andrew and his brogues, glass of wine in hand, a roll-up hanging from his mouth.

'Oh,' he said. 'Lovely surprise!'

'Sorry to intrude,' Annie began. 'I was looking for Elizabeth.'

His smile faltered. 'Well, you've come to the right place. Hey, kids.' He rubbed Caleb's head, then walked away along the hall to the kitchen.

The children looked to her for instruction. 'I think we're meant to follow,' she offered.

Halfway down the hall, cousin-ish sounds from the TV room made the children peel off, leaving Annie by herself. Now she'd have to face Elizabeth alone.

The kitchen was damp and fuggy with smoke. Saucers overflowed with cigarette butts. William and Elizabeth sat on one side of the table, Carolina and Andrew on the other, two empty bottles of red between them. Annie stood awkwardly in the doorway.

'Annie!' William exclaimed when he caught sight of her. His eyes were glittering; she could tell he was tipsy. 'Have a seat.' He patted the chair next to him. 'Vino? Or something stronger? No soju, I'm afraid.'

'Goodness,' said Elizabeth. 'Whatever she's come about, it looks serious.'

'Sorry to barge in,' she began, although she wasn't really barging, was she. 'I wanted to...' Her body felt tiny in relation to the room. 'To ask a couple of questions. Of you, Elizabeth, if I may?'

Elizabeth pulled herself from the table, her face a picture, as if someone had told her the dog had been sick in the other room. 'By all means.' She came to stand beside Annie in the doorway. Andrew sunk a little in his chair.

'I believe you gave Grace some tablets,' Annie said. 'To help with her stomach?' Why did her mother-in-law have to be so tall.

'Yes.'

'I was wondering what's in them?'

Elizabeth's shoulders lifted. 'Vitamins. Didn't she tell you?'

'She did, but which ones?'

'Dicky gut.' Elizabeth revolved to pluck her glass from the table. 'Parasites are my suspicion.' She sipped, thoughtfully. 'Could have caught them from swine, though I don't imagine she's been spending time with any of those. Has she?'

'With a...?' Annie felt herself redden. 'Not to my knowledge.' She looked down, desperate for this to end, to see Issy's diary in her mother-in-law's hand.

'Ah.' Elizabeth held the book aloft. 'Yes. Now, I hope you don't mind. I sent Stephen to fetch it when you were out for an afternoon walk a day or so ago. You've had it a rather long time. I'm sure you understand that in the circumstances...' She made a sad face. 'Hate for it to go missing. Family memento.'

The old witch had sent Stephen to *steal* it, and now she was asking for Annie's pity. 'Stephen has a key to Chapel Croft?' Annie croaked. William's not insubstantial eyebrows shot up. The room had gone very quiet.

'Man's got a key to every house on the estate.' William put his enormous palms on the tabletop and pushed himself up. 'How d'you think m'wife left all that food for you back when you arrived? Now come on, Annie, what can we get you to drink?'

'I'm not staying, I...' Annie looked around, cheeks aflame. 'I'm sure you were only trying to help, but could you please ensure you don't give my stepdaughter medicine without checking with me first? Or enter my home without telling me,' she added.

Elizabeth's nose wrinkled. 'Of course.'

'Thank you,' Annie managed. 'Now I really must get back to Chapel Croft.'

Andrew half-stood. 'Perhaps... shall I see you out, or...?'

'No need.' Annie scurried along the hall.

'I think you've rather upset the old girl,' she heard William say.

Annie knocked on the door to the TV room and pushed it open. Five heads visible over the high back of the sofa, a seventies horror film playing loudly on the television in front of them. 'Guys, we're going.' No one paid Annie the slightest attention. 'Hallo?'

Grace leant around Caleb to address her cousins. 'Good, huh?'

'Sick,' the middle cousin said. 'Can I show them *Laurin*, Marcus?'

Marcus, the eldest, snatched up the remote and paused the film. 'They won't understand it, dickhead, it's in German.'

'I can speak German,' Caleb said. 'A bit.'

Grace sniggered. 'He can say, "naked", "I love you" and "blow job".'

'Guys!' Annie yelled. The children's heads swivelled and then five pairs of eyes were on her.

'What?' Grace demanded.

'I'm going. Are you coming?'

'We're in the middle of something.' Grace pointed to the TV, as if Annie might not have noticed. 'You go.'

'You'll make your own way home?'

'Yup.' Grace turned and settled back into the sofa. Caleb smiled apologetically.

One of Andrew's boys grabbed the remote. 'Come on then, show us the German one.' They guffawed at some unknown joke. Annie closed the door.

She stood in the hallway, watched by the family portraits that rose haughtily up the wall. Issy's children belonged here. They were blood and Annie merely water. Elizabeth had sent Stephen into her home. She had given her granddaughter vitamins – if that is what they truly were – without asking. The sheer gall, the entitlement. From the kitchen, brays of laughter. They thought she'd gone home.

The stairwell was right there. Annie made a snap decision. She limped to the first floor and along the corridor, then up the next flight to the attic. Seconds after that she was feeling under the pillow in the nursery, extracting the iron key, unlocking the chest, removing the first album, and placing it on her lap. If no one was going to tell her anything, she was going to find out for herself. If Elizabeth thought it okay to go poking about in Annie's house, well, two could play at that game.

She opened the album and nearly cried out in shock.

A photograph of a newborn baby girl – a human one, not a piglet – lying in an incubator. She was on her back, skin hot pink, arms and legs spatchcocked. Her head was covered by a cotton hat. Her tiny hand clasped the index finger of an anonymous adult to the left.

The writing beneath it said: *Penelope 5/12/66.*

Penelope Dillane: that was the name on the first headstone she'd seen in the graveyard. Blood pounding in her ears, she quickly turned the page.

The same child in a terry nappy on a bright patchwork quilt. The same pattern as the ones on the beds right next to Annie now, but new, unfaded. The girl had the Dillane's distinctive blue eyes. *Six months* read the caption. Could this have been Issy and Andrew's sister?

The next page read, *One year*. The girl, naked again, bowed legs, the same adult hand to the left of the picture. Tufts of blonde hair grew from the child's scalp, her body sturdy. A yellow dress embroidered with daisies.

Annie turned another page.

Nineteen months. The little girl naked in her cot, skin puffy and covered in rashes. The whites of her eyes had gone pink. Annie could tell from the scrunched-up face, the hands balled into fists, that the baby was in pain. She forced herself to the next page.

Twenty-two months 05/10/1968. The child lay on a gurney, her eyes closed, a white waffle blanket up to her neck. Her skin had gone grey. It was clear she was dead.

A baby had died tragically and had its photo taken and preserved in an album in a child's bedroom. A snake of revulsion coiled in Annie's stomach.

On the last page before the album went blank, there was a postcard: a painting of a beautiful semi-naked woman with red-blonde hair falling to her waist. She was standing in a field of flowers. Annie frowned. Carefully, she unpeeled the postcard from beneath the plastic and turned it over. *Astarte – c. 1887 by Edward Henry Corbould (watercolour)*

Feeling distinctly out of body, Annie returned the album to the chest. Six more albums waited beneath it. Her shaking fingers crept down the pile. The spine of the second read: *Flora Dillane 5/12/1971.* Oh God.

She didn't have the stomach for it.

She locked the chest, returned the key to beneath the pillow and, trembling, passed unseen down the two flights of stairs to the hall. Loud voices came from the kitchen. She hurried to the front door. Stumbling down the inky drive, battling the wind, Annie turned left towards home.

She limped up the track, the cold gusting into her mouth, let herself in the cottage and pushed her back against the door. From the wall, Issy stared.

She went into the living room with her phone and dialled a number. The line to her Hackney flat rang once before a man answered. He had a Scottish burr. Wincing at her own lies, Annie explained she was his landlady, that she'd had some bad news: her sister had been diagnosed with cancer, and that after everything that had happened with Issy, she and the family urgently needed to return to London, and the flat.

There was silence at the other end. 'I'm sorry about your sister. We've a newborn,' the man said. 'You know that, right?'

'I know. I'm so sorry to do this to you.'

'We can't just drop everything and... We have a six-month break clause. Can't you find somewhere else until April?'

'I'd prefer not to, for the kids' sakes.' She hoped by telling the lie she wasn't manifesting bad things on Lumi.

There was a pause.

'You'll need to go through the estate agent,' he said. 'And I'll need to speak to my wife.'

'Of course.'

The call ended. Annie fell onto the sofa, put her legs up.

Before she'd had time to even breathe out, her phone pinged. It was another email from Melissa at King's.

> Dear Annie,
>
> I've done a little digging and I was right. The asterisk after the names of the students who attended King's means those pupils did indeed belong to a society.
>
> In this instance, I believe it was one they began themselves; a collection of science undergrads who, from what I can see, conducted early genetic experiments on mice and tadpoles. The society's name was 'Astarte', and its chair was the student named Elizabeth Dillane.
>
> Unfortunately, the research conducted was preserved in analogue form and for the most part has been lost (or perhaps was taken with them when the students graduated). The protocol around the keeping of records was different in those days, as you can imagine! There is one small paper I found relating to 'Astarte' in our archives, which I have photographed and attached below.
>
> I hope this information assists you in your research.
>
> Melissa

Annie clicked on the attachment. It was ten-pages of the square font particular to early word-processors.

Astarte Team Attempt Recreation of Briggs, King et al's Experiment on Cell Replication in Tadpole Embryos.

Reams of incomprehensible – to Annie, at least – research literature followed. Photographs of numbered petri dishes containing black dots. A separate photo of a fully formed tadpole. The research paper concluded with a paragraph of jargon and the names of the students involved: *Dillane, Prime, Paine, Swifton, Carey, Bell.*

Annie sat up, her eyes widening. These were the very names on the girls' headstones. Tadpoles had been their subjects, and then pigs, she felt sure. It wasn't possible that they had also tried things with their babies, was it? What about the things the woman at the museum had told her?

And now Grace was being fed 'vitamins' by Elizabeth. Issy couldn't have known anything about any of this, or she would have...

Annie got to her feet and hurried upstairs. The kids were at the Big House. And Issy's 'story' given to her by Elizabeth, the one Annie still hadn't had a look at, was inside Grace's room. Which was right there in front of her. A draft blew through the gap beneath the door. Annie pushed it open.

She clicked on the side lamp. Her stepdaughter's belongings were strewn across the bed: clothes, headphones, tampons, toiletries, a couple of paperbacks. She rifled through the open suitcase. The folder was there. She pulled it out.

A thin collection of crisp exercise paper, the school sort, hole-punched and slotted into the folder's narrow ring binder. A large circle, drawn by hand. Eight little stick-girls were lined up inside the circle holding hands. Six were equal in height, a yellow pencil line representing their shoulder-length hair, blue triangles representing skirts. Two were smaller, wearing baby caps and nappies, and had been given fat bellies and stubby little legs. These two littlest illustrations had a single diagonal line scored through their torsos in red felt tip.

Underneath, in childish script, Issy had written:

The Eye of God, a story by Isabelle Dillane, aged 11.

She turned the page.

Once upon a time in a little village in the North, there lived 8 little girls dressed in 8 pretty dresses of blue cotton. The girls were special because, the day they were born, God had played hide and seek with their mother, Astarte, for two hole Earth minutes, which blessed them and made them special in His eyes...'

Annie could feel herself losing shape.

'... In fact, He loved the little girls so much, he created them exactly alike and promised Astarte they would live forever.

But this was a fickle god, changing his mind at the drop of a (sun) hat, leaving Astarte and her subjects alone for weeks at

a time, until the little girls would know they
had to prove to Him they served only His will,
that He should return so they could show him
they deserved a life beneath His almighty lite.
The girls must never disobey or anger Him, lest
He smote them and make them only 7, or 6, or
none at all.

His older subjects promised they would keep
these special girls safe. But one day, thinking
they could be of even greater service, they

Annie turned another page. That was it. One short, terrifying fragment.

Elizabeth had thought it a good idea to hand this to her granddaughter? Annie read it again. She returned the folder to the suitcase exactly as she'd found it.

A fresh and horrible thought occurred to her: the kids were on their own at the Big House. With their cousins, but still. What if they were invited to stay the night? What if they were... she could hardly formulate the words – *drugged, indoctrinated, harmed.* She tried their phones; they didn't answer. She'd go and fetch them, bring them home. No, that might look suspicious.

She paced the hallway, panicked, confused as to what to do. She'd stay awake until they returned. If they weren't home in an hour, she'd head back over there.

She dialled Lumi's number, but her sister didn't answer. She left her a message: they were coming to stay after all, Annie explained, thank you, it wouldn't be for long. They'd be leaving Colthwaite in the next two days.

Lumi had better be okay with it. She'd been the one to offer, after all. It would mean pulling the kids out of school without notice, but so what. She'd tell them at breakfast.

She sat on the edge of her bed and waited. Every five minutes, she checked the time. She googled 'Astarte'. It was as Vincent had said, she was an ancient goddess of fertility, Assyrian origins, possibly the inspiration for Christian Easter. The glow from the screen hurt her eyes. She threw the phone onto the bed.

Forty minutes later, to her intense relief, she heard Caleb and Grace let themselves in. Their feet padded up the stairs, then there was whispering in the hallway that she couldn't make out and a click as their bedroom doors closed, one then the other. For the first time in hours, Annie felt her body soften. They were getting out of here, soon as they could.

CHAPTER THIRTEEN

Monday morning and Annie was in the car again, this time with Grace, but they weren't on their way to school: Grace had been in so much pain at breakfast that Annie announced she'd take Grace to the doctor right now, abandoning any plans of telling the kids about leaving Colthwaite. The emergency left them all in a state of confusion; she'd had to let Caleb go to school for the week in Andrew's car. Ignoring Andrew's recommendation to visit the surgery at Gillyhead – she didn't trust anyone within a five-mile radius of Colthwaite – she chose Kenworth's GP practice instead, twelve miles away. 'Lack of available doctors' would be her excuse if anyone asked why.

'All right, sweetheart?' Annie tried not to race along the lanes. Perhaps they should be heading to A&E. But that seemed a bit dramatic, and it would no doubt be a five hour wait to be seen.

Kenworth GP surgery was in a small terrace of listing houses off a depressed high street, the salmon-coloured waiting room occupied by three old women with walking sticks. She and Grace waited in silence as the old ladies hobbled, one at a time, to the practice room.

Dr Brace was a thin business-like woman in her mid-sixties. She invited Grace onto the couch and slid Grace's top over her chest as Annie waited on a chair by the desk. She palpated Grace's tummy, looking not at Grace but at the wall in front of her. 'You're sexually active?'

'No,' Grace responded with a glance at Annie. She jumped as the doctor hit a tender spot.

'Sorry. You can pull your top down now.' Dr Brace looked at Grace over her glasses. 'Is there anything you feel you'd like to discuss in private?'

Grace looked at her blankly. 'How d'you mean?'

'Would you prefer if your mother wasn't in the room?'

'She's not my mother,' Grace said quickly. 'She's my stepmum.'

Dr Brace peeled off her gloves and dropped them in the bin. 'I'd like you to take a pregnancy test.'

'Oh!' Annie squeaked, and Grace said, 'Why?'

The doctor gave Grace a look.

'But I've never had sex,' Grace insisted.

'Be that as it may, we need to rule it out.' She handed Grace a sample pot with a smile. 'Bathroom's at the end of the corridor.'

'But–'

'Please, Gracie,' Annie begged. 'Just do as she says.'

Grace went out. Dr Brace typed things into her computer. Annie squashed her hands beneath her thighs and looked around. A painting of a beach and a photo of two small children hung on the wall above the doctor's head.

'My grandchildren,' the doctor explained without looking up.

'Right.'

Grace returned red-faced. Dr Brace unscrewed the lid on

the urine pot and dropped in a dipstick. Annie found Grace's hand and held it.

'Here we are.' Dr Brace pulled the dipstick out. She frowned, her mouth slightly open.

'What?' Grace demanded.

'You are, it appears, pregnant.'

Grace let Annie's hand drop. '*What?*' She leaned so far forwards in her chair, she almost fell out of it. 'That's impossible! I've never had sex, I'm telling you!' She was up on her feet now, looking to Annie. 'You have to believe me!'

'Hey.' Annie took hold of Grace's arm. 'It's okay.'

'No, it isn't!' Grace drummed her stomach with her fists. 'It's wrong! The test is *wrong*. I want to do another.'

'It's unlikely that it's wrong,' Dr Brace replied blandly. 'I understand this sort of news can be a shock. You *do* have options. It really is going to be all right.'

'Can't she take another test?' Annie asked.

'By all means.' The doctor handed Grace another pot. Grace almost sprinted from the room.

'I don't understand,' Annie said, though she did.

Dr Brace shook her head and smiled. 'If I had a penny for every time this happens.'

'Really?'

Grace came back with the second sample. The doctor dropped a dipstick in. They waited in silence. Annie tried not to look at Grace.

Positive.

Grace groaned.

'Please try not to worry,' Dr Brace said. 'It's nothing to be ashamed of.'

'I think...' Annie said. But she didn't know what she thought.

Grace crossed her arms. 'I'm a virgin.'

'Take some time,' Dr Brace went on. 'Go home, think it over. I can pass on the names of local clinics, if that's what you decide.' She looked at Annie. 'And a counsellor, perhaps?'

'What about the tummy aches?' Annie asked.

'Not unusual. Do you feel nauseous?' she asked. Grace shook her head. 'Well, if the aches continue beyond seven days, call the practice and I'll see you again. Depending on your decision of course, Grace, we'll do a scan and go from there.'

She handed Grace a leaflet: *I'm Pregnant, What Shall I Do?* A young girl with long brown hair and a frightened expression on the front.

Annie thought of something. 'Can I just ask...' She drew Elizabeth's vitamin pot from her bag and placed it on the desk. 'Aside from possible pregnancy, is there any chance Grace's aches could be caused by these?'

The doctor frowned. 'These are...?'

'I don't know. Grace's granny prescribed them. She says they're vitamins.'

'Prescribed them?' Dr Brace squinted at the tub. 'She's a medical doctor?'

'A vet,' Annie and Grace stated in unison.

The doctor picked the tub up and turned it in her hands. 'Why isn't there a label?'

Annie shook her head. 'That's what I was wondering.'

The doctor opened the tub and sniffed. She eyeballed Grace. 'You must never take medicines without a label.'

Grace shrugged. 'I only took them for a short–'

'It's not Grace's fault,' Annie said. 'Her granny seemed to think Grace might have parasites.'

Dr Brace snorted. 'Well, now we know Granny was wrong.'

Annie got to her feet. 'Come on, sweetheart.' She took Grace's arm and guided her to the door. 'Thank you, doctor. We'll be in touch.'

They drove home in silence, Grace glowering out the window. Annie parked outside the cottage. She didn't know what to say, how to make it better. Grace leapt from the car and ran inside. Annie stayed outside, opened the car door and let the wind blow across her face.

In the cottage she found Grace face down on the bed, crying.

'My love.' Annie sat next to her. 'It's okay. It happens.'

'How would you know?' Grace asked miserably.

'We'll deal with it. Was it Adam?'

'Oh my *God!*' Grace pulled her face from the covers. 'How many *times*? I haven't had sex! Ever!'

Annie looked away. Grace was being horrible, but it was a horrible situation. Annie wasn't trained for this. It should have been Issy's job. She tried again. 'You know that's not possible if you are, in fact, pregnant?'

Those big eyes. 'It *is* possible, because I'm telling the truth!'

Was Grace a liar? What about Dougal-Douglas? And how pregnant was she? 'Could you have gone out in London before we left,' Annie asked gently. 'Say, with friends and then had a blank evening, forgotten what happened to you, and–'

Grace's eyebrows drew together. 'Was I *roofied*? Don't be ridiculous! I'm not stupid; I literally never leave my drink unattended.' Her mouth clamped shut, then opened to add something, but was interrupted by another spasm of pain and she folded in half, arms clutched around her stomach.

'Grace?'

'What's *happening*?'

'Oh shit. I'll get you a drink and a hot water bottle. Back in a sec.'

Annie hobbled downstairs and found the brandy. She poured a fat slug into two glasses. She filled the kettle.

There was a scream from upstairs. 'Annie!'

Annie flew back up the stairs. Grace was hopping about on the landing, her skirt around her ankles. There was blood tracking her thighs, her feet, and hands.

'Oh my God!' Feeling faint, Annie dragged Grace to the bathroom, scrabbling for towels. 'It's okay. It's gonna be okay. Lie on your side.'

Grace did as she was told. She'd gone quiet now, floppy. Her lips looked white. Annie stuffed the towels in between Grace's thighs, pulled out her phone and dialled 999.

'Ambulance, please. I think my stepdaughter's having a... a miscarriage. *How* long? Can't it be quicker than that?'

'How long?' Grace croaked, eyes rolling back.

'Half an hour. We'll be okay. I'll–'

Grace groaned as another wave engulfed her.

A knock at the door. 'Wait there. Don't move!' She ran downstairs.

It was Elizabeth, in wellingtons, medical bag in hand. 'Annie dear, we've a troublesome Tup to neuter, and I was wondering if I could... Is everything all right?'

'No,' Annie panted. 'It's Grace. She's–'

But Elizabeth was already in the house. 'It's okay. Where is she? What's wrong with her?' Her manner was calm yet commanding. It made Annie feel slightly less hysterical.

'In the bathroom,' she said weakly. 'I don't know what's wrong. A miscarriage?' Elizabeth was at the top of the stairwell now, tapping something on her phone.

'It's all right, Grace,' Elizabeth was saying in a loud voice. 'We'll sort this. You'll be right as rain in no time.'

'I've phoned for an ambulance,' Annie said, running into the bathroom behind her.

'Oh dear, I texted the local paramedics too,' replied Elizabeth. 'But perhaps they'll only send one vehicle?'

Together they moved Grace onto the bed in Annie's room,

laying towels beneath her. Elizabeth instructed Annie to fetch a bowl of warm water. Annie returned with the bowl. Her mother-in-law requested Annie leave the room. 'I'd like to stay.' Annie looked at Grace.

'If you wouldn't mind?' Elizabeth sounded impatient. 'More dignified for all concerned.'

'It's fine,' Grace said. 'Honestly, Annie.'

Ultimately, it was Grace's decision. It was her body, and she was almost an adult. Reluctantly, Annie left them to it.

She waited on the sofa in the living room, legs jiggling with nerves. She'd already sunk both glasses of brandy. At the slightest sound, she was up on her feet at the bottom of the stairwell. Twenty minutes passed. Finally, an ambulance arrived. It was the small kind, the size of an estate car. Two paramedics in green hurried up the stairs, packs on their backs, an oxygen canister in hand. Elizabeth was out on the landing to greet them. 'Pauline! Greg!'

'Elizabeth. How do?' The medics seemed unsurprised to find Elizabeth already on the scene. The door to Annie's room where Grace lay, was closed. Annie wanted to go in and check on her, but everyone else was in the way.

'Thank you for coming,' Elizabeth was saying, 'though really, not necessary after all. She's stable. Very early miscarriage, I'm afraid: four or five weeks. I've given her a small dose of misoprostol just to be safe, and two milligrams of diazepam.'

The paramedics nodded. After a quick glance at Annie, they said they'd double-check Grace's vitals. Elizabeth led them into the room, leaving Annie alone again.

They shouldn't shut her out. It was *her* house. Grace was *her* stepdaughter. And why hadn't Elizabeth seemed more surprised when she'd arrived and Annie told her Grace was having a miscarriage? And how did Elizabeth already know the age of the foetus? Could she tell just by looking at Grace?

Annie crept to the door, listened, turned the handle. Grace lay on the bed, legs apart, the paramedics and Elizabeth bent over her. The medic, Pauline, glanced over her shoulder at the sound of the door opening, frowned, made a shooing motion.

Annie retreated from the room, listening to the mumble of voices. Five minutes later, they reappeared. 'How's she doing?' she asked. 'Can I see her?'

'She's sleeping,' said Elizabeth, a tad breezily. 'We've given her a sedative.'

'Don't worry, Miss Park,' the paramedic named Greg said. 'She's doing well. She's to take the anti-inflammatories we've left on the bedside table and have forty-eight hours complete rest.'

'Book her in for a sweep at the hospital in a couple of days,' added Pauline.

Annie frowned. 'Two days? But shouldn't she go in now? To... check? To be safe?'

'No need. Your mother-in-law has done a solid job. It's nicer for the young ones, in general, if things aren't medicalised at this stage, unless necessary. Traumatic losing a little 'un.'

'Yes,' Annie agreed. Elizabeth gave her a look. 'I can only imagine.'

'Thank you, Pauline, thank you, Greg. I'll take it from here.' Elizabeth returned to the bedroom and Grace, the door closing firmly behind her.

Annie ran downstairs after the paramedics. 'So is that it, then? Nothing else we need to do?'

Greg laid his hand on the newel post. ''Owt else you'd *like* us to do?'

'It's just...' Annie dropped her voice. 'Grace insists she's never had intercourse, and I'm inclined to believe her.' The words sounded ridiculous, even to her own ears. 'Though unless she's Mary Magdalene, I mean...'

They didn't laugh. If anything, their expressions grew serious. 'Has Grace ever left her drink unattended?' asked Pauline. 'Has she had any evenings out she can't remember in the last five weeks?'

'Not to my knowledge. I did ask her.'

'Good.'

'Teenagers can be tricky,' added Greg. 'Got three of my own. Good luck.' They let themselves out the front door.

Annie went back to the landing outside the bedroom. 'Everything okay in there?'

'Just cleaning up.' Elizabeth emerged with a small metal bowl covered with a tea towel and several bloodied bath towels. 'These are for the wash, or the bin, not sure which. Sorry.'

Annie pointed at the bowl. 'Is that...?'

Elizabeth patted her arm. 'Some things are better left to the professionals. No disrespect.'

'Thank you for everything,' she managed. 'I don't know what we would have done if you hadn't turned up like that.'

'All in a day's work.' Elizabeth handed over the towels, collected her things and left. Annie let herself into the bedroom at last. Grace was fast asleep.

The room was clean, tidy, with no indication of a medical emergency. Annie perched on the edge of the bed and took Grace's hand, studying her face fondly. It was relaxed, the covers drawn snugly over her shoulders.

Four to five weeks pregnant? So could it have been a boy from London? And if so, who?

Annie sighed and looked away, but her gaze caught on something. On the bedside table next to Annie's alarm clock was a small squat, wide-hipped statuette: *Astarte*. Elizabeth must have put her there. Annie picked her up, turning the wooden woman in her hands. 'What are you doing here, then?' Its little eyes stared back.

She didn't want it in her house. What if Grace woke, saw it, and freaked out. The poor girl had enough on her plate already.

Swiftly, Annie hid it in her bedside drawer. She hoped that in doing so, she wouldn't bring Grace bad luck. Or at least, more bad luck.

The sound of a heavy vehicle coming up the drive, then the slow crunch of wheels as it parked. A second later the doorbell rang. Annie went downstairs.

Another ambulance. A proper big thing with flashing blue lights. Two different paramedics hopped out of the cab.

'Annie Park?' Confused, Annie stared at them both before working out what had happened.

'I'm so sorry,' Annie said. 'My mother-in-law and I both called for an ambulance at the same time. We've had two of your guys here already. They've been and gone.'

The medics looked at her in surprise. 'Who could that have been, then?'

'Oh,' Annie said. 'Greg and Pauline?'

'The Gillyhead lot? Why were *they* called? They're not Majors.'

The second paramedic sighed. 'They're closer, I suppose, but they don't have all the gear in that tiny thing. I'll talk to dispatch. No matter, anyway, long as everything's all right. She didn't need admitting, then? Need us to check her over?'

Annie shook her head. 'She's fine. Sleeping.'

'Right then.' He produced a rueful smile. 'Longer tea break for us.'

'That it is.' The other one saluted. They bid their goodbyes and drove off.

Annie went inside. She hovered in the hall. Gillyhead? Something else that didn't sit right. She pulled out her phone.

She should probably call Patrick, Grace was his daughter, after all. Plus, he was medical. Perhaps he might have wisdom to share.

'Annie, I'm glad you called! What a terrible thing.' He was at his London hospital. It turned out he'd already been told about Grace – by Elizabeth, minutes before.

Furious, she was about to mention the vitamin pills when Patrick said, 'Elizabeth asked me to come up. Grace'll need all the support we can offer in the next few days.'

'Elizabeth asked you?'

'I shan't impose; you've enough to worry about. I'll stay with Andrew at the Big House.'

The thought of them all sitting around drinking wine made her want to scream, but at least he wouldn't be in her space.

'The day after tomorrow's the best I can negotiate with work,' he said.

'Great.'

'I'll see you Wednesday, then.'

'See you Wednesday.'

She went to check on Grace again. Finding her still fast asleep, she headed out the back to Pomander. Patting the pig's hairy head, she thought things over. Grace needed time to rest and to recover. There was no question that Annie could ask the kids to up sticks and leave now. They'd wait a few days. It would give time for things to calm down. It was okay; they'd be okay.

She went back into the house, feeling uneasy, up to the bedroom to keep watch over her sleeping stepdaughter. She looked so peaceful, lying there.

Grace felt a little better the next day. She was about as enthusiastic as Annie when she learned of Patrick's visit.

'He doesn't care,' she moaned. 'It's not real. It's all for show.'

Annie tried but failed to disagree. It was kind of nice being united in dislike. They spent large portions of the next day watching horror movies together: Grace insisted scary films put life into context. Annie was just relieved Grace was out of bed and chatty. She even held Annie's hand through a particularly frightening bit, hiding her face in the sofa.

Lumi messaged Annie that afternoon saying yes, of course they could stay, and which day were they coming and for how long? Annie replied thank you, that she didn't know the exact answer yet, something had come up. She didn't want to mention Grace's pregnancy to her sister. It was private, a family matter. Annie's family.

Annie went out at dawn the next morning. She wanted to clear her head. Patrick would be arriving today; she must prepare. But it was hard to think because of the irritating buzz of a chainsaw coming from a field over the way. She'd only gone five hundred yards when the growl of a vintage Mercedes could be heard crossing the bridge behind her at end of the village: Patrick's car. Already. Damn. She tucked herself into the verge and waited.

He waved at her from behind the windscreen, the Mercedes' soggy suspension absorbing every bump. When he drew level, he wound the window down, smiling too broadly, she thought, for a visit of this nature. 'Good morning!'

'Hi.'

'Taking a constitutional?'

She frowned. 'Not really.'

'Gracie at Chapel Croft?'

'Uh-huh.' Annie drew her hand across her forehead. 'You've overshot.'

'Right. Yes, I was going to drop my stuff off at the Big House, but if you're out for a walk, I'll take advantage of the element of surprise and wake sleeping beauty myself.'

'It might scare Grace being woken by someone she's not expecting.'

'Not expecting? Have you told her I'm coming?'

'Of course I have.'

'Well then.' He beat his hand three times against the steering wheel, then once more to even things up, then another four times. Annie waited for the OCD flare to pass. 'See you back at the ranch!' He revved hard and reversed along the lane.

She watched him moving away from her. The thought of Grace waking to find a large male figure standing in her room made Annie race back after him. 'Wait!'

He'd beaten her, his voice audible upstairs as she came through the door. She hurried up to Grace's room to find him with a hand on Grace's head, and the other around his mobile.

'Much better!' Grace was saying into Patrick's phone. She looked up at Annie and smiled grimly.

'That's so good!' It was Caleb, on loudspeaker. 'I'm heading into the basement to change for fucking hockey. Catch you later.'

'Later!'

The call ended. Annie approached Grace. 'You okay, sweetheart?'

'Yes, ma'am.'

Annie knew that was code for 'help'.

Patrick turned to Annie. 'So, how've you been coping?' He seemed almost too relaxed, one leg on the bed. 'Must be exhausted?'

'I'm okay.'

'But you could do with a break?'

'Not really.'

Patrick began to fold Grace's clothes, the ones she'd abandoned on the floor. Grace looked annoyed but didn't tell him to stop. 'Dad said he can take me to the hospital this morning for the check-up,' she told Annie through gritted teeth.

'Oh,' Annie said. 'Is that what you…? We can travel in one car.'

'No need,' said Patrick. 'One parent is enough. You have a rest.'

'Thanks, but I'd like to be there,' she said.

'Annie.' Patrick smiled. 'I'm a doctor. You rest.'

'And I'm her legal guardian, with respect. I don't need a rest.'

She watched as he laid Grace's socks out, one by one, in the wrong drawer. 'As you please.' Once he'd finished, he picked up one of Grace's dresses from the floor. 'This is nice. Is it for the eclipse festival?'

'What?' Grace squinted at him. 'I don't know.'

'Maybe Grace needs some extra zeds?' Annie suggested as she made for the door. 'We'll be leaving for the hospital in half an hour.'

Patrick caught up with her in the kitchen as she bashed coffee grounds into the bin. He perched on a stool and thrummed his fingers against the counter. 'Tough times.'

She didn't answer.

'Is that a pig's head I spy poking out of that hut?' His eyes were fixed on the window. This was all she needed.

'Uh-huh. She's a runaway,' she said, lightly as she could.

'One of Lizzy and… Elizabeth and William's?'

'Yeah.'

'What's she doing here?'

'No idea.' She wasn't fucking telling him.

'Bet the kids have given her a name.'

Annie looked up, surprised he'd got that right. 'Yes, Pomander. Because of her smell.'

Patrick laughed and repeated, 'Pomander,' twice under his breath. She wondered if he'd ever had help for his disorder. Did it put his patients off?

He went close to the window. 'How did she come to be camping here in your garden?'

Annie filled the coffee pot and put it on to boil. 'She just turned up. I gave her shelter.'

'How long has she been here?' His nose was right against the glass. The coffee began to gurgle. Annie switched off the gas.

'A while.'

'She might be pregnant,' he said.

Annie tried to look surprised. 'Might she?'

'Yes, if they're hiding out, nesting. If she is, you know they generally need a bit of help with farrowing? With the–'

'–I know what farrowing means,' she snapped.

Patrick sighed. 'Help from a vet. Especially if it's their first time.'

Annie kept her lips firmly shut and poured coffee into two cups.

'When's she due?' he pressed.

'Don't know.'

Patrick tutted, then tutted a second time. She wanted to throw the cup at him. Her mobile rang. She wouldn't answer if it was Caleb, because he might be calling to bitch about his dad. But it was her old number, from her flat in Hackney. 'Excuse me.' She hurried out the kitchen to the living room and closed the door.

'We can't do anything before the six-month mark, I'm

afraid,' her tenant announced without preamble when she answered. 'As it is, we'd be staying with Wumi's parents for the rest of the year.'

A thrill of relief travelled through her. 'So that's April 10th, yes?'

'Yup.' His fury travelled into her ear.

'Thank you. I'll instruct the estate agents tomorrow. I'm really sor–'

'You're welcome.' He rang off.

April. Five months was a long time to stay at Lumi's, but it was better than here. Safer. She threw another log into the wood burner. Patrick snuck his head around the door.

'Everything okay?'

'Uh-huh.'

'Sure?'

'Time for the hospital,' she said, then called for Grace to get her clothes on.

CHAPTER FOURTEEN

Like all hospitals in the UK, Ullerforth General was roasting, busy, and over-lit. Patrick, Grace, and Annie sat on plastic chairs in the waiting area.

It was the smell that did it. Reminding her of that day. The small white room.

'Grace Dillane?' called a nurse from a pair of double doors, a sign, *Women's Health*, on the wall above her.

'Want me to come with you?' Annie asked. Grace shook her head, the scent of doom coming off her as she trudged towards the nurse, the doors swinging closed behind her.

Annie turned to Patrick. 'I hope she's all right.'

'She'll be fine.' Annie watched as he rifled through the tatty magazines on the side table. How could he concentrate? Was he aware he was tapping everything? He leant back in his chair. 'Try not to worry,' he said.

'I am worried.'

Just before they'd left Colthwaite, Patrick had whizzed over to the Big House to drop his stuff off and returned smelling of cigarettes. Perhaps the passive kind. Whatever. She wouldn't *worry* about it. 'Can we talk about how this could have happened?' she asked him.

Patrick chuckled.

'I'm amazed you think this is funny, Patrick.'

His smile disappeared. 'I think we all know *how*. The question is more *who*.'

'Or what if her drink was spiked?'

'Not a chance. Gracie's too smart for that.' Like he would know. 'I'd lay money on that boy, Donald. The one she was seeing back in London.'

Donald. Not Dougal. Not Douglas. *Donald.* How could she take care of Grace when she couldn't even remember basic info like this? 'I'm going for a pee.' She limped towards the sign for the scrubby toilet.

She washed her hands in the sink – they were out of soap and hand towels, of course. The mirror was a flat slice of smeared metal. 'Pull yourself together,' she told the fuzzy blob staring back at her.

When she returned to the waiting area, Patrick had gone. Annie looked up and down the corridor. She sat in her chair. He'd probably made a trip to the bathroom.

Ten minutes passed; still no Patrick. She wondered if he might be frantically washing and re-washing his hands. She got up and approached the reception desk. 'Excuse me, d'you happen to know where the guy who was with me went? Dark hair, late fifties?'

'Doctor Cook?'

'Oh.' Annie faltered. 'You know he's a…?'

The nurse lifted the paper register on the counter. He'd signed himself in as *Dr Cook.* 'Ah, right.'

'He went with Dr Dillane.'

'Elizabeth Dillane?'

The nurse held up the register again wearily: *Dr Elizabeth*

Dillane. Annie recognised her mother-in-law's handwriting. 'When did she arrive?'

''Bout five minutes ago.'

'Where did they go?'

The nurse pointed at the double doors through which Grace had disappeared. 'Thanks,' Annie said.

A long, empty corridor, more doors leading right and left. The corridor took a sharp turn ahead. From around the corner, low voices: Patrick's, Elizabeth's, and another woman's. Annie crept forwards, head turned sideways to better catch their conversation.

'But she's fine?' Patrick was saying.

'Well,' said the mystery woman; Annie assumed the consultant. 'There was some residual tissue we cleared under local but otherwise unremarkable. Apart – as I was about to say – from–'

Elizabeth's tinkling laugh cut her off. 'The benefits of youth. And now if you please, could we take her home?'

'There is one thing,' the consultant insisted, her volume dropping further. 'The tissue we collected, it was rather... unusual.'

Patrick said, 'Oh?' twice.

'How can I put this? It was abnormally fibrous. I'm sure it's nothing, but given that your daughter was adamant she'd never had intercourse, we've taken it to the lab for histology.'

'You're aware she's on medication?' Elizabeth's voice again, sharp now.

Annie stiffened.

'I wasn't aware, no,' the consultant said. 'That information wasn't on her notes.'

'Well, it should have been,' snapped Elizabeth. 'She's had endometriosis since she was fourteen. The poor girl has already undergone two laparoscopies and a laparotomy.'

That wasn't true. Was it?

'She's been on high-dose oestradiol for years,' finished Elizabeth.

That definitely wasn't true; Annie would have known.

The consultant said something about adding this detail to Grace's file. There was movement, the squeak of rubber soles on lino.

Annie scuttled through the double doors to the waiting area and dumped herself back in the plastic chair. Would she have known if Grace was on hormones? Perhaps Issy kept it from her, along with all the other things it was looking more and more likely she'd been hiding. She pulled out her phone and pretended to look at it. Patrick and Elizabeth came back and put themselves either side of Annie. She lifted her head, feigning abstraction. 'Oh hi.'

'Sorry to intrude,' Elizabeth said. 'I arrived when you were in the lav. I thought as I'd been first on the scene, I might have useful info for the doc.'

'*I* was first on the scene,' Annie observed.

'You know what I mean.' Elizabeth bent to tie her shoelace. 'Patch and I went for a medical chat with the on-call obstetrician.' A smart-looking gold pen rolled noiselessly from her mother-in-law's jacket pocket onto the floor. Annie picked it up and went to hand it back, but Elizabeth was preoccupied.

'The procedure went well,' her mother-in-law was saying. 'No cause for concern. She'll be discharged later. That'll be that.'

'Nothing unusual then?' Annie asked. 'Nothing abnormal?'

'Nothing,' replied Elizabeth.

Annie went back to her phone. 'You guys head off. I'm happy to wait.' She could feel the two of them staring at one another over her head.

'Actually, Annie,' Patrick said, 'Grace asked if *I* could wait.

You two can go. She said not to worry about saying goodbye, she'll see you at home.'

'Even so,' Annie was unmoving, 'I'll wait.'

'Annie.' Patrick put a hand on her arm, took it off, re-laid it. 'Grace said she'd rather it was me, and me alone. I'm sorry.'

'Be that as it may,' she said sweetly, 'you don't have a car.'

'I can wait and drive them both back,' Elizabeth offered.

Annie rose from her chair. 'Let's find out from Grace, shall we? I'll go and speak to her.'

Elizabeth stood quickly. 'That's really not a good idea. The consultant's still finishing her checks, and we should respect Grace's wishes. And you're under a great deal of pressure, Annie dear. You should rest. Here's the obstetrician now, look.'

A woman in a white coat walked hurriedly out of the 'Women's Health' doors towards a different set of doors. Annie went after her.

'Hi! I believe you're treating Grace Dillane? I'm Annie Park.' The consultant seemed confused. 'Her legal guardian,' Annie added, pointing at Elizabeth and Patrick.

'Ah, I see; I thought–'

'Is everything okay? Was there anything...' Annie dropped her voice, '...unusual about what you found?'

The consultant's eyes flicked to Elizabeth. 'Well–'

'*Code Red Dr Bahran to N.I.C.U.*' Boomed a voice over the tannoy. '*Code Red Dr Bahran to–*'

'So sorry.' The consultant ran towards the doors. 'I have to...'

Annie watched her go, then headed back to the others. 'Dr Bahran said to wait,' she lied. 'She'll speak to me when she returns.'

Elizabeth nodded. 'As you wish.'

Annie sat herself back down between the two of them. Perhaps oestradiol had been the ingredient in Elizabeth's 'vitamin' pills for Grace. Annie felt sick at the thought. She should have left the tub with the GP, asked to get the pills tested.

Ten minutes passed. Elizabeth flipped through a dog-eared travel magazine until her phone rang loudly in the sterile waiting area. She answered. Annie could hear William bellowing at the other end. 'Really? Oh dear.' Her mother-in-law turned to Annie; an eyebrow raised. 'Well hang on, you can tell her yourself, she's right here.' She held the handset out. 'It's Willy. For you.'

Annie put the phone to her ear. 'Hallo?'

'Sorry to bother you, old girl, but there's smoke coming out of your living-room window.'

Annie jumped up. 'What?'

'Stay calm, it's just a wisp. But perhaps you might want to get back here? Either you or Patch or Gracie must have left the fire burning without closing the door. Bit of ember on the carpet, maybe? D'you want me to break in and douse it?'

'Break in?' Annie looked around wildly. 'What about Andrew? Or Stephen? He has keys!'

'Can't find him,' William said. 'I think you'd better come ASAP.'

'But–'

'I'll break the lock on the door.'

'No!'

'Listen, old girl, don't be a ninny. Your house is on fire. Grace will be fine; you can go back to the hospital after.'

'Okay.' She threw the phone to Elizabeth and bundled her things up.

'Try not to fret,' Elizabeth said. 'Grace is in safe hands.'

Annie wasn't sure of that at all. 'Don't do anything!' she couldn't help saying as she hurried to the exit. 'I'll be back very soon!' She barged her way through the revolving doors and jumped into the car.

Who'd been last out of the house when they'd left? It had been her, Annie. That effing wood burner. It was all her fault. She was driving too fast again. She'd not even noticed the pain in her leg for hours. What if it hadn't been her? But they would never... Would they?

The journey took no time. The car squealed to a halt in front of the cottage. William was there with his quad bike, a trailer, the dogs, and one of Andrew's sons. There was also Stephen and his buggy. The front door looked fine. The smell of woodsmoke and burnt carpet drifted on the air.

'Emergency averted!' William called, as Annie hurried towards him. 'The wood burner door, as suspected. Stephen saved the day. No damage to anything else, at least.'

Stephen held up his keys. 'Lucky escape. Nasty burn in your seagrass, mind.'

'Oh God.' Annie surveyed the scene through the window. The room was filled with curls of smoke. There was a large black circle of carpet in front of the burner. 'Thank you so much. It was my fault. I keep leaving the thing open.'

'Rookie's mistake,' William said. He whacked Andrew's son on the back. 'Good job Marcus and I were around. We were off to Lenner's field with a Tup when he saw the plume rising.'

'So lucky,' Annie said. 'Thanks again.'

She would go inside, inspect the damage and get the hell back to the hospital. She hoped Andrew wouldn't be too annoyed: he owned the cottage, after all. She made for the hall, but the others followed behind.

'I used the bucket from under the sink,' Stephen was saying. 'Hope you don't mind.'

The living room smelt of damp charred straw. They all stood around the burnt patch. She put her hands in her jacket pocket and found Elizabeth's gold pen. She must have put it there without thinking. 'Has Dad got insurance?' Marcus asked.

William's mobile rang. He pulled it from his pocket. The device looked tiny in his massive hand. 'Elizabeth,' he announced. 'Yes?'

Annie felt a flash of panic. 'Everything okay? Grace...?'

William gave Annie the thumbs-up. 'I see. Yes, I'll tell her.' He stuffed the phone away. 'No need to return to Ullerforth, Annie. Doctor says Grace has come round and can leave within the hour. Elizabeth will bring her back in the car with Patrick.'

Annie felt suddenly exhausted. She didn't want Grace in Elizabeth's car, but she was grateful she didn't have to drive there and back again. She wouldn't trust herself on those roads feeling like this.

William slapped his palms together. 'We'll leave you in peace.'

Annie followed them out the front and waited while William and Marcus steered the quad down the track, the trailer swaying at the back. The dogs ran dangerously close to its wheels.

Stephen turned to her. 'You want to be careful,' he said as he climbed into his buggy and left.

Annie went back and forth to the living room with a nail brush and pine-scented disinfectant.

What if William had started the fire to get her away from the hospital, so that... *what?* She really didn't know the reason. She prayed they hadn't spotted Pomander.

Worried now, she went to check on the pig, who was safe in her hut, asleep. What if they'd gone through her things once Stephen had unlocked the door? Annie went back inside and checked the house: her bedside table, Grace's laptop, the contents of Grace's suitcase, Caleb's room. Nothing had been taken or moved as far as she could tell, and – a more sinister thought crossed her mind – nothing had been added. They didn't need any more Astartes, thank you very much.

Grace would be back soon. Dizzy and with her back aching, she made up Grace's bed with fresh sheets. The noisy chainsaw was back in the field. Curious, she traipsed to her own room and looked out the window at the front. The stick figure of Stephen was cutting logs behind the church and throwing them beside the platform for the eclipse party. So that was it.

Another figure appeared in the field from the direction of the Big House, long and rangy. That would be Andrew. He began hauling planks on a pulley onto the platform. His second eldest son joined him, wielding an axe, hacking at a block of wood.

Then a fourth figure, marching purposefully along the far edge of the field towards Colthwaite House: David on the phone, his neck inclined towards his shoulder.

Annie pressed her nose against the glass. David disappeared into the bowels of the Big House.

How had William and Marcus seen smoke from the end of the track when it hadn't even been a proper fire? Embers wouldn't have produced a column like that, high enough for them to see.

She checked her watch. Half an hour 'til Grace arrived home. All she wanted was to close her eyes and sleep.

The chainsaw had stopped. Out the window, she saw Stephen wipe his brow. Andrew went to his coat to fetch something. Then, stealthy as a cat, the silver Jeep Cherokee eased slowly past the lane in front of Colthwaite House. She watched it drive out the other end of the village. Stephen and Andrew watched it too, without waving, their bodies stiff and still. They clearly weren't friends. Something about this emboldened Annie. She hurried downstairs and threw on her shoes.

She was headed for the Big House. She wanted to see for herself what David was up to, all on his own in a house that didn't belong to him.

'Annie!'

Andrew had spotted her from the field and was gesturing at her. Reluctantly, she made her way towards him. 'How's Grace?' he asked, when she reached him. 'Doing okay?'

'Good, thanks. On her way home.'

Stephen drew near. He was grinning. 'Thought you'd have had enough of us for one day?' He pulled out a thermos of steaming tea and poured liquid into the aluminium lid. 'He's got his hat on at least.' He nodded at the fuzzy lemon sun.

'Let's hope it lasts,' Andrew said. 'Or it won't be much of a show.'

A pheasant scampered across the open field; Andrew's son raised the axe like a shotgun and pretended to shoot. Stephen shook out the last drips from his beaker. 'Where you off to, then?'

Annie looked away. David had emerged from a side door and was disappearing around the back of the building. He was still on the phone. 'Just getting some air,' she said.

Stephen commandeered the axe from the boy. 'That's enough of that, thank you.' He turned to Annie again. 'Nothing like a party to heal things that are broken.'

'Grace isn't broken,' she said, her tone abrupt.

'I wasn't talking about Grace.' Stephen hacked at a log. 'Was talking about the village.'

Annie eyeballed him. 'What d'you mean?'

'He means,' Andrew said, 'there's been a lot going on.'

She waited for him to say more. When he didn't, she told them she'd head home, as Grace would be back any minute. Bidding them goodbye, she headed off to the edge of the field, out of the gate, and along the lane.

She was going to find out what David was up to.

She reached the drive and snuck into the farmyard. No obvious signs of David. Perhaps he was in the big barn? She stuck her head through the door and listened. Nothing.

Then, from inside the work shed she heard his confident, irritable tone: 'Well, I'm doing it now, aren't I?'

She found a hiding spot. The shed door opened suddenly.

'Don't have a go at *me*, my dear. It was your responsibility.' In the crook of his arm, a familiar silver kidney-shaped bowl, its top covered in clingfilm. 'I'm doing it now. All right. See you later.'

Annie shrank into the shadows as he carried the bowl across the yard into the big barn. She scurried over to its left side and found the tiny opening in the slats.

In a dark corner beneath a bare bulb, David was bent over a large white rectangular chest freezer. He stopped, glancing behind him before depositing the bowl inside. He shut the lid and moved off, humming to himself.

Annie snuck further along the outside edge of the barn, keeping her eyes on him until it was too dark to see. She was now at the barn's back door – the one through which William let the boar in for the serving – when the door flung open and the vicar appeared in the doorway, arms crossed. Annie pretended to be looking for something on the ground.

'Can I help you?'

'I'm so sorry. I was...'

His expression wasn't so much cold, as entertained. At a loss, her hands went into her pockets. Her fingers met Elizabeth's gold pen. 'I was looking to return this.' She held it out for him to see, like a naughty child in front of the teacher.

'Ah, Lizzy's pen. She's at the hospital. Where you were, I believe? Until not long ago.'

'Yes, Elizabeth dropped it in the waiting room. I picked it up and kept it by accident. I thought I'd leave it at the Big House – she said she was heading straight here after, but then...' Too many words. She'd never been a good liar. 'I heard noise from the barn and thought she might be back, or... William?'

David puffed his cheeks. 'Is Grace home?'

'No.'

'Then I'm surprised you thought Elizabeth had returned.'

'I just–'

'William's up at Lenner's with a Tup.'

'Right.'

He took the pen from her, curtly. 'We were just on the phone, Elizabeth and I. A farm requires constant attention, as I'm sure you're aware. I'm to wait for her 'til she's back.' What Elizabeth would make of Annie's pen story when David related it, God only knew. 'See you Saturday,' he said.

'Yep.'

He took a step backwards into the barn, nearly but not quite shutting the door. He was waiting for her to leave. 'Bye then,' she said.

She reached the end of the driveway, looked left then right along the lane. Vincent was staring at her from his bay window.

Patrick returned Grace home just after Annie arrived back, a pack of cards in his hand. To her annoyance, he made himself at home, parking himself in the living room and teaching Grace how to play canasta. Annie fussed about them, tucking Grace in on the sofa, then hovering in the kitchen desperate to eavesdrop. After forty minutes, he left 'for a shower'.

'Well.' Annie came straight into the living room at the sound of the front door closing. 'How was that?' Grace looked so frail.

Now was not the time to tell her about leaving Cumbria, about going back to school in Hackney.

'Thank God he's gone,' Grace said.

'Are you okay, sweetheart? Get you anything? Food? Water? Stiff whisky?'

'I'm okay.' Grace sighed. 'I'm missing so much school.'

'Your brother would love to miss school.'

Grace gave her a funny look. 'Why? Because of the kids' teasing?'

'You know about that?' Annie perched next to her on the sofa. Grace nodded. 'How bad is it?'

'Well, that's subjective.' Grace stuck out her lip. 'That place is *old*-fashioned.' Her voice went suddenly small. 'Annie? Mum's story, the one Granny gave me...'

'Yes?'

'You've read it, haven't you?' Annie didn't know what to say. 'I know you have,' Grace pushed. 'It's okay, don't worry.'

'Gracie.' Annie shifted closer. 'I did. I'm so sorry.'

'Do you think the story's weird?'

'Yes,' she said carefully. 'A little.'

Grace's shoulders lifted. 'Why do you think Mum wrote it?'

'I don't know, truthfully,' Annie said. 'Your mum had a fertile imagination.'

'Okay, but she wouldn't pull that stuff just out of her head, would she? And why d'you think Granny gave it to me?'

Because she's mad. 'I don't know that either.'

There was a silence. 'You do believe me, don't you?' Grace said. 'About not having had sex?'

Annie told Grace that she did, even though the jury was still very much out.

'D'you think Dad believes me? And Granny?'

'I'm sure they do,' Annie soothed.

Grace played with the threads of blanket on her lap. 'I wish you'd waited for me at the hospital.'

Annie took her hand. 'Your dad said you'd rather I left.'

'What? No. Why would I say that?'

'For fuck's sake.' Annie sat back. So, she'd been right. 'I wanted to stay.'

'I wanted you to, too.'

This made Annie cry. She handed Grace a bad detective novel and, warmed by the rays of her stepdaughter's love but not wanting Grace to see her tears, she went to check on the pig.

Pomander was turning circles in the shed, her odd-shaped face buried in the straw. Perhaps she was close to giving birth. Perhaps Annie and the kids wouldn't even be here when she did, they'd be back in Hackney, and what would Pomander do then, all by herself?

Annie watched the trees behind the hut blowing in the wind. She thought about the figure in the woods, her long hair. There'd been so much going on, the woman hadn't crossed her mind for days.

She went into the writing shed and fired off an email to the hospital requesting they send Grace's histology report as soon as possible. A copy should be sent separately to her alone, she instructed, she should not be cc'd with Dr Dillane and Patrick Cook. An automated reply: someone from the department would respond within forty-eight hours.

Then she deleted the email and her search history, including the pages on Astarte, in case anyone came snooping, and returned to the cottage, nerves on the sizzle.

Patrick turned up again, unannounced, for dinner. Annie's mouth almost fell open at this display of bad manners, though she could hardly refuse to let him in. Leaving him with poor Grace once more, she rustled up bimbimbap with egg, marinated vegetables, kimchi and gochujang, sesame oil, and tamari. She could hear him in the living room trying but failing to pull Grace into conversation. When it was ready, Annie placed an enormous ceramic jug of hot soju in the centre of the table and called them in to eat.

'How's the writing?' Patrick asked at one point.

'Oh, you know.' She wiped her napkin across her mouth. 'Same old.' And then, because she couldn't resist, 'The Finborough called me in for a meeting.'

'That's wonderful! I heard you'd organised a trip to see them, but it was cancelled by farmyard things?'

Annie almost laughed. 'Elizabeth told you, I assume.'

Patrick nodded. 'But they'll see you another time?'

Grace was looking from one to the other.

'Yeah.' Annie took a slug of her drink.

'What's it called then, your play?'

She cleared the bowls, loaded them in the dishwasher. 'I'm afraid that's top-secret information.'

'Roger that.' Patrick stretched his arms extravagantly, half-moons of sweat darkening the pits of his shirt.

'Though if you ask Elizabeth,' she said, 'I dare say she'll tell you.'

That wiped the smile from his face.

CHAPTER FIFTEEN

Saturday at breakfast. Caleb was back for the weekend. He and Grace were sitting quietly at the kitchen table. In a terrible error of timing, Patrick had decided the previous night was a good time for the chat about smoking with Caleb. Now Caleb's eyes were firmly on his cereal, and Annie felt it was her fault. She helicoptered around them. 'You guys okay?'

'Yup.'

'Not long 'til Christmas,' she said to make conversation, over-pouring granola into her bowl. The kids grunted. *We're moving back to London,* she rehearsed saying in her head, *but not to home for a few months yet, to a nasty Lego house with my sister, far away from your old school.* She couldn't put it off forever, and Grace seemed... not better exactly, but solid at least. Once they got over the suddenness of it, they'd almost certainly be happy about returning home.

'Listen,' Annie began, 'there's something important I...' What if she'd got it wrong? What if they didn't want to leave?

'What?' demanded Grace. 'Finish your sentence. It's so annoying when you do that.'

A knock at the front door saved her. 'In a minute.' She scuttled away to answer it.

It was Patrick. Oh, brilliant. Just brilliant. Behind him the sky was milk blue, the sun low and bleaching the east to burnt orange. A vortex of leaves rustled like crisps at his feet. He was in a suit for some reason, and carried a paper bag and a bottle of orange juice. 'Pastries,' he explained. 'In case you need sustenance.'

'Thanks.' She'd no idea what he was talking about. 'How come you're dressed so smart?'

Patrick laughed and shook his head. 'Annie, you're funny.'

He pushed past, patting her arm four times as he went. The eclipse party! That's what he was referring to. It was today. She'd forgotten, remembered, forgotten again. She shuffled after him to the kitchen.

Patrick had emptied the pastries straight from the bag to the tabletop, sending a flurry of crumbs to the floor. Annie put more coffee on to boil. Her bad leg pulsed inside her jeans.

'Three pm is the actual event,' Patrick was telling the kids. 'We'll assemble in the field at two thirty. The eclipse will last around two to four minutes only. Thereafter it's eating and drinking and generally making tits of ourselves.'

'Can't wait,' Grace said with a glance at Annie.

'I think Grace might need to take it easy,' Annie told him. 'We mustn't rush her recovery.'

Patrick let out a dismissive tut. 'She'll be fine. She's tough, my girl. Aren't you?'

'I'm not a *girl*, Dad.' Grace extracted the oblong of chocolate from her pastry and put it in her mouth.

'Well, I don't think she should go,' Annie insisted, and Caleb nodded in support. She didn't want Grace and Caleb disappearing off at a village festival. It would be dark and chaotic; God only knew what Vincent, or Elizabeth, or any of them had planned.

'Annie, their grandparents are expecting them,' Patrick said.

'We'll see.' Annie nodded at the kids; they nodded back at her across the table.

She knew suddenly, and with absolute clarity, that they would support the escape to London. It made her want to pick up their stuff right then, march out the door. But Patrick was here. He'd let Elizabeth know and then William might arrange another tractor event in the road.

No, they'd make their escape *during* the party. It would be so busy, Elizabeth and co would be less likely to miss them. Grace could rest in the back of the car. She'd tell the kids as soon as Patrick left. They'd better be good at packing quickly.

———

Patrick, however, didn't appear to want to leave. He'd been in the hallway on the phone to his hospital in London for almost an hour, discussing a patient.

Annie paced the living room, furious. Why wouldn't he go? There was already activity on the lane: the beeps of four-by-fours reversing. Unable to talk their father down, Caleb and Grace had disappeared upstairs to get ready.

And now Noah was yapping at the end of the track, which meant her in-laws were on their way to her. The threat of their arrival was enough to motivate her to hide upstairs.

She snuck into Grace's room. Grace was brushing her hair. 'Thanks for knocking.'

'Gracie,' Annie urged, shutting the door behind her. 'I need to tell you something. Both of you. It's important.'

Grace nodded, as if she knew what was coming. 'I'll get

Caleb.' She ran out the room. A second later, Annie heard her say, 'Oh!'

'Gracie!' Patrick was at the top of the stairs. 'Where you off to in such a hurry?'

'Going to fetch Cal for a clothing conflab.' Grace's voice was high up in her throat. 'It's time, right? Cal! Come on!'

The doorbell rang. Too late. Annie shook her head at Grace as they passed on the landing and, like a man to the gallows, headed downstairs.

When she opened the door, Elizabeth stood in front of her in a green silk ankle-length dress. Next to her, filling the rest of the porch, was William, wearing what appeared to be a deerstalking cape.

'You look... nice,' Annie managed.

'Ready?' Without waiting for a reply, William headed back down the track. 'Come on, Lizzy, we don't want to be late!' Elizabeth did as she was told.

Caleb and Grace appeared at Annie's shoulder. 'Do we have to go?'

'*No.*'

Grace leant into her ear. 'What were you going to tell us, me and Cal?' But Patrick was behind them now, like a bad smell.

'C'mon, kids. No time to lose!'

'Dad, Annie says we–'

'I'm not taking no for an answer.' He linked arms with the kids and dragged them along the track. 'No party poopers.'

Grace looked back at Annie, helpless. The blue sky was already on the turn: a mix of grey and yellow. Grimly, she set off after them. They turned out the gate onto the lane.

The lane was glutted with muddy four-by-fours parked along the verge. She spotted the silver Jeep Cherokee amongst them. Interesting. Perhaps she'd meet the man in black trousers milling about in the field. Perhaps she'd be brave enough to ask him why he passed through the village at five miles an hour on the regular, and why when he did so, no one smiled or waved. Fuck it, even the woman in the woods might be there, all smiles, long hair swinging.

William was chattering away to the children. 'The next total eclipse isn't for another ninety years. At which point the weather will be ghastly and we'll be long gone. This is the first clear sky we've had since the partial in 2006.'

They passed Colthwaite House and turned down the path towards the church. Frank Sinatra's 'White Christmas' blared from speakers.

The population of Colthwaite seemed to have swelled overnight, because the field was now packed. Annie stared, wide-eyed, at the sheer amount, greeting one another in their smartest clothes. The only explanation she came up with was that Colthwaite must invite their neighbouring villages too.

Even she could acknowledge the field looked pretty: the platform garlanded with evergreens and ribbons; fairy lights swagged from poles. There was the platform, an edifice. That explained the amount of sawing over the last week, then. On its top was the criss-cross support for the roasting spit and the dead pig impaled on a pole, livid red; beneath it a small unlit pyre circled by a ring of metal.

The far end of the field had been cordoned off, a sign warning – FIREWORKS! DO NOT CROSS! – placed in front of it. A bonfire had been built in another corner, picnic tables and chairs laid out far from the danger of spitting logs.

'Work to do,' William announced, and headed off with Elizabeth towards the platform. Caleb and Grace stayed by her side; she could feel something coming off them, like sparks. Energy, perhaps. Or fear.

Andrew's three sons appeared. 'Dude,' said the one called Marcus, commandeering Caleb's arm. 'Come hang with us.'

'Er–' Caleb looked at Annie.

'*Dude*,' the youngest boy echoed. They dragged Caleb away.

'I'd better go with him,' Grace said after a moment, and left.

Annie called after her, 'Gracie, you shouldn't be–'

'Relax.' Patrick put a hand on her shoulder. Trust him to be the one to stick around. 'Let me give you a tour,' he said smoothly and pulled her into the crowd.

She should have told him she didn't want a tour, certainly not from him, but she had the escape plan – all she needed to do was keep her head down before scooping up Grace and Caleb, and they'd be away.

Her eyes passed over the church. The bones of the dead, rattling to Sinatra. 'What's this festival in aid of again?'

Patrick gave her a funny look. 'Who knows? Chance to have a few drinks, whatever. There's a couple of little traditions they do, the usual.'

'What sort of traditions?'

'Oh.' He rolled his eyes. 'Country stuff. Maypole-y things.'

'A *Maypole*? But it's November.'

'Maypole *type* things.' Something caught his eye. 'Look, someone wants you.'

It was Stephen on a straw bale in front of the platform. In his hand, a large metal tripod. 'Annie! You all right?'

'I don't know!' She headed towards him, pleased to dilute Patrick with another person.

Stephen was grinning. 'You'll be fine.'

'That's what I keep telling her,' Patrick said. 'She doesn't believe me.'

Annie raised an eyebrow at the tripod. 'What is that?'

'For Elizabeth's telescope,' Stephen explained. 'To see the eclipse. It goes on the platform.'

'Of course.' This was so weird.

Noah appeared, fixing his sights on Annie's boots, a precursor to Elizabeth, who swished up in her long green dress. 'Isn't this gorgeous? Don't look so scared, Annie.' She was laughing. 'It's just a party.' Then she was gone again. Annie hadn't realised she'd been looking worried.

'Shall we?' Patrick took her arm once more.

Annie forced a smile. 'For sure.'

Over in the corner, Grace, Caleb, and the cousins had been joined by some other teens. A boy was swigging from a bottle of cider. He passed it to Grace. 'Alcohol's the last thing Grace needs,' Annie muttered.

'Oh, let her have some fun,' said Patrick.

The vicar arrived beside her. 'Now, you two...' He was carrying a large box and was accompanied by Margaret in a voluminous hot pink trouser suit, her blue hair sticking up like a loo-brush. In her hand she held a small hessian bag. Patrick turned to talk to someone else. *Finally.*

'What's that for?' Annie was sure she'd seen the bag somewhere before.

'This?' Margaret held it up as if only just realising she had it. 'It's–'

David cut her off with a tut. 'Don't spoil it, Margaret.'

'No,' Annie pressed. 'Do spoil it. What's it for?'

'It's a cowl.' Margaret's eyes flicked to David.

'A cowl?' Annie said. 'How d'you mean?'

'It's difficult to explain...' Margaret shook her head. 'To honour the–'

David dumped his box on the ground, the contents rattling alarmingly. 'Oh stop, Margaret dear. You'll find out soon enough, Annie. You might even enjoy it.' He bent to open the box. It was full of pairs of opera glasses with shaded lenses. 'Kick off's in twenty minutes.' He thrust a pair into Annie's hands. 'You'll need these.'

'Oh,' Annie said. 'Thank you.'

'God's watching.' He pointed at the sky. 'Going to be a blinder.'

'I hope not.' Annie put her eyes to the eyepiece: the view was almost black.

'Not keen on dressing smart?' Margaret enquired.

Annie pulled the binoculars from her face. 'I would have done if... I didn't know today would be so formal.'

'Don't worry your pretty little head about that,' David told her. 'It's simply a tradition, not a mandate.'

'What's going on over there, then?' Annie asked, noticing a large group of people now assembling at a corner of the field.

David tapped his nose. 'Wait and see.'

Andrew's Labrador waddled up, all soulful eyes. It licked Annie on both knees. She patted its head. 'She likes you,' David observed. 'She's keen on older women.'

'She has good taste,' Annie said.

This made Margaret laugh. 'You tell him, Annie.'

Vincent hobbled towards them, acknowledging them with a waggle of his stick. 'Vincent!' David cried. 'About time, old sausage.' Vincent looked even older than usual in a long dark coat, the tails trailing. She could barely look at him now she knew about his past.

'Annie,' he began wheezily, 'but you're in mufti? "When in Rome" and all that?'

'I wasn't aware it was smart dress.'

''Course you weren't.' Vincent tapped her arm. 'One of Andrew's wretched sons was no doubt sent to tell you but forgot.'

One of those blasted hunting horns blew nearby, making Annie duck instinctively, eliciting laughter from the surrounding men.

The group that had assembled in the corner were now passing something out from the back of a flatbed truck over their heads. It was large and wide and wooden, and resembled – at least from this distance – a vast spider's web. 'What is that?' she said.

'I told you she asked a lot of questions,' Vincent said to David.

Fine. Let them not tell her. She'd be gone soon enough and wouldn't get to find out probably, anyway. She scanned the rest of the field: Elizabeth was mounting the ladder to the platform, William following behind; Stephen was securing the telescope to its tripod. The Sinatra went off with a clunk. People began to gather around the platform.

Annie checked for the kids: she could see Grace's blonde hair shining amongst a gaggle of teenagers on the other side of the field. Okay. Good.

'Ladies and gentlemen!' Elizabeth cried. 'Welcome to the annual festival celebrations, and a very special one at that!' A cheer went up. 'And goodness me, we've *just* made it in time.' She nodded at the sky. 'We'll now count down the preliminary moments, everyone: five, four...'

The crowd joined in. '...three, two, one!'

Like a magic trick, the light in the sky dropped several shades to sickly yellow. People oohed. Annie tried to ooh with them. The group with the wooden spider web began to carry it towards the centre of the field. 'The Opening of Astarte has survived another year!' Elizabeth proclaimed. A smattering of applause.

So here it was: the Astarte festival. Brilliant.

The wooden web was brought in front of the platform and turned upright onto its ends. Close up, she saw it was made from woven branches and sticks. It looked old, home-made, and rather beautiful. It was also far larger than she'd initially thought, with a hole, like a shark's mouth, at its centre – big enough to pass a person through.

She stood on tiptoes to keep tabs on Caleb and Grace, but there were so many people around Annie now, they were impossible to spot. A circle of hands was beginning to form, around the web. David grabbed Annie's. 'Come on!'

'What's happening?' she said as he pulled her along. 'What's it for?'

Vincent was holding David's other hand and Margaret was three away from him. She must go along with it, until she could get to Caleb and Grace and whisk them away. Seconds later, the kids appeared. But they were far away on the opposite side of the circle. Annie called for them, but they didn't hear.

'Let us pray!' thundered Elizabeth from the platform. Everyone bowed their heads, murmuring along while her mother-in-law intoned the Lord's Prayer. Annie looked around. Grace and Caleb were staring at her.

'Let's go in a minute,' she mouthed, and they nodded. They had no idea exactly how far she meant to take them.

Elizabeth was still speaking. 'Before we view the glory of the sun and moon in alignment, before Astarte is fed, we must feed ourselves with the festival offerings, and a dance.'

William struck a match to the pyre beneath the pig on the spit, its pink flesh in vivid contrast to the yellowing sky. Flames grew quickly and the skin hissed and shrivelled. Someone cried 'Amen!' as the sky turned from yellow to brown.

'Glasses at the ready, everyone!' Elizabeth commanded.

David said into Annie's ear, 'We're minutes from the eclipse.' His breath was hot and his grip too hard. 'The best is yet to come.'

That was it. She couldn't stand any more. 'I forgot my phone!' she cried, snatching her hand from his. 'It's back at the cottage.'

'What do you need a phone for?' He put his binoculars to his face.

'To film the eclipse.'

He glared at her. 'Can't you just enjoy it for what it is?'

'I promised my sister I'd live-stream it.' She stepped back, out of his reach, but then Vincent appeared at her side.

'What's all this?'

'Annie's forgotten her phone,' David said, crotchety.

Vincent shook his head. 'Oh, you won't need that.'

But Annie was moving further back, putting distance between herself and the two men. 'I promised! It's at Chapel Croft. I'll only be a sec.'

'But you run the risk of missing it altogether!'

She was faster than either of them, she reasoned, even with her bad leg. But they didn't follow and, once she'd gestured for the kids and they'd hurried to join her, she began to feel better.

They left the field and stepped on to the lane. She pulled the children towards her, 'Listen,' she began. 'We need to–'

'What the fuck is going on?' Grace interrupted. 'What's with the sticks contraption, why is everyone being so strange?'

'And who's Astarte?' Caleb added.

'Listen to me now,' Annie said. 'We need to leave. Not just the party, but the village. We need to leave Colthwaite. We need to go home, back to London. Right now.'

The children's eyes grew round. 'What? Why?'

'I'll tell you everything, I promise, but there isn't time now.' They nodded, trusting her, waiting for instructions. 'Go to Chapel Croft.' Never had she loved them more. 'Wait for me there. I need...' What did she need, exactly? All they *needed* was to leave. Wasn't it?

But what about evidence? If they'd done something, anything, to harm Grace, to cause her bleed, Annie wanted to go to the police. For that, she'd need what was in the kidney-shaped bowl. The bowl that was in the freezer in the barn. That was what she needed. Forensic evidence. Proof. 'There's something I have to do,' she told them firmly. Caleb's head was shaking no. Annie put her arm on his. 'Please,' she said. 'Trust me. It's important.'

'You're not leaving?' said a voice. It was Patrick, hanging over the field's gate.

'I left my phone at the cottage,' she said. 'I want to film the eclipse.'

'Er... okay.' Patrick looked at the children. 'But no need for you guys to go; you'll miss it.' When no one said anything, he grabbed Caleb and Grace's hands and pulled them round. 'Executive decision. Back to the party, you both, for some fun.' The children looked back helplessly at Annie.

'I'll be back very soon.' She told them. 'Promise.' They'd be okay. He was their father, after all. Despite everything, she believed he'd never deliberately hurt them.

She swung around, turned left and ran into the woods on the other side of the lane, scrambling through the cover of the trees towards Colthwaite House, her leg whingeing.

The driveway up to the house was empty, and so was the farmyard. She scurried across the lane and into the yard, ran over to the large barn and slipped inside.

She switched on her phone's torch and crept her way past the machinery and animal pens until she reached the open rear section. The chest freezer sat in a corner against the wall. She went to it, her mouth set.

The lid was up. Frozen meat was piled up, labelled in bags: *lamb leg*; *pig cheeks*, each with a date. No silver kidney-shaped bowl. But she'd seen David put it here. She stood in the darkness, thinking hard. She knew where it would be.

With trembling fingers, she punched *1943* into the lock on Elizabeth's work shed door. It clicked open. Glancing over her shoulder, she slid inside.

She'd almost forgotten how antediluvian the shed was: the

grubby walls, the mess, the hum of padlocked fridges beneath the countertops. The place smelt strongly of chemicals. She walked the length of the shed: beakers, centrifuge, test tubes labelled with numbers and letters, written directly onto glass in erasable pen. There was a microscope, a glass slide waiting on its stage, something stained pink beneath its microfilm. Outside, the wind was building. She reached the far end. No kidney-shaped bowl. It had to be here somewhere. Her eyes re-scanned the clutter.

There. At the rear of the starboard counter, almost hidden behind the centrifuge, the silver kidney-shaped bowl. She *knew* it. She went to it, slowing as her eyes took in the dried blood above its rim and down the side. Heart hammering, she peered inside: more dried blood, nothing more. She took a photo. She had a strong sense she'd missed something.

The fridge directly beneath her was unlocked. It was the only one not locked in the entire shed. She grabbed the handle and pulled.

The smell inside was overpowering, a mix of parmesan cheese and disinfectant. Two things sat on a shelf: a white unlabelled bottle, and a small package the size of a cod fillet wrapped in white plastic. Feeling nauseous, she pulled the package onto the countertop and peeled it open.

A tiny curled pink thing the size of a fingernail in a mess of tissue. A wave of revulsion overwhelmed her, and she turned suddenly, knocking a beaker to the floor where it shattered noisily into pieces. She must take a photo of the... *thing.* If it was evidence she needed, this was it. Steeling herself, she leaned back in for a closer look.

It looked a lot like a pig foetus. The torso was deeply curved, a stump at one end like a tail and four tiny, shorter stumps. Not Grace's, after all. She let out a breath.

She took several photos at different angles, then returned it to the fridge. She swept the smashed beaker fragments towards the skirting with her shoe. Their presence meant Elizabeth would know for certain someone had been here, but Annie and the kids would be gone by then, safe in the car on their way to London.

The sound of claws on cement in the yard. Annie tensed. Noah. His arrival almost certainly preluded Elizabeth's. Annie looked about in panic: there was nowhere to hide.

Too late anyway. Here was Noah, slipping around the half-open door, ears alert, pink tongue poking from the corner of his mouth. He stopped at the end of the shed, fixing her with chocolate-coloured button eyes. Annie waited, hunch-shouldered, for Elizabeth, but she didn't come.

'What are you doing here?' she hissed at the dog after several moments. 'Fuck off.'

Noah cocked his head to one side and trotted through the shed towards her. She watched intently as he sniffed the floor around her legs; she mustn't give him reason to bark. Now he was nudging his nose into a narrow gap between the rear door of the shed. Something behind it had caught his interest. A second later, he widened the gap, pulling at it with a foreleg, then edged his muscly body through to the other side. She poked her head around the back door to see where he'd gone.

To her surprise, she met a further room, small and full of shadows. Two flickering TV monitors were propped on a desk, one on top of the other. Beneath them was a small radio transistor spitting out static. Noah panted at her from the corner. 'Good dog,' she told him and stepped inside.

The monitor screens relayed grainy black-and-white feeds of the front drive into Colthwaite House, the shrubs moving stiffly in the breeze, and – more peculiarly – the front steps of Blea Crag. Annie stared, confused. Were they burglar deterrents? There seemed to be an awful lot of surveillance going on for such a remote place.

She scanned the rest of the room. There were walled shelving units with plastic lidless containers. When she peered into several, she saw they held long rolls of wide bandage, medicines for wound cleaning, and bottles of something called – she angled her phone torch at them – 'Natron'. She snapped a photo of each one.

On the floor beneath the shelf there were some smaller round tubs. She shone her torch on them: *NUMBER* 23, *NUMBER* 24, *NUMBER* 26 each one said, with accompanying dates – all this year.

She pulled 23 out and opened it: brown pig-feed pellets. A smell of rotting vegetation. This must be the pigs' 'specialist diet'. Noah trotted up beside her and stuck his nose in. She pushed him away.

Numbers 24 and 26 contained the same-smelling pellets. She was about to push them back into place, but there behind the tubs was something else. Annie leant closer. A second line of tubs, hidden in the darkness: *GRACE, POLLY, NUMBER* 66. Panic rising, Annie edged them out.

GRACE. She pulled at the corner of the lid. Same vegetable stink. More brown pellets. These must be the so-called 'vitamins'. They were identical to the things in Grace's bottle. She took a photo.

Why did Polly have a tub of her own, and why was it separate to Grace's when she was away at the rehab centre? And what, or who, was Number 66? She pulled them open.

Both *POLLY* and *NUMBER* 66 contained identical-looking pellets to Grace's, though she knew there would be subtle differences in composition, or they'd have been stored together.

Picking one up, she turned it in her fingers. They were

capsules, not pellets – easy to split in half and open, then add to food if someone was unwilling to take them.

A sound came out of the transistor: someone humming aimlessly. Annie sat up and stared at the radio. Who was that? Did they know they were being overheard? The next moment the humming stopped, and the person's footsteps could be heard moving away from the microphone, then the click of a door, then more static.

Annie went back to what she had been doing. She swiftly documented the tubs and pellets with her camera, then returned them to their original position.

Sitting back on her haunches, she cast her eyes about the room. There would be more things stored here, she felt certain; secrets the family didn't want known. There, beneath the lip of the desk sat two narrow drawers. She pulled them open.

The first held memory cards, gaffer tape, glue, and batteries. The second held a box file marked *Sequencing*. Inside the file were folders, labelled and numbered. They held thick wads of computer printouts on photocopy paper: a repeated series of letters – A, C, G and T – in unending lines. The words: *SPLICING WOULD HAVE OCCURRED IN THE ABOVE SNIPS* typed at the bottom. Each folder also had a single microscope slide stuck to the bottom, the slide containing a smear of pink dye.

She quickly took photos of each one before snapping the box file shut. She should leave now – the children were waiting for her in the field; people would be wondering what was taking her so long. She was only meant to be collecting her phone from the cottage.

A large stack of correspondence sat at the back of the second drawer. She had to know what was in it. She *had* to.

Printed invoices, purchase-orders for chemicals and pharmaceutical equipment, 'CRISPR kits' from a place called

Bio Labs in Dallas, Texas, bills from a German company, Zuchunftstechnologie, for "Wachstumsstimulanzien".

Annie hurriedly typed *CRISPR* followed by *CRISPR kits* into Google.

CRISPR is a technology that can be used to edit genes. The essence of CRISPR is simple: it's a way of finding a specific bit of DNA inside a cell. The next step in CRISPR gene editing is to alter that piece of DNA. CRISPR stands for "clustered regularly interspaced short palindromic repeats." The CRISPR system is made up of two components: a protein called Cas9 and a guide RNA, a string of nucleic acid molecules with a certain genetic code. Put them together, and they create a tool you can use to tweak an organism's genome

The kits could be bought from the US, it said, and used by anyone with a rudimentary grasp of science and a centrifuge.

Underneath, at the very bottom of the drawer were two cream vellum envelopes held together with a note marked *family correspondence (photocopies)*, both addressed by hand – one in Issy's name, one in Andrew's. She pulled Issy's out and unfolded the paper. It was dated two years ago.

> *Dearest daughter Isabelle,*
> *As you know, your father and I are terribly proud of*
> *you. We've supported you throughout your career as well as*
> *during other, harder, times (periods of your more "personal"*
> *life choices, for example). We know that Patrick, too...*

Annie looked up. Patrick? What had he got to do with anything two years ago?

...has been most generous in such matters. I think you'll acknowledge that in no small part we have contributed to Grace maturing into a wonderful young woman, despite having been raised amongst the questionable "advantages" of London. Neither I nor your father ever approved of your moving away and I don't mind telling you that I have for many years worried for both yours and Grace's health, living in such poor-quality air, given our genealogical propensity for respiratory oedema.

You are no doubt aware that it will soon be time for you and the children to return north to continue – and complete – our work. It is of the utmost importance that we maintain a watchful eye on you and Grace as the years progress.

We very much desire you honour our wishes, and that Annie, your "wife" as you refer to one another, will not prove troublesome in the matter.

If anything were to happen to you, God forbid, I require your solemn vow that you'll send Grace to us, come what may. It is a small sacrifice on your part for what is likely to be a huge step forward for mankind (and womankind) and for the collective well-being of everyone, here and beyond. Goodness knows, but we have suffered enough in the name of progress.

I trust you will do the right thing. It is with great regret that I must write that any dissent in this matter will end badly for you, the children, and Annie.

"Why have you delivered yourselves unto death, having power to partake of immortality?"

Yours always,

Mother

CHAPTER SIXTEEN

Annie sat back heavily. It was too much to take in. What did Elizabeth mean, *send Grace to us?* and what about *respiratory oedema, continuing and completing our work,* and most terrifying of all, *things ending badly* for Issy, Annie, and the children if Issy failed to comply? And where had Issy hidden her own copy of this letter, the original copy? Had she even received it? If she had, she'd made damn sure Annie never found it.

With trembling hands, Annie folded the letter into its envelope and pocketed it. She eyed the one addressed to Andrew. She'd no doubt it contained words of equal misery. From the field she heard *oohing* and *aahing* noises. Noah's ears pricked. She must leave.

She stuffed Andrew's letter into her pocket and scuttled into the main section of the work shed, closing the little door behind her. Checking she hadn't left anything behind, she made for the door, Noah at her heels.

The light in the sky had changed again: dun-coloured, almost black, the sun fully hidden now, its beams sneaking round the moon's edges. Exultations came from the field. *The*

Eye of God, David called it. But it was not God's eye she need fear. These people. Her own wife.

She flew down the drive and along the lane, the dog giving chase. She must get to the children, pull them from the field, get out of here.

A single gunshot rang out high up on the fell. It was followed by a squeal that could have come from anything. Or anyone.

She stood on the lane, legs shaking. The kids were safe with Patrick, weren't they? What if they weren't? He'd been mentioned in Elizabeth's letter. What if he'd led them away somewhere, onto the fell and—

She raced across the lane and up into the trees. There was no way she was letting harm come to the kids. Noah followed, running beside her with excited eyes.

'Go home!' she panted, but the dog, like Annie, was on a mission. 'Go *on!*' She almost kicked him in the direction of the field. He barked before running on to the lane.

Up she went through the thickets, lungs on fire, the sound of the festival receding.

Pomander. Grace, Polly, their diets all supplemented. *Goodness knows, we have suffered enough.* Issy had hidden all of it. A secret life Annie knew nothing about. This hurt so much it almost burned.

She pushed on until she reached the perimeter of the large pheasant enclosure, the same spot she'd seen the woman with the long hair. It lay in shadow, but at its far reaches the clearing containing the shepherd's hut glowed in the odd light from the eclipse. It must be at its fullest now. People would be angry she had missed it, would want to know why. Annie peered through the trees: there was no sign of Grace or Caleb, no sign of anyone. All she could hear was her own breathing and the creak of the trees.

Perhaps she'd imagined the shot? It might have come from the field – a shot of celebration – the sound bouncing off the fell instead.

She was about to turn, head back down the hill, when she noticed the pen's padlocked gate hung open. She stood, staring at it, when a sudden movement drew her attention. It came from inside the pen thirty metres up the hill and it felt definitively human. Annie's spirits faltered. 'Grace?'

Another shift in space ahead, closer now to where she stood. A sliver of light slid across the forest floor. As it did so, behind a tree, the corner of a waterproof jacket.

'Hello?' Annie hissed, stepping forwards. 'Grace? That you? Who's there?'

A figure emerged, slowly. Not Grace. Straggly fair hair. A young woman. A girl, really. The one she'd seen before. The first thing Annie was struck by was how very like Issy she was: tall, striking, a Dillane. The second was that the girl held a shotgun in one hand, the barrel pointing at the ground.

The girl lifted her free arm, as if to signal she meant no harm, then put a finger to her lips. She gestured at the trees around her. Perhaps she was trying to warn Annie, let her know that someone else was here?

Annie mustn't put herself in danger, for the kids' sakes as much as her own. But equally, it was clear this girl needed help. The waterproof coat jutted proud at her belly. She was standing in the middle of the forest, her shoulders raised as if in appeal, seemingly pregnant. She certainly didn't appear threatening, despite the presence of the gun.

The girl beckoned for Annie to follow, then darted back through the trees towards the clearing. Annie watched her departing back, blonde hair flying. All she could think of was Issy, and the next moment she was pushing through the open gate and chasing after her.

The girl was faster than Annie, even in her pregnant state, and gained ground, crossing the open section of the clearing and disappearing through the little door at the front of the shepherd's hut. Annie, heart thrumming, belted after her through the rickety door just as the sun pulled itself from the moon's grasp and daylight began to be restored, the sky returning from brown, to yellow, to blue.

Annie stood, panting, in the doorway. 'Hallo?' The girl was nowhere to be seen. Stephen had lied: the hut was by no means his hang-out but looked to be someone's actual home. The walls were panelled in ageing tongue and groove. There was a modest kitchen area in one corner, a single bed, a sofa, a short bookshelf of paperbacks, a small dining table, and a radio. Another even smaller room led off to the right. She was relieved to see the shotgun in the corner, its barrel facing down.

The girl emerged from the small room, her waterproof coat hanging open, exposing a slim body with a hugely swollen belly. She seemed awfully young to be pregnant. She hung her coat over a hook on the wall, then turned. Immediately, Annie opened her mouth to speak, but the girl shook her head.

'Why?' Annie mouthed. 'Who's listening?' When the girl didn't answer, Annie asked, 'Was it you that fired the gun?'

The girl nodded. 'Why?' Annie demanded. She looked eerily familiar.

'To let them know I'm ready,' the girl whispered.

'Let who know?' Annie pressed. 'Ready for what?'

The girl looked out of the window. Her appearance was so like Grace it was uncanny. As Annie studied her, waiting for an answer, it dawned on her who it was she was talking to. '*Polly?*' she exclaimed. 'Is that you?'

The girl whipped round. 'Ssh!'

It was Polly, of course it was. Andrew's daughter; the ever-absent child. Not in a medical centre, but here, living in the wood. Not bipolar, but pregnant. So young! And... a *prisoner?* This seemed a strange place to spend time voluntarily. Annie raised her hands in peace. 'What are you doing here?'

Polly reached across the table for a pen and paper. She began to write in fast, spiky hand. *It's not what it looks like. My dad's a good man.*

Annie took up the pen: *I don't understand. What do you mean?*

Polly shook her head: *I let off the shot to say I'm ready. They'll be here soon.*

Annie stared at the words. *What are you doing up here?* she wrote. *Are "they" your grandmother and Vincent, and are they keeping you hidden?* Her hand was shaking so much she drove the pen right through the paper. *And if so, why?*

Polly looked at her for a moment. *It's not my dad's idea,* she wrote.

Whose idea is it?

The society, Polly wrote. *They've been keeping me hidden from you, and Grace, and Caleb. Until you're ready.*

Annie looked up, sharply. 'Ready for what?' she said out loud.

Polly shook her head and put her fingers to her lips once more.

Why not? Annie wrote. She remembered something: the transistor in the back room of the shed. *They're listening, aren't they?*

Polly hesitated, then wrote: *Go back to London.* She underlined the words several times, then whipped the paper away before Annie could write on it again, tore it into pieces, and clutching them in her fist went to the other room.

If she hadn't heard Polly's shot, she never would have come here, she'd have gone back to London never knowing that Polly was living in a hut in the woods. It was all too surreal. She took a photo of the room while Polly was gone, then stared out the window to the clearing. Polly said the gunshot was to signal she was ready; people might arrive at any moment. Annie mustn't be here when they did.

Polly came through the bathroom door and made a shooing motion with her hands.

'But you have to let me help!' Annie said. Polly simply reached behind her, yanked the door open and pushed Annie out into the clearing.

'I'm fine!' came her voice from the other side of the door. 'I don't need help.'

Annie spoke into the door. 'What are your grandparents doing to you?' she said. 'How did you get pregnant?'

A second later, Polly's face appeared, ghost-like, at the window. 'Go!'

There was nothing else Annie could do. She headed downhill towards Chapel Croft. What had Polly meant, it wasn't what it looked like? She must remain focused on the most important things: packing the essentials, collecting the kids from the field – though how she'd manage that, she couldn't imagine, she'd have to make up some major lie – then jumping in the car and leaving. Down in the bowl of the valley, an insistent bass thumped through the speakers.

Now she heard the buggy moving along the lane. Stephen, probably, on the lookout for her. She veered in a sideways direction, her legs carrying her further downhill. There was Chapel Croft at last, nestling against the hillside to her right. She slipped down the last slope until she was directly above the back garden, then skidded the remaining thirty yards, arriving on her bottom on the grass.

She dusted herself off. Something felt different. She looked around.

Pomander: she was gone. The table had been pulled – or

knocked by the pig herself – to one side. Annie felt sick at the thought that Pomander might have been captured, then taken to the field. She'd find out soon enough when she went for the kids.

She hurried into the writing shed and snatched up her laptop. She ran to the back door of the cottage. Her keys weren't in any of her pockets. Prickles of fear rose on her arms. The key to the car was attached to that set of house keys. It was the only one. If she'd lost them, they wouldn't be able to leave.

The music in the field had switched to an English-sounding madrigal. A cheer went up.

She needed to think. The keys would almost certainly be nearby. Grace and Caleb had left theirs in the cottage: she distinctly remembered seeing them on the kitchen table before they'd headed to the party. In her distracted state, might Annie have left hers in there, too?

There was nothing else for it: she limped around the garden until she found a rock, limped back to the door, took off her jacket and wrapped it around the rock, then slammed it hard through the glass panel closest to the door handle. The glass exploded into the house and skidded across the floor. She stuck her hand through the hole and slid the bolt from the inside.

The kids' keys were on the kitchen table just as she'd thought, but not hers. She must have dropped them, then. What if they'd fallen out in Polly's hut? Or worse, in the work shed, or the secret room?

She flew upstairs, pulled a holdall from the cupboard and jammed in her laptop. She threw clothes into the bag, another pair of shoes, personal items, the letters to Andrew and Issy that she'd taken from the work shed. She ran into the kids' rooms, grabbed armfuls of clothes from their bedsides – thank God they'd barely unpacked after school. She dumped the bags in the hallway by the front door. No car keys. She'd have to go on a search.

Her phone pinged. It was an email from the hospital. Grace's histology report. Annie scanned it, quickly. A list of medical terms, and at the bottom:

> There were several foreign cells present, appearing at first glance to be consistent with porcine stem cell DNA, though this could be a mistake on the part of the lab, or a contaminated sample, and needs establishing. As such, a second investigation has been ordered and the slides sent to Porton Down. The consultant in charge of the case has informed the patient's father and will be in touch with him in due course.

Porcine stem cell DNA? Inside Grace? No, that was a mistake: she'd ingested the wrong supplements by accident. That accounted for it.

Annie changed her outfit, splashed water on her face, and left the cottage for the field, the kids' keys in hand. Evening was drawing in. Her arms around her chest, she pressed along the path, head down.

Porcine stem cell DNA. Issy's daughter. *Annie's* daughter.

Someone was running towards her. 'Annie!'

Margaret. Annie didn't want to talk to her. She didn't trust a single soul in this wretched village. 'I'm heading back to the field,' Annie muttered, but Margaret wasn't giving up.

'Wait! I haven't... There's something I need to tell you.'

Annie tried to move around her, but Margaret grabbed her

arm. 'Please!' She pulled Annie back towards Chapel Croft. 'For Grace's sake.'

Annie went stiff. 'What? What about Grace?'

'It's not his real name,' Margaret urged.

'What? Who?'

'My husband: Colin Paine. That's not his real name. His name's Christopher. Christopher Dillane.'

Annie frowned. 'Margaret, if this is a–'

'It's not a joke. He's Elizabeth's brother.'

Annie stepped back. 'She doesn't have a...' The blonde hair, the height, the piercing blue eyes. 'She has a *brother*?'

'It was his portrait that hung on the stairs at the Big House above Andrew's,' Margaret was saying. 'They took it down before you came in case you asked questions.'

'I'm sorry, I don't understand. Why is Christopher pretending to be Colin?'

Stephen's buggy buzzed along the lane somewhere up ahead.

'The blessing!' Margaret said. 'Oh God, we must go back to the field. Meet me at Chapel Croft after the fireworks. I'll explain everything, I promise.' She scurried away.

'What blessing?' Annie panted, running after her. 'Who's being blessed?' But Margaret slipped through the gate into the field and vanished.

Annie followed her through, wedging herself in against the hedge in the hope no one would see her. Get the kids, find the car keys, that was all she needed to do.

Processional dancing was going on around the wooden platform, to music played by someone on a drum, another on a pipe. Everyone was holding hands. On the platform, the pig sizzled. A bonfire raged in the far corner, its orange flames licking the sky. It was too dark to make out anyone at this distance. She'd need to head into the fray to find the children.

As she made her way towards the centre, Stephen's buggy bumped noisily through a rear gate: inside it, Stephen and a smaller person in a dark coat. It drew near and Annie recognised Polly.

Pregnant Polly. Polly who, not fifteen minutes ago, had shooed her away. Polly, who'd known Stephen was on his way to collect her because she'd alerted him with a shot on her rifle. Who had known that *this* – whatever this 'blessing' was – was about to happen.

He helped Polly up the steps of the platform, where Elizabeth and William waited, arms wide.

Annie cast her eyes around: there was Caleb and Grace! In the processional circle, Patrick in between them, holding fast to their hands. She pushed hard against the dancing crowd towards them.

Patrick saw her coming. He broke out of the line and came right up in front of her. The kids ran up behind him. 'Everything okay?' he asked.

Annie shook her head. 'I've lost my... house keys.' Patrick smiled, put an arm around her shoulder. His lean was a little too heavy for her liking. 'Could you not?' She ducked out from under him. Polly was being led to the front edge of the platform by William. 'Caleb, Grace, d'you want to–'

'The blessing only takes a couple of minutes,' Patrick cut her off. 'What's the rush?'

Caleb was throwing her nervous glances. 'Like I said,' Annie told Patrick, raising her voice over the music. 'I've lost the keys to the cottage. I'll take the kids, hunt for them: sharp eyes.'

Grace and Caleb nodded at her with enthusiasm. 'Great idea.' Patrick had no choice but to let them go.

Annie chivvied them across the field, the drumbeat thumping through the soles of her feet.

When they reached the gate, Annie thrust their own sets of

keys into their hands. They looked at her in confusion. 'I smashed the glass at the back door of the cottage,' she explained. 'The car key was with my house keys. I need to find it or... Listen, you go home right away, do you hear? No matter what happens, do *not* leave Chapel Croft. Wait for me there. Don't answer the door to anyone.'

'But if the back door's broken, anyone can get in,' Caleb reasoned.

'But they don't know it's broken,' she told him. 'You're quite safe. Just do as I say.' She wasn't going to have them hiding out on the fell.

At that moment, the music died and a hush descended on the field.

'Go!' she said. 'Please.'

This time, there was no Patrick to stop them. Annie watched as they hurried along the lane, their silhouettes melting into the sky.

CHAPTER SEVENTEEN

'Everyone!' Elizabeth's voice boomed through the speakers as Annie stepped through the gate. Instantly, Patrick was back. 'Where are the kids?'

'They've gone to the cottage to look for me,' she lied.

'I thought you needed their sharp eyes?'

She looked him square in the face. 'Fuck off.'

His smile faltered. 'Now that's not very nice.' He linked an arm through hers. 'It's okay, I know you've been under a great deal of stress. Why don't we watch the blessing and then I can help you look?'

She didn't want his help. She didn't want him anywhere near her, but Elizabeth was at the front of the platform next to Polly, mike in hand, and Patrick had Annie firmly in his grasp. 'Patrick,' she told him, 'get off me, please, I–'

Several people around her turned and told her to shush.

Ahead, Elizabeth cleared her throat. 'Tradition dictates that after prayers and dancing comes the blessing. This year, to echo God's bathing us in glory and beneficence through His mighty eclipse, we have a special person that I just know we've all been longing to see.'

The crowd were lapping it up, cheering and clapping. They probably had no clue about the shepherd's hut. Like her, they no doubt believed she'd been at a retreat.

Elizabeth handed the mike to Polly. 'Thank you,' came Polly's breathy voice. 'I'm thrilled.'

'Let us bless this blessed gift.' Elizabeth reached forward and flung Polly's robe wide, revealing her belly.

'Amen!' cried the crowd.

Elizabeth was nodding at William. He went to the pig on the spit and carved away a slice of its flesh with his knife, then returned to his wife, who took it, the meat resting on its blade, and fed it to Polly. 'May your loins be forever fruitful,' she intoned. Polly dutifully chewed and swallowed. 'And now...' Elizabeth looked around, grandly. 'Where are you, David?'

David climbed onto the platform. The crowd applauded. He took Polly's arm and lead her gently down the steps to stand before the upright wooden web. 'Prepare for your blessed journey through the Mouth of Astarte,' he decreed.

People moved to form a ring around the structure. Annie looked at Patrick. He shrugged. 'Tradition,' he said. 'Another couple of minutes, then I'll help you look.'

The crowd were pulling the small brown hessian sacks, the same as the one Margaret had carried, over their heads. Annie's eyes went wide.

They were not, in fact, sacks but hoods with pointed tops and cut-outs for eyes, like the Ku Klux Klan. She felt herself shrink backwards, away from them. It was impossible to tell who was who. She remembered suddenly where she'd seen the hoods before. On the rail in the attic room at Colthwaite House.

She turned to Patrick and let out a cry of surprise. He was also wearing a hood. 'This is for you,' he whispered, handing her one of her own. She batted it away.

'Are you fucking kidding me?'

'Oh, Annie,' Patrick sighed. 'It's just a bit of fun.'

She moved around him. 'I need to find my keys.'

'Listen,' he grabbed at her sleeve. 'You're on someone else's land. You must do as they do. You can leave in a minute. For now, just... assimilate.'

She glared at him, standing there in his hood. 'No.'

David's voice boomed from somewhere. 'May Astarte bless this baby with precious gifts!'

To cheers from the crowd, Polly began clambering ungainly through the central hole cut into the wooden structure. As she made it out the other side David cried, 'May she be forever protected and healthy!'

The crowd moved to queue beneath the platform, and William began to hand out slices of pig meat.

Annie wheeled across the field, eyes down for any sign of the keys, then headed for the gate. A hooded someone put themselves in her path. They were small and holding a large stick. 'What is it, Vincent?' Annie snapped.

'The wanderer must depart again so soon?'

Two further people appeared at his side, men judging by their height, one a lot taller than the other.

'Gentlemen – whoever you are...' she said. 'I'd love to stay and chat but–'

The taller man removed his hood. It was Colin Paine. *Christopher Dillane.* He was frowning. He looked so like Andrew, she noticed now. As alike as Issy to Elizabeth.

'Annie,' he said.

She didn't like the way he said it, like a threat. She shot a nervous glance around the field. Elizabeth and William were on the platform with Polly, smiling and dancing, oblivious.

'Did you get your phone?' Vincent asked. She could just see his eyes behind his hood. 'Capture the eclipse? Wasn't it magnificent?'

'Yep,' she managed. 'Amazing.'

'But how peculiar...' Vincent's hood swivelled to look at the other men.

'Most peculiar,' the third man chimed: it was David's voice. His hand went into his pocket and he pulled out her house keys. He dangled them in front of her face. 'I believe these are yours?'

Annie stared. Her car key. Her means of escape. Not lost, but in David's pocket.

'It would have been impossible,' he said, 'for you to retrieve a mobile that, according to you, had been locked in the cottage–'

'–without your house keys?' Vincent finished.

Annie made a stab for them, but David was fast and snatched them away.

'Can I have them back now, please?' She replayed the last encounter she'd had with him. He'd been right next to her in that circle at the start of the festival, her jacket pocket gaping.

'Fireworks in a minute,' commented Christopher, replacing his hood. 'You wouldn't want to miss those, would you?'

'Grace is unwell,' Annie said firmly. 'I need to–'

'Come, Annie.' Vincent was laughing at her softly, as David took a step towards her with a waft of familiar marzipan scent. 'The problem is,' Vincent went on, 'we simply don't want you to go.'

'But I have to,' she squeaked, her heart beating fast now. 'Grace isn't feeling good.'

Vincent was in front of her and Christopher and David were either side. She looked for Margaret – even Patrick – but it was dark and everyone was in hoods. If she could just stay calm, if she could not show fear.

Christopher loomed at her shoulder. 'Boys, do you know what I'm thinking?'

'What?' replied the others.

'I'd love to talk to her, really talk, if she would do us the honour? What do you think?'

Vincent was nodding. 'What a good idea.'

'What? Talk? I can't, I have to...' Her breathing grew shallow. She pushed her elbows out. 'Can you move away a bit?'

'But we should try to find somewhere quiet for our talk,' the vicar pressed. 'It'll be impossible to hear in a minute, with the fireworks.'

That was it, she'd had enough. Without thinking, Annie stepped hard onto Vincent's foot, catching his shin and sending him stumbling. She blundered away, hardly seeing, desperate to get home, to get the kids, and ran slap into William.

'What's the hurry?' He grabbed her at the waist, pinning her arms at her side. She fought against him, but it was useless. The other men joined him.

'Let me go!' Her voice was trembling now. 'What is it you want from me?'

'We don't want anything, old girl.' William's tone was gentler than his grip. 'Just a short chat to clear things up. Promise.'

A short chat. The first fireworks exploded, making her jump. William's arms wrapped more tightly around her. 'Easy now,' he said.

A shower of red, gold, and green sparks rained from the sky. Another, then another. Collective sighs came from the crowd, whose upturned hooded attention was directed elsewhere, not at her. She went unnoticed at the side of the field, surrounded by men. She was on her own.

They started to propel Annie in the direction of Colthwaite House. 'Where are we going?' she asked. 'Why can't we talk here?'

'Too noisy here,' David told her.

'But don't you want to see them?' she tried.

'Stop fretting,' Vincent complained as they pushed her across the grass. 'We've seen the fireworks a million times. You've been anxious, Annie. You've questions we've been waiting to answer.'

What was he talking about? She hadn't stopped asking questions since she'd arrived in the village, and all she'd been met with was lies.

'A chat in the warm,' David was saying, 'then you can get back to the field – or home – as you wish.'

Annie didn't trust a word he said. If the plan was to be honest, the preliminary wouldn't have required hostility. They led her through the bottom gate and across the drive, in front of Colthwaite House, gravel crunching under foot. She wondered which of the many rooms they would take her to.

'Nearly there,' David remarked, as they passed the house and carried on towards the farmyard.

'What? But—'

'For God's sake, Annie, *relax*,' said William. 'We're not going to hurt you.'

A cold bar dropped through her. More fireworks lit up the night sky. She needed to call for help. But everyone was in the field. Apart from the kids.

William steered her through the farmyard. 'Bet you're longing for a cup of tea.'

What would the kids do if something happened to her? And where was Patrick? He'd been glued to her side all day; now she needed him he was nowhere to be seen. They arrived outside the large barn.

'In here.' David pushed her through the door.

The infrared lamps were on. Injured sheep lay in pens along one side, their diamond-slitted eyes watching in the red light as the group led her on.

'The Big House is busy,' David was saying. 'Pregnant with

caterers preparing the buffet. We'll be more comfortable where it's warm.'

What caterers? She hadn't seen any caterers.

They led Annie to the rear, where the heat didn't reach, the area where she and William had 'served' the gilt. Another freshly slaughtered pig hung upside down from a hook attached to the pulley. It swung gently back and forth. Blood had oozed from a cut in its neck and pooled on the concrete. Nearby lay a mound of straw.

'Hang on.' David dashed into the darkness and returned with four mucky crates as fireworks popped and fizzed outside. He placed the crates in a semi-circle, leaving one on its own at the centre. He gestured at it. 'That's for you.'

'I'm fine standing,' she said.

'*Sit*,' Christopher ordered, sharply. 'There's a good girl. Quicker you do as you're told, the quicker we'll all get back to the party.'

As if to show her how it's done, he sat on one himself. The others followed suit.

Annie sat. There was an awkward hiatus. God, it was freezing. The crate was hard beneath her bottom, and the smell coming from the dead sow was terrible. She wondered what – or who – it was they were waiting for.

William shifted. 'Any moment we'll–'

Efficient footsteps outside. Claws on cement. The four men rose. Elizabeth and Noah stepped through the door at the far end of the barn, the infrared light framing their outlines ghoulishly.

'About time!' William bellowed as Noah raced straight up to Annie. He circled her once, then licked the end of her boot.

'Dogs really do love her,' she heard David say as she shuffled back on her crate. She made some quick calculations. Her phone and penknife were in her jeans pocket. Behind her was a large mound of straw. The men in front of her were strong but slow, though there were four of them, and Elizabeth too, of course, but only one of her.

Christopher tripped away into the darkness, returning a second later with an extra crate. 'Here, you take mine,' he told Elizabeth. 'The rats have been at this one.'

'Apologies for the delay,' Elizabeth said, perching on Christopher's crate, legs to one side. 'Polly needed help getting into the buggy.' She looked around. 'Where's our son?'

'In the field,' William said. 'Couldn't leave Marcus in charge of that spit.' The four men looked at Elizabeth like naughty schoolboys.

Elizabeth turned her attention to Annie. 'I believe we owe you an apology.' It was so cold in the barn that Annie could see her breath condensing as she spoke. 'We haven't quite given what I believe legal parlance terms "full disclosure". You've been doing investigations of your own, I hear. Which is a good thing.'

'Is it?' Annie doubted that.

'Truly. You're family,' Elizabeth told her. 'The time has come where we must share with you what it is we do.' She lifted an eyebrow. 'I know what you're thinking.'

'What's that, then?' Her mother-in-law was using her God voice; it pissed Annie off as much as it scared her.

'You think we're mad,' her mother-in-law said. 'But we're entirely rational. Allow me to explain–'

From the field, the high-pitched circular scream of a Catherine wheel took Elizabeth's words from her mouth, and her and the men's attention were pulled in the other direction. Annie quickly slid her phone and knife from her pocket and hid them behind her back.

'And the Angel of the Lord appeared to him in a flame of fire from the midst of a bush,' David intoned, turning back. 'So he looked, and behold, the bush was burning with fire, but the bush was not consumed.'

'They declared Galileo insane, Annie,' Elizabeth began again, 'when he claimed Earth revolved around the sun.'

'So?'

'Each of man's great discoveries has been greeted with suspicion and cries of madness throughout time.' Elizabeth rearranged herself on the crate. 'Now, I may be speaking out of turn here, and you don't have to answer me, but do you have any idea what it's like not to be able to have a child?'

Annie looked Elizabeth right in the eye. 'No.'

Elizabeth sighed. 'We're on the same side, Annie, you and me, and...' she gestured to the four men, '...them. In the past, generations of women grieved their unborn. There was the invention of IVF in the early seventies, it's true, but what about those women for whom IVF wasn't suitable, those who we now understand have genetic SNP's – "snips" - polymorphisms in their DNA sequencing, or other problems with their DNA? What if you happened to be a scientist and through science and hard work discovered how to eradicate this suffering? If *you* had the means to realise your discovery, would you? Allow yourself to unhook from present-day societal belief structures – societal ethics – for one moment and think about it.' She sat back.

'It would depend,' Annie said eventually, 'on what I had to do to achieve it.'

'Well.' Elizabeth got to her feet. 'If you chose to take the doing-something-about-it route, the path to realising such a thing wouldn't be easy: moral problems, ethical ones, things that go wrong.' Annie saw a look of genuine pain pass between Elizabeth and William. 'We've toiled against the odds, endured heartbreak and personal sacrifice in the name of science to bring others' happiness to light.'

'I'm still not following,' Annie said, prompting a 'huh' of

irritation from Elizabeth. From the field, the puff-puff sounds of smaller fireworks, cries of pleasure.

Vincent struggled to his feet. 'If I may, Lizzo, you're being a little vague. You seem like a straight-talking sort of person, Annie, am I right?'

'You are.' Annie searched his face for a chink of uncertainty; weakness; *something*.

'I'll tell it to you straight, then. Science isn't pretty. All this cloak and dagger stuff, it served a purpose. We couldn't let you in first for fear of scaring you.'

'What,' Annie said, 'are you talking about?'

'I gave you a tour of the house, yes?' said Vincent. 'The library door was locked, then later it was unlocked, do you remember that?'

She remembered. Of course she did.

'That was on purpose.' He seemed pleased with himself. 'So you'd find things out – the albums were a start – on your own. Step by step.'

'But... why?'

'We had hoped you'd venture up to the nursery that night too. But that particular investigation took longer to achieve.'

Elizabeth's trip to help William with the sheep, leaving her alone in the Big House: that had been a ruse? And the man sitting beside her was her *brother*, a man they were all still pretending was someone else entirely. None of it made sense. Unless you were mad, of course, then it took on a twisted logic of its own.

'Don't pull that face.' Vincent tutted. 'Perhaps we got it wrong, but that was our intention. Now for a little more hard science, if I may?' Vincent puffed out his chest. 'I think you know that our background is medical. That we met at university?'

Annie nodded.

'We've been helping women who can't conceive due to their DNA since 1961,' he went on. 'That's pre-IVF. But do you see us in the papers? Do you see us winning Nobel Prizes? It's been a long, hard and painful road. We've sacrificed our own happiness and experimented when perhaps we shouldn't. Over the years, the dead grew in our wake, things became grim and tiring; dark nights of the soul, but we persevered. Around 1984, we felt we had no choice but to suspend our work. Medical guidelines would never have let us... and I'd had a... mishap.' He looked at his feet. 'I shan't go into details, though no doubt through your investigations you know about that too.' When Annie said nothing, he pushed on. 'In 1987, there was a breakthrough in genetics. Not *our* breakthrough, sadly, but one we could use none the less. The discovery of a small organism in water that could edit its own genes, fix things inside itself that were broken. This was the dawn of CRISPR, a gene-cutting tool that–'

'I know what CRISPR is,' Annie interjected, unable to stop herself. 'I read it in your research papers.' What was the point in lying anymore?

'Good.' Vincent seemed impressed. 'With the advent of CRISPR we've recommenced our work on a more successful level, eradicating previously ineradicable mutations; this involves trying new things, experimenting. We're still working.'

Trying new things: Polly, Grace, Number 66. 'You used your own families as guinea pigs,' Annie said.

Elizabeth frowned. 'No one has been hurt.'

'Grace?' Annie said loudly. 'What about Grace? Her miscarriage? She was pregnant; you fed her pellets from a tub! And *who* made her pregnant?'

'We kept Grace on an excellent food supplement,' Elizabeth said.

'Is that what caused her miscarriage, that supplement?'

Annie turned to William. 'Why did she supplement her? What was wrong with Grace?'

'Goodness,' Elizabeth snapped. 'Nothing was wrong with her.'

David muttered, 'If she had a scientific bone in her body...' He picked up his crate and set it down beside her. 'Let's get some things out in the open: no great breakthroughs come without cost. Grace was on a cocktail of vitamins, minerals, growth-hormones and co-factors to increase her chances of an in-vitro foetus cleaving to its host. The host being Grace.'

'"An in-vitro foetus"?' Annie stood quickly. '*You* impregnated her?' She could feel the blood draining from her head. She fell backwards off the crate, landing in the mound of straw. 'But why? How? When did you...?'

'Calm yourself,' Elizabeth told her. 'Your becoming hysterical isn't helping. The supplements are part of the protocol. It's a method we've used with each expectant mother in the village for the last forty years, me included.' Her mother-in-law took a breath. 'With tweaks. Science marches on: we march with it.'

'When?' Annie croaked. 'When did you do it? Put a baby inside Grace?'

'During the drinks party,' David said as if it was perfectly normal. 'Grace was asleep, sedated, in the nursery. All terribly quick. Painless.'

'*What?*' While Vincent had distracted her with the hunt for the portrait of Issy, her stepdaughter had had things done to her that she'd not consented to and still had no knowledge of.

'Now you've frightened the poor girl.' William peered down at her. 'Too much information too quickly. Am I right, old thing?'

'It's a simple procedure, Annie, the implantation,' Vincent said. 'Please don't alarm yourself. Why,' he looked to Elizabeth, 'none of the girls were ever aware it was happening.' He took a step forwards.

'Don't!' She shuffled backwards, nudging her phone with her, until she and it was up against the barn wall. 'How could you? It's like...' She searched for the words. 'Medical rape. You raped my daughter!'

There was a deathly silence. David let go of a long, slow breath.

'Your daughter?' Elizabeth said at last. '*Step*daughter, no? If we're going to insist on facts, let's at least be consistent.' She beckoned the men to her. They huddled together whispering amongst themselves.

Annie swiped frantically at her phone behind her back, desperate to unlock it, praying the last thing she'd done with it was make a call. What they'd told her was diabolical. She clicked the volume button at the side as low as she could, then blindly pressed her finger onto what she hoped was the right part of the screen. It was a wild guess, a stab in the dark, but miraculously, a second later, a faint ringing reached her ears. Thank *God*. Who had she last called? Caleb? Lumi? *Please*, she prayed, *whoever you are, pick up*.

'Hallo?' said a voice.

Elizabeth's head spun round. She marched towards Annie, reached around Annie's back and plucked the phone from her hand. 'You won't be needing this – oh!' She put it to her ear. 'It's you! Hallo, dear.'

'Caleb?' Annie called. 'Is that you? Are you okay?'

'Yes, she's here,' Elizabeth said, ignoring her. There was a pause. 'Come and see for yourself.' She clicked off and pushed the phone into the pocket of her green dress.

Not Caleb, then. Could it have been Stephen? But she'd never called Stephen from her phone. A moment later, there were footsteps outside the barn, a figure slid through door and came towards her.

'Annie.' It was Patrick.

'Tell them to let me go,' she said, as he dropped to his haunches in front of her.

'Not just yet.' His voice was low, bemused. 'I'm sorry. All we want, Annie, is for you to understand.'

'You're... you're involved in all this?'

'I am,' he said. 'Let me explain. When I was a junior doctor struggling to make sense of my vocation in the organisational shitshow that is the NHS, these guys took me under their wing. The work they're doing is frankly astonishing.' He stopped to rub his nose. She could see he was working out how much he could say.

'Did Issy know?' she asked. 'About you?'

Patrick gestured at the others. 'These fearless pioneers are what modern society, modern medicine, is missing. Forging the great unknown. Religion has lost its power. Humans are miserable, spiritually bankrupt beings. We crave ritual. No wonder the country is falling apart.' She watched as he repeated the words 'falling apart' under his breath. 'We could make a real difference to peoples' futures here. CRISPR *is* the future.'

'Did Issy know?' she repeated. 'And what about Grace?' she demanded through gritted teeth when he still hadn't answered. 'How do you feel about what they did to your daughter?'

Christopher let out a snort.

'Well,' Patrick said, stepping back. 'I tried.'

'There are more people here in Colthwaite, Annie,' Elizabeth said, defensively, 'contributing to our work, helping in any ways they can. Far more than you can imagine; fighting the good fight against nature, its aberrations. We look out for our own. Protect one another. Help one another. Presently, you are by yourself in the village; you could benefit from our support, and we from yours.'

By herself in the village? She wasn't staying here, not for one single minute longer than she had to, and they were off their rockers if they thought she was going to help them.

'All we're asking is access to Grace as she matures,' David explained, as if it were perfectly reasonable. 'She plays a vital role in our work.'

'You want me to keep Grace here so you can experiment on her?'

'We're this close,' Vincent held his thumb and forefinger an inch apart, 'to cracking it, Annie. The whole thing. CRISPR has changed everything.'

'And when we succeed,' Patrick picked up the thread, 'you can say you've been part of something truly magnificent, historical, improving lives. You'll be able to say: "I was there. I contributed".'

'An insignificant village in the north,' David added, 'plagued by centuries of poverty, hardship, and misfortune becoming one of the wealthiest spots in the land. View it as an act of charity, if that helps.'

'It was never our intention,' Elizabeth said, 'to cause harm to you, or to Grace. To anyone, in fact.'

Annie still couldn't understand what exactly it was that they had been doing. All she knew for certain was these last few weeks had been nothing but a breadcrumb trail to get her to fall in line, and now she needed to get the kids and go straight to the police. 'Your *daughter*,' she repeated, glaring at Patrick.

Christopher pushed a lump of straw across the floor with his shoe. 'Technically, she's not his daughter.'

Annie's eyes flicked up. 'What?'

'Yes, you might as well tell her.' Patrick sighed. 'She deserves to know.'

'Know what?' Annie's body went still, like an animal about to spring.

Elizabeth looked to her brother. 'She won't understand.'

'She ought to know,' Patrick insisted. He was blinking hard.

'Issy is...' Christopher spoke with exaggerated care. 'No, sorry, Issy *was* Elizabeth.' He turned his palms up.

'What do you mean?' The skin on her scalp felt tight across her skull.

'Fashioned from Elizabeth's DNA. A clone,' he said. 'A replica.'

Her head began to pound. The pain of it made her wince.

Christopher was still talking. 'And Issy gave birth to Grace, yes?' How could he still be talking? 'And Grace is also a clone. From Issy's DNA, which is Elizabeth's DNA. Do you see?'

Annie staggered to her feet. Her head felt heavy.

Christopher turned to Elizabeth. 'We shouldn't have told her.'

'Stay calm, Annie. No good will come of grand gestures, sudden decisions. Grace is me,' Elizabeth said. 'As well as my daughter, Isabelle. It's beautiful, in a way. Think about it.'

Think about it? No, Annie wasn't going to think about it. Annie's darling wife. Annie's own stepdaughter. She forced her head up, her eyes meeting Elizabeth's. 'Did Issy know?'

No one said anything. They were all looking at her.

'She didn't, did she? How did you get the... clone into her without,' her voice was rising, 'her knowing? Did you drug her, like Grace? I'm right, aren't I?'

'Shush shush,' Elizabeth crooned.

'It isn't difficult if your subject is sedated,' David said. 'Issy came to learn of it in time, of course. The cloned embryo,' he brushed his hands together, 'became Grace.'

Annie saw everything suddenly: Issy had found out who she truly was, who Grace truly was, late in the day, and her world had turned upside down. The threatening letter from Elizabeth and William had been the tipping point. Issy had asked her to move to Colthwaite whatever the circumstances, not for selfish reasons, but to protect them all – Issy, Annie, and the kids. Any lies, any withholding of the truth had been an act of love. No wonder she had suffered the aneurism. Her heart had probably given out in shock.

'Annie?' Vincent implored. 'Please. We know it sounds awful and confusing presented all at once like this, but you must understand we've been trying to *help* people, to mend what was broken. We need you to help us in return, to allow us to complete our work anonymously, and in peace.'

'Help you?' How *dare* they. 'You monsters!' she screamed. She pressed the safety catch on the penknife and the blade flicked out. She whipped it back and forth in front of her.

William lunged, but Annie dodged out of his way, moving out beyond their circle with surprising ease. She ran between the animal pens for the door, but it was dark, and she tripped, crashing to the floor on a tangle of hurdles, bashing her head, the penknife spinning from her hand. An intense pain shot through her skull, and she felt warm liquid begin to trickle down her face.

'Oh Annie.' Elizabeth hurried over. 'What did you think you were doing?'

'What a shame,' she heard Vincent say. 'I was convinced she was going to... Oh look, her head.'

Annie scrambled to her feet, the barn spinning around her. Blood was in her eyes and she couldn't see clearly. Then William was at her side, twisting her arm, pushing his leg into the backs of her knees, and she was heading down again, gently, towards the floor.

'You're hurting me!' she cried, as he leant a good portion of his weight onto her chest. 'I can't breathe! Please!'

'You're hurting her, Willy,' Elizabeth said. 'Stop that.'

William released Annie and she gulped air. 'Sorry,' he muttered, brushing himself off. 'Too used to the animals.'

She watched him as he picked her penknife up and pocketed it.

'And now you're hurt, Annie.' Elizabeth bent to pat at Annie's head with a tissue. 'Silly girl. You may need another stitch.' She turned Annie's head to the side. Annie didn't have the juice to fight it. 'It's all very well this talk about consent, you know. Things have changed since our day. The feminist brigade has proven an enemy to its own cause many times over the years. All this outrage is a waste of energy. Can't they see they're ruining things for themselves? People *die*, Annie, as I'm sure you're aware.' Her eyes flickered with something real; Annie wondered briefly if there might be even the faintest chance of getting through to her. 'And yes,' Elizabeth went on, 'it is a tragedy. However, these days not only can we create new life from its inception, but we can bring old lives back, give someone another throw of the dice. Think about that. Issy isn't dead: she lives! In Grace.'

No, Annie thought, Grace was her own person. She struggled to speak through the pain. 'But your version of helping people so far has been by recreating yourself.'

'Despite appearances, it's not an act of narcissism,' Elizabeth demurred. 'Throughout history, great scientists have experimented on themselves at the outset. First do no harm. Or try not to.'

David was by her side, drawing a syringe tipped with a long needle from his jacket. 'This may give us some time?'

Annie felt her blood pressure drop.

'Ah,' Elizabeth was saying. 'Must we? I suppose we must.'

'We need your co-operation, Annie,' David said, close to her ear. 'We need your word.' He removed the plastic cover of the needle and pressed the syringe stopper up, flicking the liquid until it squirted from the needle's tip. Annie could smell marzipan. That was the odour coming off him, then: this, whatever this was. 'It's a sedative,' he explained. 'Nothing more. Try not to worry.'

She turned her head away, her eyes squeezed shut. Her legs scissored helplessly. This was it. Nothing more she could do.

William and Christopher rolled her onto her side. She made no sound. She'd gone limp, bovine. Porcine. She wasn't in her body, she was somewhere else, floating above herself.

'We're terribly sorry,' one of the men said.

'Annie, it's temporary.' Elizabeth's voice. 'Until we've sieved our options.'

She felt the needle point at her neck. 'Don't squirm,' David's voice. 'There's a good girl.'

Someone placed their hand over her mouth. The needle went in. The hand released. She let out a whimper.

'You'll be asleep before you know it,' someone said.

'Fuck you,' Annie whispered, barely audible. Elizabeth made a tutting sound.

'Now, now. Though as it turns out "fucking me" is exactly what you've been doing. For the last twelve years, in fact. Isn't that strange?'

Annie's head was so heavy it stuck to the floor. 'It's not just genes,' she slurred. 'Epigenetics, nurture.' What dim light remained was fading. 'Issy was nothing like you. *Nothing.*'

'What's she saying?' one of them asked. 'Can you understand?'

The barn swelled and contracted, its outlines swirling like water down a plughole. Left behind was only the faint pop of fireworks, the exclamations of the villagers.

CHAPTER EIGHTEEN

Annie and Issy tucked up in bed in Hackney, Annie spooning her wife's body, one leg and an arm curled around her like ivy.

She gasped into consciousness, her eyes opening into darkness. Strange noises. Heavy breathing. Steady drip. A bleat. Scuffling. Something in her mouth: soft, salivary. She was upright – or was she? Her brain a muzzy wetness. Cold, damp around her bottom, down her leg. Trousers, too low at the hips. Horrible smell; rancid milk. Taste of acid and iron. Tongue dry. Thick. Dripping. A searing tearing sensation between her shoulder blades. Something had her by the scruff of the neck. A separate sharp pain behind her ear.

Stop, she ordered, forcing her mind to go blank. *Organise your thoughts.*

She was in the barn. The others put her there. A rough material was tied at her mouth to gag her. Her hands were bound at her back. She couldn't lift her head. Her feet dangled into nothingness: they were bound, too. Her jacket collar was up around her ears; she could feel the stiff fabric brushing her lobes. Nearby, animals rustled in their pens. She moaned softly. An owl hooted.

It wasn't ropes she was hanging from: too hard, too cold at her neck. She flailed and the restraints squealed, metal on metal, as she began to swing gently back and forth. She knew, then, where she was. She was on a hook off the metal runner, hanging from chains, like the pigs. The metal loops nudged at her skull. A hot flush of terror washed through her.

She twisted her head, squinted through the darkness at a large shape hanging several feet away: a fat belly, four trotters. She looked down; all she could see was her chest rising and falling. They couldn't keep her here forever. They had to return. They had to. Beads of sweat broke across her forehead. No phone, no knife. No sounds of the party outside. The rancid smell. Was it coming from her? What time was it?

Pins and needles began to spread around her hands and feet, and a dawning awareness of a stabbing pain at the base of her neck. She scrabbled for a thought to cling to. The fell, where the sheep were grey and hobbling, their backsides caked in diarrhoea. No.

Issy.

A fresh burning pain under her armpits.

Grace.

She swayed gently. Only this moment. This one. Then this.

Crunching of feet on gravel. More than one person, their treads out of step. It could be Elizabeth and David. Christopher and Vincent. Or Patrick–

'Hello?' A man. A northern burr. A beam of light scraped across the walls of the barn. She watched as it passed over the tractor, the shelves, the cat, finding her at last, the glare forcing her eyes to close.

'Oh God.' A woman, also northern, the steps moving swiftly. 'Look what they've done.'

'Jesus effing Christ.'

Annie recognised the voice: Stephen. She let out a strangled noise, wriggled like a fish at the end of a line.

'Don't worry, pet. We're here.' The other voice was Margaret's. She stood in front of Annie now, her head level with Annie's feet. 'We'll get you out of here, promise.'

Margaret disappeared into the black. Annie heard her say something about pressing the button, and Stephen answering, *no don't.*

'What's that smell?' he was saying. He was behind her, the twine binding her wrists and ankles loosening. 'There now.'

Blessed relief. Instinctively, she kicked out. 'Easy.' He put his knife on the ground and laid a hand gently on her leg. 'I'm not going to hurt you.'

Margaret returned with a ladder, and Stephen wrapped his arms about Annie's waist and lifted her body off the hook in one motion. She'd lost all strength and collapsed over his shoulder. 'It's okay.' He moved downwards rung by rung then laid her carefully on the ground. 'Gonna take this off now.' He untied the gag. 'You're not to make a sound.'

Annie gulped air.

'Water.' Margaret turned to Stephen. 'She needs water.'

'And take my jacket.' Stephen shrugged off his coat, put it over her. 'It's covered in your sick, anyway.' That's the rancid smell: her sick. He pulled a flask from his pocket. Annie downed the water greedily. 'Slowly, slowly,' he was saying.

'Thank you.' When she spoke, her voice was weak. 'What time is it?' She began to shiver uncontrollably.

'Three twenty in the morning.'

'Look at her,' Margaret told Stephen. 'We need to get her

away fast. I put something in Christopher's whisky; he's out cold, but it won't last long.'

Stephen pulled Annie to her feet. 'They'll be back here first light. Can you walk?'

'Thank you,' she said again. 'Are the children okay?'

'They're fine. Sssh.' They steered her through the barn and out the door, Stephen supporting one arm, Margaret the other. The wind was arctic outside as they crept across the drive, as far from the Big House as possible.

On the lane the trees swayed. The night sky seemed to have drawn closer to Earth, pressing on Annie's head. She leaned hard into Stephen. The children must be frantic.

'You keep this to yoursen',' he told her. 'What they said to you. They didn't mean to hurt Grace.'

Annie's thoughts pulled themselves into focus. She must say nothing. If she put a foot wrong, Stephen and Margaret would abandon her. She didn't have the strength to make it home alone.

'Her miscarriage,' Stephen went on. 'It wasn't supposed to be like that.'

The miscarriage was only part of their transgression. If it hadn't been for the miscarriage, Grace would have had a genetically altered baby. One with porcine DNA.

'Their people are everywhere,' Margaret warned. 'Even the police. The chief's daughter up here, she's...'

Even the police? Annie kept her eyes on the ground. The *police?* Up in Cumbria?

'Yes.' Margaret nodded, as if Annie had answered her.

'If you speak about it, you'll put your children in danger,' Stephen said. 'Other peoples' children too.'

She'd see about that. Maybe the police here in Cumbria were up to no good along with the village, but not in the south, not in London, where she was heading – tonight, as soon as she could.

'Now you understand why I told you about Christopher,' Margaret whispered. 'To stop this from happening; to protect you.'

No, Annie didn't understand any of it. They were heading to Chapel Croft. That was all that mattered. They were nearly there.

They rounded the last bend in the lane. The moon appeared from behind a cloud. Annie looked behind her, beyond the Big House, beyond the farmyard. The remains of the bonfire glowed in the field at the back of the church, the faint sulphur smell of fireworks drifted on the wind.

Stephen coaxed her on. 'Watch where you're going.'

Chapel Croft was in view. A lamp in the living room still on. Annie faltered. 'Will they be watching, Elizabeth and...?' she asked. 'Will one of them be there?'

Stephen shook his head. 'The way they operate, it's not like that. Their science is ordered; the rest is chaos. Can't you see how old everything is: the equipment, the houses, the people? The way they dealt with you?'

'They know you want to protect the children,' Margaret said. 'They're confident that if you were to get away, you wouldn't say anything.'

Well, they were wrong about that. Grace and Caleb. Waiting for her in the warm. They were at the gate leading up to the track. As if the bones had been removed from her body, Annie folded inwards, collapsing onto the ground.

'There now.' Stephen swept her up and carried her up the track, his profile clean against the crescent moon. Suddenly, they were in the porch, the bulb flickering in its housing. He put her down, reached for the door handle.

Annie stiffened. 'Patrick!'

'He drove out the village an hour ago,' Stephen soothed. 'But he'll be back soon enough. Calm. Breathe. Don't want your kids more worried than necessary, do we?'

The door swung open. The children were right there. Grace flung herself into her arms.

'Oh, Annie!' She wound herself round Annie's neck. It was one of the best things Annie had ever felt. 'We didn't know if it was you.'

Annie rubbed her daughter's back – her *daughter*, no matter what Elizabeth said. 'It's okay,' she told Grace. 'I'm okay.'

Caleb clung to her. 'What's happened to your face? You smell awful. Are you okay? Dad was with us and then he said he was anxious about you and that he's going to the police. He's bringing back the chief constable.'

Annie turned to Stephen. He paled. 'Oh God.'

From around the living-room door, Andrew appeared, his face drawn. 'It's okay,' he told her as she stepped away. 'I'm on your side, I promise. I just...'

'He's safe,' Stephen reassured. 'He's here to help.'

Annie didn't trust that. She didn't trust any of it. 'We need to leave,' she told the children. 'Now.'

'Go where?' Grace said. 'What's going on? Our flat's got people in it.'

'Lumi's.'

'Lumi's?'

'Just trust me.' Annie pushed her way into the hall, pointed at the bags lined against the wall. There was the tiniest pause, then both children nodded.

'But, Annie,' Caleb said, 'Pomander's in trouble. She's been crying in the woods. Dad wouldn't let us go to her.'

'It's her time,' Grace stated. 'I know it. We have to help get her babies out.'

On cue, a squeal came from behind the cottage. Grace was

glaring at her. Annie knew she'd never be forgiven if she refused. 'Quickly then.'

Stephen said, 'You'd better mean that. Me, Andrew, and Caleb'll pack the car.'

'I'm sorry, Annie,' Andrew called pathetically as he followed Stephen out the front door. 'I'm so sorry.'

Pomander hadn't gone far. Once they were in the back garden, they could hear her whimpers nearby. Her lumbering form emerged from the trees. She waddled towards her stone hut until she reached the doorway, then stopped. Grace, Annie and Margaret went to her.

She lay down, sprawled on one side. She was panting, shivering, her teats swollen and leaking milk. One back leg was cocked, her tail twitching. Annie took a look at the pig's rear end. Four tiny legs poked from the pig's vagina. Annie stared at the legs, blue and wobbly, like jelly.

'They're coming!' Margaret cried. 'But the first one's stuck. We need Stephen.' She ran off. Grace let out a wail.

Stephen, Caleb and Andrew raced around the side of the cottage. 'It's breech.' Stephen dropped to his knees. 'Go to the house, Cal. Get oil: baby oil, cooking oil, anything. Get washing-up gloves!' Caleb stumbled away.

'Aim that torch here, would you?' Stephen's head was low by the sow's bottom. He rolled up his sleeves. 'You'd better get on with it, Number 66. These lot are leaving in three minutes.'

Number 66. Pomander. It was Pomander. Her disfigurement, Elizabeth and William's desire to capture her. Why they hadn't euthanised the pig when caught.

Margaret shone a torch at the pig's rear. It was an awful sight. Blood ran in a steady stream.

'She's going to be okay, right?' Grace said. 'Her baby?'

'Bab*ies*,' Stephen corrected. 'This one needs to come out now. There'll be others, waiting behind it.'

Pomander groaned. Caleb returned with a bowl of soapy water and the oil and gloves. Stephen pulled on the gloves, slathering them in oil. He pushed his hand inside the pig, making slow twisting motions with his forearm. Pomander's panting intensified. 'It's okay, lass.'

A moment later, a grey-blue piglet slithered out. It flopped onto the ground. Pomander's head lifted briefly, then dropped back with a thud.

Annie stared at the tiny lifeless animal. It was small, partially covered in a white cawl, and very dead. Pomander licked at the remains of the cawl, making little grunting noises, nudging the piglet with her nose.

'Oh no!' Grace cried. 'No!'

There would be no little piglets following behind. Stephen rocked back on his heels, wiped his brow. 'I'm sorry.'

'Something's wrong with it,' Grace whispered. 'Look. What *is* it?'

Annie leant in for a closer look. The piglet had a narrow neck topped by a humanoid head, complete with human-baby nose, ears, mouth, and tiny glued-together eyes. She glared at Stephen. 'What the fuck is that?'

'They call it "grafting",' Stephen said. 'It's part of their experiment; their work.'

Grace drew closer to Annie. 'What's he talking about?'

'Go inside,' Annie instructed. She couldn't meet Grace's eye. 'Finish packing the car. You too, Caleb.'

'But I–'

'Go!' Annie barked. The children hurried away. Stephen and Margaret swiftly cleaned Pomander, collecting the placenta that had slipped out after the dead piglet.

That little malformed foetus wrapped in white paper in the work shed fridge. It could have been Grace's baby after all. Anything was possible.

Andrew hovered nearby. 'Annie, I...' He dropped his head. 'I feel I must explain myself.'

'No need,' she told him, roughly. She'd heard enough Dillane lies.

'I'm not a bad man.'

That's what Polly had said. But he *was* a bad man. He was weak, easily manipulated. They all were. Issy hadn't been like that. All of her actions had been attempts to protect those she loved, not hurt them. Not lock them in shepherds' huts in woods or move portraits around houses as decoys.

'What's going to happen?' Annie demanded. 'To Polly? Her baby? Will it look like this one?'

Margaret tutted. Andrew turned away. 'It's... you wouldn't understand.'

'You're right; I wouldn't.' Annie spat the words out, the anger injecting her with fresh energy.

Stephen emptied the bowl of soapy water onto the grass. 'We've taken care of Polly best we can.' He nodded at Andrew. 'She wanted for nothing.'

'But she's my responsibility.' Andrew's voice had a wobble in it. 'I need you to know, Annie; Polly agreed to it, to everything.' Then more quietly, 'Eventually.'

Annie looked up, sharply. 'With coercion, you mean?'

'*Everyone* agreed to what happened to my daughter,' Andrew said. 'Agreed unanimously. We hid her on the fell on account of you.' Stephen rested a hand on the other man's back, but Andrew shook it off. 'She needs to know.'

Annie was furious now. 'On account of *me*? Don't you dare blame me for your actions!'

'There's no blame,' Margaret said, gently. 'But you're not from here. How could we have explained the years of suffering? And even if we could, would you have understood?'

Annie stared at the dead piglet, its misshapen head. 'No,'

she said. 'I still don't. Why are you helping me now? Why have you remained silent all this time?'

Stephen and Margaret exchanged glances. 'They buy you, the Astarte society, buy your silence. We all wanted a piece of it, one way or another, see. Childless people, drawn to settle here via word of mouth.'

'But not you,' Annie said to him. 'You grew up here. You have your own children.' She blinked. 'Don't you?'

Stephen looked up at the sky. 'Well...'

She followed his gaze: hundreds of stars, pricks of light in a navy firmament.

'The Ancients,' he said, 'stood as we stand now, creating gods from nothing but air. I've mouths to feed. I'm not proud. They paid me well for my silence.'

The children appeared at the kitchen window. They beckoned to Annie, urgently, then ran out to her, eyes wide. 'Dad's car! It's coming! Are the police going to be with him? What's going on?'

They took one look at Annie's face and stopped. 'It's bad he's back?' Caleb said. 'Isn't it?'

Stephen ushered them around the side of the house. 'I'll take care of the sow for you. Don't fret.'

By the car, Annie pushed her hand into her pocket for the key. 'My key!' she exclaimed. 'It's... I had it and then–'

They were truly screwed. Patrick would be upon them any moment.

'Here.' It was Andrew, handing her the key to her car. 'They had it. I'd heard them talking about taking it earlier. Then when I went to visit my folks when you were...' He shot a glance at the children. 'I took it back for you. It was in Dad's coat.'

Annie snatched up the key. 'Thank you.' He was good for something at least. 'Gracie, you sit with your brother in the back.'

They'd be safer behind her. She climbed in, pushed the key into the ignition. The dashboard lit up. All those numbers. What if she fell asleep at the wheel and they crashed and burned on the motorway?

Margaret took Annie's hands through the open window. 'You can do this. Be safe. Don't return.'

'Will they...' Annie was aware of the children behind her, 'look for us in London?'

Andrew shook his head. 'My parents only want to continue their work. They lost so much in pursuit of it, they must, to give their lives meaning.'

Annie looked from Margaret to Stephen to Andrew. 'Thank you. For helping us.'

Patrick's car would be over the bridge, on the approach. 'Go on then,' Andrew said gruffly. 'Go.'

Annie closed the window. Margaret pressed her mouth against the glass. 'Leave the back way, past High Tarn via Gillyhead.'

Annie's car crawled silently along the track and out the gate. She kept the headlights off, the children silent in the back. Once on the lane, she gathered speed, coasting away as the beams from Patrick's Mercedes swung into her rear-view mirror. She watched them, her breath held, until she could be sure he hadn't followed.

She flicked the headlights on and opened the engine, focusing on the tarmac. Behind the adrenaline a tiredness sat deep in her bones.

'It's Granny, isn't it?' Grace whispered at last. Annie glanced back. Her stepdaughter's eyes were smooth with tears.

'Not now, sweetheart.' There was still so much Annie herself didn't understand. 'I'll tell you, but not now.'

It was only when they'd joined the motorway that Annie felt her shoulders drop. She put the radio on low, shoved a stick of gum into her mouth. It would be 7am when they arrived in London. They'd stop at a motel on the edge of town. She couldn't deal with Lumi's questions yet. She needed sleep first. And New Malden was miles beyond the M1 anyway.

'Will we be going back to our old school?' Caleb asked drowsily.

'Yes,' Annie replied.

'Oh,' he said. 'Happy about that.'

CHAPTER NINETEEN

The motel room was large and hot and just off the North Circular. The roar of early morning traffic penetrated the sealed windows. The room had two double beds: Grace and Caleb asleep in one, curled into each other like animals, Annie in the other.

Annie stared at the flicker of the TV, the sound off: unbelievably, a farmer was showing a young girl the correct way to hold piglets to check their sex. She'd had enough of pigs to last a lifetime. She hit the remote and the screen went black. On her mobile, five missed calls from Lumi.

Annie lay back on the pillows. Her neck was sore, her whole body burned. She studied the ceiling, which was ugly and made of stippled cardboard panels. Not a pig in sight. It was as if she'd never been to Colthwaite, as if it had happened to another person.

She sat up, suddenly. She'd left Issy's portrait at Chapel Croft. It belonged to Andrew, but still.

She rolled off the bed and went to her bag, returning with the photocopied letters from William and Elizabeth; the ones for Andrew and Issy. She placed them in front of her.

Dear Andrew, the one she'd not yet read began,

> *Your father and I write to you with the best of intentions. You've been a good son and a loyal and hardworking colleague over the years. But there is a matter over which we're both extremely worried.*

Annie guessed what was coming.

> *It concerns Polly's attitude; her reluctance to play her part in our work, in what we all know is a long but definitive road to discovery. She was a rebellious and unstable child, demanding answers to things that she couldn't possibly have understood at her delicate age and were not her business in the first place. Do you remember the time she broke into my private shed (I've no doubt you do)?*
>
> *When her periods started, and she refused to take even the most basic supplements despite hard evidence that these would benefit any young woman, things grew more urgent. The almighty brouhaha that followed, while you and Carolina worked to change her mind, I need not remind you of. Now, only two years later, we find ourselves in a similar situation. Of course, Polly must not be forced to agree to anything, though I feel she hasn't quite grasped the significance of her role, how vital she is, how our work cannot be completed without her compliance.*
>
> *Astarte has reached a decision and humbly requests that you change her mind or failing that, you insist. If you're unable to do so, we as her grandparents will be forced to act; not something we wish to do, in truth. I'm sorry it must be like this. I hope we understand one another.*
>
> *We trust you will do the right thing.*

Yours,
Mother and Father (on behalf of Astarte)

Annie put the letter down. She felt deeply sorry for Andrew, living as Issy had under the cosh of tyrannical parents, their threats, their bargaining. He must hate them, as she, Annie, did. No wonder he had helped her escape.

It was 8am and time to ring Lumi. Her sister would be worried.

'Annie!' Lumi cried on answering. 'I've been calling and calling and–'

'I'm sorry. And we're fine,' Annie said. The children were awake now, their eyes open. She smiled at them. 'We're okay. I can't... we're coming to you today, if that's all right?'

'Of course it's all right. Jesus. Jamae, what's going on?'

Annie glanced at the children. 'I'll explain later.'

'As long as you're safe,' she said. 'What time will you be here?'

'Soon. I need to sort some things out first.' That made the kids sit up.

There was silence at the other end of the line, then, 'Just so you know,' Lumi's voice had dropped a register, 'George is prepping a big case, so the kids'll need to be quiet.'

Annie rolled her eyes at Caleb and Grace, and they chuckled. 'No problem.'

'And, Annie? Have you thought about how they'll get themselves to school? It'll take hours.'

'I don't know yet, Lumes. We've just woken up. As I say...' She glanced at the letters beside her. 'We've had quite a night.'

Lumi must have turned her head because when she spoke her voice sounded farther off. 'Annie?'

'Yes?'

'Be safe, little Jamae.'

Grace was looking at Annie with big eyes. 'Everything okay?'

Annie packed a small bag with the letters, her laptop, some other bits. 'Uh-huh. I've got to go somewhere. You stay here 'til I'm done.'

'Where?' Caleb asked. 'How long will you be?'

'Maybe a couple of hours.'

His shoulders went back. 'But *where?*'

She picked up the bag, slung it over her shoulder. 'I'm going to the police.'

'The *police?*' Grace was on her feet. She paced back and forth in front of her, and threw on her coat. 'I'm coming with you.'

'No, Gracie,' Annie told her. 'Stay here 'til I've made a statement, in case...'

Both children were on their feet now. 'In case *what?*' Caleb demanded.

'Danger,' she whispered. There was a silence. 'I don't actually know what I mean by that, or even...' Annie's hands dropped to her sides. 'I'm trying to be honest.'

Caleb put a hand over hers. Annie felt herself soften. 'Are our lives in danger?' he asked.

'*No.* I don't... they're not.'

He sat heavily on the bed.

'Please,' Annie implored. 'Try not to worry. We're safe here. Get some breakfast at the buffet. It's included.' That made them smile. 'I'll be back soon. Then we'll head to Lumi's, promise.'

She left the children closed-mouthed on a tumble of covers.

***

The police station was thirty minutes' drive from the hotel, but it took nearly an hour thanks to traffic. Annie parked up and limped through the doors.

The reception was full, people waiting in sticky plastic chairs with wearied, fearful expressions. A solitary police officer behind thick glass was taking notes from a young woman with two children at her feet. She didn't speak English; the police officer remained resolute in his attempts not to understand.

Annie took a ticket from the dispenser and sat watching the digital wall counter for the next twenty minutes. Finally, her turn. She approached the desk. The officer didn't look up. 'How can I help?'

'I'd like...' Now she was here, she didn't know how to start. 'To report a crime.'

The officer's head lifted. He was young and looked tired, with a good day's growth of beard. He pushed a leaflet through the grille towards her: *How to report a crime.* 'You can fill that in now, or on the internet at home. Internet's quicker.' A crackly voice on the walkie-talkie attached to his shirt rattled out something unintelligible.

Annie pushed the leaflet back at him. 'I need to report it to *you*, here now, in person.'

The officer sighed, adjusted his stance. 'Right. Ib?' he called over his shoulder. 'Ibrahim? Got a minute?'

A second officer emerged from the back room, younger than the first. 'What?'

'This woman wants to report in person. Can you? Shift's about to end.'

'Who's gonna do the desk then, you muppet?' asked the man called Ibrahim.

'Melanie's off break.'

'Fair enough.' Ibrahim stepped up to the glass and gave Annie the once over. 'Is it happening now, your crime?'

Annie blinked. 'What?'

'Is the crime happening now? Do we need to scramble a car?'

'Oh.' Annie considered. 'It *is* happening now. But not in the way you might think. No need for a car.'

The officers looked at one another. Ibrahim shrugged. A buzzer sounded and the locked door separating the waiting area from the rest of the station clicked open. 'Come through.'

She followed him down a maze of brightly lit corridors to a windowless side room. In it, a table and two chairs. The walls were white Artex squares, like the motel.

'Have a seat.'

Annie sat. Ibrahim sat opposite and slapped a pen and pad onto the tabletop. He took some basic information: name, age, etc. – she hesitated over which address to give but settled on the Hackney flat – then he drew a line from one side of the page to the other.

'Right.' He looked up; pen poised. 'Describe the nature of the crime.'

'Crimes against humanity,' she said. Ibrahim's brows shot up. 'Yes. Also kidnapping, false imprisonment, false impregnation, and...'

Ibrahim brought his hands up. 'Woah. Hang on, hang on. False *impregnation?*'

Annie nodded.

Ibrahim looked confused. 'And it's you that's the victim of these crimes?'

'Not the impregnation.' Her palms dampened. 'But yes to the other parts. It's not just me; there are lots of victims. These crimes have been going on for years.'

Ibrahim stopped scribbling. 'What?'

'Their "work"...' Annie stalled. 'That's what they call it. A group of scientists. A university society called "Astarte" after an ancient proto-Christian goddess.' It sounded insane, even to her own ears, and it was coming out all muddled.

Ibrahim was giving her the expression she would give someone if she'd just heard the same thing. 'Come again?'

'Let me start again,' she said. 'At the beginning.'

She explained things as succinctly as she could, laying out details, bringing out the letters to Andrew and Issy as evidence, displaying the photos on her phone. Ibrahim barely glanced at them, but at least he recorded everything in looping longhand.

'They said they'd hurt me if I went to the police,' she finished. 'Hurt my kids.' Her gaze slid sideways. 'My stepkids.'

Ibrahim put his pen down. 'Okaaaay.'

He skimmed several pages of the statement, then shook his head. 'What you're saying is... your in-laws, along with the other people named here – the... Dillane family, and the others – are carrying out illegal genetic experimentation on animals and human females? Am I correct?'

'Yes.' Annie saw herself through his eyes: a post-menopausal woman with a buzz-cut and paranoid delusions. 'It sounds far-fetched, I know. But it's true.'

'And in which borough is this alleged crime happening?'

'Oh.' How had she forgotten to mention that? 'In Colthwaite. It's a village. In Cumbria.'

Ibrahim leant his elbows on the table and put his head in his hands, pressing his palms either side of his ears. There was a small bald patch at his crown. Nothing happened for several moments until finally he pushed the pad to one side.

'Ms Park. I'm very sorry; if these crimes are happening in Cumbria, you need to file the report *in Cumbria*.'

'No.' Annie shook her head. 'That's the whole point!' She waved the letters at him. 'I can't. They're in on it.'

'Who's in on it?'

'The *police*. Up there.'

Ibrahim rocked back on his chair. 'The police are in on it?'

'That's what Ste... that's what the "Keep" told me.'

'The keep?'

'The gamekeeper. The ranger. For the pheasants.'

'Right.' Ibrahim squinted at the wall, as though hoping someone might walk through it and rescue him. 'I accept you believe these things happened to you, and to others – but it does sound a little... There might be a few problems persuading–'

'I know but–'

'You really will need to take it up with one of the Lake District constabularies.' He stood, folding the cover of the pad over his notes. 'We've no jurisdiction in the Met to investigate crimes outside Greater London. Not in this instance, anyway. What I can do is pass your statement to the Lake District police department located closest to the village and allow them to take it from there.'

'No!' She almost leapt from her seat. An alarmed-looking Ibrahim took a step back. 'You can't,' she said more gently. 'There must be *something* you can do?'

He held his hands out. 'I'm sorry.' That, apparently, was that.

She placed the letters on the table. 'Here,' she said. 'You keep these. As evidence.'

'They're not originals,' Ibrahim said. 'They're photocopies, so they don't count as–'

'Be that as it may,' she said flatly. 'I'll send you JPEGs of the photos I took in the shed via the police reporting service online.'

She returned to the car. Of course the police weren't going to believe her. She hardly believed it herself.

Back at the motel she found Grace and Caleb still on the bed, watching TV. A small squat statuette of Astarte lay on its back on the shelf by the window.

'What's that doing there?' Annie cried. 'Where did you get that?'

'You tell me.' Grace glowered. 'I found it in your bag when I went looking for shampoo.'

Annie paled. She'd left it in her bedside drawer at Chapel Croft, she knew she had. But then she was in such a rush packing. She must have accidentally dumped it into her bag with everything else. Unless someone had put it there?

'It's okay, Gracie.' Annie strode over, picked up the statue, went out of the room and down the emergency stairs. She threw it hard into the bin in the lobby. It made a thunk as it hit the bottom. 'Good riddance,' she told it.

Lumi greeted them at the door with a smile, and a tray of freshly baked dasik biscuits just like Annie's. Annie took four, more out of habit than hunger. She could see in the set of her sister's face she was desperate for answers, but she took Annie's warning glance as intended and held her tongue.

The house was characterless but large, and they could each have their own bedroom. The square beige rooms full of square beige furniture were a relief after the drama of Colthwaite House. It was a blessed relief, too, to dump her bags and step into a shower. Later, after dinner, she told Lumi everything while the kids watched TV in the other room. Lumi listened carefully, not interrupting, not even when Annie paused in the middle to collect herself.

'Bloody fucking hell,' was all she said once Annie finished. She took Annie in her arms and gave her a hug. Annie fell into it gratefully: she'd expected not to be believed.

'Oh, this is nice,' she said, resting her head on Lumi's shoulder.

'We're going to sort this,' Lumi was saying, her hand rubbing Annie's back. 'We'll take those fuckers to court. George has contacts.'

The thought of court made Annie feel tired. Lumi went to put the kettle on. 'Have you told the kids yet?'

'Not all of it. I don't know what to say. How to... I mean, I hardly get it myself.'

'Tell them. They probably know anyway. Tell them now.'

Annie went into the other room and sat between Grace and Caleb. She told as much as she dared: about the society, the experimentations on pigs, that Annie had been in danger of some sort. She told them Patrick was loosely involved, but only in a medical capacity. She told a lie about Grace's pregnancy: that the hospital had confirmed it was endometrial tissue and not a baby after all. Grace took in this information slowly, her eyes cast at the floor. 'I told you I wasn't pregnant,' she said. 'You didn't believe me.'

'Forgive me,' Annie replied. If there was a heaven for good parenting, Annie would surely go to it.

'So, let me get this straight,' Caleb cut in. 'All that happened in the short time we were there? We'd hardly arrived.'

'I know,' Annie said. 'It's hard to accept. I'm so sorry.'

He looked the other way. 'Not your fault.'

'You okay, baby?' She put a hand on his knee.

'Did Mum know?' His voice was very quiet.

'No,' she said. It was partly true.

He nodded. 'Will we still see Dad?'

She considered her words carefully. 'I'm not sure that's a good idea. Do you want to?'

'Was he going to hurt you?'

Annie could feel the weight of his gaze. 'I... I don't think he was.'

'We don't want to see him,' Grace said, finally. 'Do we, Cal?'

Caleb shook his head. 'I guess not... no.'

Grace turned to face Annie. 'You know we didn't even *want* to go to Colthwaite in the first place?'

Annie looked up in surprise. 'What? But you said–'

'For Mum,' Grace said. 'We wanted to for Mum's sake.'

How had Annie not realised? Had she not been paying attention; had she been lost in her own grief? She searched for signs of Issy behind Grace's eyes but couldn't see her there.

'But we wanted to go there for your sake too, Annie,' Caleb added. 'We thought it was what *you* wanted.'

'For my sake?' she stammered.

'Yes!' The children said in unison. They loved her. They really loved her.

'I think Mum would have understood,' Caleb said at last. 'That we didn't want to go, that we left. Don't you?' He looked so vulnerable.

'I do.' Annie leant in and squeezed him. 'I honestly do.'

CHAPTER TWENTY

On the second day, she'd just confirmed with the school when the kids would start back when the phone rang.

'Am I speaking to Annie Park?'

'You are.'

'This is Clarence from Hackney Lettings. How are you today?'

'Fine thanks.' Annie had no idea why estate agents insisted on asking how you were; like they cared. You could be dead on the floor, long as they were getting their money.

'Just wanted to update you,' he said. 'Had a call from your tenants. The husband's taken a job in Manchester. They'll be moving north in a month.'

'A *month*?' Annie couldn't get the word out fast enough.

'I assume this comes as good news?'

'Yeah! Yes! Amazing news.' God knows, she deserved some luck.

'You get to keep their deposit, as technically they're the ones breaking the contract.'

'Even better.' Annie thought suddenly of the tenant's baby. 'No, wait. Clarence? On second thoughts, waive their deposit.'

On the seventh day, more news: not one, but two letters arrived. They were addressed to the Hackney flat; the tenants had kindly forwarded them on. The first was postmarked 'Ambleside', the other – typed and official-looking – had a blue rectangle stamped 'Ullerforth Hospital' on its back.

Heart thumping, she went to her bedroom. She ripped open the one from the hospital first.

To the parent/guardian of Grace Dillane,

Porton Down has confirmed the stem cell samples taken from the patient were consistent with those from a pig foetus.

We are still investigating if the sample could have been tampered with, or if the histology became contaminated or mixed-up somewhere along the chain.

In the meantime, the sample and various results have been passed to a geneticist at Imperial College London, who has requested further testing, and that the patient make an appointment at her earliest convenience.

Herewith, two forms: one consent to be signed and dated by the parent/guardian and returned in the envelope provided. The second, a questionnaire that the specialist requests the patient fill in herself and bring with her to the consultation.

With best wishes,

There was an illegible squiggle beneath, and the name: *Professor Belinda Grant, Head of Gynaecology, Ullerforth General.*

Annie re-folded the letter along with its various forms and questionnaires and pushed them back into the envelope. She hid them below a pile of books on the bedside table.

Grace was not going to be told about the letter, nor was Annie going to sign any forms. The matter was over. Her daughter would not be going anywhere near a hospital any time soon.

She stared at Lumi's spare room, the cream bedding, the magnolia walls. She took out the second letter, the address written by hand. *Please God,* she thought, *let it not be Elizabeth.*

It was from Margaret.

Dear Annie,

Forgive me writing to you like this, but as soon as you left, I felt I must put pen to paper. I realise you left us without knowing or understanding things and I imagine you may have many questions. Someone owes you a fuller explanation, so you're able to put things into context, and perhaps – who knows? – forgive us all. You're a good person and you deserve good things. Being clear of mind will help you move on, at any rate.

I will save you the group's history; I think you're aware of their beginnings at King's. Please excuse any repetitions. It's a complicated, messy business. I will try to start at the beginning.

Christopher and I met young. We longed to have a child, but nature wasn't kind. We both had fertility issues; a bleak prognosis. When Christopher and Elizabeth went to university together and founded their society, Astarte, they made it their mission to help us. I think the name started out as a bit of a joke, but then, for reasons I cannot remember, it stuck. The group were unconventional and brave: experimenting on themselves and so on.

Because it was myself and my husband who were the subjects in their experiments with infertility – a matter which was an ethical hot potato at the time – Christopher felt he must change his name. I'm sure you know that around the same time, a group of scientists – Purdy, Edwards, Steptoe, et al. – were conducting secret IVF testing, to terrible press. He didn't want to gain a bad reputation: were Astarte to succeed having used themselves as subjects, people would dismiss their findings due to conflict of interests, or worse, write them off as cranks.

When they'd finished at King's and we'd migrated as a group to Elizabeth and Christopher's family home in Colthwaite, David discovered other interests and moved from medicine to theology to become the vicar here, while Vincent set himself up as the village GP (Elizabeth had by this time met and married William).

Initially, their work was attempting to implant Elizabeth and William's fertilised egg into my body. When that failed, they tried a second time, by fertilising my eggs with William's sperm. Another failure.

The group then discovered, quite by accident, that they already had the solution to our childlessness – mine and Christopher's – under their very noses. Something entirely new, something so different that they believed using themselves in the actioning of it was not only necessary, but essential. That they would later be viewed by the world as true geniuses. This moment was the turning point, I suppose, when things began to get out of hand. This was their discovery:

A fertile sibling's DNA (Elizabeth's), so closely matched to my husband's, gave them an entirely different method of impregnation. Using Elizabeth's DNA they created a clone, ex vitro, grew the clone to a certain number of weeks and implanted it into my womb. The clone was accepted by my body, the host – this was their stunning, unexpected success.

Shortly after this, the other IVF team, the ones in the press, in another part of the country, also had an unexpected success: a woman, pregnant. Wonderful news, of course, but the press then went into overdrive, the scientists, the woman involved, all vilified, hounded. Astarte determined they must keep their own success secret at all costs, until such time as deemed appropriate.

They quickly needed further subjects, of course, one person wasn't going to be enough to prove anything, so they expanded to the locals. Those that were native were largely unwitting volunteers. Vincent handed out pills to the womenfolk. God knows what they were, but they rendered the women infertile. Their infertility meant they were far more likely to choose the system Astarte peddled as the cure, and as recommended by Vincent himself, their trusted GP. It was a system that guaranteed a child. It was unethical and carried out with uniformed consent, which is malpractice and against the Hippocratic oath, as you may be aware. Their system was to take the women's stem cells, doctor them, create clones of Elizabeth's DNA (because it was her DNA that had worked the first time), the women would take Vincent's drugs, be implanted with the clone, and hey presto, a baby.

If you're wondering why I co-operated, why I let them put anything into me in the first place, I only hope you understand how desperate I was. As desperate as those women undertaking illegal IVF in Purdy and Steptoe's group.

So many things went wrong here. I shan't list them all. Life can be cruel when you mess with nature.

Penelope was the first child we lost.

Penelope. It had been poor Margaret's baby.

Flora was our second. Technically, they were Elizabeth's children. Well, Elizabeth herself, her clone – but I was their "mother". It was a terrible time.

I was also, and I don't mind admitting this, terrified. Look what they did to you. They were ruthless; so utterly convinced they were doing good they'd stop at nothing.

When we lost Flora and Penelope, it became clear Elizabeth and Christopher shared some inhospitable gene mutations. The other women's children quickly followed the fate of the first. Such grief, such shame, such sadness.

Astarte tried to fix things: they believed by pushing on, they would absolve themselves, and at the same time forge more discoveries. They began to broaden their reach, tinkering with sick villagers' DNA to eradicate genetic mutations, a thing that had until this time been impossible. You see how so much of it was driven by good intentions? After that, things got worse.

They began to use swine cells, doctoring them, mixing them with human cells, implanting them into women and vice versa. Cloned foetuses, human-porcine hybrids, cloned stem cells to fight disease, there was no stopping them. Their justification: that modern science used pig hearts, thyroid, and other organs to ameliorate human disease, so why not fertile sow's wombs, sow's embryos? What started

*out as a desire to better the plight of humans, a healthy
fascination with science began to morph. Their "work"
changed, became twisted by greed and narcissism. They
began to preserve bodies for later investigation. I found it
unconscionable.*

*David, in particular, had a chilling Mengelian
approach: having decided to move sideways into the church,
he became frustrated with the slow pace of Astarte's
discoveries, and developed his own system, something he
dubbed "The Eye of God". It worked like this: two females
of the Dillane's younger generation would be implanted
with Elizabeth's clone to continue her "line". This,
unfortunately, was the work you were an unwitting
player in.*

*Grace and Polly were the "volunteers" with which to
"complete" their work. The total eclipse falling at roughly
the same time as Grace's arrival in the village, they took as a
good omen. Grace carries the faulty gene, Annie, the one
that affects Christopher, Elizabeth, and poor Issy. Were you
aware? Because Grace is Elizabeth, she is Issy.*

Annie was not aware of the Dillane's faulty genes. How
could she have been?

*Astarte have done one great thing, at least. The
CRISPR technology integrated into their recent work was
used on Grace to eradicate her genetic abnormality; they
dealt with it whilst implanting the cloned embryo. It's a
swift process, painless, and it may have saved your
stepdaughter's life. Christopher and Elizabeth have altered
their own gene expression in the same way. They are no
longer under threat from a genetic ticking time-bomb. You*

won't know this, but they tried to bring Issy here to do the same for her, to fix her using CRISPR: she refused. She wanted nothing to do with them. I'm not sure, in truth, that she was cognisant of the full extent of their work, as I lay it out for you now.

Polly doesn't carry the faulty gene; she's a daughter born to Andrew and Carolina in the natural way. She's the control.

So, then there was Grace and Polly, both pregnant for a time with the next generation's newest clone. Despite Astarte's successful work on eradicating Grace's DNA mutation, the clone inside her failed to graft, and they had to use porcine stem cells (I am sorry to tell you) to stimulate and stabilise the gene expression within her. But even with their best efforts, life continues to be random. Grace lost her baby. Polly's clone, on the other hand, grafted well.

I've nothing more to lose by telling you all this, do you see? It was solely to protect others, the young women like Polly and Grace, that I've kept their secret. The whole thing started all those years ago because of me, and I feel responsible.

I hope you can forgive me, forgive us all, and make sense of what it is I've written. I know it will be hard to understand.

Christopher and I did eventually have another child. One of our own. A late blessing, conceived in the natural way. Christopher's convinced it was not an accident but due to the work Astarte had done, though I don't believe that for a second. Her name was Rebecca. She reached the age of eleven before Christopher's gene mutation (pre-CRISPR) took her from us. We love and miss her every day.

I send you and Caleb and Grace all the very best.

Margaret

Annie slumped. She stayed there, unmoving, staring at her hands for a long time.

The way Margaret told it, so much of it made sense: the early experiments of Astarte not being that different to that group of three scientists racing ahead with IVF in the sixties. But you could use twisted logic to make sense of anything if you tried hard enough. When the group had gone off-piste, grown strange and impatient, that's where her understanding stopped.

She pulled the little box of Issy's ashes from her T-shirt drawer. She kissed the box, put it back. 'I love you,' she told it.

Somehow, she got the children off to school. Lumi and George went to work, and Annie was left alone. The silent house overwhelmed her, and she forced herself out to wander New Malden High Street, her head still spinning.

Their 'work' was the opposite of the way she'd always understood science, understood medicine. *First, do no harm.* Yes, that.

New Malden had hardly changed: small-town life, too much traffic funnelling through the main road. New flats had sprung up. There was a Greggs in place of old Pam's bakery, a Nandos where Ji-Hoon's grocery used to be. She walked all the way around Furniture Village rerunning Margaret's explanation. Whichever way she looked at it, she couldn't forgive them.

Later still, she took Caleb and Grace for dinner at Pizza Express. Annie had two beers. Grace had one. After much complaining about life being unfair, Caleb settled on a Coke.

She watched Grace closely: the living, breathing version of Issy in different skin. When she thought of it like that, she grew dizzy.

'To Mum.' Caleb's eyes creased at Annie. He meant her, he was talking about her. 'And to Mum.'

'To our Mums.' Grace raised her glass. 'And not to Dad.'

Her face collapsed and she began to cry. Annie put her arms around her.

'Why is Dad so...?' Grace took a ragged breath. 'It's like, do you think all his weird habits, his tics and OCD are because he's feeling guilty? About us? About being involved with... *them*?'

'I don't think we'll ever know for sure,' Annie said.

Grace wiped her eyes. 'You know I cry when I'm happy, right?'

Annie kissed her cheek. 'Gracie, I'm sorry for all you've been through.'

Grace sniffed. 'You've been through it too.'

'Be that as it may, you're incredible both of you.'

'Well, *I'm* incredible.' Caleb put a hand over his sister's. 'Grace is pretty average.'

'*Incredibly* average.' Grace laughed suddenly, then tucked into her pizza.

Grace's DNA had adapted long before they'd doctored her cells with CRISPR. She was nothing like Elizabeth, nothing like Issy. She was her own person, as Issy was before her.

Christmas was three weeks away and Annie had done nothing in preparation. Grace had asked for a jumpsuit from Uniqlo, Caleb said he didn't mind what he got. They were due to move back into their flat shortly after New Year, which meant they'd be spending most of the festive period in New Malden with Lumi, George, and their grown-up kids.

Secretly, Annie was relieved. She wasn't up for Christmas as a single parent this year, despite Lumi's annoyingness. It would be nice to have the extra company. She was spending large portions of each day in a state of hypervigilance: there'd been no contact from Patrick, but she doubted that would last, and when he raised his head, she'd have to be ready.

Caleb and Grace didn't seem to mind about Christmas in the boring beige house either. And Annie and Lumi could do the cooking together, the way they used to as children. Now that would be something.

She'd even been managing a little writing at George's desk in the tiny box room, the one Lumi grandly referred to as 'The Study': some revisions on *Bambisexual* based on notes from the Finborough Theatre, a little work on *Kimchi Trout Sandwich*. When Lumi asked what project Annie was busy with one night and Annie told her the title, her sister had thrown her head back and laughed. 'Grandma Halmi would have *loved* that!'

She was hanging washing on the line in Lumi's back garden when the call came. She pulled it from her pocket. Vincent's number. This was worse than Patrick.

The old man's name flashed on and on across the screen. She waited, the phone shaking in her hand, until the call rang out. A voicemail icon popped up. Annie put the phone to her ear.

'*Annie,*' Vincent said in his trembling baritone. '*I think we all know where we stand. No need for lengthy explanations. You understand there are important things happening in Colthwaite in the name of science. We trust that you and the children are doing well. We trust that we will not hear from you again, and we give you our solemn promise that if you keep your mouth shut, you'll hear nothing from us in return.*

'*We do have one final request – a small thing, really – that you allow Lizzo's, excuse me, Elizabeth's, associate in London to take a blood sample from Grace, and that this practice continue once a year for the next five years. It is vital to our work. Elizabeth would be happy if you'd prefer and it's more convenient, that you arrange for the blood to be taken yourself and sent by courier. I will forward the necessary information – dates, number of vials, etc. – via email in due course.'*

There was a short pause.

'We knew about the missing pregnant sow hidden in your back garden. We thought it best not to interfere. I hear it birthed a stillborn. I dare say you found it upsetting – perhaps as a result you may better understand the sacrifices and suffering we endured for the betterment of mankind. Take care, Annie.'

Annie deleted the message. Take blood from Grace and send it to him? Was he entirely mad? Yes, that's exactly what he was, of course. Completely and utterly insane. She picked up the washing basket and went into the house.

Lumi was waiting for her in the hall. 'Done?'

'Done.'

'Will you help me pick a Christmas tree in town?'

'Sure.'

Lumi's hand went onto Annie's shoulder. 'I've missed you, little Jamae.'

'Oh.' Annie didn't know what to say. 'Thank you. That's kind.'

'I've been sad thinking about when we were kids,' Lumi went on, 'and poor lonely Appa, without Mum.'

'He had Grandma Halmi,' Annie reminded her.

Lumi pulled a face just like Appa's. 'Not the same.'

'I'm just saying.'

Her sister's expression softened. 'I'm glad you're safe. I don't want to lose more family members.'

'Have you been having therapy?'

Lumi frowned. Her mouth opened and shut.

'I'm *joking*.' Annie gave her a hug. 'I've missed you too, Lumes.'

It was as if in the intervening years, Lumi's personality had changed. Or perhaps it was Annie who'd changed. Either way, Annie thought, it proved genes alone did not determine outcome.

CHAPTER TWENTY-ONE

Early morning light crept through the basement sash. The egg-yolk colour felt warm on her eyelids. Annie bolted upright, then remembering she was home fell back onto the pillows. This was the way of things each day. Not up north, no longer at Lumi's, they were back in Hackney at last. *Home.*

She rolled over, throwing an arm across the pillow on Issy's side, longing for the heat of her wife's body, the soft up and down of her breath. A sun ray streaked a graphic shape on the white cotton where Issy's fan of hair would shine like echoes from a star. In the room next door, Grace was on the phone, the bloop of WhatsApp messages travelling through the wall.

Annie swung her legs out of bed – the injured one barely ached now – and opened the curtains. No fields, but from her position in the basement she could see a slash of blue sky above the pavement. It was a school day. A bright day. Her chest lifted. She was going to the Finborough later for her meeting.

Across the hall the bath tap went on: Caleb. It amazed her he made time for a bath before a whole day of lessons. At his age she'd be up last minute, straight out the house with barely a slice of toast.

Annie shuffled to the kitchen. The sun only reached the back of the flat late in the day, and hardly at all in the morning until April, and she had to switch the lights on to make coffee. While it brewed, she watched the birds in the backyard pecking at the feeder. The coffee came to a throaty boil. Annie poured liquid into a cup. Her phone began to ring.

Caller ID hidden.

Her body stiffened. What now? What if it was Patrick? Checking the kids weren't in earshot, she slid her finger across the screen.

'Annie Park?' A woman's voice, businesslike, a Cumbrian lilt.

'Yes?'

'This is Detective Inspector Monk from the Professional Standards Department at Ullerforth Constabulary. Is this a bad time?'

'Professional Sta...?' Annie grabbed her coffee cup and took it out into the yard, closing the back door behind her. 'No, it's fine. What's this... Why are you calling?'

'I'm calling about crimes you reported to Sergeant Khan of the Met Police at Tottenham station on November 28th; crimes you allege took place in the village of Colthwaite.'

'Oh.' Annie squinted at the salt and pepper shakers through the kitchen window, side by side behind the oven like two fat soldiers. 'Yes?'

'In your report you claimed police officers here in Cumbria were involved. You left two photocopied letters with Sergeant Khan and sent him photographs as evidence. Is this correct?'

'Yes, but he said he couldn't do anything about it because he was based in London.'

'Well, thankfully Sergeant Khan had second thoughts. He sent them here to me. And let me tell you that we take these things very seriously in the PSD.'

'Oh!' Nature was random, there was no predicting it. 'Thank you. Thank you, that's very good.'

'I want to let you know that we had already reopened a cold investigation into similar matters prior to your report.'

'Had you?' Similar matters? What had that been about?

'Yes, but since you made your claim, we've opened a second case as well. We believe the two cases are linked. Strictly speaking, I'm not supposed to give more details at this stage, but our aim is to gather as much evidence as possible as quickly as we can. Would you be prepared to meet with one of our officers to give a second witness statement?'

Annie baulked. 'Go back up north?'

She could hear DI Monk's smile as she spoke. 'Reading through the statement you gave to Sergeant Khan, I'm guessing you'd rather not, am I right?'

'I'm afraid so.'

'That's not a problem. One of our officers can travel to a halfway point to take your statement if necessary, or even come to London at a push, if we have the budget.'

'That would be amazing.' Annie focused on her hand. Her skin was smooth and tan, with freckles. 'How... how did you...' She had about a million questions. 'Would you mind me asking if others have come forward? To give evidence, I mean?'

DI Monk drew a breath. 'I'm going to level with you. We have another witness, yes, who says he's willing to go on record. Someone loosely involved.'

'Is he named Stephen?' asked Annie. 'The Keep? I don't know his surname, sorry.'

'I'm afraid I can't reveal their identity.' DI Monk paused. 'What I can tell you is that the witness's daughter had a baby recently and...'

'Polly?' Annie said quickly. 'Polly's had her baby? It's *Andrew*, the witness?'

'I'm afraid I can't say.'

Annie couldn't believe her ears. '*Andrew's* going to help with your investigations?'

'The witness felt he had no choice but to come forward after he saw his daughter giving birth in a barn in Colthwaite.'

'The barn? At Colthwaite House?' Polly next to the sows and sheep in the straw beneath a lamp. Near the hooks.

'I really shouldn't...' DI Monk let out a heavy sigh. Annie had the impression she was struggling not to tell everything. 'She started birthing in the barn but fell into difficulties. Fortunately, the witness overruled members of the village and called an ambulance. Once the girl was at Ullerforth General, the on-call doctor cross-referenced her notes with those of your stepdaughter's and–'

'Is it okay?' Annie asked. 'Polly's baby?'

Monk's voice softened. 'The baby's bonny. Six and a half pounds. Ten fingers and toes. A girl.'

A girl. A clone. A replicant. Issy, yet not Issy. The line had gone silent. 'Are you still there?' Annie asked.

'Yes, I'm here,' DI Monk said. 'I think I should probably also tell you my father used to be Detective Super here at Ullerforth, covering Colthwaite. He's retired now. He had an open case in the seventies – insider dealing and administration of illegal medical drugs to members of the Colthwaite community. The case went cold due to lack of evidence. Let's just say he's been conducting... *unofficial* investigations of his own more recently.'

'Unofficial?'

'You passed him several times in the village, he said. Around seventy. Wears a scarf. Drives a Jeep. Has a way with cameras.'

'*That* man?' Annie exclaimed. 'In black trousers? The Jeep Cherokee?'

'That one. He read your report. He's tried to keep an eye on the place over the years. He doesn't give up, my dad. Once he's got the bit between his teeth, he won't let go.'

The boulder-cam. The camera in the trees. Those were his devices. No surprise that images from those hadn't been on display in the secret room at the back of Elizabeth's work shed.

'In the meantime, we're seeking a warrant to enter the mausoleum at Colthwaite church.'

Annie gave an involuntary shiver. 'Because?'

'It's been brought to our attention that there may be some... er...' The sound of Detective Inspector Monk swallowing. 'I'm not sure how to put this. The witness raised some questions around who might be inside the mausoleum, and the unusual method in which they were interred.'

'"Who might be in...?"'

'I'm sorry, Ms Park. I know this will be hard for you. The witness believes there's a strong likelihood your late wife is in there.'

'Issy was cremated,' Annie said weakly. 'The funeral was held at the church.' She had Issy's ashes right here at the flat. Some were sprinkled at High Tarn.

'I'm sure that's true, but there are some bodies in there, nonetheless, and we will need to investigate them. According to the witness, there may have been disturbances to the bodies at some point.'

'Disturbances?' They could have taken Issy's body and handed Annie someone else's remains. They could have–

'Ms Park? You still there?'

'Yes.'

'This must be upsetting,' said DI Monk. 'I'm sorry. I want to be as transparent as I can.' She wanted to be transparent; all Annie wanted was to get off the phone.

'Now I've your details,' DI Monk was still talking, 'someone will email you shortly to set up a date and time for your second statement. I do have to warn you the statement may be used at a later stage if the matter goes to court.'

Annie didn't have words.

'We'll do our best to bring them to justice, I promise. My dad's convinced we've a chance,' said DI Monk before the call ended.

Disturbances. Tampering with lonely bodies in a dirty, drafty shed. She looked out over the yard. In another universe, a different version of Annie would meet Polly's baby in a romantic setting. They'd fall in love, the cycle repeating itself. The thought made her want to puke.

Her coffee had gone cold. A couple of birds were fighting over a clump of stale breadcrumbs soaked in rainwater, the fat ball Caleb had put out only two weeks previously was already gone. A lone seagull swooped in, commandeered the table and hoovered up the bread.

An investigation was under way. It might not result in a thing. She didn't know what to think except this: she'd nail them herself if she had the chance.

Through the window she saw the children heading into the kitchen. She chucked her coffee down the drain and went inside, laid out breakfast. She talked about birds and bird feed, the weather. The kids chomped cereal.

'I love you, Mum,' they told her, one after the other as they left.

'I love you too,' she said, closing the door behind them.

The little theatre was in the upstairs of a pub, the building itself between two busy roads near Earls Court. Annie lugged her bag, heavy with manuscript and laptop, all the way on the Tube.

Now she stood outside sweating, with a sore neck. She checked her watch: early, as usual.

Inside, the pub was empty save for one woman behind the bar idly jabbing the keys on her phone. She looked up as Annie entered, smiled, went back to jabbing. Over the speakers, a radio DJ kept a patter going. A fruit machine flickered from a corner. The whole place smelled of old beer and toilet cleaner. Annie stood for a moment in the centre on the sticky floor, eyes wide, in sensory overload. She felt strangely elated. On the way here, she'd worked out what she was going to do. Or try to, anyway.

'You must be Annie?' a voice said behind her. A young man in glasses, and an attractive woman with a haircut exactly like Annie's. 'Aku,' the man said, offering his hand. 'And this is Sam. Shall we go through?'

Annie smiled. She'd assumed Sam would be a man. The woman whose name was Sam smiled.

The meeting room was upstairs next to the auditorium itself, small and hot, the narrow sash fogged with condensation. She thought briefly of the writing shed. 'Thank you so much,' she said. 'For getting me in.'

'We're thrilled you're here. Please.' Sam gestured to the chair on one side of the table. Annie sat. They settled themselves opposite. Annie laid out her laptop and manuscript carefully.

'Long journey?' asked Sam.

Annie sat, straight-backed, hands resting in her lap. 'From Hackney.'

'That's funny.' Sam ran a hand across her undercut. 'We heard you'd moved to Cumbria.'

'Didn't work out.' Annie made a face.

Sam put her head on one side. Her irises were the colour of walnut halves.

'Not a fan of the countryside?' Aku asked. 'All that silence?'

'Oh no,' Annie found herself saying. 'I loved the silence. It was more...'

'...the people?' Sam finished. A sly smile, a little flirtatious perhaps.

'Exactly,' Annie agreed. 'The *people*. Not all of them, though.'

'Well,' Sam tapped her temple, 'I've no doubt it's all been fed into the databank.'

'It has.'

Aku cleared his throat. 'You know we're big fans of yours, Annie. We've been trying to put on one of your plays here for a long time.'

'You have?' How had Annie not known? Could this be happening at other theatres: people in love with her work, yet somehow unable to let her know?

'Is this the revised version?' Aku was gesturing at the *Bambisexual* manuscript.

'Yep,' Annie said. 'With the changes we discussed on the phone.'

'Wonderful.' Sam did her funny smile again.

Annie gulped air. 'So, listen, there's something else. I did a lot of new writing in Cumbria. A play based on my grandmother, which I'm still going at...' She must say it now, or it would never happen. 'But, um, this may sound weird so bear with me.' She spread her palms face down on the table. 'I have a third proposal. *Not* the play you have here, and not the one about my grandmother either. Another one.'

Aku drew back his chin in surprise. 'Another one?'

'One I think – I *hope* – you might consider. It's set in the north, in a small village, a small community–'

Sam laughed. 'No prizes for guessing where your inspiration for *that* came from.'

'Exactly.' Annie smiled. She felt a little dizzy. 'It's a... thriller, I suppose.'

'Oh.' Sam leant forward. 'I love a thriller. What's the premise?'

'Well, it's hard to... It involves a comer-in, an elderly cabal, pigs, young women...' Annie paused. 'And replicants.'

That got their attention. '*Replicants?*'

'Human clones,' Annie clarified.

Aku pushed his glasses up his nose. 'It's not usually the sort of work we'd put on here. But go on, tell us more.'

'It's not a subject that appears, at first listen...' Annie was deeply conscious of Aku and Sam's polite faces, 'to be within the realms of... theatre.'

'Or within the realms of reality, even?' Sam raised an eyebrow.

'Yes, that too.'

Aku said, 'Where in your brain did you pluck this from?'

Annie took a sip of water. 'Long story.' Something was happening. Something in the room.

'Are you okay?' Sam was asking.

Annie could feel Issy. She was here, with her, right now. The sensation was strong, as if she could reach out and touch her. 'I'm fine,' she said. She took a breath, smoothed her trousers. 'I know exactly how I want to get this piece onto paper. And honestly, I think it could blow the roof off.'

Sam didn't smile, didn't dismiss her. She was looking at Annie hard, with genuine artistic interest. 'In what way?'

'I think it could become a... national sensation.'

The truth – the whole story – was going to come out, if Detective Inspector Monk and DI Monk's father were right about it. Why shouldn't Annie, one of the victims and main players in the story, be permitted to speak out?

Sam was smiling again. Her teeth were very white. 'And have you started? D'you have sample pages?'

'Not yet – I could get them to you by the end of the week.'

Perhaps there were laws around open cases, and Annie would be prevented from mounting the piece due to ongoing investigations, but God, she was going to try. She'd change the names, the places, and caveat with: *the following is a work of fiction. Any similarity to actual persons living or dead, or actual events, is purely coincidental.*

'Well, I'd be fascinated to see something on this long story.' Sam threw a glance at Aku, who nodded in agreement.

'I promise you won't be disappointed,' Annie told them. 'And in the meantime, you have the latest draft of *Bambisexual* right here.' She pushed the manuscript across the table.

'This *new* new piece,' Aku said. 'The one with replicants. Does it have a title, or...?'

'Oh yes, it has a title.' Annie leant back in the chair, one leg swinging beneath the table. She felt as strong as a tree blustering on the fell. 'It's called, *The Drift*.'

She felt Issy smile at her from across the room.

THE END

ACKNOWLEDGEMENTS

I'd like to thank my publisher, Bloodhound, in particular Tara, Rachel, Betsy, Hannah and Abbie, for all your hard work and your faith in this book. Thanks as ever to my wonderful agent, Laura Macdougall, and to the wider team at United. A massive thank you to scientist extraordinaire Matthew A. Child at Imperial, for the chat about centrifuges and gene editing over beers, for your amazing science tips – your knowledge and time have been invaluable. Thanks also to fellow author Hayley Dunning for putting me in touch with Matt in the first place. To Sophie Ward and Rena Brannan. To the Faber Academy alum, authors Deborah Appleton and Chloe Timms, for their unending support and for their sharp eyes as early readers. Thanks to Francis Cleverdon at Hatchards, to Rhiannon and Charles at Waterstones Kensington, and to booksellers and book readers everywhere from the bottom of my heart. Lastly, thanks to John and Kit, forever and always.

Susannah Wise is an actor, author and screenwriter who grew up in London and the Midlands. Susannah studied at the Faber Academy, graduating in 2018. Her debut novel, *This Fragile Earth* was released in 2021 (Orion/Gollancz), and her second, *Okay Then That's Great*, in 2022 (Orion/Gollancz). Both books were longlisted for the Mslexia Prize. She has also had poetry published online and in print. She lives in London with her partner and son.

A NOTE FROM THE PUBLISHER

Thank you for reading this book. If you enjoyed it please do consider leaving a review on Amazon to help others find it too.

We hate typos. All of our books have been rigorously edited and proofread, but sometimes mistakes do slip through. If you have spotted a typo, please do let us know and we can get it amended within hours.

info@bloodhoundbooks.com

www.ingramcontent.com/pod-product-compliance
Lightning Source LLC
Chambersburg PA
CBHW030524190726

48283CB00006B/1756